Darwinian Feast

By
Sheila Berglund

Version 1.0 November 2025

Published by Sheila Berglund

ISBN: <u>978-1-7369358-4-2</u> (Paperback)
ISBN: <u>978-1-7369358-5-9</u> (ebook)

To the dreamers of dread—
those who find wonder in the wound,
and beauty in the feast.

❧ Chapter 1 - Gertie

The year 2128

My name is Gertie. Well, Gertrude, really, but everyone calls me Gertie. It's the name my parents gave me when I was born. I never knew my parents. They left me in the woods when I was just a baby. I always wondered why. Did they not want me? Were they trying to give me a better life? I liked to believe that. It's easier than thinking they didn't care. Times were different back then, or so I've been told. Sometimes it scares me to imagine what they went through back then. But I'm grateful they gave me a name, etched in soot on the swaddle I was wrapped in. A name meant to be seen.

Gertie.

I don't know who changed it to Gertrude. Probably the sisters at the orphanage. They tried to call me Gertrude, but I never answered. I'd only respond to Gertie—the name on the swaddle.

I still have it to this day. The same cloth, worn thin with time. Whenever the soot faded, I'd trace the letters back in coal, then ink. That was until Miss Linda stitched over them in dark blue thread. Now it will never fade.

I wear it around my neck like a scarf. A reminder that someone, once, loved me enough to give me a name.

I'm twelve years old, and a student at Greyburry Prep School, in Trivel House. I came here when I was four, right after the revolution. That was when the new government took over the orphanages and shut down the child labor camps. Like all the newbies, I started in kinder, but by seven, I'd already earned my way into secondary school.

Only the best kinder students make it to secondary school. The rest get sent to the colonies. They say it's not as bad as the camps—but it's not good either. I've heard the stories.

I plan to stay at Greyburry. No matter what it takes.

Trivel House is the best secondary school in all of Greyburry. It sits high on a hill near Mascot Lake, and we've got the fastest runners in school, me being one of them. Well, among the secondary students, anyway. Living next to the lake is the best. In summer, we'd sometimes take class trips there, even camp overnight. You can still see Trivel from the campsite, but it feels just far enough to be fun.

On our first trip out, Edgar, one of the kids in my class, got scared of the dark and had to go back to the dorms with aide Gabby. Edgar was afraid of everything, so no one was surprised when he cried to go back to his room.

What was strange, though, was that we never saw him again.

Lady Bader, the school nurse, said he had appendicitis and was sent to the infirmary before being transferred out of Greyburry. Everyone thought it was odd to get expelled over something so minor. But I figured that if you're missing a piece of your body, maybe you're just not cut out for excellence.

There are thirty-two houses in Greyburry: twenty-one kinder, ten secondary, and just one senior house. The Down House.

Each house has its own colors and mascot. Trivel's colors are purple and gold, and our mascot is a lion. I've never liked purple and gold. I prefer the pink and black of the Down House. I've always dreamed of making it there someday, but then I remind myself: You will make it.

The Down House isn't like the others. It's a finishing school. Only the best of the best go there, like me. Besides, I'm ready to leave secondary school. The classes are dull, and most mornings I lie in bed until the aides give last call for breakfast. Then I drag myself up to get ready. But not today. Today is Thursday.

Thursday means marmalade Danish with sweet cheese filling. It's the best thing they serve all week and definitely worth getting up early for.

I'm out of the shower and done brushing my teeth before the crowd descends into the bathroom. I don't like waiting for the sinks while the older girls apply makeup and fuss with their hair. Back in my dorm, I slip into my school uniform and am once again reminded of how much I hate purple and gold when Siri pops her head in the dorm door.

"Wait for me. I just need to brush my teeth real quick," she said.

"Okay, but hurry," I moaned. "It's Thursday, and I don't want to miss out on the good Danish."

"I promise," she said, disappearing into the hall.

I lay back on my bed and started fidgeting with the charms on my purity bracelet. Six banded charms so far. Only three other girls in Trivel have six. That's something.

My happy heart and genotype charms came first, then my purity charm, but everyone has those. You wouldn't be at Greyburry if you didn't. What I'm most proud of are the others: the free thinker, the behavior champion, and the winged talaria I earned for winning the secondary school sprint.

Sometimes I imagine what it would feel like to earn the challenge hawk or the scholar roll—maybe even the golden rattle.

Growing impatient, I got up to leave when Siri raced back into the room.

"Let's go!" she cried.

As Siri and I made our way down the hallway toward the secondary cafeteria, the school sirens blared, stopping us cold. The sound was sharp and loud, like something had broken in the air.

We froze, locking eyes.

Siri's face lit up with shock and a curious grin.

"What? Is it happening, is it really happening?" I asked, breath catching. Oh, how I wanted it to be true.

"I think so. Look!" Siri pointed as students poured into the corridors, shouting and laughing. We hugged, bouncing with joy.

The sirens could only mean one thing.

Challenge Day.

Challenge Day is the best day for two reasons. First, you get to slack off on your studies. Second, and most important, it's how you get into the Down House. In fact, it's the only way into the Down House. You never know when it's coming, either; some years, just once; others, multiple times. It's always a surprise.

Each Challenge, one class is chosen to compete. And at the end of the games, the top students are placed in the Down House. The best of the best. Like me.

Siri and I raced out of the dorm, through Trivel's front gate, and into the central courtyard near the Greyburry fountains, where kids from every school congregated. Students from the House Woodstock in gray and blue were there. So was Everly House in their green and yellow, too many schools to count. The courtyard buzzed with chatter.

"I can't believe it. There hasn't been a Challenge in almost a year!" A student from Wessington House cried.

Everyone speculates who it will be.

"Ridgehaven for sure," said an older boy with thick black glasses.

"No, Delta. Delta is due." Argue a group of boys from a rival school.

My stomach growls. In all the excitement, I almost forgot it was Thursday.

I pulled Siri aside. "We'd better get to breakfast. We don't want to be late and miss the Danish," I said.

"You're right. Let's get back before Miss Lacy sees us out here, not that she'd care on a Challenge day," chuckled Siri.

Siri and I ran to the secondary school cafeteria and took our place at the end of the line, where everyone was talking about the Challenge.

"Do you think it will be us?" said a girl from my class named Leesa.

"Probably not. Trivel never gets picked, not since I came to Greyburry anyway," I said as I peered over the crowd toward the breakfast trays. I'd better not miss out. I desperately wanted to push my way past the group, but decided it wasn't worth losing my chance at getting my perfectly polite charm and stayed put.

"They usually choose the academic houses anyway," said Siri.

"That's not true," said Ferris from the Viceroy House. "Chicory got picked two years ago."

"Oh yeah, they had four challenges that year," said Ian. "Four!"

Taking my turn through the line, I see there are still plenty of trays full of sweet Danish and let out a sigh of relief.

"Oh heaven," I drooled as I picked up a Danish, then another, and placed them both on my tray. Not wanting to look greedy, I took another and held it in my hand before moving on to the juice.

At our usual table, I watch Fiona sip her tea and scowl. I was glad I didn't have to drink the tea yet. Everyone says it's terrible. Not all girls in Trivel have the tea, just Fiona and a few others—the early bloomers, as Miss Lacy called them.

After breakfast, I hurried to homeroom. I had just reached the door to my class when someone yelled my name. It was Eva. She was twelve, too.

"Gertie, did you hear?" said Eva.

"Everybody heard!" I exclaimed as we entered room 24B.

Inside, the room buzzed with energy, every student talking at once, their voices bright with anticipation.

"Do you think they'll announce the winners at lunch?" said Rayleigh.

"Of course, they always do," said Judah.

"Settle down, everyone, take your seats and settle down," said Miss Becky as she tried to corral everyone to their desks. "Lunch break will be here before you know it, so do your best to concentrate until then."

Homeroom was a blur. We were all too excited to think. Even the teachers never cared about studies on Challenge days. I did my best in my second-hour reading class. The book was one of my favorites, but I couldn't concentrate, so I sat staring at the pages, wondering what it would be like to win. I glanced toward Judah, who wasn't even trying to hide his excitement. He smiled and crossed his fingers, and I crossed mine too.

The morning flew by, and before I knew it, lunch hour had arrived. Groups of students flocked to the cafeteria and gobbled lunch. I sat in my usual spot at the Trivel table with the rest of my classmates. After clearing our trays, we sat anxiously, awaiting the news. Finally, the cafeteria's lights dimmed, and the room fell silent as Greyburry's Headmistress Padma appeared on the overhead balcony. The winning school's color banner hung next to her, rolled up tight and tied with golden tassels. Hanging from the ceiling overhead was the purity flag with its newly sanctioned vertical infinity symbol. Siri grabbed my hand and let out a squeal.

I stared up at the purity flag and frowned. "Why'd they have to change it? I liked the infinity symbol better the other way. It's stupid now, it doesn't look like an angel anymore," I said.

"They changed it to protest the old treaties and to signify progress flowing upward, not stagnant," said Karen, a braggy know-it-all from my class.

"Yeah, well, I think someone messed up and put it upright by mistake, and they were too cheap to change it," said Homer. Everyone laughed except Karen.

"Good afternoon, students, and welcome to Challenge Day!" Padma beamed as she raised her arms high above her head. The cafeteria roared to life.

"Okay, everyone, settle down, please. Take your seats so I can reveal the winning class banner." Padma's voice rang out, smooth and bright, as she waved us back to our chairs.

I loved Padma. Kind and stunning, with chocolate-brown eyes that sparkled when she spoke and a smile that could light up even the darkest day. She had a way of making you feel like the most important person in the room, even when that room held hundreds of students, like today.

The chatter faded, and the room fell into a hush.

Padma stepped toward the banner, her movements slow, almost teasing. She reached for the tassel, turned, and gave us one last dazzling smile before pulling the golden rope. The banner snapped open with a crisp flutter, revealing the purple and gold flag of the Trivel House. My seat bounced beneath me as the students at my table jumped to their feet.

"Is it us? Is it Trivel?" cried Siri.

"Of course, it's us. Look at the colors!" said Ian.

"It's true. Miss Grayson and Miss Ellie are joining Padma on the balcony right now," said Leesa.

Miss Grayson and Miss Ellie were the lead teachers at Trivel. The three ladies stood smiling down at us while holding hands. It was true. They picked Trivel for the Challenge!

Trivel was still celebrating while the teachers quickly escorted the other schools out of the cafeteria. No one outside the winning house could be here for the Challenge. It's a secret. Even the teachers weren't allowed, nor did they know what the skill tests would be. The room emptied except for the Trivel students, and we all nervously took our seats as Miss Ellie addressed the room.

"You should all be honored. There are many fine schools here at Greyburry, and I expect each of you to do your best today. Make Trivel proud!" The students cheered.

"Now, there are eight spots at Down House. Five girls and three boys. Maybe more, depending on the scores." The room erupted in chatter.

"Only eight spots?" said Siri.

"That's less than usual," I said.

Linus looked worried. "Yeah, that means thirty of us won't make it. That means we won't see each other again."

Linus was right. If your house went up for the Challenge, those not selected can't stay at Greyburry. That was the whole point of the Challenge. You didn't even get to say goodbye. Down House was only for the best, and there's no point keeping you around if you don't win. That's the only bad part about the whole thing. But if you win, it's worth it. At least, I thought so.

"She said maybe more," I said.

"You didn't think we were all going to go, did you?" said Ian.

"No, but that's not very many," whimpered Linus. "Now I wish we hadn't gotten picked at all."

"Why? We'd get sent away after tenth year anyway, at least this way some of us have a chance," said Leesa.

"At least we'd all be together," Linus pouted.

Leesa rolled her eyes.

I knew why Linus was concerned. There was no way he'd win anything. I never knew how he got into Greyburry in the first place. I always knew I would do well in the Challenge, even though I didn't know what the skill tests would be. I'm good at math and solving word problems. Oh, and did I mention I was the fastest runner? Linus, on the other hand, not so much.

The cafeteria doors swung open, and a tall, thin woman with short black hair wearing black slacks and a light blue jacket entered the room, my new favorite colors.

"I want everyone to meet your Challenge Captain, Winnimere Truss," said Miss Ellie. Winnimere waved as she glided up the stairs in her shiny black heels. Reaching the top, she gave Padma a quick hug and turned to address the crowd. She waited while Padma, Miss Ellie, and Miss Grayson disappeared out the back exit of the balcony before she spoke.

"Hello, students. As Miss Ellie said, my name is Winnimere, and the handsome fellow standing in the doorway is Abfundt, our Challenge Judge."

Our heads snapped toward the door in unison, followed by a nervous round of laughter. The figure in the doorway was more beast than man and anything but handsome. Abfundt stood stoic, arms crossed across his chest, his frame so massive it nearly blocked the entrance. He wore full leather, the kind that creaked when he moved. His black hair hung in tangled clumps, partially hiding the eyepatch over his left eye. A thick beard swallowed most of his face, but the scars on his cheeks remained exposed.

He growled and stepped forward. The floorboards groaned under his weight.

Inside, he paused and raised a hand above his head. Seconds later, six steel drones hovered in from outside. Disc-shaped and gleaming, like Adfundt, they barely fit through the doorway. They circled the room with slow menace before settling near the ceiling above the balcony.

"And those are your Challenge Marshals," said Winnimere. "The Marshals see everything and report back to Abfundt and the Challenge proctors."

Just then, as if on cue, four overly energetic proctors burst through the cafeteria door wearing matching red tracksuits, each grinning ear to ear.

"Please welcome your Challenge proctors, Jade, Quinn, Blaine, and Destiny," said Winnimere.

We all cheered as the proctors circled the cafeteria, slapping each of our hands as they passed before standing at attention in the center of the room below the balcony.

"The proctors are here to administer the skills and monitor your performance. There will be five skills in all. We specifically designed each one to test your problem-solving, analytical strengths, tactical abilities, and how you respond to stress," said Winnimere.

"Tactical abilities?" whispered Leesa.

"Yeah, what's that?" said Judah.

"Remember, the proctors cannot and will not help you. They will give you instructions for each skill only once, so pay attention." Winnimere's tone had become increasingly hostile, and my stomach gurgled. I probably shouldn't have eaten all three of the Danishes this morning.

"There will also be no cheating! The Marshals will watch your every move, and anyone caught cheating or breaking the rules will be removed from the Challenge and dealt with accordingly. Questions?"

Linus sheepishly raised his hand.

"Yes, you there. What's your question?" said Winnimere.

"What exactly are the rules?" he said.

Winnimere laughed. "Other than no cheating, the rules are subject to interpretation."

"What does that mean?" whispered Siri. I shrugged. This wasn't what I was expecting, for sure.

"Now, if you complete the skill, you will move on to the next round. However, if you fail at any skill, you will be immediately removed from the Challenge. And don't get cocky. The skills are not always what they seem. Does everyone understand?"

"Yes," we chimed in unison.

"Good. Your first task is to return to your homerooms within five minutes. When you hear the Challenge alarm, you may proceed," said Winnimere.

We looked around, confused, and started murmuring to one another.

"That's really our first skill? Five minutes to get to homeroom?" I said.

"I can make it in three if I stroll," Ian said.

"She said not all skills are what they seem," said Leesa.

We stood, confused, scanning each other's faces for answers. No one moved.

The task was simple, too simple. Walk back to your homeroom. That was it.

How could that possibly measure problem-solving or tactical skill? It felt like a trick. A test wrapped in something so ordinary it became suspicious. I glanced at Siri, who shrugged, her brow furrowed.

Was this part of the Challenge? Or something else entirely?

"Wait now. Everyone, sit back down. I know you're all eager to get started, but I have a quick message from President Bruno that he asked me to share," said Winnimere.

Winnimere gestured toward the ceiling, where a large electronic board, generally used for school announcements and schedule changes, descended with a soft mechanical whir. The screen lit up, and a giant golden purity cross took shape.

Then the treaties began.

"Through sacrifice and cleansing comes rebirth and prosperity…"

After the reading, the cross dissolved into a thousand purple butterflies, and President Bruno appeared, sitting in a high-back leather chair positioned between two flags—the flag of the Western Front and the Purity flag.

"How old do you think he is?" whispered Leesa.

"At least a hundred," said Ian. We all giggled.

Once celebrated for his looks, President Bruno rarely made an appearance now that age and decades of hard living had taken their toll. Portraits of a much younger Captain graced the walls of nearly every building in Greyburry, as well as the back cover of our textbooks, though none of them looked anything like the man sitting before us today. He was still handsome, in a way. But older. His hair was shaded too dark, and his face was too touched up, but other than that, he looked okay, for an old person anyway.

The room fell silent as he began to speak.

"Good afternoon, students. As you know, peace and purity have always been the aim of the new world. In the past, we've struggled with population control while trying to raise viable, sturdy, educated children to help our species flourish and bring us victory over our enemies. Children now outnumber adults by almost three to one. Inbreeding, sins of lust, and procreation of the ill and unfortunate have taken a toll and fostered an environment unsuitable for growth. Which is why we gather here today."

President Bruno continued, his voice steady, almost soothing.

"To celebrate those who have risen above physically and academically. Those who embody the principles of the new world, discipline, clarity, and genetic integrity. Greyburry remains one of our strongest bastions. A place where excellence is not just inherited, but earned. Where the weak are redirected, and the worthy are refined and rewarded."

A few students sat straighter. Others tried not to tremble.

"The Down House will open its doors again this season. Selection will be swift. Final. And those chosen will carry our future on their backs."

President Bruno paused to take a sip from a mug sitting on the desk in front of him. He set the mug down and adjusted the flesh-colored mask covering the right side of his face. I wouldn't even have noticed it had it not moved when he drank.

"There are no simple choices. We learned that years ago. We must weed out the meek, the inbred, and the unsullied," he said.

"What does he mean by 'weed out'?" whispered Leesa.

"What does he mean by 'meek'?" said Linus. I looked at Linus with his cleft lip and lazy eye. I knew what President Bruno meant, but I just shrugged.

"We conduct these Challenges to protect and foster the livelihood and prosperity of our people and ensure we are producing the highest quality stock." He smiled, but it didn't reach his eyes. "It is a privilege to be here. Not everyone earns such a place, and not everyone keeps it."

A few students shifted in their seats."

I looked around at the other students, and they all looked just as confused as I was. This seemed like an odd speech for such an honor.

"And with that, I wish you all good luck. Let us begin."

The screen went dark, and a second later, the lights snapped on. Above us, the Marshals buzzed to life. Their steel bodies whirred and clicked as they broke formation, circling the room in slow, deliberate loops. Red lights blinked beneath their bellies, casting sharp shadows across our faces.

"So we just go now?" said Ian.

"She said to wait for the alarm," I said.

We all stood, anxiously waiting for the alarm, when Bucky, one of the younger students, ran to the center of the room and cried out.

"I'm scared. I don't want to do this anymore." Tears fell from his eyes as Bucky raised his hands toward the balcony as if asking for a hug. Staring down at Bucky with a look of disgust, Winnimere puckered her lips and let out a wad of spit that landed on Bucky's gold collar.

Bucky looked down at the blob hanging from his shirt and began to sob. "Why?" cried Bucky.

"Come on, Siri, let's move closer to the door," I said.

"Shouldn't we help him?" she said.

Siri was right.

I turned toward the cowering boy but stopped. Above Bucky's head, a Challenge Marshal hovered, its undercarriage pulsing with red and blue light. A hatch slid open with a hiss, revealing something dark and glistening inside.

The other Marshals began to circle. Faster and faster. Their buzz grew shrill, like a swarm preparing to strike. The crowd didn't move. Couldn't. We stood like statues carved from fear.

Bucky looked up, eyes wide and wet, then took a step back toward the tables. The alarm sounded.

"And the Challenge starts now! The clock is ticking. Five minutes to return to your homeroom," cried Winnimere, but no one moved nor took their eyes off the Marshal stalking Bucky.

"I said go!"

On cue, the Marshal zipped to the ceiling, paused, then fired. A stack of round metal blades shot from its hatch, spinning like coins. They tore through Bucky's torso, front to back, with a wet, mechanical precision. The razors clattered to the floor, streaked with blood and cafeteria grime.

Bucky collapsed, face-first, into the spreading pool beneath him. For a moment, silence. As if the room itself had stopped breathing.

Then the screams came. Students bolted in every direction, chairs overturned, trays scattered, the air thick with panic and the stench of blood.

Above it all, the Marshals circled the crowd, their metal bodies humming like wasps.

I dropped Siri's hand and dove under the table as the first attack began. Siri turned and sprinted toward the cafeteria door, but one of the Marshals intercepted her, flying past with a shriek of metal. As it passed, the drone began to change. Its top popped open, and its sides folded outward like wings. The outer shell twisted and collapsed inward, feeding itself into a new shape.

It wasn't a drone anymore. It was a gleaming robotic dragon, alive, wings stretched wide. Its mouth opened, glowing from within. Then came the fire.

Siri screamed as the flames hit her, her body folding to the ground in a smoldering heap of purple and gold.

I couldn't move. I couldn't speak. I just stared, frozen, as the dragon hovered above her like it was proud of what it had done.

Another Marshal shifted midair, its body stretching and reshaping into a giant bird. Metal wings flapped with a deafening clang, and long talons scraped the ceiling as it swooped over the screaming crowd.

From its beak, it spat small lead balls, fast, precise, like bullets only larger. One rolled under my table and stopped near my foot.

Tick. Tick. Tick.

The sound was slow at first, steady. Then it sped up. The orb began to spin, trembling as if it were alive. I didn't think. I just kicked. The orb flew into the middle of the room, bounced once, and exploded near the exit. The blast tore through the crowd, and one student who'd almost made it out now crumpled in a heap of smoke and blood.

I stared at the wreckage, heart pounding, unsure how I felt about saving myself at the cost of so many others. I knew one thing: making it to the door was no longer an option, so I crawled under the table to the furthest end of the cafeteria near the windows, where Eugene, a boy from another Trivel homeroom, leaped out of an open window to the grassy field outside. Following suit, I pushed myself through the tiny opening and fell to the ground just before an army of razors whizzed overhead, barely missing my skull.

Remembering the Challenge, I jumped to my feet and raced to the main entrance to Trivel house while Eugene headed towards the lake. I thought about reminding him of the Challenge, but didn't—one less competitor.

Running down the hall towards my class, I fell in line behind a group of students scrambling to reach safety. I pushed my way past a small boy at the tail end of the group. The boy screamed as he fell to the ground. It was Linus.

Linus reached for my hand. "Gertie, please," he cried as he lifted a hand, but I didn't stop to help. I jumped over his quivering body and raced to room 24B, where I quickly took my seat seconds before the alarm sounded.

Smiling and clapping her hands, proctor Jade entered the room. "Congratulations," she said. "You all completed the first skill in the allotted time."

Looking around the room, I'm surprised and a little disappointed at how many students made it. Eva, Leesa, Fredric, Puck, Judah, Bailey, and Sadie all sat perfectly still at their desks. Four others were missing, but I couldn't remember who, other than Linus and Siri.

"Are you all ready for their next skill?" I look over at Leesa. Blood from a gash on her forehead ran down her face, and her uniform was a mess. She looked back at me and smiled, and I nodded.

One skill down, only four more to go.

❧ Chapter 2 - Maya

The year 2116

"Calm down now. You took a pretty hard hit to the head by that stump, and that hand of yours looks infected. What were you doing in the water, anyhow?" Said a man with a concerned smile and crimson-stained shirt that stood out like death's calling card.

"Huh, what? Where am I?" Surrounded by curious faces, I tried to sit up but fell back as rockets of pain shot across the back of my head. My hair and clothes were wet. The type of wet that warrants addressing. I touched the spot on my head where the pain resonated and choked back cries at the sight of my bloody fingers.

"Is this blood? Is this my blood?" I said.

"Now, now, don't you worry, it's just a gash. It should heal up in a couple of weeks," said a man with the furthest face. "I'm much more concerned with that hand of yours."

"We'll get you to Doc Brown, and he'll stitch you right up. Get your hand cleaned up, too," said the face of a woman kneeling next to me.

I lifted my head and saw more faces, tiny ones, splashing and playing in the pooled water near the river's edge. Wading nearby, women, their mothers perhaps, filled cooking pots with the same water I was likely plucked from. Another face appeared. His smile was warm and kind. He took hold of my arm and wiped away mud with a towel.

"Now, what do we have here?" he said.

"Just found her in the water. She's young, has the marking behind her ear," said another face.

"Ah, so she does," said the man holding my arm.

"No, it's not true," I muttered as I tried to pull away.

"Calm down now, don't wiggle. This will help you relax," he said as he jabbed something sharp into my arm. Not so kind, after all.

"Stop," I mumbled. "Get the children out of the water. It's not safe."

"Shhh," soothed the face.

"Get away from me, don't touch me," I spat.

"No, no, dear. Don't worry. We won't hurt you." I wished I could say the same.

"No. It's the blood. There's dirty blood in the water," I moaned.

"Poor thing. She's hysterical," said a face. Someone tried to lift me by my other arm, but I yanked it away.

"She's in shock. We need to get her out of those wet clothes. How long before that shot kicks in, Doc?"

"Right about now…" said the doctor.

❧ Chapter 3 - Gertie

The year 2128

"Okay then, on the count of three, I want you to remove the tokens from your bag. There are three sets of five tokens. Each set contains five matching finishes. You will have 60 seconds to separate each set until you have three matching stacks of five," shouted proctor Jade as she paced the floor in front of us.

Frantically, I opened the top of the desk and looked inside. "What tokens, where?" I said.

Jade counted the students. "Hmm. There are eight of you. That's too bad. There are only six bags," she shrugged as a Marshal zoomed into the room.

"Only six? What does that mean?" said Eva. Jade didn't answer.

The Challenge Marshal hovered quietly overhead as screams of joy and horror spread throughout the hall, as the other classes started the second skill. Desperate, I scanned the room but didn't see any tokens or bags. Finally, the Marshal roared to life. It spun and hummed as it released several small burlap sacks from its underbelly. Leesa jumped from her seat and grabbed one mid-air while the rest of the bags bounced off the floor and scattered around the room. Five in all remained. Remembering what Jade said, the rest of us scrambled to the floor. I quickly retrieved one bag, returned to my seat, and promptly untied the rope holding it closed. I dumped the contents onto my desk as Eva cried out.

"They're all gone. This isn't even fair!"

"I don't have one either," said Puck.

A desperate Eva rushed to my desk and tried to take my tokens. "Share with me," she pleaded.

"No! Get away from my desk," I said, swatting her hand as the Marshal dove in. Eva slumped to the ground and cried, but I ignored her and began studying the contents of my bag.

Inside were fifteen coin-shaped tokens, each etched with the face of a current or former government official, including President Bruno. Five of the coins were flat and smooth, five had a rough texture, and the faces on the last five were raised—five matching sets of three. I quickly separated the piles by their texture and sat back. Three stacks of five, like

Jade, said. Except for Eva and Puck, everyone figured it out and completed the task in plenty of time.

"Great job!" shouted Jade. "Now do it again, this time with five piles of three matching tokens. You have sixty seconds. Go!"

"Five piles? I don't get it," said Leesa. I looked around the room. No one seemed to get it. I rearranged the tokens on my desk, but it made little sense. President Bruno, smooth. Colonial Lindeman, rough and rigid, ex-President Feister, raised. I looked over at Sadie. The smile on her face and fast-moving fingers told me she'd figured it out. The Marshal hovered above her and signaled her completion with a loud chime. Sadie let out a sigh and sank into her seat as beads of sweat dripped from her forehead.

The Marshal spotted me staring and zoomed overhead, and I immediately went back to my own pile. Shuffling through the tokens, it finally came to me. There were five presidents, five colonials, and five generals. The textures had nothing to do with it. I separated the piles by each president, the generals who served under them, and finally, the corresponding Colonial. The first few were easy: Bruno, Nguyen, and Elders. Next came Bailor, Smithers, and Yeager, followed by Feister, Beck, and Bishop.

I struggled with the last two. Sensing my frustration, the Marshal hovered above my head. He waited, but after swapping Colonial Lindeman with Colonial Ali, the Marshal approved my piles and moved on to its next victim, Fredric, who completed his task just seconds after me. Screams erupted from the other side of the room, where Eva lay face down near the doorway. A long metal rod shot from the Marshal had pierced her skull and protruded out of her forehead. The rod made a melodious tap-tapping sound against the tile floor as the muscles of Eva's body twitched to the tune of death.

"Oh, did I forget to mention you can't leave the room until the challenge is complete? Oops, my bad," blushed Jade.

Smoke hissed from the Marshal's undercarriage as it spun, locking onto Puck, who'd vaulted over Eva's body and bolted for the door. He yanked it open and ran into the hall. The Marshal gave chase, but before it reached him, an axe whirled out of nowhere and struck Puck square in the forehead. He staggered, turned to face the class, eyes wide and empty, then collapsed backward. Puck was dead.

Abfundt emerged. Silent. He planted a boot on Puck's chest and wrenched the axe free. The crunch of Puck's bones beneath Abfundt's weight sent nausea crawling up my throat, but I stayed frozen.

Without a word, Abfundt wiped the blade clean with his shirt and walked away.

"Very nice, everyone!" cried Jade as the alarm sounded. "Last round. You now have only forty-five seconds to stack all fifteen tokens in chronological order, making one tall stack. One two three, go!"

Careful not to jiggle the desk, I stacked my coins until I had a completed tower and 20 seconds to spare. I sat still and waited for the clock to run out. Jade walked by each desk, examining everyone's completed stack.

"Well, this is no good," she said as she passed by each one.

"What's wrong?" said Sadie.

"I don't know. It just seems too easy," sighed Jade.

"What do you mean?" I said. "None of it's been hard."

"Well, we need to do something about that then," she said, motioning to the Marshal. The Marshal sped to the center of the room, right above our desks, and shot tiny red, rubber balls that one by one hit each desk, destroying everyone's stack. We all watched as our tokens scattered to the floor near our feet. Scrambling to find my tokens amongst the mess, I retrieved all the pieces and quickly re-stacked them before arching my body over them to avoid further hits from the Marshal.

"I'm missing a Colonial Ali. Who has my Colonial Ali?" cried Leesa as she frantically scanned the floor around her desk. I looked over at Judah, who'd also completed his stack, and watched as he secretly slid something into his shirt pocket. Leesa's Colonial Ali, no doubt, but I didn't call him out; instead, I went back to protecting my stack while ignoring Leesa's pleas for help. The alarm rang out at forty-five seconds, and I sat back and let out a sigh. On all fours, Leesa was frantic as she continued to search for her lost token.

"Times up, return to your seat," said Jade.

Leesa returned to her desk and started sorting her remaining pieces.

"I said, time's up," said Jade.

"But, but... One of my tokens is missing. I need more time to find it," stammered Leesa.

"Oh, that's so unfair," chided Jade. "Well, by all means, look."

Leesa lowered herself to the floor and searched for her missing piece while the Marshal landed on her desk and sucked her existing tokens into its undercarriage. Judah reached into his pocket, retrieved the stolen token, and let it fall to the floor near Leesa's feet. Leesa shot Judah a dirty look, grabbed the token, and jumped back into her seat, only to find her remaining pieces gone.

"Wait, what are you doing?" Leesa cried. "She said I had more time!"

Jade snorted as Leesa threw Captain Ali at the Marshal sitting on her desk. The token bounced off the top of the metal beast and disappeared under Miss Becky's credenza. The Marshal lifted itself off Leesa's desk, hovered above her head, then fired her tokens back at her with such force that the tiny metal objects pierced her skin. Leesa screamed as the tokens shot into her face and chest and embedded themselves into her organs. I held tight to my desktop as the room spun, and the sweet vomit lying in wait in my stomach entered the room, splattering onto the floor near my feet. I looked down at the sugary remains of the day's meals and smiled.

Only three skills left.

❧ Chapter 4 - Maya

The year 2116

The only thing worse than the pain in my head was the desert oasis forming in my throat. I reached out to search for Gertie's swaddle, but it wasn't there. Frightened by my missing baby, I jolted upright and found myself sitting on a cot in a small hut. There's just enough light from the curtain covering the doorway to tell I'm alone, surrounded by empty baskets and fruit drying on racks.

I kicked the jumbled blankets from my legs and swung my bare feet onto the floor. The cold earth felt good against my tired feet. Sitting on a table next to the cot was a cup of water. I grabbed it with my newly bandaged hand and guzzled it empty.

"Hello?" My head throbbed, and somewhere nearby, I could hear the soft rush of water. It made me think of the faces. I stood up, bracing myself against the cot, and shuffled toward the curtain. Outside, the sun was already high. The air smelled like damp earth, strong coffee, and smoked fish. It was morning, and time for breakfast.

Clothes drying on tree limbs swayed in the breeze near a large communal fire that crackled with new wood. I recognize a shirt and a pair of pants hanging amongst the drying laundry. They were mine.

"Hello," I said again, but no one replied. The six other huts surrounding the fire were quiet, too. Water pots nestled in the fire steamed and shook as they boiled dry, while skewers of fish lay burned amongst the embers as if forgotten by the cook.

I listened for any sign of life, but there was nothing. No chatter from the women as they worked, nor shrieks of laughter from children playing in the distant river. No sounds of men chopping wood or riding on horses outside the fort. Maybe they went somewhere together, but where and why would they leave the fire unattended? I'm reminded of my head wound and run to the nearest hut.

Empty.

A hastily tossed washbasin lay in a puddle near the door, where its once-clean contents mingled with the mud. What happened here?

De-evolution.

No, that can't be it. There's no blood, no ripped flesh dangling from the trees or smeared on the ground.

De-evolution.

I moved from hut to hut, finding each empty except for the evidence of the day's activities left waiting for their owners to return. A pair of unfolded jeans sprawled across a newly made bed. A baited fishing rod and a fresh can of worms. A duffel bag packed with dried meat next to an overfilled canteen that dripped water from its lid. Exiting the last hut, I wandered through the fort towards the river, passing empty stables and abandoned watchtowers.

Outside the fence, the river surged on, loud and restless, as if trying to drown out the silence left behind by its missing neighbors, but something floating in the current snagged my attention. Not a person but a horse.

Its bloated body drifted slowly, limbs stiff, eyes gone. It rocked against the dam like it was waiting for something. Overhead, the birds circled, curious and hungry.

De-evolution

Gagging, I stumbled back to the hearth, tore my clothes from the tree limb, and sprinted to the hut where I'd slept. I changed quickly, hands shaking. Then I returned to the fisherman's hut, grabbed a frayed black jacket from the chair, and tied it around my waist.

As I turned to leave, something yellow caught my eye beneath the chair. I bent down, picked it up, and froze.

A neon yellow armband. Bold black letters across the front: **DUTY**.

My stomach dropped. It was the same kind worn by the prisoners at Intermountain. The same one Jobe stole the day we went looking for Markus.

"Jobe?" I called out, tearing through the hut, searching for anything familiar, a shirt, a comb, those sloppy shoes. Nothing.

I checked the other huts. Still nothing. Just the yellow armband, bright and unmistakable. Was it Jobes? Or had one of the men kept it as a souvenir from a past life behind fences and watchtowers?

I tried to believe that. Tried to believe Jobe hadn't been here. But the thought clung to me.

And Gertie, what about her? The travelers must've reached the fort sometime yesterday. What happened to them? What happened to my little girl?

Leaving her with them had felt right. There was no life for her with me. But Jobe. Jobe was different

I slipped the yellow band into my pocket and stepped outside. The sky was a piercing blue, too bright and clean. It reminded me of that day in Proper. The day Father Jameson came back with his men. The day everything changed. I used to dream of change, just not like this.

I tilted my head toward the heavens, closed my eyes, and rose onto my toes. Then, like a child chasing magic back at my library, I clicked my heels together three times. Nothing. With a sigh heavy, I turned and walked toward the river.

✢ Chapter 5 - Maya

The year 2116

Hours had passed since I'd left the fort, but the faces were still nowhere to be found. The riverbank was marked with fresh footprints and scattered horse droppings. Signs of movement all around, but no people. Just the steady rush of water and a few birds wheeling overhead.

The sun hung high now, merciless. My dehydrated body felt like it might fold in on itself. I sank to the edge of the river, pulled the yellow duty rag from my pocket, and wiped the sweat from my brow.

"Hello?" I called out, voice cracking. "Is anyone out there?"

The only sound was that of the river and the faint rustle of the trees as they tousled with the wind. I reached back and touched the wound on the back of my head. It was sticky and wet, but it didn't hurt anymore, nor did my hand, and I wondered if that was a good thing.

I cupped water in my palm and drank. My stomach churned, growled, and threatened to revolt. I rolled onto my side, shut my eyes, and tried to breathe through the nausea.

Then a memory surfaced. A holy man, maybe. His name I couldn't remember, but his words lingered:

"For the living know they will die, but the dead know nothing."

Then it came back, the water, the faces pulling me from the river, the blinding light, and the face of Jesus, gazing down on me. I thought I was dead then. Maybe I was right.

I sat up, brushed the dirt from my cheek, and smiled. Of course. It was the only explanation that made sense. No one survives a blow like that. And I remember drowning, clear as day, lungs full, body sinking into darkness.

I looked toward the sky and smiled again. For some, the truth might have shattered them. But I felt relief.

The dead don't hurt. They don't kill. They don't die again. At least I didn't think so.

But if I'm dead, then what now? This place wasn't Hell, and there's no way I'd ever end up in Heaven. So where was I?

I thought about the holy man again and remembered his name. Father Dillon. Purgatory. That's what he called it—a place for the undecided. For the souls who weren't ready, or maybe never would be.

God's waiting room, where the clocks tick without hands and the doors never quite open.

Was that what this was?

The river, the silence, the yellow armband. The absence of pain. The lack of certainty.

Maybe I wasn't meant to know. Perhaps that was the point.

By the waters edge, I saw a boot half-buried in the mud. Jobe's boot, maybe. But if I were dead, and Jobe had been here, was he dead too? Or was this place not just for the dead, but for the lost?

I looked up at the sky, so blue it felt cruel. If God was watching, he wasn't saying much. Was my fate that difficult to decide?

I was still trying to make sense of things when I heard shouting ahead. I jumped up and ran toward the noise. About half a mile up the trail, the river split in two, and there in the water, at the fork, a man on horseback was beating another man with a whip.

The rider gripped the whip tightly, swinging it with practiced force. The victim stood waist-deep in the water, blood streaming from fresh wounds. He kept lunging toward the horse, bouncing off the river bottom, but the rider struck again and again, keeping him back with each lash. The man screamed with every blow, but he didn't retreat.

On the riverbank, a small boy stood alone. Maybe four or five years old. He was crying, watching everything unfold, frozen in place like he'd seen it all before.

"Is Mum alright, Pa? Did you find Mums?" cried the boy.

"Stay back, Jax," shouted the man on the horse. The young boy hunched to the ground and wept for his mother, but I knew somehow she wasn't coming back.

"Are you alright?" I asked, but the boy didn't respond. He sat trembling, head buried in his hands, shoulders shaking.

I took a step toward him, then froze.

In the river, the bloodied man stopped screaming. The rider had lowered his whip, staring as if hypnotized as the man in the water began to laugh. Not wildly, but with a strange rhythm, like he'd found something beautiful in the pain.

He stopped reaching for the horse and started to spin. His arm lifted and circled above his head as he turned again and again, the water around him spiraling red. Without the river, it would've been a dance, one I knew too well. One I'd seen before back at Proper.

My legs gave out. My stomach twisted. Whatever water was left in my stomach came up as I dropped to my knees and screamed, not at the man, not at the rider, but at the little boy.

"Run, run away!" I shouted.

The boy turned. His eyes were trembling, pink, wet, and unnatural. "But I have to find my Mum," he said, voice thin and broken.

I screamed. The sight of his Kuru-stricken gaze knocked the breath out of me, and I fell hard onto the ground. My hands scraped the dirt as I scrambled backward, heart hammering.

In the river, the horseman raised his whip one last time. The final lash tore through the man's flesh, and his body went limp. Blood bloomed around him as he drifted downstream, limbs slack, eyes open. His face was unmistakable; it was the same face who'd given me the shot just yesterday.

The horseman turned his mount, rode to the river's edge, and scooped the boy into his arms. Then he came toward me, slow and deliberate, the boy clinging to his chest.

"I'm sorry," I whispered.

The man spat at the ground near my feet, then raised his voice and began reciting scripture.

"Come out of her, my people, so that you don't share in her sins or her diseases," he shouted. "Her plagues will come in a single day: death, mourning, and famine. She will be consumed by fire, for mighty is the Lord who judges her."

He gripped the boy by the waist. The child didn't struggle, just stared, trembling, eyes wide and pink with sickness. The man drew a knife and, without hesitation, plunged it into the boy's chest. Then, with the same hand, he dragged the blade across his own throat.

They collapsed together into the river. The water swallowed them whole. The horse bolted, hooves kicking up mud as it vanished into the trees.

I fell backward, my head striking the ground with a sickening thud. Pain burst behind my eyes as I curled into myself and sobbed.

The year 2128

"Congratulations, you have all completed the second skill." Jade walked over to Leesa and kicked her lifeless leg. "Well, almost," she chuckled. "Your next skill starts in one minute in the History Lab. One, two, three, go!"

The remaining five of us jumped to our feet and raced to the History Lab at the opposite end of the building, where we found proctor Destiny standing at the front of the room.

"Take a seat. Quickly, take a seat," shouted Destiny as we entered the room where four other students sat waiting. Seconds later, three students from Ian's homeroom raced in and took their seats. Ian wasn't one of them.

Anxious, we all looked around the room for clues as to what the next skill would be, but there was nothing. After the one-minute alarm, Destiny pulled the door shut and locked it.

"I guess this is it," she said as she pulled down a whiteboard at the front of the classroom, revealing the word *Spelling Bee* written across the top, along with a doodle of a bee waving hello.

"Ok, you all know how this works. I will give you each a word, and you will have 10 seconds to spell it correctly or, oh wait now," giggled Destiny. "I almost forgot," she shook her head in embarrassment, and opened the locked door where two impatient Marshals hovered out in the hall.

"Silly me," she said as the Marshals entered the room and took their place on either side of the whiteboard. "Ok, we will start at the front and move across from left to right. Destiny looked straight at me and fired off the first word.

"Pioneer," she said.

"Pioneer," I stuttered. "P, I," I stopped and cleared my throat.

"Six seconds," shouted Destiny.

"P, I, O, N, E, E, R. Pioneer," I said.

"Correct!" said Destiny. I smiled and looked at the student sitting next to me. Her name was Gilly, a girl from another class. Gilly quickly spelled her word, ambidextrous, and I cringed. Not only was she correct, but I would have missed that one.

"Nice," said Destiny. "Now you," she said as she approached Pearl's desk. Pearl wiped a bead of sweat from her brow and gulped air.

"Your word is judiciously," said Destiny.

"Judiciously," said Pearl. "Can you please use it in a sentence?" Destiny rolled her eyes and huffed.

"Very well. If you don't spell judiciously correctly in the next five seconds, I will have my Marshal judiciously take your head." As if on cue, one Marshal dove to life and hovered above Pearl's desk.

"Judiciously, J, U, D, I, C, I, O, U, S, L, Y, Judiciously," blurted Pearl.

"Very good," said Destiny. Pearl lowered her head to the desk and gave an audible sigh.

Round after round, Destiny fired words at each of us while the Marshals darted from desk to desk. With each round, the words became harder, but we spelled them all correctly, that is, until round four when Morten misspelled carcinogen, and Sadie missed blasphemy. Sadie's head was still spinning near Morten's dismembered body when Destiny delivered my next word.

"Your word is soliloquy," said Destiny.

"Soliloquy?" I said. My heart raced, and my stomach turned. I'd never even heard of this word. "Soliloquy, S," I paused as tears filled my eyes. "O." Just then, the alarm sounded, and the Marshals returned to their spots near the whiteboard.

"Times up," shouted Destiny. "Aren't you the lucky one?" she whispered as she passed my desk.

I nearly fell out of my seat with relief as Destiny instructed the remaining students to go to the next skill. I stepped over Sadie's crumpled body, careful not to get too much blood on my shoe, and followed the others down the hall to Room 14B, where only six other students and two marshals waited. Proctor Quinn entered the room holding a stack of papers and placed one face down on each of our desks.

"Welcome to the fourth skill," said Quinn. Conner reached for the paper on his desk, and Quinn slapped the boy's hand. "No, no, hands down. Do not touch the math exam until I say so," he said.

The room buzzed at the mention of math, and everyone looked at Bailey, who sat up in her seat and smiled as she rubbed the math charm on her purity bracelet.

"You will have forty minutes to answer a series of mathematical problems," said Quinn, as he paced the floor. He stopped at Bailey's desk and scowled as if annoyed by her smugness.

Quinn held out his hand. "Give me those," he said.

"Give you what?" said Bailey.

"Your eyeglasses," he said.

Bailey reached up and touched the pretty tortoiseshell frames of her glasses. "But I can't see without them."

"Give them to me!" screamed Quinn. Desperate, Bailey looked to each of us for support, but everyone, including me, ignored her stares.

"I will not repeat myself," sneered Quinn as the Marshals glowed red. Bailey slowly removed her glasses and handed them to Quinn.

Conner let out a nervous laugh before lowering his head as one Marshal turned its glass eye on him.

"Enough! We've wasted enough time already. You have forty minutes to answer all the questions. Turn your exams over and start now!" shouted Quinn. The Marshals spun to the ceiling and circled the perimeter of the room as we turned over our exams and quickly began to work.

There were twenty questions in all. The first ten were basic arithmetic, and I breezed through them in under fifteen minutes. The next few were word problems, slightly trickier but still manageable. I kept my eyes on the exam, trying to block out Bailey's panicked muttering as she stumbled through the questions, and the soft sighs of confusion from Pearl and another girl whose name I couldn't recall.

I was nearly finished with the final question when I felt a shift in the air beside me. Pearl had leaned in, her eyes flicking toward my answers. I slid my hand over the page and kept writing.

A Marshal noticed.

It lowered from the ceiling like a spider and hovered above Pearl, who froze beneath its shadow. Then, a thin strand began to spool from its core. It was white, sterile, glistening, and spun in slow circles around her head.

Pearl screamed.

She tried to stand, but the filament wrapped her face, then her arms, and her chest. She thrashed, legs kicking, the plastic cocoon sealing her from the waist up. Her cries turned to gasps. Her gasps turned to silence.

Then she slumped forward onto her desk.

The Marshal retracted into the ceiling, its filament trailing. Around me, pencils scratched paper. A cough. A sniffle. The ordinary sounds of a math test resumed, as if Pearl had never existed.

Sitting one row ahead and just to my left, Judah turned to me, lifted his exam, and shrugged. The bottom few questions were blank. I shook my head, went back to my last problem, and quickly filled in the missing angles of the isosceles triangle before returning my exam to the facedown position. Judah squirmed as Quinn counted down the last ten seconds of the skill. With only three seconds remaining, Judah frantically wrote a series of numbers and x's for his last questions and turned over his exam.

He looked back, and I smiled and nodded, acknowledging his completion. Judah shook his head and opened his mouth to scream, but no sound came out. I knew his answers were wrong, but I raised my eyebrows and crossed my fingers anyway.

"Times up, everyone stop, pencils down." Quinn rushed to Bailey's desk and slapped the exam from her trembling hands. "I said pencils down!"

Bailey's exam wafted to the floor and landed near my feet. The problems were blank. Bailey dropped her pencil, lowered her head onto her desk, and wailed. Quinn quickly retrieved the remaining exams, gave them a quick once-over, then tossed them in the wastebasket near the door.

"Aren't you going to grade them?" said Judah.

"No," said Quinn. "I said you had to answer all the questions. I didn't say they had to be correct." Judah let out a cry of relief and raised his hands in the air, while Bailey slowly lifted her head off her desk. The look on Bailey's face was not that of the sweet twelve-year-old girl I remembered from this morning's breakfast but rather that of a deceived animal.

"What did you say?" Bailey sneered.

"What are you deaf to?" Quinn laughed. "Or perhaps you're just not as smart as you think you are?"

Bailey's blind eyes burned with fury as she shoved her desk aside, her body trembling with rage and fear. A sweet, acrid stench of adrenaline filled the room as she staggered toward Quinn, arms swinging wildly. Quinn stood by the door, unmoved. His face held a quiet amusement, as if he'd seen this play out before.

Above them, the Marshals skittered across the ceiling, waiting for the signal.

Bailey was just feet away from Quinn when the first Marshal struck. A rope shot from its undercarriage, looped with surgical precision, and caught Baily by the ankles. She was yanked forward, face-first, the breath knocked from her lungs as her head slammed against the ceramic tile near Quinn's feet.

The sound of a shattered skull echoed.

The Marshal reeled her in, rope winding fast, until Bailey hung limp and unconscious, suspended just above the floor like a broken doll.

Then the Lab door burst open.

Several students rushed in and took their seats without a word. Behind them came Winnimere, Abfundt, and the three remaining proctors. Winnimere glanced at Bailey's dangling body, chuckled, and began counting the students. "Nineteen, impressive, don't you think so, Abfundt?" said Winnimere. Abfundt growled. "Well, I'm impressed. Wait, does that one there count?" said Winnimere, pointing to Bailey. Quinn shook his head no.

"Ok, well, "Eighteen, that's still a record. How in the world did so many in your class complete the math skill?" said Winnimere. "Jade had six, and Destiny only four."

"I had to alter the rules a bit," said Quinn, nodding toward Bailey.

"Oh, Joy," Winnimere clapped. "I do love it when things go off the rails. This will make for an interesting final skill for sure."

A lump grew in my throat. Only one skill left, and there were still eighteen of us remaining. There would have been fewer had it not been for stupid Bailey and her smugness.

"Speaking of your final skill, you will all return to this room after a break. Our Marshals need time to recharge, and I could use a rest and a warm toddy myself." Winnimere winked at Abfundt.

The lights circling the Marshals dimmed as they fell into a straight line near the ceiling, including the Marshal holding an unconscious Bailey.

"You have one hour before your last skill. Take some time to relax and get something to drink, then everyone is to meet right back here, where Blaine will be waiting. Do not be late." Winnimere turned to leave, then paused.

"Oh, and by the way, the campus gates are open," she said. Heads jerked back and forth as we processed what Winnimere said. 'What does that mean?' mouthed Fredric. I shrugged.

"Abfundt be and dear and escort me back to the dorms, will you?" Winnimere held out her arm, and Abfundt placed his in hers, and the two left the room.

❧ Chapter 7 - Maya

The year 2116

Death was confusing.

Hours had passed since the man killed his son and then himself. I only knew this because the sun had shifted across my skin, dragging the day behind it. Time didn't tick here; it drifted, like dust in a slow-moving storm. They were only trying to help me, back at the fort. And now they were dead because of me. Jobe might be dead, too. I tried not to think about it, but the thought kept circling: if I'm already dead, wouldn't they be dead too? And if that's true, can someone die again? Is there a second death, a deeper one? I rubbed my eyes and let out a long sigh. Maybe this is just how it works in God's waiting room.

I hadn't moved since the incident. There didn't seem to be a point. Leaving would only complicate things. Dead or half-alive, God had surely made up his mind, and after everything, it was clear I wasn't headed for Heaven. So I lay still, waiting for the earth to open up and swallow me whole. Hell felt inevitable. I belonged there.

But as the sun began to set, I started to wonder what was taking so long. The light faded, and shadows stretched. Maybe that was the plan, to be taken in the dark, when this world was quiet, and no one would notice.

I imagined the thing that would come for me: ten feet tall, hooved, with spiral horns that scraped the sky and arms thick as tree trunks. It would grab me by the waist and snap me in two, then drag my mangled body down into the pit. I'd spend eternity there, tortured by Kuru-infected zombies, their eyes pink and trembling, their mouths full of laughter and rot. That seemed more fitting than simply falling into the earth. As darkness fell, I thought about standing up and meeting my demon head-on. But I didn't. I stayed where I was, arms folded across my chest, eyes closed, waiting. I listened for the sounds of fate: low growls, the thud of heavy footsteps, the crack of giant knuckles ready to strike. But none came—only crickets, chirping in rhythm with the river's flow.

It was peaceful. Too peaceful. The kind of quiet that felt like a lie. Hard to believe a demon was on its way.

By morning, I was frustrated and exhausted. I hadn't slept, not even a minute. My throat was dry, and I had to pee so bad it stung. It got me thinking again, do dead people pee? I figured they must. So I stood, didn't bother with a bush, and let it happen right there.

Afterward, I walked to the river, knelt, and drank handfuls of water. All night, I continued to try to convince myself I really was dead and that this was all a test. The idea of being alive was unbearable. Too much to face. So I pushed it away and let myself wonder what came next. If I'm still here, maybe I still have a chance. Maybe God is more forgiving than I thought.

Pastor Dillon used to preach about God's forgiveness. One sermon stuck with me, about choices, and how even the smallest decision could change your life in ways you couldn't imagine. Good or bad, it didn't matter. What mattered was proving yourself worthy. If you could do that, he said, God would welcome you in all his glory. No matter what you'd done in the past.

If that's true, then maybe Hell doesn't have to be my final stop. Perhaps I could do something worthwhile while I'm here. Something that shows I'm still a good person. And besides, this mess, this blood, this death, it wasn't all my fault. Not entirely.

Maybe I could make it home. To Sister Kate and Father Jameson. And Anell, sweet Anell, and her tomboy Gertie, who I'd named my own child after.

I shook the memory away. There was no time for that now. I had work to do. I had to earn my salvation. I wasn't off to the best start, but I could turn it around, I was sure of it. I stood, brushed the dirt from my pants, and took a breath. The air was cold. I shivered, not from fear, but anticipation.

Being dead was freeing. For once, I was in charge. I had a purpose. And nothing could hurt me anymore. At least that was what I hoped.

∾ Chapter 8 - Maya

The year 2116

My mind raced as I set out on this strange new journey. I didn't know where I was going or who I might meet. I didn't even know where I was or if this place had a name, but I was determined to find out. Anything was better than ending up back at the fort.

I kept close to the river, heading north, or so I thought. Sometimes the banks were thick with cattails and spiny weeds, and I had to climb to higher ground to get past. I sang old hymns from church and told myself stories to fill the silence, to distract from the hunger gnawing at my gut and the pain pulsing in my hand.

When night fell, I curled beneath a tall tree and slept harder than I ever had. But by morning, the pain in my hand was worse. It had swollen to twice its size, and dark lines crept past the gash, winding up my arm. My head burned. Dead or alive, I knew I was in trouble. If I didn't find food and medicine soon, I wouldn't last.

The idea of enlightenment now felt foolish. I considered turning back; maybe there was still help at the fort. But then I smelled it, smoked meat. And I heard singing.

I bolted upright and ducked behind a tree, heart pounding. The sounds came from uphill, a few hundred yards from the river—a man's voice, warm and steady. Half of me wanted to run. The other half wanted to investigate.

"Come on, don't be afraid, think about what you've been through already," I said out loud. "How are you going to prove yourself if you're too afraid?"

I figured there was no harm in taking a look. I'd be quiet and careful. If I didn't like what I saw, I'd slip away before anyone noticed.

I crept up the hill, placing each foot with care, avoiding the crunch of dry leaves and brittle twigs. I listened for other voices, but heard only one, the man's.

"Dearest Matilda, oh, stunning Eileen, women I fought for, so lovely and clean," he sang.

At the top, I crouched behind a thick bush and peered through the leaves.

The man sat on a stump beside an open fire, humming as he turned sausages on a homemade skewer. Behind him sat a three-wheeled motorbike, tethered to a wagon unlike anything I'd ever seen. The wagon had four wooden wheels: two smaller ones in front and two larger ones in back, and a staircase that led to an arched awning and a dark red door.

It reminded me of a book I once read about Roman gypsies and their traveling wagons. But theirs were pulled by horses. This one was far more elaborate with carvings in gold and bronze that curled along the corners and across the top. On the side, in bold, ornate lettering, a sign read:

Sebastian Sheets Carnivále Extraordinaire!

I held my breath as I watched the man inspect his sausages. Drool had begun to form in the corners of my mouth, and I was still trying to determine whether or not to flee when the man started to speak.

"Y'all can come on out now and grab a seat. Ain't no use hidin', I know you're there. Besides, it's mighty rude to be eatin' in front of company."

I was startled for sure, but his voice was calm, gentle even. Not what I expected. It made me pause, made me listen. His words were slow and melodic, and there was a bit of an accent I couldn't place. He didn't sound like a crazy person or baby wrangler, not like any of the ones I knew, and I knew plenty.

I stood up and stepped into the clearing. "You can see me?"

The man looked over at me and smiled. "I can now," he said.

"How did you know I was here?" I said.

"I could smell you coming from a mile away, eucalyptus ointment and fear, I think. Oh, and that stomach of yours wasn't too quiet either," he said.

"Oh, well, I'm just passing through. I'd better just go back to my friends," I said.

"C'mon over here an' have a seat with me. I know you're alone, saw ya sleepin' under that ol' tree last night," he said. "Sit." He gestured toward another seat on the other side of the fire.

I hesitated and looked back toward the river and then again at the man. His eyes were dark brown yet sparkled like the night sky; he had long, brown hair that lay wild just past his shoulders, and a wry, crooked smile that made my stomach quiver.

"Well, come on now, I ain't gonna bite, and I reckon yer starvin'. I got more than enough for both of us. Plus, you look like ya might just keel over. You feel alright?" he said.

My stomach growled again. "I'm okay, just a little hot and hungry," I said.

"Then it's settled. Sit," he said again.

"Okay, maybe for a bit," I said. I did need food and felt like I might just 'keel over' soon, so I walked over to the fire and sat down.

"What's your name, young lady?" he said. The question took me off guard for some reason. I didn't know what to say. When you think about it, Maya Jameson is no more, and I also wasn't exactly sure how things worked in the afterlife with warrants and all, and I certainly didn't need any trouble right now.

"I don't have one, not anymore," I said. Given our circumstances, I was sure he'd understand, but he just looked puzzled.

"What you mean? Everyone has a name, don't they?" He said.

Flustered, I blurted out the first name I could think of. "Prudence, I think," I said.

"Prudence? You don't look like any Prudence I've ever met. More like a Molly or Olive."

"Fine, then you can call me Olive," I said. The man lifted an eyebrow and cocked his head.

"Sorry. But I'm not really sure who I am right now." I lowered my voice. "You know what I mean, right?"

The man laughed. "I certainly do, sweetheart. I've been down that road myself a few times." He smiled at me with the most charismatic smile I'd ever seen, and I wondered what he'd done to find himself out here. Was he, too, waiting on God's wraith?

"That's a pretty necklace," he said, pointing his skewer at my neck. "It's a purity charm, right? And I bet you got that marking behind your ear, too."

I nodded.

I guess that means you're hiding from something other than the screening patrol," he laughed.

"Oh, that, no, I'm not," I said, touching my charm. "Do they still care about that out here?" I said.

Was there no reprieve from the DOJATE even in the afterlife?

"That I don't know, I try to keep out of politics and certainly away from the DOJATE," he winked. "Now here, take this and eat. There's plenty," he said as he shoved a sausage my way.

"Are you sure? I don't want to take your food," I lied. I wanted nothing more.

"As I said, I have plenty, plus one thing I learned in my life was not to turn away those in need. And you, my dear, look to be in need," he smiled and extended his skewer again.

I grabbed the sizzling meat and joggled it in my hand while it cooled. I desperately wanted to shove the entire sausage into my mouth, but took tiny bites instead—bites like those a Heaven-bound girl might take.

"Now let me see, Olive, no, not an Olive. But, I know, I'm going to call you Poppy," he said.

"Poppy? Why Poppy?" I asked.

"Only 'cause it's the purtiest, most beguilin' flower of 'em all. Just like you, my dear." He winked and flashed a smile that tickled my insides and turned my face hotter than it already was.

"Yes, Poppy, it is," he said.

"What's your name?" I asked between bites.

The man frowned, then sprang to his feet with exaggerated flair. "Why, you must think me the rudest soul alive!" he said. "Allow me to introduce myself. I'm Sebastian Sheets, and this here," he swept his arm toward the wagon like a magician unveiling a trick, "is my Carnivále Extraordinaire."

He bowed low, as if to an invisible audience, then straightened with a grin that shimmered somewhere between charm and madness.

That's when it hit me, why he felt so familiar.

Sebastian had Val's presence. Not quite as tall or rugged, but the same magnetic pull, the same easy confidence. And something else, too. Something darker. His wild hair and mischievous eyes reminded me of Danger, the deranged lunatic whose daughter killed Val. The resemblance was subtle, but it crawled under my skin.

I glanced around, searching for signs of a carnival: tents, performers, music. But there was only the wagon, the fire, and Sebastian.

He caught my confusion and shrugged, settling back onto the stump. "Well, right now it's kinda just a one-man show," he said, poking at the sausages. "But you just wait. One day, I'll have the biggest, most amazin' carnival you ever saw. Attractions so wild, folks'll travel from way out yonder just to catch a glimpse."

His voice was full of conviction, but something in his eyes flickered, like he'd already seen it, or maybe dreamed it too many times.

"What kind of attractions?" I asked.

"Mostly oddities," Sebastian said. "Freak show stuff. Things that make your stomach turn and your eyes pop."

"Like a bearded lady?" I said, remembering a book I'd read about circus performers.

"A bearded lady? Nah," he scoffed. Sebastian leaned forward, elbows on his knees. "You ever seen a man with no skin? Or a girl who speaks in tongues she's never learned? I met a boy once who could cry blood on command. Real tears, too. Not stage tricks. That's what I'm after. The real stuff. The kind that makes you question what's possible."

He stared into the fire for a moment, lost in thought. "It'll be the most amazing show anyone's ever seen," he said softly, then blinked and snapped back to the moment.

"So there are others out here like us?" I said.

"What do you mean like us?" he said

"People... waiting for judgment?" I said. My voice was starting to slur, and my head felt heavy.

"There are people all over these parts. Not so sure about judgment, though. Everyone gotta go in front of the Lord at some point," he said.

"I see," I said, wobbling a little and nearly dropping my sausage.

"Are you okay? You seem a little out of it," Sebastian said.

"Yes, I'm fine," I replied. "I just didn't expect it to be so busy here." I looked around, confused. Father Dillon never mentioned other people when he talked about this place.

Sebastian tilted his head and laughed. "You're an odd bird, aren't you?"

"Why would people want to see that? The oddities, I mean," I asked.

"It's the mystery," he said. "People are drawn to things they don't understand. That's why freak shows are so popular. They want to be seduced by the grotesque."

He leaned closer to the fire and grinned.

"Want to know a secret?" he whispered.

I nodded.

"I already have my first attraction," he said. "Wanna see?"

"I do," I said, still chewing.

Though the idea of being seduced by the grotesque sent chills up my spine, I doubted he had anything so elaborate housed in that tiny wagon. Even though Sebastian reminded me of Val, I couldn't help remembering Val's warnings about strangers and all the trouble I got in with Percy, but this felt different for some reason. It felt safe.

Sebastian jumped to his feet and headed to the back of the wagon. He opened a small hatch and pulled out a box no bigger than a shoe. But before he could say anything, he noticed a smudge on the wagon's side and paused to wipe it clean with his sleeve.

"It's an actual Romani wagon," he said proudly. "And that's my bike, the Flying Cruiser." He pointed at the motorbike with a grin. "Found them both in a junkyard in Diego. The bike was in decent shape, but the wagon took me three years to fix up. Now it's better than new." He looked at me, eyes shining. "Come see."

Still holding the box, he ran to the front of the wagon, dashed up the stairs, and threw open the big red door.

I walked up the stairs and peeked through the doorway. My eyes widened. "It's so much bigger than I expected," I said. "And so lovely."

Inside, the wagon looked like a tiny home. At the far end was a raised bed. Cabinets made of dark wood lined the walls, with shiny brass knobs and hinges. On one side sat a red couch with a high back and soft, velvety pillows. Across from it was a small dining table with two chairs. The table legs were carved to look like lion paws, and the wood matched the cabinets.

"It's magnificent," I said.

"I know, right?" Sebastian jumped into the wagon and knocked on the top of the table. "Hand-carved, ya know? I stumbled upon it in Cowtown and fixed 'er up myself. And over there is the sitting area, just right for entertainin' or catchin' some peace and quiet." Sebastian plopped down on the sofa and continued admiring his handiwork.

"Plenty of storage space too, and look in here," Sebastian said, jumping to his feet. He opened a small door next to the table and pulled out a package of frozen meat.

"My very own ice chest," he said proudly. "Finding ice is the hard part, but once I get it, it lasts about a week. And check this out, both sides swing open."

He pulled a lever above the ice chest, and the entire side of the wagon lifted.

"Open-air living at its finest," he said with a grin. "And if I pull this bottom part out, wala! You've got an outdoor table for selling things at the market."

I wanted to ask where you'd find ice or a market in a place like this, but I decided to go along with it.

"What do you usually sell?" I asked, impressed by how clever and practical everything was.

"Mostly my special tonics and elixirs," he said. Sebastian opened a side cabinet, exposing an array of bottles of varying sizes and shapes. I leaned in for a better look, and Sebastian slammed the door shut.

I caught a glimpse of one of the labels and laughed. "Love potion?" I said.

"Yes, and it works too," he said.

"Where did you get love potion?" I said.

"Oh, a good showman never reveals his secrets," he winked.

"Well, I'm impressed," I said. "It's not just beautiful, it's cozy and useful too."

"Wait, I almost forgot the best part," Sebastian said. He opened the rectangular box he'd been holding and gently pulled out a small green turtle.

"This, my dear Poppy, is the first of many," he said, stroking its shell.

"It's just a turtle," I said.

"Oh, but not just any turtle. Look." Sebastian gave it a little shake, and the turtle slowly poked its head out, or rather, two heads.

I leaned in, surprised. "It has two heads?"

"He does," Sebastian said.

"Is it real?" I said, reaching out to touch one of the heads. The turtle disappeared back inside himself.

"Of course, he's real, and his name is Banjo," said Sebastian. "Found him near a dried-up creek bed a few months back. Thought he was a rock at first."

"That's amazing," I said. I was fascinated by the tiny green two-headed turtle named Banjo. I'd never seen anything like it. Not even in my books. This trip through the afterlife was going to be crazy.

"This is what I'm talking about, but I need more! Bigger, more bizarre. Something no one has ever seen before," he said.

"Wait. Why does he only have one name?" I said.

Sebastain frowned and cocked his head. "What do you mean?"

"Well, he has two heads. Shouldn't he have two names?" I said.

"Huh? I never thought about that before. But, hmm, you know what, no. He has one heart and one soul, so he gets one name," he said.

"That doesn't seem fair, does it, Banjo?" I said as I stroked the top of his shell. Sebastian winced at the sight of my soiled bandage.

"What happened to your hand?" he said.

"It's nothing," I said, pulling away.

"It doesn't look like nothin'. Here, let me look at it." Sebastian removed the bloody, soiled rag from my hand and gasped at the smoldering gash. "What in the world? It looks like someone stabbed you," he said.

"Someone did stab me," I said flatly.

"Who dressed this?" he said.

"I don't know, one of the faces. They cleaned it, too," I said.

Sebastian shook his head. "This doesn't look clean at all. That eucalyptus oil doesn't work on a wound like this." Sebastian squeezed my hand. Yellow and black pus oozed from the gash, releasing a putrid stench.

"What is all that?" I said.

"That, my dear Poppy, is an infection. A bad one," Sebastian said as he wiped the pus with a clean rag.

"How bad?" I asked.

"Bad enough to kill you. You're lucky to still be alive with that much sepsis."

"Alive? What do you mean by 'alive'? I'm already dead, right? Tell me I'm dead." I said.

Sebastian chuckled. "No, not dead. Maybe a little confused, but definitely not dead. Not yet anyway."

"Then this isn't purgatory?" I asked, pulling my hand away.

"Purgatory?" Sebastian touched my forehead and frowned. "You're burning up. You need to lie down." He tried to help me by putting his arm around my shoulder.

"No, don't touch me," I said, pulling away. "I thought I was dead. I thought I was safe." I scrambled toward the door.

"It's still in me!" I screamed.

I reached for the door, but the walls of the wagon seemed to close in around me. Then everything fell away. I was back in the river, alone, struggling to breathe.

Drowning.

Drowning.

Drowning.

Chapter 9 - Gertie

The year 2128

After Winnimere and Abfundt left the lab, the proctors followed suit, leaving the final eighteen of us alone for the first time since the Challenge began.

"What do we do now?" asked a boy named Fritz, his voice low. A faint buzzing from the ceiling reminded us we weren't truly alone.

"Let's get out of here," said Chad, an older student from another class. "We need space to figure out our next move."

We followed Chad to the fountains outside Trivel. It was getting dark, and the area was empty. The walkways connecting the schools were silent; everyone else was still under lockdown until the Challenge ended.

Once there, we formed a loose circle around Chad, who had quickly become our leader.

"Listen," he said, "we should head to the river beyond the grounds. If we move fast, we'll make it before time runs out. Once we're there, we scatter."

"Won't the Marshals come for us?" said Gilly.

"The bracelets can't have that kind of range. By the time the Marshals finish recharging, we'll be too far away to track. They won't be able to find us," said Chad.

"He's right. I say we run for it," said a girl named Prill.

"But what about the Challenge?" I said.

"And leaving the grounds is forbidden," said a girl named Yoli.

"Don't you understand? You're going to die. We all are. No one can win," said Chad.

"That's not true. People win all the time. That's how you get to the Down House," I said.

"True, but how? Think about it. These skills can't be the real test. I think this is the final skill. You remember what Winnimere said in the cafeteria. Not all skills are what they seem. This could be what the whole thing is about," said Chad.

"You know, you might be right," said Judah. "That makes more sense than a spelling bee."

"Yeah," chimed some of the students.

"Ok, then it's settled. We run. Now, come on and follow me to the river. From there, it'll be every man for himself." Chad turned and raced past the fountains towards the entrance to Greyburry. Judah and a handful of others followed, leaving me and the rest of the students behind.

"What do we do now?" said Yoli.

"We stay here. We're not supposed to leave. It's a trick," said Fredric.

"I don't know, but it seems like this whole Challenge has been a trick," I said.

"It doesn't make any sense. How do we win if the skill is to run so far that they can't track us? No, we need to stay and be back in one hour, like Winnimere said," said Fredric.

"But why would they open the gates? I think it's part of the Challenge to escape," said Gilly.

"I don't know. Maybe Chad's right. This could be a twist," I said. "What if they want to know who's the fastest runner?"

The group fell silent as we each contemplated our next move. Finally, Gilly broke from the group and raced towards the gates.

"I think we should follow them. Yoli, come with me?" I said. Yoli looked to Fredric, who frowned, then shook his head.

"Fine, I'm going," I said, turning and running toward the path that led to the Greyburry gates. The others were already far ahead, but I caught up quickly, falling in near the back of the group.

Then I heard it, a faint whirring sound from above.

I stopped and ducked into a thicket of brush near the fence that bordered the Down House. Holding my breath, I listened. Crickets chirped in rhythm, and the wind rustled through the trees. Up ahead, I could hear Chad and the others passing through the gates, leaving Greyburry behind.

I started to rise, but the whirring returned, louder this time.

I sat back down and looked up. At first, the sky was empty. Then the whirring grew louder, and five round shadows appeared above the trees, drifting slowly and with purpose.

Marshals.

Hidden in the bushes, I watched as the Marshals drifted toward the gates and vanished into the night. The band of my purity bracelet buzzed and burned against my wrist. I hadn't made it far enough.

Panic set in. Should I swim across the lake to the point? Or run the two miles to the far side of campus and hide near the kinder dorms? Was Chad right? Were we supposed to escape? Or was Fredric?

I didn't have time to decide. I chose the kinder dorms. They'd never find me there.

I jumped to my feet and raced around the back of the Down House. I'd have to stay low past secondary row, but after that, the path to kinder was wide and quiet, tucked between thick trees. If I sprinted, I could make it in under ten minutes.

The sound of the Marshals powering up in the woods told me they were in kill mode now. The others were probably already dead.

I ran around the back of the Down House and slipped in a patch of mud. I got up, wiped myself off, and froze when I heard a loud knocking from above.

I crouched in the brush and looked around. The Down House was mostly dark, except for a few lit rooms upstairs. The knocking came again.

I looked up and saw one of the older girls standing in a window. She was staring at me and waving.

She tried to mouth something, but I couldn't understand. I shrugged, and she disappeared. A few seconds later, she came back holding a letter board. She scribbled something down, then turned it around so I could read it.

The board said, *GO BACK.*

I pointed toward the gates, confused. The girl shook her head and started writing again.

Back to Trivel. It's how you win!!!!

Of course. It wasn't a race, it was a trick. I waved to her, then turned and ran toward the main path back to Trivel. Time was almost up.

When I reached the room, it was quiet. Fredric and Yoli sat in the first row. Proctor Blaine stood at the front of the room, arms crossed, staring out at four rows of desks, five seats in each. Way too many, I hoped.

Each desk had a small plastic tablet on top.

I stood in the doorway, waiting for instructions. Blaine didn't say a word.

The clock above his head ticked down.

One minute left.

"What am I supposed to do?" I said—still nothing from Blaine.

The clock wound down to twenty seconds when two more students rushed in, pushed me out of their way, and took seats. It was Olivia and the girl whose name I couldn't remember. I followed suit and took a seat as Lester raced in behind me.

"What's this?" said Olivia.

"It looks like a slide puzzle," said Fredric.

"It is a puzzle," huffed Lester as he picked up the tablet.

Ten seconds left on the clock. Waiting for the final alarm, I studied the slide puzzle but didn't dare touch it. Not yet. It was just like the ones we used to play with at kinder. There were only nine slides, and although they were mixed up, it was easy to tell they were pictures of a cow.

The alarm sounded, and a single Marshal entered the room and hovered near the front just above Blaine. The Marshal's glass eye flashed red as it voiced a robotic countdown that started at sixty. Fifty-nine, fifty-eight, fifty-seven...

We all sat in silence, watching the clock tick down. Blaine didn't move. He didn't speak. Just stood there, arms crossed, eyes fixed on us like we were pieces in a game.

"He's counting down from a minute," Yoli said, her voice tight.

"Is it the puzzle, then? Is this the final skill?" Olivia asked.

"It has to be," Lester replied, already adjusting the pieces on his tablet.

I followed his lead, sliding my own tiles into place, trying to stay calm. The room felt heavy, as if something were about to shift.

Then the door burst open. Gilly ran in, breathless, and dropped into an empty seat—the only one from Chad's group to return.

No one spoke. No one welcomed her. We just kept working, waiting for the clock to hit zero. The robotic reading of the seconds continued as we finished our puzzles one by one.

"Done," yelled Fredric with nineteen seconds to go.

"Done," said Yoli, followed by Lester, who also threw his hands in the air.

"Finished," cried Olivia. "What about you, Neddie?" she said to the girl whose name I didn't know.

"Yes, I'm done," choked Neddie.

"Done," I shouted as I slid my cow's head into its rightful slot. Gilly finished her puzzle next, but didn't speak. Her face was red with welts, her purple vest smoldered, and she reeked of burned hair and feces.

Glenn and Raleigh, two more of Chad's team, entered the room as the Marshal's countdown struck zero.

"Times up," said Blaine.

Glenn and Rayleigh, covered in mud, grabbed hands, moved to the back of the room, quietly sat on the floor, and embraced as Winnimere and Abfundt entered, followed by the remaining proctors.

Winnimere beamed from ear to ear. "Do we have some winners?" she said.

"Six," said Blaine. The Marshal shone a light on my desk and the other five winners' desks.

"Only six? That's less than last time, isn't it, Abfundt?"

"About the same," muttered Abfundt.

"Such a clever-looking bunch, though," said Winnimere.

Gilly looked around the room and began counting the finished puzzles. Hers was number seven, but her desk wasn't lit.

"What about me? I finished too," shouted Gilly. Blaine shook his head at Winnimere and pointed to the clock.

"She came back after the hour was up," he said.

"Oh dear, I'm afraid you were late," Winnimere feigned regret as she shook her head. "You remember what I said. Don't be late."

"Only by a second, and there are only four girls. You said there were five spots. I finished the puzzle in time," said Gilly.

Winnimere marched to Gilly's desk and kicked Gilly's feet. "Why mud?" said Winnimere.

Gilly sat up straight and folded her arms. "I… I was outside on break," she said, voice shaky.

"There's no mud outside," said Winnimere. "Abfundt, did you see any mud?"

"The only mud I saw was near the gates," Abfundt replied.

"Near the gates?" Winnimere raised an eyebrow. "What were you doing out there, hmm?"

"Nothing… We were just on break," Gilly mumbled.

"Admit it. You tried to run," Winnimere said.

"You said we could!" Gilly cried.

"I said no such thing," Winnimere laughed. "I said the gates were open. That was a warning, not an invitation. But you ran anyway."

"But I came back," Gilly said, her voice breaking.

Winnimere turned to the rest of us. "You need to understand something. Runners never win."

"But I came back!" Gilly shouted.

"You came back too late! I said, don't be late!" Winnimere screamed, spit flying from her mouth.

Gilly covered her face and sank into her seat.

"Repeat after me. Runners never win. Repeat it!" Yelled Winnimere.

"Runners never win," eeked Gilly.

"Everyone say it," said Winnimere. "Runners never win. Say it!"

"Runners never win," we all chimed.

"Do you remember what I said at the beginning? That the tests are designed to test a particular attribute?" We all nodded.

"What do you think this silly little puzzle tests?" No one said anything.

"Loyalty," sneered Winnimere.

The room fell silent. Winnimere straightened her blouse, whipped the corners of her lips with a tissue, and addressed the winners.

"Now, the six of you follow Blaine to the Down House. Miss Ivy will have your things moved over in the morning." I stood just as Winnimere stopped at my desk, looked down at my mud-covered skirt, and frowned. I froze.

"Go on now," she said. "You won't want to be here for this." With that, I quickly made my way to the door just as the remaining Marshals entered the room.

ᴇ CHAPTER 10 - POPPY

The year 2116

"Alrighty then, not too bad," Sebastian said. "But this time, make sure the axe head's pointed at the target. And line up your left foot like this." He stepped behind me and gently turned my hips to face the tree stump.

I tried to focus on the axe, but it was hard not to notice the sweat on his bare chest or the strength in his arms. His breath was warm on the back of my neck.

"Keep your arms steady when you throw," he said. "And don't take your eyes off the target."

He stepped back, and I threw the axe as hard as I could.

It hit the ground a few feet in front of me and bounced into the bushes.

"I can't do it," I sighed.

"Of course you can," Sebastian said, brushing dirt from the axe head. "You're just lettin' go too early. Bring it down to eye level before you let it fly. Stay steady in the middle, hold tight, and release clean. Watch me."

He stepped into position, swapping places with me. He moved with ease, the sun catching on the sweat along his bare shoulders as he raised the axe behind his head. The muscles across his shoulders and back flexed in quiet coordination, each one tightening with purpose. His biceps flexed slightly as he lifted the axe, forearms tight and steady while he found his balance. I tried to focus on the throw, on the steps, but my eyes kept drifting to the curve of his back, the way his muscles moved under his skin. I watched as his torso shifted with each motion, his abs tightening as he exhaled and swung forward.

The axe spun through the air in clean rotations and hit the stump dead center, right on the carved X. He turned and smiled. I looked away, pretending to study the stump, but the image of him stayed with me.

"Bullseye!" he shouted, grinning widely.

I stared at the stump, then at him. "I'll never be that good."

"You will," he said, walking back toward me. "You just need to keep practicing."

He handed me the axe again, his fingers brushing mine. "It's not about strength," he added. "It's about rhythm. You find your rhythm, and the axe will follow."

Sebastian stepped back, arms crossed, watching. "Alright, Poppy. Show me what you've got."

"What's the use? I have no skills," I said, staring down at my hands.

Sebastian leaned back against the stump, arms crossed, a half-smile tugging at his lips. "What you need is some confidence. Just like that time in Austin, we could've cleaned that guy out of a whole heap of credits, but you got cold feet."

I looked up, frowning. "He was on to me."

"Nah, he wasn't," Sebastian said. "You got scared, that's all. I told you, always size up your mark. That guy was flashing credits like he wanted to be robbed. Tan line on his ring finger, nervous laugh, kept checking his watch. He was begging for it."

I didn't answer. I remembered the man's eyes, too kind. I'd hesitated.

"You've got everything it takes to be a world-class con," Sebastian said, stepping closer. "You just don't believe it yet. But that's okay. Stick with me, kid. I'll teach you."

He smiled, and something in me gave way. My knees went soft, and I hated that he noticed.

But he didn't tease. He just stood there, steady and calm, like he'd already decided I was worth the trouble.

"I guess," I said, not sure what I was agreeing to.

Sebastian turned and walked back to the wagon. He grabbed his shirt from the steps and tossed it over his shoulder.

It had been two months since I stumbled upon him near the river, and he still amazes and intrigues me to this day. Though I wasn't dead like I'd hoped, I was close. Sebastian nursed me for two weeks before the infection was completely gone. Now we were a team of sorts.

"So," I said, brushing dirt from my pants, "what's for dinner?"

Sebastian lit up. "Oh, you are in for a treat tonight. Flame-broiled lobster with hollandaise, fingerling potatoes au gratin, and for dessert, apple tart with fresh whipped cream."

He paused, then grinned. "Or… leftover cram sausages and biscuits. Your call."

I laughed. "Hmm, hard to choose, but I'm going to have to go with the cram sausages."

"Excellent choice," he said, already heading inside. "Vintage flavor. Slightly rubbery. Pairs well with lake water. Though someday I am going to treat you to that lobster dinner. I promise." Sebastian winked.

Cram sausages weren't as bad as they sounded, though I didn't know what was in them, nor did I care to. They were a staple all over the region, and we had no trouble trading up or stealing them whenever we ran out. I was tired of the same thing every day, though, and was looking forward to my lobster dinner.

When we met, Sebastian was on his way down south to his hometown near the ocean, where he owned a family plot of land that he named Jubilee. It was there that he planned to build his magnificent *Carnivále* and invited me to come along. I learned this wasn't the same south as where the boys and I talked about going; it was the southern south, not the Safe-Zone south, but I decided to tag along anyway.

I'd been thinking a lot about the twins lately, but decided I'd be better off with Sebastian for now. Sebastian saved my life, after all, and I didn't want to leave him. I knew traveling alone while looking for the twins would be dangerous, and I'd convinced myself it was for the best, for now, anyway. The boys would want me to be safe after all, and I knew once we settled, I could regroup and figure out how to get to them. Besides, there was something more important out there I needed to find first.

Sebastian was curious about who I was, where I'd come from. But I never mentioned Proper, Sparks, the twins, or Gertie. And I certainly never spoke of my dirty blood. After a few weeks, he stopped asking. I figured the less he knew, the safer we both were.

Maybe one day I'd tell him. But not now. Not until I knew Gertie was safe.

If I'd known I'd find Sebastian, I never would've left her in the barn that day. Never would've let the river take me. Never would've ended up at the fort, spreading sickness like a curse. That part still haunted me, the way the faces looked at me when they dragged me from the water, the way they tried to help.

Now that things were different, I searched for Gertie everywhere we went. Every baby in a stroller, every swaddle tucked under a stranger's arms, I looked. I hoped. I imagined her face, older now, changed maybe, but still hers.

Someday, I'd find her.

I had to.

After supper, I sat by the fire and watched Sebastian chop wood. With every smooth swing of his axe, his muscles danced. When he was done, Sebastian lifted his shirt to wipe his brow, exposing one of his many tattoos.

"Where did you get all those?" I said.

"All those what?" he said.

"Tattoos," I said.

"Oh, you mean these?" he grinned as he flexed his left bicep, making the tattoo of a half-naked lady wiggle like she was dancing. "Here and there, mostly when I was young," he said.

"Why?" I said.

"That's just what people do in prison," he said.

"Prison?" I said.

Sebastian flashed an evil smile. "Yes, my dear. You're not the only one with a past around here."

"Why were you in prison?" I said.

Sebastian laughed. "You tell me your secrets, and I'll tell you mine."

"Hmmm," I grunted. Sebastian tossed the axe aside and joined me near the fire, where, like most nights, he'd stare into the flames, lost in thought. I knew what he was thinking about and didn't dare disturb him. Sebastian wasn't always fun-loving and had an unpredictable madness about him I couldn't explain, but I was drawn to him. He was obsessed with getting his carnival up and running and talked about it constantly. I knew he'd stop at nothing, and I wanted to be there for him however I could, even if it meant we would only ever be friends. I wanted more, of course, but couldn't allow it to happen. If anything, I learned the hard way with Eric. I'd say I got lucky, but that would be a lie. Too many people died because of our love, and I couldn't let that happen again.

Life on the road with Sebastian wasn't always easy, but it was thrilling to say the least. We had no credits, but that didn't stop us from getting the things we needed. Sebastian taught me how to persuade people to get what I wanted and, if that didn't work, how to take it anyway. We traveled from town to town, stealing bread from storefront windows, clothes from unattended laundry lines, and tricking people out of their belongings. Sebastian was a master of conversation and captured the locals' attention, while I snatched up anything I could.

I thought about the twins often, but the yearning to find the Free-Zone to search for them faded more and more each day until I convinced myself I didn't know where they were and I'd never be able to find them, but the truth was I was falling in love with Sebastian, forbidden love, of course, but love nonetheless.

Riding Sebastian's motorbike with our ornamental wagon in tow, the two of us raced along the backroads near the southern waters, eliciting stares and comments wherever we went. The roads were battered and bumpy but free from DOJATE checkpoints, grid units, and, best of all, warrant boards.

The roads were dangerous, so besides his two-headed turtle and abundance of homemade elixirs and medications, Sebastian also carried a small arsenal of weapons, primarily axes and swords. He also had two rifles hidden away under his mattress. At night, we'd find a secluded place to camp. We'd eat dinner by the fire. I listened to him go on and on about his plans for *Carnivále*, then we'd take shelter in our ever-shrinking wagon, which was bulging with loot and all my new treasures.

Sebastian loved to spoil me. Mostly with books, whenever he could find them. But it didn't stop there. Over time, I'd collected bags of costume jewelry, secondhand clothes, body creams, and oils with scents that lingered on my skin.

One afternoon, he sweet-talked a traveling merchant out of an entire trunk of scarves and beaded chains. He brought them to me like offerings, laying them out with a flourish, calling me "Her Majesty" and bowing low like we were in some grand palace instead of a dusty roadside camp.

I scolded him, told him he didn't need to do all that. Said the books were enough. But the truth was, I loved the attention. The way he looked at me like I was worth something. Like I was more than a girl with a broken past and a wagon full of stolen things. I didn't really need the gifts. But I needed the feeling they gave me.

And Sebastian knew that.

Sebastian woke from his trance, tossed his stick into the fire, and looked up.

"Will you read to me again tonight?" he said.

"Of course," I said, holding up our latest read. The story of a snobbish southern belle whose life unraveled when a long-forgotten war broke out in pre-cannibal America.

It was one of my favorite books from my library back in Proper. I cried for two days after Sebastian gave it to me, and couldn't bring myself to read it until recently. I knew he was curious and confused by my actions, but he didn't press. It had only been a few days since I started reading, but we were already halfway through. He loved the story just as much as I, and after each chapter, when I'd put the book down, he'd beg me to go on.

"Ok, but only three, no, four chapters tonight. I need to do some work on the cruiser tomorrow and want to get an early start," he said.

"So we're staying here then?" I said as I moved closer to share my blanket.

"Just for another night, we're running low on everything. We're not too far from Bastrop. We'll be able to stock up there. I've got to warn you, though, stay close to me. The people of Bastrop are a bit eccentric."

"Eccentric how?" I said.

"They're a bit off and kinda quirky, ya know? Might be the sorta folks you'd see in a Carnivále. Of course, who knows, we might just come across a three-eyed cow or a knife-swallowing big gal. Wouldn't that be something?" he smiled.

"And put them where? There's hardly enough room in the wagon now," I laughed.

"We'll just strap them to the roof," he joked.

I started reading. Seven chapters later, I closed the book. "Where was Georgia exactly? I've never seen it on a map," I said.

"Georgia? You mean the Cube," he said.

"What's the Cube?" I said.

"The center of the nuke that wiped out the southern bunkers back during the drills. Took out three states in all. Georgia, Western Florida, and parts of that other state. What was it called? Alabama, I think. Now it's nothin' but a dead zone," he said.

"Where is it?" I said.

"East of here, not too far, really. About half as far as we've come," he said.

"Well, that seems far," I yawned.

Sebastian chuckled. "Keep reading."

"No, this is a good place to stop, and my eyes are getting tired."

"Ahhhh," he whined.

"Come on, off to bed with you," I said as I swatted the top of his head with the book. Inside the wagon, Sebastian plopped down on the sofa he had made into a separate bed and patted the cushion for me to join. I shook my head, climbed into the bed that once belonged to him.

Though nothing less than a gentleman, Sebastian made no effort to hide his feelings for me, but he never acted on them. I did my best to act disinterested in his casual flirtatious comments, but the truth was, I wanted nothing more than for him to know I felt the same way, but I couldn't. Sebastian let out a long sigh, settled in under the blanket, and began to sing.

"I'm just a love-struck grifter."

"No lady to call my own."

"Fell in love with a girl named Poppy, with a heart made out of stone. La, la la la la…."

"Stop!" I laughed. "Go to sleep."

❧ Chapter 11 - Gertie

The year 2132

By the time I left the nursery, it was nearly dark outside. The warm summer breeze had turned chilly, and I wished I hadn't forgotten my jacket that morning when I left the dorm, but I didn't really mind. Fall would be here soon, my favorite time of year.

"Almost home," I sang as I headed through the Greyburry campus to the path that led to the Down House. Twirling as I walked, I pretended I was wearing a fancy party dress rather than the faded green smock I wore to work in the nursery kitchen. My dress flowed straight to the ground, with pink and purple flowers across the bottom hem. Maybe I'd get one like it tomorrow for the ceremony. Girls always got a new dress for their ceremony.

They caught me counting the babies again today. Luckily, it was just Brie. I still remember the look on her face when she came into the nesting center.

"Gertie, what are you doing here?" she snapped. "You know you're not allowed."

"The tests came back today. I wanted to see for myself," I said.

"Well, get back to the kitchen. You shouldn't be in here." Brie dropped her clipboard on her desk and politely showed me the door. "If Dara sees you, she'll have a fit."

"Okay, I'm going," I said, leaving the room.

There were only eight babies left. Yesterday, there were eleven. I had to check on number three. Number three was still there. I knew he was perfect. Sadly, numbers five and six were gone. So was number two, though I knew she wouldn't make it. Born too soon, she never gained the weight, and this morning, Noel and all her belongings were gone from her room. No room at Greyburry for someone who makes sickly babies. That's what Lady Eleanor always said. But number three was there, and that made me happy. I secretly named him Arto. He is such a cutie with his crooked smile and perfect little nose. I hoped that if I ever had a baby, he'd be just as perfect.

Arto would make it to Ascension at the kinder school, and his mother, Beatrice, with her two golden rattles, would leave Greyburry with honors. It's her second perfect baby in two years. Girls at the Down House are obligated to have two perfect births.

If you don't produce, you're sold at the labor auction or married off to tradesmen while they send your partner to work in the corps and fight the war against the North. To lead the perfect warriors to a perfect victory. The ideal weapons, built by expert engineers at the Western Alliance's Department of Justice. But if you succeed, you're allowed to go anywhere you like with a stipend for life. You can marry who you like and make all the babies you want and keep them, perfect or not.

I walked past the Bevel house, the secondary school near the edge of campus. Its flag hung low, and the doors were locked. They wouldn't open again until the following kinder graduation.

I stopped and thought about Summer, a Bevel girl I met in the infirmary a few weeks ago. She'd slipped and hit her chin and needed four stitches. She was sweet and gentle, and she reminded me of Siri. But Summer didn't win her Challenge. Just like Siri, she was gone. I stood there for a moment, staring at the flag, thinking about how quickly people disappeared around here. How easy it was to forget them.

Just a few more twirls, and I made it to the main gates leading to the Down House. Sitting outside their new dormitory were the newbies from Bevel. There were only seven Challenge winners this last round: five boys and two girls. Ever since Abfundt took over as captain, the tasks had become more grizzly, and I heard the first skill wiped out most of the class. A race around the lake on a course riddled with booby-traps and devilish harlequins wielding gas-powered saws. **The Marshals had shapeshifted into Adlets and lay in wait among the bushes, attacking the students as they ran past.** Most of the students were ripped to shreds or lost their heads before making it halfway around the track. I would have made it, though. I was always a fast runner.

I waved to the victors as I passed, but they didn't wave back. Instead, they just stood there with that look on their faces. The same look Trivel had our first week, the look of terrorized appreciation.

Entering the cobblestone courtyard outside Senior Hall, I stopped twirling for fear of tripping. I headed up the stairs to the common area, where a set of curious eyes peered out from behind the window curtains. It was Fedric. His face lit with excitement when he saw me coming, then he darted out of sight. I knew they'd been planning something. They had all been so coy all week, but I knew something was up. The Governess frowned at birthday celebrations, but it was one of the small things she'd let slide on occasion. I knew mine wouldn't be anything fancy, given that tomorrow was the ceremony, but it would be something special, and it was.

Most of the Down girls my age were there, along with Asher and some of the boys. Esther and Adelyn baked a small cake, and everyone signed a homemade card. We sat around the fireplace playing cards and talking about each of our first days at Greyburry until curfew, when Lady Lucy emerged from her lookout, cleared her throat, and casually opened the doors leading to the boys' side of the dorms. No words were needed. We all knew the rules. Unsupervised mingling and staying up after hours were strictly forbidden. The boys retreated to their dorms, and Lady Lucy locked the door behind them.

"Okay, girls, off to bed and no chatting until dawn. Tomorrow is the ceremony, and everyone needs a good night's sleep. Especially you five up for Binding. We want to look our best now, don't we?"

"Yes, Lady Lucy," we all chimed as we headed to our dorms.

That night, I tried to fall asleep, but couldn't stop thinking about my birthday and tomorrow's ceremony. I pulled out the book Asher secretly gave me at the party and fumbled through the first few pages before putting it back in its hiding place under my pillow. I couldn't believe he wrote it himself. He was always the clever one. I loved to read, but anything outside our school textbooks was forbidden at the Down House, and if Lady Lucy found it, we'd both be in hot water for sure.

Asher was from Wessington House and had already been at the Down House for nearly a year before I arrived. All the girls wanted to be paired with him; he was the one everyone whispered about in the dorms. But he wasn't matched until I came along.

He was taller than me, with messy blonde hair and bright blue eyes that almost glowed in the dark. His teeth were perfect, even the crooked canine that stuck out just a little. Somehow, it made him look cooler. If I'd had a choice, he would've been my first pick. But I doubted I was his. We loved each other more than anything. But not that kind of love. Girls didn't interest Asher. And that was a secret I'd carry to my grave. Like so many other things, that kind of thinking was forbidden here at Greyburry. If someone found out, he could be sent to the coal mines. The coal mines, if he were lucky.

We'd been paired since the day I arrived, chosen by the council after our DNA testing. Somehow, I got lucky. Asher and I clicked right away. We became best friends, and it stayed that way. Not everyone was so fortunate. Privy, a girl a year older than me, was paired with Gabriel, and she hated him from the start. I didn't blame her. Gabriel was loud, rude, and always ready to argue. They were complete opposites, and it showed.

But Asher and I had everything in common. We loved books and card games. He was a runner, just like me, and we'd sneak off to the lake trail whenever we could. Afterward, we'd swim to cool down, racing each other to the far bank, laughing until our sides hurt. He was kind. Smart. Charming in a way that made people forgive him, even when he pushed too far. His sarcasm got him in trouble more than once, but he always smiled his way out of it.

I loved him more than anyone.

We were committed to making things work, at least for us. But every night, I prayed. I prayed that it would be enough. That my body wouldn't betray me. That I wouldn't be found out. Because here, even love could be dangerous. My cycle had never been normal. Lately, it had stopped altogether. A sign of imperfection. A flaw. Lady Bader had started asking questions last year. She watched me closely, her eyes sharp and cold. So I started faking it. Every month, like clockwork, I'd show up at the infirmary for my feminine supplies. And every month, she'd say the same thing.

"Glad to see we got you on track. No room for an irregular cycle here at Greyburry."

I'd nod, smile, and walk away. But inside, I was terrified.

I rolled over in bed and promised God my eternal faith if he'd grant us success in our upcoming endeavor. Girls were always excited for Binding, but I was terrified. Not so much for myself but for Asher. I'd never forgive myself if something happened to him—something because of my flawed self.

I finished my prayer, closed my eyes, and tried to relax. Tomorrow was the day, and no matter how scared I was, what had to be done would be done. I'd had the tea for almost two years now. At least that would stop, for today was my 16th birthday, and tomorrow my Binding ceremony, where Asher and I would come together to fulfill our obligations to the treaties.

Fulfill or die.

❧ Chapter 12 - Poppy

The year 2116

Sebastian wasn't wrong when he called the people of Bastrop eccentric. They greeted us like magistrates in their newly slaughtered sheepskin shawls and flamboyant antlered head dressings. Much to Sebastian's disappointment, though, they didn't have any three-eyed cows or knife-swallowing fat ladies, so after trading what little elixir we had for gasoline, more cram, and a box full of deer antlers, and despite an offer to stay, we left. Sebastian didn't seem concerned by the place or its unusual inhabitants, but I was. It reminded me of the camp where Percy and his Green Beast left me for dead, and I was more than happy to leave.

Later that day, the cruiser overheated again, and we had to pull over on a dusty dirt road to let the engine cool down. I made our afternoon meal while Sebastian worked under the hood. From the look on his face, I could tell the cruiser needed more than just a quick fix. It required real repairs: repairs that would cost real credits, something we didn't have.

"Can you fix it?" I asked.

Sebastian groaned and threw his wrench to the ground. "It'll get us by for a while," he said, "but not all the way to Jubilee."

"So we're not going?" I asked.

"Oh no, we'll find a way. Don't worry about that."

"I'm glad," I said. "It'll be nice to get off the road."

"You're going to love it down there," he said.

"Really? What's so great about it?"

It was a question I'd asked before and already knew the answer to, but letting Sebastian talk about his beloved home always calmed him down. And right now, he needed it.

Sebastian beamed. "The bayou's beautiful, and the food, nothing like it. You haven't lived until you've had fresh Gulf oysters, straight from the water. That's where I'm from, so you know it's gotta be good."

I laughed, but stopped when I saw something behind him, movement on the road. A group of people walking up the hillside, heading straight for us. Sebastian stopped talking and turned to follow my stare.

"What do we do?" I said. Typically, a group of strangers wouldn't be an issue, but things were different out in the middle of nowhere, and after leaving Bastrop, I couldn't help but think these parts weren't as safe as Sebastian did.

"Just follow my lead. If anything happens, run inside and get my rifle. Not the big one, the shorty up under your bunk," he said. I nodded.

I was always a little nervous having the guns in the wagon, but I was glad we had them today. It was the first time we'd come across anyone since we left Bastrop. Although the people there treated us kindly, I couldn't help but notice the abundance of tall metal sheds and discarded bones littering the community's roadsides. Sebastian said they were archaic signs leftover from the drills, much like the burn mounds near Proper, but they still made me nervous, as did the oncoming entourage.

As the group approached, I could tell they weren't marauders or wrangles or even residents of Bastrop. They were young and carried their belongings on their backs like the travelers who took Gertie, but they resembled the gypsies the boys and I followed to Sparks so long ago. There were three men and two women with a small burro tied to a rope. Sebastian eyed the unsuspecting group, then turned to me and winked.

Two men and the women stayed back while the group leader approached Sebastian. A pipe dangled from the young man's mouth while his dusty, wide-brimmed hat flapped with the wind. His bare feet were nearly invisible underneath his long mustard trousers held up by one lone suspender.

"Friendly greetings, sir! It's truly a wonderful day now, isn't it?" he said, puffing his pipe.

"Friendly greetings indeed, but not such a wonderful day for us," sighed Sebastian.

"What then?" said the man as he waved an all-clear to his companions.

"I can't get the darn thing to start, and my wife needs medical. She's with child and not feeling well," he said.

Taken aback by Sebastian's claim, I cringed, lunged out my belly, and took hold of the wagon railing to help support my newfound condition.

"Get back inside, dear, and take a rest," said Sebastian. I retreated inside the wagon, but left the door open just enough to peek outside.

"Let me take a look at that engine. I haven't seen one like this in a while." The man reached out and presented his hand to Sebastian. "I'm Brother Johnathon, by the way. And that there's my wife, Miss Debby, and her kin," he said.

"Nice to meet you. I'm Sebastian, and that was my wife, Poppy."

"Well, Sebastian, let's see what we have here." Brother Johnathon jiggled and poked under the cruiser's hood, then summoned Sebastian to start it up. Sebastian turned the key, and the engine roared to life.

"See, there you go," said Brother Johnathon.

"Hallelujah!" cried Sebastian. "I just hope we can make it all the way to the clinic." Sebastian placed his hands on top of his head and gazed toward the sky. "Please, Lord, watch over us during our long journey to Ivy."

"Ivy? Why not Berryville? There's a medical facility there, too, and it's only a couple of hours north," said Brother Johnathon.

"Oh, they only take credits in Berryville. No, we have to get to Ivy, where we can trade," said Sebastian.

"Trade? What y'all got to trade?" said Brother Johnathon.

"A couple of pounds of sausages. Good sausage, too, not that cram stuff," said Sebastian. Brother Johnathan looked back at his companions and raised an eyebrow.

"Well, we ain't had a bite in a while, but we just got a handful of credits ourselves. Sold 'bout all we had over in Huntsville. We gotta save it to get transport up north 'fore the weather turns," he said.

"What about the burro, then?" said Sebastian. The man looked back at Miss Debby. She frowned and shook her head as she stroked the burro's knotted mane. I knew the woman with the burro would be a hard sell, so I grabbed a sausage, threw on a shawl to cover my non-existent belly, and went onto the porch.

"See here," I said, holding out the sausage. "These are the good ones, like he said."

The others looked intrigued, but Miss Debby wouldn't take her eyes off her furry friend.

"You won't be able to find transport that will take that burro anyway, you know. We could take him to Berryville and get a good price. They got plenty of farmland up there. He'll have a nice home. I'll make sure of it," said Sebastian.

"Well, you might have a point," said Brother Johnathon as he shifted his pipe and eyed the sausage in my hand.

"Save us a day or two, that's for sure. Maybe save my wife's life." Sebastian lowered his head and wiped a fake tear from his eye. I covered my eyes and wept as well. Sebastian came to my aid and helped me back inside the wagon.

"Come now, dear. You need your rest," he said. Inside the wagon, Sebastian pulled the remaining cram from the ice cooler.

"That's all we have," I said.

"I know," he said.

"Don't give them all of it," I said.

Sebastian laughed. "I'm not giving them any of it." Sebastian placed the sausages in a burlap sack, went back outside, and presented the lot to the group.

"There's a full dozen here. Made by an old farmer's widow back in Lubbock. None of that cram paste in these," he said.

Brother Johnathon peered into the bag and swallowed. "Those are some nice sausages," he said.

"I'll even throw in some biscuits," said Sebastian.

The man turned to his companions. "He's got a point 'bout the transport. Ain't no way we'll find one that'll take Barnaby along. These folks here are good, Miss Debby. I reckon they'll see that he gets a proper home," said Brother Johnathon. The group looked at the woman holding the rope, and she reluctantly nodded.

"Then it's settled," said Sebastian. "Let me wrap these in ice for you."

Sebastian raced inside, tossed the sausages back in the cooler, filled the burlap bag halfway with ice, and then dropped a bag of sand he used to hold the wagon's pop-out lever in place. He covered the sand with more ice, wrapped the whole thing in more burlap, and topped the bundle with a few of the biscuits I'd prepared for lunch.

"Go get on the cruiser and wait for me. I've got this wrapped pretty tight, but by the look of those ladies, they're gonna want to dig in right away," he said.

Outside, the travelers removed their belongings from Barnaby's back, and Brother Johnathon and another man helped Sebastian lure the scared animal up the front steps of the wagon while I waited on the cruiser. They tied the burro to the front door and roped off the stairway so he couldn't fall off. Miss Debby shot Sebastian a dirty look.

"Oh, don't you worry about Barnaby. He'll be fine, it's a short drive to Berryville, and we will go nice and slow," said Sebastian as he handed Brother Johnathon the bag of frozen sand.

"Thank you. Wow, you wrapped them pretty tight."

"Yep, that ice will last all day. Ya gotta keep 'em fresh, so don't take 'em outta the ice till ya got the fire goin'. Ya don't wanna let 'em go bad," said Sebastian.

"Will do," said Brother Johnathon as he grabbed Sebastian's hand and gave it a vigorous shake. "And good luck to you and your wife. We will keep you in our prayers."

Sebastian bowed. "And you, ours."

Sebastian jumped on the cruiser, revved the engine a few times, and we sped away, leaving the group smiling and waving on the side of the road. We headed north, away from where the traveler had come, and stopped at a fork in the road only a few miles later. There we saw a hand-carved sign that read, 'Right to Dapper and left to Berryville'. We turned right and didn't stop until we passed through Dapper, then parked in a clearing near the town's border. Sitting on the steps, eating lunch, and watching Barnaby kick at the dirt, I gave a heavy sigh.

"Now don't tell me you're feelin' guilty?" said Sebastian.

"No. We do what we do," I said, repeating what Sebastian would say after every good grift.

"Exactly," he said.

"I'm just sad because you gave them almost all the biscuits," I said.

Sebastian chuckled. "That's my girl."

∽ CHAPTER 13 - GERTIE

The year 2132

My palms were slick with sweat, but I didn't dare wipe them on my new dress. It was long and pale, the kind of white that showed every flaw. The color of purity, they said. The color of obedience. The color that made sloppy girls look guilty.

Still, I loved it.

It hung loose on my frame, shapeless like all the others, but mine looked better. The lace around the collar and sleeves was soft, not scratchy, and the way the cuffs flared at my wrists made me feel like I belonged to something meaningful. All the girls up for Binding wore the same style, but mine fit me best. Simple. Clean. Virginal excellence.

Our feet were bare, scrubbed until the skin stung. No shoes allowed. We were to walk as we came into the world, quiet, exposed, and vulnerable.

Each of us had a flower crown. Handmade. Chosen carefully. Mine was a ring of baby's breath, small and white, like the color of the dress.

"Hold still," Shelby said, her fingers brushing my scalp as she placed it on my head.

I held my breath.

"Hurry up. I don't want to be late," I said.

"Alright, almost done. Oh, how I wish I could be there tonight. I remember my Binding like it was yesterday. All the boys looked so handsome, and the dinner was spectacular." Shelby sighed and stepped back to admire her work.

"Okay, finished. You look beautiful," she said.

"Why, thank you, ma'am," I said as I twirled and practiced my formal curtsy before joining the other girls in front of the bathroom mirror. We were all busy admiring ourselves when Lady Lucy came and corralled us out.

"Come out, ladies, you don't want to be late now, do you? The Governess is already in a mood and won't be pleased if you're delayed," she said.

Lady Lucy was the primary aid at the Down House and acted as a buffer between us girls and the Governess, though I never really trusted her. She'd been known to turn girls in for even the most innocent infractions just to keep on the Governess's good side.

I finished fussing with my bangs and took my place behind the other girls at the end of the line. I was the youngest in this year's ceremony, and had it not been my birthday just yesterday, I'd have another whole year before I was eligible for Binding, which would have been fine with me. Nevertheless, most girls were excited, though I didn't know why. The thought of being bound never appealed to me, Asher, either, and with my medical limitation, let's just say we were in for a challenge. We'd worked out a plan to make it work, though, and I was at least excited about that.

We followed Lady Lucy out into the common room, single file, heads high like we'd been taught. The other girls from Down House were already waiting to see us off. Even the newbies from Bevel, in their matching gray frocks and annoyingly silly head scarves, were there. Oh, how I hated those head scarves.

The room was quiet, too quiet. The clock on the wall chimed six times, each note sharp and slow. And right on cue, Governess Marigold entered. She wore her usual long black dress, high-necked and spotless, her arms folded behind her back, as if she were carved from stone. She didn't speak. She didn't smile. She just stood there, tall and still, her eyes scanning the room like she was counting sins.

Marigold was beautiful, everyone said so. Tall, graceful, with skin like porcelain and hair pulled tight into a perfect twist. But her beauty was buried under that scowl she always wore, the kind that made you feel like you'd done something wrong just by breathing.

No one dared move.

"Well, don't you all look lovely," said Marigold. We all stood tall and silent as she circled us girls like Farmer Dillinger inspected his hogs before the annual Greyburry auction.

"Such a beautiful night, isn't it, Adalyn?"

"Why yes, Governess," said Adalyn.

"Beautiful night for a ceremony indeed." Marigold sighed. "Too bad, though. There seems to be a bit of nasty business we need to tend to before dinner. Such a shame, especially on the night of the ceremony, but as you all know, these things cannot be delayed," she said.

"Yes, Governess," we all chime in unison, everyone except the newbies from Bevel. The look of terror from breaking protocol was clear on their faces, but Marigold didn't call them out.

Nasty business, that's what Governess Marigold called it when someone was to be punished. A lump grew in my throat, and I prayed that whatever it was didn't involve me. Had Brie ratted me out to Dara about being in the nesting center and counting babies? I hoped not. That was grounds for a lashing, for sure.

"As you may have noticed, Lenore is gone," Marigold paused as if to choose her words. I had noticed we all had. Rumors said they found her with someone other than her partner, Stanley, but no one knew for sure.

"Now, I will not get into any dirty details, but must I remind you why you are all here? Why you're afforded such privilege when others are not? Do I?"

"No, Governess." Getting the hang of how things are done, the Bevel girls chimed in at 'Governess.'

"Then why do these things keep happening? It's very clear. You are each paired based on what is best for your future child, not on what is best for you. Love or social dynamics have nothing to do with it; rather, what will result in the strongest, most perfect baby," she said.

I nearly huffed at that statement. My child? How about President Bruno's child? No one leaves Greyburry with a child. Everyone knew that.

"Having said that, Lenore and Gregor are no longer students here at Greyburry. I hope that the rest of you will take this warning to heart," she said.

I knew something was going on, but the news about Gregor shocked me. I looked around the room for Jeddy, Gregor's partner. I hadn't noticed her before, standing next to the Bevel girls in the same gray frock and dismal headscarf. She was back to square one. I felt so bad. She had to start over, drink the tea, and face the threat of not getting paired. Back to kitchen duty and living in the smaller dorms, and no ensuite. Plus, if no suitable pairing was made, she would have to leave Greyburry.

"I wish that were all the nasty business, but it's not." Marigold shook her head as she walked to the fireplace and retrieved Gunther from above the hearth. The sound of twenty-six girls sucking air into their lungs filled the room.

Gunther was the name of Marigold's whip. There would be lashings tonight, but who? I thought about the babies in the nesting center again and held my breath. Marigold slapped the tip of the whip across the palm of her free hand as she walked to the center of the room, where the senior-bound girls stood petrified.

"Daisy, come here, please," she said.

"What? Why me?" stuttered Daisy.

"I said come here," Marigold repeated. Daisy stepped out of line and trudged to the center of the room. Tears flowed from her eyes, and her lips quivered as she stood face to face with the Governess.

"Tell me again about the tea?" said Marigold, slapping the whip harder against her hand.

"Drinking the tea is forbidden after binding," whimpered Daisy.

"Yes, it is. Now tell me why you think it's okay for you to continue to have it?"

"But I haven't, I swear it." Fists clenched at her side, Daisy trembled as she spoke.

"Liar!" sneered Marigold. Everyone knew Daisy and Patton had struggled to conceive, but never imagined Daisy was avoiding her duty.

"No, it's true. I haven't touched it, not even once, since I've been bound."

"Then what is that?" Marigold motioned to Lady Lucy, who removed a towel hiding a box of the special tea on a nearby table.

"Lady Katherine found this under your bed when she was doing rounds."

"That's not mine," said Daisy.

"Assume the position," said Marigold.

"But I said it's not mine," insisted Daisy.

"And I said, assume the position." Marigold grabbed Daisy by the hair and pushed her to her knees before unleashing a series of lashings across Daisy's back. Daisy remained stoic. To struggle or cry out would surely earn her more than the usual ten for such an offense. After her lashing, Daisy got up and resumed her place in line with the others. Marigold returned Gunther to his rightful spot above the mantle, and we all resumed normal breathing.

"Oh, Governess, what about Miss Clair?" said Lady Lucy.

"Oh, her," sighed Marigold. "Clair will not be joining us this evening. Late last night, Clair went into early labor and sadly lost her baby."

We all gasped in disbelief. Some girls cried out. Clair was everyone's favorite, including mine. She was always laughing and dancing about. Some nights she'd sneak into my dorm, and we'd whisper stories and secrets for hours. My heart ached, knowing she'd lost her baby, and I hoped I'd have time to sneak away to the infirmary tonight to say goodbye before she was gone.

"Don't feel sorry for that repugnant little ingrate," sneered Marigold. "Clair knew the rules and *CHOSE* to break them just like the others." I shot Jeddy a curious look, and she shrugged. What could she have done? My stomach turned. There would be no reason to sneak away to see Clair tonight. Clair was already gone. "Let me ask you all something. What's the first thing that happens when you're expecting?" No one responded.

"Anyone? Bethel?"

Bethel looked confused. "I received the precious honor charm?" she said.

"No, not that. What is the first appointment you had?" said Marigold.

"Oh, I met with Lady Bader."

"And what did you and Lady Bader talk about?"

"Nutrition, what to eat and what not to eat. To make perfect babies," said Bethel.

"Exactly. Here at Greyburry, we do everything possible, give you all the tools needed, and coddle you through your pregnancies so you can fulfill your one requirement. So, you can do your job. To make a perfect baby!" Marigold was practically screaming by this time, and the Bevel girls looked more frightened than usual. I wanted to go over and give them each a hug and tell them they'd get used to it, but that would warrant lashings for sure.

"What is your one job, ladies?"

"To make a perfect baby," we all sang.

"That's correct. Please understand. Milk is murder. Sugar is murder, and I don't think I even need to remind you of smoking or drinking alcohol," she said. Katrina, one of the Senior girls, grunted in agreement. Marigold looked pleased.

"Why is dairy murder, Katrina?"

"Dairy makes stupid babies," said Katrina, loud and clear.

"Yes, that's right, and what about sugar, Gertie?" said Marigold.

"Sugar makes sick babies," I said.

"Correct!" Marigold graciously wiped a bit of sweat from her brow, straightened her dress, returned her hands to their usual spot behind her back, and smiled.

"Now that's enough nastiness for one evening." Marigold turned to the five of us girls. "Come, girls, let's all make our way to the dining hall and greet the council. Smiles everyone. Our special guests will arrive soon. Everyone else, back to your dorms. I will see you all tomorrow," she said as she glided out of the common room and into the hall with the five of us girls in tow.

The other girls, in their standard pecking order, silently returned to the dorms. Daisy walked just as tall and proud as everyone else. The only sign that something had happened was the tiny red stains forming on the back of her pink and black dress.

I couldn't help but feel bad for Clair. We all knew Clair didn't get lashed that night or leave Greyburry. Something far worse happened to her. Something they forbid us to speak of.

Clair never smoked or drank, but she liked to eat, especially sweets. I caught her frequently sneaking Danish and milk from the kitchen, something forbidden when you're with child. Her baby suffered the price, and there was no need to waste any more time on Clair. Clair murdered her baby before it had a chance to live; according to the law, she too had to die.

⇄ CHAPTER 14- POPPY

The year 2117

Winter arrived, as did the rain, and it continued for twenty-eight days straight. It wasn't the welcome relief to a hot, summer dry spell type of rain either. This was nothing less than the sky's wraith in the form of wind and water.

We'd parked the wagon near the outskirts of Sabine, a small town near the gulf and not too far from Sebastian's home, almost three months earlier. Not because we wanted to or thought it was a good place to stay, but because it was where the cruiser finally died. Sebastian was beside himself, knowing we were so close to Jubilee, but we had no way to fix the cruiser, especially once the rain came.

Sebastian was frustrated. Jubilee was so close, and now we were stuck. But even with the cruiser broken, he didn't give up. He built a small covered trailer for Barnaby and hooked it to the wagon. Then he started mixing new batches of elixirs, hoping to sell them in town once the weather cleared.

Even with the rain and cold, I loved our time alone in Sabine. The days were quiet, slow, in a way that felt safe. I'd sit inside and read out loud for hours while Sebastian worked at the table, mixing potions from fermented potatoes and discarded pharmaceuticals he'd collected during his travels.

Barnaby would perch on the porch, sitting upright like he was part of the conversation. He'd listen to my voice and beg for scraps, his ears twitching every time I paused.

At night, Barnaby would shuffle off to his trailer, curl up in the blankets, and fall asleep without a sound. Sebastian and I would stay up late talking and test the day's batch of elixirs. He grew more frustrated each night, muttering about the weak potency, the dull effects. He wanted something sharper. Something that would sell.

When the rain let up, he'd walk into town alone, searching for better ingredients, roots, powders, anything that might give his elixirs the edge he needed. I stayed behind with Barnaby, watching the clouds roll in again, wondering how long we'd be stuck.

One particular day, Sebastian came back breathless, his face flushed with excitement. It was one of the few sunny days we'd had in weeks, and he looked like he'd just outrun the storm itself. In his arms were two things: a thick paperback book and a large brown sack that clinked with every step as he rushed up the stairs.

I grabbed the book before he could pull it away.

"Oh my, what is this then?" I said, laughing as I flipped through the pages. The cover showed a shirtless man with bulging muscles and loose drawstring pants. In his arms was a blonde woman with a corset barely holding her in. Her head was tilted back, lips parted.

"The Devil's Passion?" I read aloud.

"Just a little something to spice things up," Sebastian said with a wink.

I raised an eyebrow. "What, no food?"

I peeked into the sack. Inside were bottles of all shapes and sizes, filled with white powder. Some were labeled. Most weren't.

Sebastian grinned. "Better than food. These are going to change everything."

I didn't ask how. Not yet.

But something about the way the powders shimmered in the light made me nervous.

"You should've seen it," Sebastian said, breathless, shaking the bag of jars like it was full of treasure. "The town square was packed. First sunny day in weeks, and it was crawling with vendors and shoppers. That place is going to be a goldmine."

"But no food?" I asked.

"Oh, there was plenty of food, alright," he said, flopping onto the couch. "But I had to run. Pulled a one-man grab-and-go on some fat fool selling this stuff. He chased me for half a mile before he collapsed. I circled back, grabbed the rest, and got out of there."

He laughed, still catching his breath. "So much easier with two people."

I picked up one of the small brown bottles and pulled the cork. A sharp scent hit my nose and stung my eyes.

"Smells like the stuff Sister Page put on my gums when I had a tooth pulled," I said.

Sebastian grinned. "It's poppy dust. The real stuff. Not that fake chemical junk. Made from the most precious flower in the world."

He looked at me, eyes bright.

"My Poppy."

"I heard this stuff is dangerous," I said, remembering that the sisters back home had to keep it locked up in the Keep.

"Nothing wrong with a little danger," Sebastian smiled.

For the next three days, he barely slept. He hovered over his two-burner stove, mixing poppy dust and liquids, muttering to himself like a man possessed. Every batch had to be tested, of course. He'd sip, wince, scribble notes, and start again.

One night, after feeding Barnaby, I came back into the wagon and found Sebastian face down on the floor. I tried dragging him to the sofa, but he was too heavy. So I threw a blanket over him and left him there.

By morning, he was up with the sun, eyes bloodshot, hands shaking. He looked like he'd been dragged behind the cruiser for miles, but he didn't stop. He kept working.

That night, he handed me a cup filled with emerald green liquid. It glowed faintly, and the scent was sweet, like fruit and sugar. "I present to you my latest creation… Poppy's Poison," he said.

"It's pretty," I said. "What's in it? How did you get it so green?"

He just grinned.

"And people are going to buy this?"

"Hell's yes, they will," he said. "We'll have enough credits to fix the cruiser and buy lumber when we get to Jubilee."

I stared at the cup.

It shimmered in the light.

I wasn't sure whether to drink it or throw it out the window.

"Why would anyone want this?" I asked, sniffing the sweet, glowing liquid. "It smells good, but…"

Sebastian leaned in, eyes wild. "People want to escape. They want something that cracks open their heads and lets the light in. We'll give them a ride they'll never forget, whether they want to or not."

"I don't know," I said, watching the green swirl in the cup.

"Just try it."

I took a sip. The taste was bittersweet, sharp at the back of my throat. I choked a little.

"What's in this?" I asked, wiping my mouth.

"Just the right mix of poppy dust, elixir base, and a hint of root juice for flavor and color."

"I'm not going to end up on the floor, am I?" I said, taking another sip. My tongue went numb. My face flushed. It reminded me of the tonic they gave me at the clinic back at Intermountain, but it didn't make me feel scared or lost.

It made me feel warm. Detached. Like my thoughts were floating just above my head, watching me from the ceiling.

"Not too much, my Poppy," Sebastian said.

"But you said a little danger was good," I murmured, reaching for the bottle.

Sebastian watched me take a long swig of the elixir, then stepped forward, took my face in his hands, and kissed me, deep and hard. I wanted to pull away. I should have. But I didn't.

I'd wanted him for so long, and the elixir made it easy to forget why I ever hesitated. My selfish temptations took over, and I let them.

The next morning, I didn't wake up on the floor, but I ended up there anyway. I tried to stand, missed, and rolled off the bed. I hit the ground with a thud and stayed there, staring up at the ceiling.

"Oh Lord, what did I do last night?" I whispered, dragging myself onto my knees. The wagon was quiet. Too quiet. Sebastian wasn't in his bed. Or mine.

I looked around, and my heart started racing. The stove was cold. Sebastian's coat was gone—no sign of him anywhere.

Had something happened? Had I done something? The bottle from last night sat on the table, half-empty, glowing faintly in the morning light. Something wasn't right.

"Sebastian!" I shouted, voice cracking. "Sebastian, where are you?"

"I'm here, I'm here," he said, stumbling into the wagon, hair wild and eyes bleary.

"You're alive," I sighed, relief flooding through me.

"Of course I'm alive. I feel like I got hit by a railcar, but yeah, still breathing."

"Oh, thank God."

He looked down at me, confused. "Why are you crawling around on the floor?"

"Looking," I muttered, reaching under the table.

"For what?"

"My skirt. Possibly Jesus," I groaned, flopping onto my back.

Sebastian chuckled, rubbing his temples. "I warned you about the elixir. Might've gone a little heavy on the dust. Woooeee, that stuff packs a punch."

He bent down and handed me a small cup filled with something red.

"Here. Try this one. It'll make you feel better."

I stared at the cup, then at him.

"You sure this isn't going to send me to the moon?"

He grinned. "Not this time. This one's for the landing."

"I don't trust you," I said, eying the crimson juice.

"Don't worry. It's just crushed tomato and cayenne," he said.

I drank the juice, wiped my mouth, and let out a loud belch.

"Sorry," I said.

"Don't be," Sebastian laughed.

"What exactly happened last night? We didn't do anything, did we?"

"Well, let's see…" He scooped me off the floor and dropped me gently onto the sofa. Then he tossed me my skirt and sat down beside me. "We kissed. Then you pulled away and bolted outside. I chased you, and you started yelling about dirty blood and white rabbits in cages. You were talking wild."

I groaned.

"And then," he continued, "you took off your skirt, threw it at me, and ran face-first into a tree."

I cringed and covered my face with both hands. "Please tell me you're lying."

He just chuckled. "Wish I could, oh, how I wish I could." Sebastian shook his head as if bewildered, then pointed to my face. "You even got a bit of a scrap or two on your forehead there."

I rubbed my hand across my forehead. He was right; it was pretty scraped up. With all the pain already in my head, I hadn't noticed.

"I thought you might be flirtin a bit at first, with the skirt and all, but then the bashing into the tree part confused me, so I brought you inside and put you in bed," he said in his serious tone that he only used when he was pretending to be serious but was making fun.

I peeked at Sebastian through my fingers, and I could tell by the look on his face that he thought the whole thing was hysterical.

"I hate you," I whispered.

"Oh no, you don't, you lovvve me," he teased. "Said so yourself. Many times. Many, many times. Poppy loves Sebastian…"

❧ Chapter 15 - Gertie

The year 2132

I'd only been inside the grand dining hall once. It was after I won the Trivel Challenge. The victors got a full tour of the Down House grounds, including the coveted room. Headmistress Padma led us there herself, but warned us never to enter again unless invited.

Back then, I didn't think much of it. The room was sunlit, sure, but the light felt thin. The dusty blue curtains hung stiff, like they hadn't been touched in years. The candle operas were cold and dark, and the fireplace looked more like a brick mouth than a source of warmth.

Even the grand dining table seemed sad, with its high-back chairs flipped upside down, as if someone had left in a hurry and never returned.

The air smelled strange. Not rotten, but old. Like the living quarters of Lady Greyburry, who died a few years ago. That same mix of unwashed hair and eucalyptus cream.

When I stepped into the dining hall that night, I could hardly believe it was the same place.

The candlelight flickered softly, casting shadows that danced across the walls. Once faded, the curtains now hung crisp and clean, tied back with golden tassels that shimmered like jewelry. They framed the starry night beyond like a painting.

The dark mahogany table stretched long and proud, no longer forgotten. It was dressed in white china and crystal glassware that caught the glow and scattered it like stars. At its center rose a towering arrangement of pink and white purity flowers, laced with baby's breath and sprigs of rosemary.

The walls were lined with portraits of leaders, both current and long forgotten. The largest—and most absurd—was the life-size painting of President Bruno above the fireplace. The smell of fresh paint gave it away as new, though the image showed a younger Bruno, shirtless, golden-haired, his skin flawless. He crouched over a lamb, knife in hand, blood dripping. It was theatrical, exaggerated, and designed to make him look powerful. To me, it was just another sign of his swelling ego.

Across from the dining table sat a pink velveteen sofa that looked so soft it could swallow you whole. Nearby was a baby grand piano, where Lady Evelyn sat ready to play.

The whole room was fancy and impressive, so much so that it almost made me forget how strange things were about to get.

Headmistress Padma and the Elders stood in front of the fireplace, smiling proudly as the five of us girls curtsied one by one. We'd been trained for this moment, every movement rehearsed. We greeted each Elder with the proper words, then took our places beneath the purity cross mounted on the wall.

Lady Evelyn began to play, soft and slow, as Governor Anders and the boys entered the dining hall. They were barefoot, just like us, and walked in their assigned order, my Asher leading the way. Their outfits matched ours: off-white tunics with flowing slacks, simple and pure.

Each boy greeted the Elders, then stepped beside his partner. Asher didn't look at me, but I felt him there, steady and close.

The music stopped.

We lowered our heads.

Padma opened the treaties and began to read. Her voice was calm, clear, and heavy with meaning. I held my breath as she reached the final line.

"Through sacrifice and eradication comes rebirth and prosperity…"

After the reading, Padma and the Elders took their seats at the dining table, followed by Governess Merigold and Governor Anders, then finally the ten of us up for binding. Asher squeezed my leg under the table and gave me a smirk.

"Are you okay?" he whispered.

"Of course. We got this," I whispered back as a well-organized team of kitchen staff descended upon us with trays of food and pitchers of drink.

As the course began, I couldn't help but stare at each couple and wonder who'd be the first to fulfill their reproductive duties. Obviously not Asher and me, that much was clear. But someone would.

Casper and Whitney, maybe. They got along and were both healthy, but my bet was on Cameron and Esther. They'd been in love since the day they were paired. And even though pre-binding relations were frowned upon, if it hadn't been for the tea, they probably would've met their birth quota by now.

Then there was Yoli and Trevor. Never a stranger-looking pair. Yoli had that kind of beauty that made people stop and stare, wild red hair, emerald eyes, and the kind of confidence that didn't need permission. Trevor, on the other hand, reminded me of a boy from my old class at secondary school. His name was Bucky. He used to eat paper and cry during spelling tests. I tried not to laugh, thinking about him.

Next to Yoli sat Privy and Gabriel, who looked completely uninterested in each other, or in anything, really. They barely spoke, barely moved. It was hard to tell if they were bored or just numb.

And then there was Asher and me.

We weren't romantic, not in the way people expected. But we were close. Real close. The kind of close that didn't need words or flowers or long looks across the room. We understood each other. We trusted each other. Our love was different. Stronger, I thought. We could do anything together.

And that mattered, especially after tonight.

Dinner was incredible. We feasted on duck and roasted vegetables, and hibiscus water instead of the usual tea—no more tea for us.

Lady Evelyn played cheerful music on the piano, and for a moment, everything felt light.

Then came dessert. Chocolate pudding. I scraped every last bit from the bowl, licking it clean before setting my spoon down. I felt a little guilty, thinking about Clair. But I ate it anyway. She knew the rules.

Privy gave me a sharp look when he saw my empty bowl. Her pudding sat untouched in protest. But I didn't care. If anyone here had a sweet tooth, it was me. And no amount of restraint was going to bring Clair back. Besides, who knew when I'd get pudding again?

After dinner, Headmistress Padma gave each of us our fertility charm. Then she read a few passages from the bible, her voice calm and steady, like she'd done it a hundred times before.

"And you, be ye fruitful, and multiply; bring forth abundantly in the earth, and multiply therein."

When she finished, she led us toward the couple's wing on the west side of Down House, far from the dorms. It covered three floors and had two entrances, one outside near the Down fountain, and a hidden one that connected directly to the grand dining hall, but this would be the only time we'd be allowed to use that one.

We stepped into the first-floor foyer, which had four rooms known as Quads. Each Quad contained four couples' suites and two shared bathrooms. At least every room had its own sink. Our rooms were on the second floor, laid out exactly like the ones below. Asher grabbed my hand as we climbed the stairs. He squeezed it tight, and I squeezed back.

No one spoke as we reached the second-floor foyer. The air felt thick, like it had been waiting for us. One by one, each couple stepped into their assigned Quad, found their room, opened the door, and vanished inside.

No goodbyes. No glances. Just the soft click of doors closing, one after another, like a countdown.

It wasn't my first time in the couple's wing. I'd started moving things over weeks ago. Once you're bound, you're not allowed back in the dorms unless something happens, like with Jeddy. It's forbidden.

But this was my first time here with the others. And knowing Privy and Gabriel were in the room next to ours didn't sit well. It meant we'd be sharing a bathroom. I shrugged it off. With everything else going on, it probably wasn't the worst thing.

I sat on the edge of the bed while Asher paced. The room was small but tidy. The bed looked comfortable, and each side had a nightstand with a lamp, and a fresh fire was already burning in the fireplace.

Above the bed hung another painting of President Bruno, shirtless again, riding bareback on a black stallion. His face was turned just enough that it felt like he was staring straight at me.

It was disturbing for sure.

"What's this guy got against clothes?" Asher said.

"I don't know, but I can't look at this anymore." I jumped up, grabbed a blanket, and threw it over the painting. Then I sat back down, trying not to think about it.

"Are you ready for this?" Asher asked.

"Maybe," I whispered. "Don't you think we should wait a little longer?"

He shook his head, leaned over, and kissed my cheek. Then he dropped to the floor, pulled the rug aside, and started lifting the floorboards.

"Quiet," I said. "Someone might hear you."

He placed the boards gently on the bed and reached into the hole we'd made weeks ago. He pulled out two travel packs, one for him, one for me. Then he grabbed a pair of heavy wire cutters from his bag.

"Where did you get those?" I asked.

"From Powell's work shed," Asher said.

"Will they work?"

"I think so. I've seen Powell use them to cut the iron rods near the gate," he whispered.

"I hope you're right," I said, holding out my arm.

Asher took my wrist and looked at the purity bracelet. Then he placed the wire cutters around the thick metal band. He squeezed the handles hard, his face turning red and the vein on his forehead popping. After a few seconds, the cutters snapped through the metal.

I pulled the broken bracelet off and watched as all my charms fell to the floor.

"That wasn't too bad," I said.

"Now you'll have to do mine," Asher said.

I looked at the cutters and shrugged. "I don't think I'm strong enough."

"You've got this. Use both hands and keep your pressure steady," Asher whispered.

I gripped the cutters, jaw tight, mimicking his technique as best I could. The metal resisted, biting back with each failed attempt. A few muttered curses slipped through clenched teeth before the bracelet finally gave way with a soft snap.

"Such language," Asher teased. "We're breaking all the rules tonight."

"No allegiance to the treaties here," I replied, brushing the broken charms into my palm.

We tucked the remnants of the bracelets and charms, along with the cutters, into the hole beneath the floorboards, slid the slats back into place, and smoothed the rug over the evidence. Asher crept to the window and eased it open.

"It's a bit of a drop," he said. "I'll go first, then help you down. Just like we practiced."

"Wait," I whispered, freezing as soft footsteps creaked across the floorboards outside the door.

Asher raised a finger to his lips. We held our breath. Whoever lingered outside didn't move on.

Without a word, Asher crossed to the fireplace and stirred the embers, coaxing a crackle from the flames.

"Chilly night," he said, voice casual but too loud.

"Yeah," I added, fumbling for normalcy. "They said it might rain. Maybe we should put our clothes back on?"

Asher smothered a laugh. The footsteps resumed, then faded into silence. "Gertie! You almost made me pee my pants," he said.

"Sorry, I didn't know what to say, you caught me off guard," I shrugged.

"Well, at least they left," he said as he grabbed his pack and slung it over his back.

"Wait. One last thing," I said. "I brought these up this morning, but didn't have a chance to pack them." I reached between the mattresses, pulled out my swaddle and the book Asher gave me for my birthday, and shoved them inside my pack.

"Oh, God forbid we don't forget that ratty old thing," said Asher, reaching for my swaddle.

"Hey, it's sentimental," I said, pulling away from his reach. My pack hit the bedside table and knocked a thick leather-bound book to the floor.

"What in the world is this monstrosity?" said Asher as he picked up a book and began flipping through the pages. Embossed on the front cover was the purity cross.

"Check this out," Asher said. "Binding for Excellence," he read aloud in a mock-heroic tone. "A thrilling tale of nutrition, obedience, and how not to terrify your gestational partner. I give it zero stars and a mild rash. Look, they even included diagrams. Did they really think we'd sit down and absorb this treaty-soaked propaganda?"

He tossed the book onto the bed like it had personally offended him.

"Consider yourself lucky," I said. "Marigold made us read it cover to cover in class."

"Of course she did," Asher said, laughing. "Marigold probably laminated her copy and sleeps with it under her pillow."

I laughed.

"Let's get out of here before she returns with her clipboard and that smile that says, 'I've already reported you to the Council, but I still believe in your potential,'" he said.

The second-floor window of our room pressed up against a steep wall of packed earth, just shy of the Down House's back fence. Privy and Gabriel's room sat caddy-corner, their window tucked around the corner. Luckily, the room directly beside ours was vacant, but we still had to be careful.

Asher leapt from the ledge with the confidence of someone who'd failed at this maneuver enough times to perfect it. He landed on the slope, skidded halfway down, and threw his arms out like a gymnast sticking a dismount.

"Ten out of ten," he whispered, bowing to the dirt.

I tossed him my pack, swung my legs over the sill, and eased myself down until his hands found my feet. As he lowered me, I walked my palms down the wall, slow and steady. We'd rehearsed this escape nearly twenty times, each descent a little smoother and a little less likely to end in a twisted ankle.

Feet on solid ground, I snatched my pack and followed Asher behind the woodshed, where he'd carved out a narrow tunnel beneath the fence just hours earlier. We dropped to our knees and crawled through the damp soil, emerging into the overgrown yard behind the abandoned Bevel house. From there, we sprinted toward the loading docks behind Greyburry's central kitchen.

Working in the nursery kitchen, I knew the delivery schedules by heart. Mondays brought poultry, Wednesdays produce and fruit from the local farms. But today was the second Thursday of the month—seafood day. The truck from the southern coast would arrive sometime in the late evening; Greyburry was its final stop before heading back to the Trident colony overnight.

Perfect timing. Almost too perfect. By the time anyone noticed we were missing, morning would be well underway, and we'd be halfway to Hope Island.

It was a narrow window, but it was all we had.

We couldn't afford to get caught. That wasn't just a risk; it was a death sentence. But staying was its own kind of death. I hadn't wanted to go through with Asher's plan at first. He made it sound like a caper, like we were characters in one of his stories. But when my cycles started slipping, and the signs became harder to ignore, I knew we had no choice.

Those deemed unworthy after binding were quietly removed. Officially, they were 'relocated', but everyone knew the story of Clair and what happened to students like her.

❧ Chapter 16 - Poppy

The year 2117

It was cold that morning when Sebastian and I packed our supplies onto Barnaby's back and got ready to head to Sabine. Without the cruiser, we couldn't bring the wagon. Instead, we made do with what we could strap to Barnaby's back: jars of our newest elixirs, including Poppy's Poison, a clutch of handmade voodoo dolls I'd stitched from string and buttons, scarves dyed in mixed hues, and bundles of cured fish Sebastian had caught and smoked himself.

"Sorry, lil buddy," Sebastian said, patting Barnaby's flank. "Till we get the cruiser running, you're our noble steed and mobile storefront for the day."

Before leaving, Sebastian and I each took a shot of Poppy's Poison, then the three of us, me, Sebastian, and Barnaby, started down the road toward the town square.

"Ah, nothing like a little kick in the morning," Sebastian said with a grin. He took another sip of the green elixir, then leaned in and kissed me, pushing the rest of it into my mouth.

"Watch it, sir, I'm a bound lady," I said.

"Indeed, you are," he grinned.

Other than kissing, nothing happened between us that first night I drank the Poison. But it didn't take long before I stopped resisting Sebastian's advances. Once he knew how I really felt, he didn't hold back. He told me we were meant to be together, and I believed him, even with everything I was hiding.

He knew I was nervous about being physical, so he took his time. I wanted to believe it would all be okay. I kept telling myself that the "dirty blood" stuff was Maya's problem, not mine. If we did end up being intimate, nothing bad would happen. It hadn't with Eric, and I'd had a perfectly healthy child. And I was Poppy. And Poppy was supposed to be perfect, too.

Still, I couldn't risk hurting Sebastian. So complete intimacy was off the table. He said he understood, and for now, he seemed okay with it. But I knew that wouldn't last forever. And that scared me.

Sebastian and I walked into town holding hands. He was in a great mood, singing, humming, smiling the whole way. Even Barnaby seemed happy, trotting along to the rhythm of Sebastian's songs.

When we got to the town square, we found a spot to set up shop between the Trinity Faith Church and Dilbert's Pub.

"This is perfect. Best of both worlds," Sebastian said as he helped me unpack and set up our things.

I glanced around, uneasy. "What if the guy you took the poppy dust from comes back?"

"Let him," Sebastian said with a grin. "If he tries anything, I'll punch him in the face."

I knew his good mood wasn't just about us being together. We were so close to the bayou now, and he could feel it. He was focused on making enough credits, by selling or scamming, to fix the cruiser and get us to Jubilee.

We finished setting up the table, and Sebastian got Barnaby ready.

"Alright," he said, winking. "You know the drill, smile big and reel in the suckers. We've got plenty of elixirs, but save some of that Poppy's Poison for my special lady and me."

"Of course," I said.

"Keep an eye out for anything good, fancy watch, fat wallet," Sebastian said.

"I know," I replied. "I'll give you the signal if someone looks promising."

"That's my girl," he said, giving me a quick pat on the backside. "Now go work your magic. I'll be over there charming moms into paying for kiddie rides on Barnaby."

As if he understood exactly what was coming, Barnaby let out a low whine while Sebastian led him off toward the crowd.

My job was always the same: flirt with the men, sell elixirs, short-change them when I could, and spot anyone rich enough to rob later. I wore my best skirt with shiny beads, a low-cut blouse, and added a bit of rouge to my cheeks. Even while working the crowd with Barnaby, Sebastian always kept an eye on me.

The square got busy fast. After church let out, the street was full. Lots of women stopped to look at my scarves and trinkets, but I focused on the men. One of them caught my eye as he pretended to be interested in the voodoo dolls, but I could tell he was watching me.

"Careful," I said. "You don't want to put a hex on yourself by accident."

The man jumped, dropped the doll, and started to walk away.

"I'm just teasing, sugar. What's your name?" I called after him.

He stopped, turned, and pointed to himself. He was a little chubby, dressed in a freshly ironed brown tweed suit with a matching vest. I figured he'd just come from church.

"Who, me? Uh… my name's Henry," he said, stumbling over the words.

"Henry," I said with a smile. "That's a strong name for a strong man. Want to try one of my magic elixirs? Just two credits."

I tried not to laugh. My fake seductive voice still felt silly, even after all the practice with Sebastian. It had taken me a while to say the lines without cracking up.

Henry glanced around, then stepped closer to the table. "What kind of elixir?"

"Well," I said, "that depends."

"Depends on what?" he asked, wiping his sweaty hands on his pants.

"On what you're looking for," I said, leaning forward a little. "Do you want luck? A good high? Or maybe true love?"

I smiled and licked my lips.

"True love? Really, you can do that?" Henry said. Sweat was gathering on his forehead and upper lip as he pulled out his wallet. "What do you think I should try?" he said. I smiled and stood up.

"Love potion it is." I poured a cup of one of the less potent elixirs and extended my hand. I didn't think Henry could handle anything too strong.

"I call it the Devil's Candy," I said.

Henry smiled, set the credits down, and reached for the cup of bright yellow liquid. But before he could grab it, a woman came up behind him and slapped his hand away.

"No, thank you," she said sharply, grabbing his arm. "Henry! What did I tell you about women like that?"

Henry shrank back as she pulled him into the street. "Sorry, gotta go," he muttered.

"Suit yourself," I said, drinking the elixir and slipping the credits into my corset. The woman turned and gave me a nasty look before disappearing into the crowd.

By midafternoon, we'd sold nearly all the elixirs and most of the fish. I was tired and ready to leave, and Barnaby looked just as worn out. Sebastian was nowhere in sight, so I started packing up on my own. I took a handful of trash over to the community bin when I heard a strange sound coming from a truck parked in front of the pub. It sounded like someone crying.

I turned to look and saw something strange, a large cage in the back of the truck, half-covered with cloth. Inside was a man, struggling and trying to break free.

At first, I ignored him. But then he started to speak.

"Miss Maya, is that you?" wept a familiar voice. I stopped and turned back.

"Who is that?" I said.

"It's me! It's Loki!" the voice wailed. "Please, help me, this is a blue day indeed!"

I turned, pulled back the cloth, and there he was: Loki, the dwarf from the creepy church at Sparks. He was crammed into a cage, limbs flailing like a trapped possum, his robe was stained with something that looked suspiciously like jam and something that definitely wasn't.

"What on earth are you doing in there?" I asked.

"They say I've got warrants, three to be precise!" he cried, pressing his face against the bars. His breath fogged the metal, and a bit of drool slid down his chin. "I told them, I'm a man of the cloth! A servant of the divine! A collector of sacred toenails! But no, in I went, like a common criminal!"

"But how? Who did this?" I said.

Loki sniffled. "Oh, please, Miss Maya. You must help get out of this portable jail. I'm too dainty for prison!" he said.

Loki looked just like I remembered, grimy, smelly, with brown teeth and wrinkled yellow skin. Still, something in me said I should help him. Not because I thought he was innocent, and not out of pity. It was that awful little face, pressed between the bars, that stirred something deeper. A memory. Not mine, exactly, but Maya's. The quiet girl. The scared one. The version of me that hadn't learned how to bite back yet.

I thought of the first time the twins and I arrived in Sparks, how Loki stood outside his wicked congregation, preaching nonsense with wild eyes and sticky corn-soaked fingers. He reminded me of my time with Figgy and Thomas T and how kind they'd been to the twins and me, how they'd made us feel safe for a moment.

I didn't save Loki that day for him. I did it for Maya. "Hold on a minute. But listen, you have to call me Poppy, okay? Poppy's my name now," I said.

"Okay, Miss Poppy, please…" Loki begged.

"I'll be right back," I said, scanning the crowd for Sebastian. I spotted him juggling for a group of kids while their mothers watched, smiling at him as if he were the main attraction. I pulled him aside and led him toward the truck.

"A little jealous?" he teased.

"Not even close. I need your help. We have to save Loki."

"Loki? What's a Loki?" he said.

"A friend. From before. We need to take him with us," I said.

"A friend? We don't have room for a friend. Especially not a Loki," he said.

"We can't just leave him locked up. Who knows what they'll do to him?"

"Even if I wanted to, we've got Barnaby and all our stuff. There's no space for anyone else."

"But he's a small person. Like, really small and pretty gross. And a trickster, kind of an oddity. Honestly, he's a little evil, and I think you'll like him," I said.

Sebastian stopped and raised an eyebrow. "You mean a dwarf?" he said.

"Yes, he's over here. Come look," I said, leading Sebastian to the truck where Loki sat sniffling behind the bars.

Sebastian leaned in. "Well, now, that's something. Every Carnivále needs a good dwarf."

"Please, kind sir, rescue me from this cruel injustice," Loki said with a wide grin. His breath hit us like a wall, rancid and sour, with a hint of something fermented. Sebastian gagged and stumbled back.

"Holy crap, he's hideous! I love him," he said.

"A bit unkempt, maybe," Loki sniffled, "but hardly hideous."

"Show me who did this to you," Sebastian said.

Loki pressed his face against the bars, his yellow skin squishing like old fruit. "It's them, it's them over there!" he screeched, jabbing a stubby finger toward a couple across the street. "Those two are the captors!"

Sebastian squinted. "Those two? The ones shoving pickled eggs into their mouths?"

Loki nodded furiously. "Don't be fooled by their good looks! They're agents of injustice! They lured me with promises of candy and cream ale and then—*bam!*—cage!"

Sebastian looked at me, half amused, half unsure. "Well, he's got flair, I'll give him that."

Loki rattled the bars. "I demand liberation! And maybe a snack."

"Okay, I'll take care of them while you get the little guy out, hide him somewhere, and wait," said Sebastian.

"Got it," I said.

Luckily, the bounty men who'd snatched Loki weren't men at all; they were two women loitering near the food stalls, stuffing their faces with free samples.

The first was tall and rail-thin, with a face shaped like a stretched-out potato and greasy hair. She moved slowly and blinked with the confusion of someone who'd just woken up from a nap. She seemed harmless.

Her partner was anything but. She was built like a brick oven, with a belt full of tools meant for pain: a thick black whip, a collapsible metal rod, and a brass glove clearly designed to rearrange someone's face. Her leather vest was tight and covered in territory patches. I wondered if she was Jupiter Kane's long-lost twin sister, the one they kept locked in the basement when company came over.

Sebastian spotted them and lit up like it was showtime. He strolled toward them with that easy charm of his, already tossing out compliments and juggling tricks like bait. I slipped back toward the truck, trying to look like I belonged there, and kept my eyes on the cage while Sebastian worked his magic.

"Can you two lovely ladies help me? I think I've been robbed," Sebastian said with a smile.

"Robbed?" said the bigger woman. "What do you mean?"

"By your beauty," he said, laying it on thick. "It's stolen my heart."

The skinny one blushed. The big one just stared at him.

"You serious?" she asked, raising an eyebrow.

"Only when I'm lucky enough to meet women like you," he said, tossing a small apple in the air and catching it behind his back.

The skinny one giggled, covering her mouth like Sebastian had just told the funniest joke in the world. Her partner wasn't amused. She planted her hands on her hips, frowned, and wiped a smear of egg from her chin. For a second, I thought she might punch him.

Sebastian took a step back.

"In all seriousness," he said, smoothing his tone, "can I interest you ladies in a taste of my magic elixirs? A shot of Blue Grenada, perhaps? On the house. I'd love a woman's opinion on my newest batch."

The big one didn't react, just stared him down. But her friend nodded eagerly, eyes bright with curiosity.

"No funny business, I swear," Sebastian said, placing a hand over his heart and smiling. "My stand's right over there, next to the big furry guy named Barnaby."

"What is it?" asked the big woman.

"He's a burro," Sebastian replied.

"Not the donkey, you dingbat, the Blue Gralava stuff," she snapped.

"It's pronounced Grenada," Sebastian said smoothly. "It's an exotic elixir made from fermented potatoes, blueberry mash, and a touch of honey. Tastes like springtime."

He kissed his fingers and winked.

The big woman tilted her head and frowned. "It got booze in it?" she said.

Sebastian rolled his eyes. I could tell the big woman was testing both his charm and his patience.

"Yes," he said flatly. "There's *booze* in it."

That was all it took. The two women followed him to our table, chatting and laughing like they'd known him for years. I stayed behind at the truck, working on the cage.

I pulled a pin from my hair and tried to open the lock, but my hands were shaking. The pin kept slipping and falling to the ground. I needed something thicker, like a paper fastener or nail.

Meanwhile, Sebastian was stuck playing host. The two bounty women were laughing louder now, cheeks flushed and eyes glassy from their third round of elixir. The big one had taken to poking Sebastian in the chest every time she made a joke, and the other kept leaning in like she was trying to solicit a kiss.

Sebastian smiled, though the effort showed. His eyes darted to me, then to the women, then lingered on the elixir bottle—as if calculating how much more it would take to knock them out.

He poured another round with the grace of a man deeply regretting his charm.

"Hurry, Miss Poppy," Loki whispered, gripping the bars with his grubby fingers.

"I'm trying, but this hairpin's useless," I muttered, fumbling with the lock.

"Here, use my collar pin," he said, producing a two-inch brass pin topped with a tiny golden pineapple.

"You had this the whole time?" I asked, shaking my head.

The pin slid into the lock as if it were made for it. After a few quick turns, the latch popped open, and Loki tumbled out with a grunt.

"Oh, praise Jesus, I'm free!" he cried.

"I didn't see Jesus picking that lock," I said, waving the all-clear to Sebastian.

"No, no, it was you, Miss Maya, I mean Poppy. My savior," Loki said, scrambling to his feet.

We ducked into the crowd, crouched behind a fruit stand, and watched as the two bounty women staggered back toward their truck, laughing and swaying from too much elixir.

"What happens when they see I've absconded?" Loki whispered, eyes darting nervously.

"I don't know. Just be ready to run. Sebastian will distract them," I said.

But it turned out we didn't need a distraction. The two bounty women climbed into their truck without even glancing at the cage. The cage door swung open behind them, clanging against the metal as they sped off, completely unaware. We watched as the truck swerved down the road, nearly flattening a bread stand before disappearing toward the edge of town.

Loki and I met Sebastian back at the table. We packed up the last of our things, loaded Barnaby, and hurried home.

Back at the wagon, Sebastian cleared a space beside Barnaby and cooked Loki a massive plate of cram and biscuits. The little man devoured it like he hadn't eaten in days, then waddled to his bed and collapsed without a word.

Sebastian and I sat by the fire, the quiet settling around us was nice. For the first time all day, things felt calm.

"So," he said, poking at the flames, "how exactly do you know that little weirdo? You didn't date him, did you?"

"What?" I nearly choked on my tea. "Don't be ridiculous!"

"I just want to be clear," he said, smirking. "If I'm walking into some kind of three-way reunion, hookup with your ex, I'd like a heads-up."

"I'm going to slug you," I said.

"Well, you never tell me anything. What am I supposed to think?" he laughed.

"I didn't date him. I hardly even knew him," I said, rolling my eyes. "He's from a place I used to live. Sparks. He was a pastor or something like it. Ran a weird little church. No romance. Just a strange chapter in my life."

Sebastian leaned back, tossing a twig into the fire. "So tell me then," he said, his voice quieter now, less teasing.

I looked at him and saw the quiet hurt behind the smile. He'd told me nearly everything about his past, laid it out like a map, and I hadn't even given him my real name.

That night, for the first time, I told Sebastian something true. Just a sliver. I kept it light, just enough to satisfy the moment. I told him about growing up in Proper with the twins, and our time in Sparks, about Thomas T. and Figgy, about the strange little church, and the way Loki used to preach like he was rooting for the wrong team.

I didn't tell him how I got to Sparks or why. I didn't mention the Jameson Eight, what happened to Marcus, my dirty blood, or especially what came after I left. Those parts still made my chest ache if I breathed too deeply.

And he didn't push. Just nodded, listened, and seemed content with what I gave him.

For now, anyway.

That week, we returned to the market every day, and luckily, the two bounty women never returned. We managed to rack up a decent stash of credits, almost enough to finally get the cruiser fixed. But then Sebastian got greedy and decided some of it should go toward Carnivále, and that he could handle the repairs himself with a few new parts.

Several days passed. Then several more. Blue Grenada flowed freely, poppy dust hung in the air like fog around his head, and Sebastian was no closer to fixing the cruiser than he was to launching it into space. Frustration took over. He kicked at the dirt, hurled bike parts into the trees, and snapped at Loki and me like we were the ones who broke it.

Even poor Barnaby wasn't spared. One day was particularly bad, and the poor Burro retreated to his trailer, tail tucked and ears drooping. Loki and I didn't wait for our turn. We slipped away and headed into town, leaving Sebastian to rage alone in the clearing, surrounded by broken parts and empty bottles.

Loki and I had become quite close in the short time since he'd joined us. It was nice to have someone other than Sebastian to talk to, and being different himself, he understood me. Though I never told him my secret, he seemed to know something was strange about me. A dark secret. Maybe he'd heard about me at Sparks when the bounty men came looking for the boys and me, or perhaps it was just his own keen perception. Either way, he never mentioned it, and neither did I.

It was a Tuesday, and the market was slow. Most vendors came in on Friday and stayed the weekend. Loki and I got a coffee and scones at Mabel's and walked along the street admiring the day. A few hours had passed, and I figured Sebastian would either be passed out or dead by now, so we decided to turn back when a familiar sight caught my eye and turned my stomach.

It was a bus parked next to one of the empty vendor stations: a large green one, the Green Beast. Leaning against the bus, smoking a cigarette while counting a stack of credits bigger than I'd ever seen, was Percy, the human trafficker who befriended me at Sparks only to sell me to a gang of baby wranglers. I couldn't take my eyes off his vile, smug face as he ogled his cash, likely earned by stealing and selling other young girls on the black market.

"Hey, Loki," I said.

"Yes, Miss Poppy," he replied.

"I think I've got our cruiser problem solved."

"Really? How so?"

I nodded toward the Beast.

Loki squinted. "Hey, I've seen that guy before."

"Yeah, so have I," I said, tossing my scone to the ground. The sweetness had curdled in my mouth, leaving a sticky, bitter taste. It was the taste of revenge.

"What do you want to do then, Miss Poppy?"

"I want to take that bus."

He looked at me, then at the Beast, then back again.

"Well," he said, brushing crumbs off his coat, "I suppose it's a good day as any for a little grand theft."

ᴄ Chapter 17 - Gertie

The year 2132

Crouched behind the kitchen garbage bins, Asher and I waited, nerves buzzing, for the Thursday transport to arrive. He kept leaning out to peek around the bin, while I gnawed at what was left of my fingernails.

"You're sure there's a place to hide?" he asked for the fifth time.

"I'm sure," I said. "The refrigerated box doesn't sit flush with the back of the trailer. There's a gap behind it. It's small, but big enough. I saw it once when I stayed late one night to help with the deliveries. The driver said it was to keep the bins from slamming against the cab and scratching the paint."

Asher nodded, but his eyes didn't stop scanning the alley. The silence between us was tight, filled with the distant hum of the kitchen freezers and the sour stink of old cabbage. "I hope you're right," he said..

"I am," I said. "So get your jacket ready. It's going to be cold in there."

Asher pulled out his jacket and tied it around his waist, and I grabbed my swaddle and wrapped it around my neck.

He groaned. "Ugh, not that again. It's not gonna keep you warm."

"It's for good luck," I said.

"It looks like a dirty napkin," he muttered. "And it smells like one, too."

"No, it doesn't," I said. "Besides. It's gotten me through tough times in the past."

"Yeah, like what? A haunted laundry basket?" he said, peeking around the bin again. "If we get caught, I'm blaming the swaddle."

"Fine. But if we make it, you owe it an apology."

"Not happening."

The two of us fell silent as we waited for what seemed an eternity. The stench from the day's discarded food wasn't enough to break our spirits, but the overdue transport was.

"And you're sure they're coming?" said Asher. "It's been hours."

"I'm positive. There's never been a missed delivery." I said. It was true, they never missed a Thursday delivery, but I couldn't help but feel a little nervous and was contemplating heading back when the headlights of the seafood truck slowly turned into the back lot behind the kitchen.

The bright red cab with attached living quarters, pulling the extended white trailer full of fresh seafood, was a glorious sight.

"Gulf of Mexico Marina Transport," read Asher.

"That's it," I said. Mexico, the land of freedom, was just a day's journey away.

"Get ready," he said.

"I am," I said, grabbing hold of the straps to my pack.

The driver circled the back lot once before backing the truck up to the elevated loading dock near the kitchen doors, where Asher and I crouched just a few feet away, hidden behind the bins.

He climbed out of the cab, hopped onto the dock, and pressed the buzzer on the wall. A moment later, Jester, the pantryman, opened the door.

"Beau, you're late," Jester said.

Beau scowled and spat a wad of chewing tobacco onto the concrete. "Got sidetracked in Albuquerque. Highway was out. Had to cut through some back roads to make the Santa Fe drop. Damn, Grid repairs or some other crap like that."

Jester didn't flinch. "Anything good this time?"

"The usual," Beau grunted, unlocking the trailer doors. "Shrimps, perch, and a crap ton of tuna."

As the two men started unloading boxes and disappeared into the kitchen, Asher grabbed my hand. His grip was tight, eyes locked on the trailer's open door.

"Now!" said Asher. We jumped to our feet, darted across the platform, and leaped into the back of the trailer. The fish coolers were huge and nearly took up the trailer's entire width. There was just enough of a gap that Asher and I squeezed through before ducking down behind the cooler just as the men returned for their next load.

"Hey, Beau. How far down are you going this time?" It was Godfrey, one of the kitchen cooks.

"All the way to Nola. Why?" said Beau.

"Pick me up some of them crawdads, will ya? My wife wants to make a pot of that etouffee Clarice brought to the festival last year," said Godfrey.

"Sure thing," said Beau as he slammed the trailer doors shut, muffling the sound of the men's conversation.

"What are crawdads?" I whispered.

"Shhhh, I don't know, some kind of fish, I guess," said Asher.

A few minutes later, the truck engine roared to life, and the trailer vibrated beneath us as Beau slowly pulled away from the kitchen dock and out the front gates of Greyburry, taking Asher and me with him.

95

❧ Chapter 18 - Poppy

The year 2117

"Hello, kind sir, could you be a friend and help us with some directions? We seem to have gotten ourselves turned around," huffed Loki, dabbing his forehead with a handkerchief.

Percy paused his work on the Green Beast's engine, grabbed a jug of water, and took a long swig. Without a word, he handed it over.

Loki accepted it gratefully, drank, then passed it to me. I took it and set it down near the front tire, careful not to knock it over.

"Of course. Where are you two headed?" Percy asked.

"Back to our camp near that old cemetery," I said. "I don't know how we got so turned around. And this heat is brutal."

Percy nodded toward the road. "Cemetery's that way."

He paused, squinting at me. "Have we met? You look familiar."

"I don't think so," I said.

"No, I'm sure of it," he said.

"I just have one of those faces," I offered.

Percy raised a brow and smiled, not convinced. "So what brings you two out here anyway?"

"We were heading north to see family," I said. "Had a motorbike, but it broke down. Been stuck here ever since. Sure wish we could get a ride. Know of any transports nearby?"

Percy shook his head. "Not around here, no."

"You wouldn't be headed north, would you? We have credits," I said.

Percy frowned, giving me a slow once-over. A con man himself, he could smell a hustle from three miles away.

"Credits?" he asked. "How many?"

"Hundreds!" Loki declared, throwing his arms wide in the air. "Perhaps more, depending on how you feel about antique buttons and a half-eaten scone."

I slapped his arm. "Loki."

"What?" he whispered, eyes wide. "People love scones."

Percy's smile faded. He squinted at me, the gears clearly turning. We looked too desperate. No one with real credits begged for a ride from a stranger.

"Sorry," Percy said, turning back to the Green Beast's engine. "I'm staying put for a while. Heading west later in the year."

But I saw it, the flicker in his eyes, the way his shoulders stiffened. He recognized me. And now he was pretending he didn't.

"No worries," I said calmly. "We'll find another way. Thank you for your time."

Percy didn't respond. He was already halfway back under the hood of the Green Beast, pretending not to hear.

Loki tugged on my arm and gave a half-shrug, like he wasn't sure what to do next. I just smiled and shook my head. He didn't know what had happened between Percy and me, and he didn't need to. This wasn't his revenge; it was mine. All he had to do was play his part. I pointed to my satchel, then to the jug.

Loki's eyes lit up, but his voice dropped to a whisper. "Ah," he breathed, nodding slowly. "The old wala, wala, in the wata wata. Classic."

"Good luck to you," Percy called from beneath the hood of the Green Beast.

Loki extended his hand with theatrical flair. "Same to you, good fellow. May your bolts stay tight and your gaskets leak wisdom."

Percy grunted as I handed Loki a vial of poppy dust from my satchel.

"Have a blessed day," Loki said, as if he were giving a sermon, then tipped the dust into Percy's water jug. He dropped the empty vial into his coat pocket, and we slipped away toward the town square.

"How long should we wait?" Loki asked, eyes wide and voice hushed.

"It depends," I said, giggling. "But it won't be long. You dumped the whole thing in."

"Oh dear, he won't die, will he?" said Loki.

"I hope so," I muttered.

We returned to the Beast an hour later and found Percy slumped over the steering wheel, unconscious. The empty water jug lay on its side next to his feet.

"Okay, let's get him outside and remove his clothes," I said as I pulled Percy from the seat and dragged him down the steps. I loosened his belt and removed his pants and shirt. Then we dragged Percy's naked body into the bushes and tied his arms behind his back with his belt.

"Take the clothes and throw them in the back. I don't want him to find them when he wakes up," I said, climbing into the driver's seat.

"Oh, Miss Poppy, you are evil," Loki whispered with a grin. "Do you even know how to command this behemoth?"

"We're about to find out," I said, turning the key.

The engine sputtered a few times, then roared to life. I scooted forward so I could reach the pedals. I'd never driven before, but I'd watched Cleaver Stevens drive his old tractor back in Proper plenty of times. One pedal to go, one to stop, and the wheel to steer. Simple enough.

I pressed the right pedal. Nothing. Tried the left—still nothing.

Loki leaned in. "Maybe it needs the fuel?"

I sighed. "Or maybe it needs me to figure out how to drive. "Why won't you go already?" I said.

"Try the stick," said Loki, pointing. "You take it out of stop and put it in go before you hit the pedals."

"Oh, right, the shifter," I said. I grabbed the long metal lever and pulled it down from P to R, then gently pressed the gas.

The bus lurched backward, rolled over a clump of bushes, and I slammed the brake hard.

Loki screamed. "Don't kill us, Miss Poppy! I'm too young to die! I haven't even finished my memoir!"

I looked back at him. "You have a memoir?"

"Work in progress," he said, clutching the seat. "But I've got a title: Doom comes in small packages: The Loki Story."

I blinked. "That sounds fascinating, I think."

"Oh, it is… It's got everything, sin, redemption, betrayal, and a raccoon named Dennis."

"Dennis?"

"Yes. He's pivotal."

I rolled my eyes and reached for the shifter again. "Hold on, it might get bumpy while I swing this thing around that tree," I said. The bus gave a low groan as I nudged the shifter into Drive. Loki clutched the seat like it might fly out from under him.

"Swing around the tree?" he whined. "Miss Poppy, this vessel is not a dancer."

"It's fine, stop being so dramatic," I said, easing my foot onto the gas. The Beast rolled forward, slow and heavy.

Loki peeked out the window. "If we hit that tree, I'm blaming your lack of formal training and your questionable footwear."

"I'm wearing sandals," I said.

"Exactly."

We crept past the tree, going a bit too fast, maybe, its branches scraped the side of the bus. I gripped the wheel and held my breath as the rear end of the bus bounced over a fallen branch.

Loki crossed himself as if he were auditioning for sainthood. "If we survive this, I'm adding a chapter called Death Ride: How I Survived the Murder Bus."

"Sounds delightful," I said, swerving onto the street and flooring the gas.

As we drove off, the town of Sabine shrank behind us, its crooked rooftops and faded signs swallowed by distance. Percy was still out cold, tied up, and tucked away in the bushes like yesterday's trash. I didn't know how long the poppy dust would hold, but I knew we had a head start.

Loki leaned forward, peering out the window. "Do you think he'll remember us when he wakes up?"

"I hope he remembers everything," I said. "Especially the part where we took his bus."

Loki smiled, soft and strange. "Revenge tastes like scones and smells of gasoline."

Chapter 19 - Poppy

The year 2117

Despite being less than two miles away, the ride back to camp took over an hour. I managed to get us there in one piece, with only minor damage to a lonely street sign that had the misfortune of standing too close to the road outside town.

As the Green Beast rumbled into camp, Sebastian stepped out of the wagon, shotgun in hand, his scowl ready for trouble. But when Loki popped his head out the window and waved like a party queen, Sebastian's face lit up.

"What in the world?" he shouted, slapping his leg and doing a little dance. "Where did you get that?"

"We burgled it!" Loki cried, arms raised like he'd won a prize.

I slammed the brakes. Loki flew to the floor, and the bus skidded sideways, kicking up a cloud of dust. Sebastian jumped clear just in time.

"Okay, marvelous job," he laughed, coughing through the dust. "But no more driving for you."

He climbed aboard, retrieved the keys, and gave the dashboard a pat of approval. "Wow. This is perfect. Just perfect. Tell me how you did it."

"Later," I said, scanning the horizon. "We need to get out of here before the owner wakes up."

Sebastian nodded. "Say no more. Let's hitch up the wagon and get the hell out of Sabine."

We worked late into the night, attaching the wagon and Barnaby's trailer to the Green Beast. It took some clever handiwork on Sebastian's part, ropes, clamps, and a few muttered curses, but after a handful of adjustments and one near disaster involving a loose axle, we had all three lined up and ready to roll.

By sunrise, we were leaving Sabine behind.

Sebastian had wanted to take the cruiser and sell it for scrap, but he couldn't figure out how to make it fit, so we left it behind, half buried amongst the trees, and headed north.

Now that we had a full-size vehicle, Sebastian was itching to explore a bit before heading to Jubilee. He suggested a detour to the Flats, a stretch of desolate earth and scattered homesteads where, according to him, oddities were abundant, and he was right.

In Guthrie, we met Sven, a freakishly strong simpleton working the fields on a nearby farm. He barely spoke, but could lift a hay bale with one hand and a goat with the other. No one asked him to; he just did.

Then came Big Alice. She had no sword-swallowing talent, but she was enormous and hilarious, and Sebastian adored her from the moment he saw her working a vegetable stand at the Edaville market. He tried to charm her into handing over free food, but lost a fistful of credits when she beat him at a game of three-card monte without breaking a sweat.

Our last recruit was Boris, from Sulphur, a colony still sealed behind high barrier walls built during the scourge. The settlement reminded me of Proper. It's bleak town square, lifeless faces, everything so gray and quiet. Boris had no particular freakish ability, unless you counted being tall, ugly, and followed everywhere by a devious little monkey named Clyde, who thankfully rarely left his shoulder.

It surprised me how easily Sebastian convinced them to join us. But I suppose the promise of Carnivále was greater than whatever world they'd been living in.

Team in tow, we headed south toward the southern shores, stopping when we needed to refuel, restock, or stretch our legs. The Green Beast held together better than expected, and our motley convoy rolled on like it had purpose.

Sebastian talked non-stop about Jubilee, what we'd see, who we'd meet, and how his plans for one *Big Show* would finally come together. I even started to believe it. The closer we got, the more real it felt. Like maybe this time, things wouldn't fall apart. It was really going to happen. I could feel it.

But that all changed the day we reached Galveston.

It was a beautiful morning at the Peach Street Fair, but Ringo the goat, the newest member of our Carnivále family, had been increasingly hostile all day. Maybe he missed his goat mother, or perhaps it was the fake horn Sebastian had glued to his forehead, a broken deer antler held in place with watered-down paste.

We'd found Ringo during a midnight raid on a farm outside Alpine, a deserted, sour little place just south of the Flats. I begged Sebastian to leave him be. He was skittish, half-starved, and clearly not meant for life on the road. But Sebastian was desperate. He wanted an act that would lift our ragtag operation into something grand, something worthy of his name and the years he'd poured into it. I didn't know exactly how poor Ringo fit into that vision. But I figured I'd find out soon enough.

The crowd at the fair was intrigued, eager, even. They paid big to see their first unicorn and lined up for the free elixir samples that came with each ticket. Everything was going smoothly at first. Alice and Loki handled the tickets and poured the drinks, while Boris and Sven managed the "talent."

We were on our sixth viewing of the day and about to wrap things up when Sebastian insisted we go one more round. No one asked Ringo how he felt about it. He was tired, hungry, and clearly done performing.

Then an unruly fat kid came at him with a stick.

Ringo panicked, bolted for the Green Beast, and disappeared inside, leaving his fake horn and a shocked crowd behind in the dust.

A group of men, drunk on elixir and disappointment, shouted and rushed the wagon. Sebastian tried to fight them off, but there were too many of them.

I stood frozen, watching it unfold. I couldn't believe their anger. Did they honestly think we had a real unicorn?

Sven and Boris did their best to hold off the drunken mob, fists flying, elbows swinging. Loki, Big Alice, and I ran for cover inside the Beast. Clyde, ever loyal, hissed and spat from Boris's shoulder, but that only made things worse, and someone threw a bottle at him that shattered against the side of the bus.

The men beat Sebastian bloody. They tore the sign from his beloved wagon and made off with a week's worth of earnings, laughing as they went.

Sven and Boris hauled Sebastian's beaten body into the Beast, and we peeled out of the fairgrounds with what remained of the mob chasing after us, shouting, throwing rocks, and kicking up dust. The Green Beast roared down the road, and behind us, Peach Street burned, not with fire, but with fury.

Later that night, parked near a secluded estuary, Sebastian and I walked down to the beach and built a small fire while the others turned in. I cleaned the cuts on his head and wrapped his wrist, but there was nothing to be done about the bruises blooming across his face.

He lay back in the sand, staring up at the stars. I sat beside him, brushing the grit from his hair.

"It really was a good idea," I said. "If it hadn't been for that stupid kid."

"No," he said, sitting up abruptly and jabbing at the fire with a stick. "You saw their faces. They loved it until they realized it was fake. Fake like me."

He shook his head, jaw clenched. "It's trash. All my ideas are trash. Carnivále will never happen. I'm a fraud, and they knew it."

"Don't say that," I said. "We had one bad day."

"One bad day is all it takes," he muttered. "You and the others should leave while you still can."

I didn't answer right away. I watched the flames dance, listened to the waves roll in, and felt the weight of everything he was saying.

"We're not leaving," I said finally. "We just need to get to Jubilee. Once we're there, the acts will come together."

He didn't argue, but he didn't agree either. He just stared into the fire, shoulders tight, pride wounded.

"There's nothing else," Sebastian said, staring out at the fire. "Carnivále's finished. I've wasted everyone's time chasing a fantasy. You'd all be better off if I just walked into the ocean and disappeared."

"Don't say that," I said. "You can't leave me. Not ever." I felt a lump rise in my throat. He wasn't wrong. If Carnivále died, so would Sebastian, maybe not literally, but everything that made him who he was. Sebastian had always been dramatic, but this felt different. What happened at the market had cut deeper than the bruises on his face.

I took a sip of elixir and wiped my eyes.

"There might be something else," I said. "But we have to be careful."

"Careful?" Sebastian scoffed. "Of what, another mob? Another empty crowd? We've already been beaten, humiliated, and robbed blind. What else is there to lose?"

"No," I said, my voice low. "It's not about them. I have a secret that could help."

He turned to me, eyes narrowed. "What could you possibly be hiding? You've got no more than I do." Sebastian stroked my hair. "Oh, you beautiful thing. Those eyes, those lips, that hair. What could you possibly have that could fix all this?"

His voice was soft, but something in it stirred a heat in my chest, not desire, exactly, but devotion. Dangerous devotion. I would walk through fire for this man. I would bleed for him. I would do worse.

I looked away. "It's something else. Something no one can ever know."

He rolled off my lap, brushing sand from his coat. "What then?"

I didn't answer right away. My heart was pounding, not from fear, but from the weight of what I was about to say. I'd kept it buried for so long, wrapped in silence and shame. But Sebastian had saved me, fought for me, loved me in ways no one else ever had. Not Eric, not Val, not even the twins. Only Gertie came close, and I felt her soul with me every day.

But Sebastian was here. And he was unraveling.

"I love you," I said quietly. "More than anyone. And that's why I have to tell you."

He didn't speak. Just stared at me, waiting.

And somewhere behind him, the waves kept rushing the shore, angry and cold, as if warning me not to tell.

"You said once you wanted an Adlet," I said.

He chuckled, then stopped. His gaze sharpened like he knew I wasn't lying. Like he knew what I was going to say, and he wanted to hear it.

"Go on," he said.

"What if I told you I could make one?" I whispered.

He sat up slowly, the firelight catching the bruises on his face, making him look half-savage. His eyes gleamed with something wild.

"So your secret is dark?" he asked.

I nodded.

"How dark?"

I looked down at my hands. "It's my blood."

Sebastian's smile twisted, not cruel, but hungry. He took a long swig of elixir, then handed me the cup, his fingers brushing mine.

The waves crashed behind us, louder now, like they'd heard something they didn't like. And for the first time, I felt the weight of what I was about to unleash, not just a creature, but a truth that couldn't be buried again.

"Show me," he growled.

❧ Chapter 20 - Gertie

The year 2132

The ride to the Trident truck yard took a couple of hours. When we arrived, Beau hopped out, flung open the trailer doors, and climbed inside. Asher and I crouched low behind the ice bins, trying to stay hidden. Another man joined Beau, and the two of them started sorting through the slushy remains in the coolers.

Water dripped from the lid above, landing cold on our heads, but we didn't move.

"Here, take these," Beau said.

"Thanks. You want me to dump the ice?" the man asked.

"Nah, leave it. It'll melt by the time I get there. Keeps the box cool anyway," Beau replied.

"Alright. Appreciate the shrimp. You coming down to Libby's for a drink?"

"Can't. Got two big drops this week. Need sleep."

"Night then."

"Night."

The trailer doors slammed shut, the chains rattled, and the lock clicked into place. I exhaled slowly.

"We're locked in for the night," I whispered.

"Yep, no going back now," said Asher.

"Asher, what if someone finds out we're gone before we leave here?" I said.

"They won't," he said, pulling me close. "Besides, even if they did, they'd never think to look for us here. We're safe," he said. I pulled away and sat up.

"It's so dark in here," I said.

"Lie down and try to rest," he said as he positioned himself on his back, using his pack as a pillow.

"I'll try." I took my pack, laid it next to his, and cuddled up against his arm.

"Asher."

"Yes, Gertie."

"Never mind," I said.

That night at Trident was the longest of my life. Even the steady rhythm of Asher's breathing couldn't calm me. I didn't sleep. I didn't

"

even try. Every creak from the cab, every cricket chirp, every stray voice from the yard sent a fresh wave of panic through my chest.

Asher had said no one would think to look for two Greyburry escapees in a seafood truck. He was probably right. But what if he wasn't?

By morning, I was still wide awake. I knew it was morning by the thin light slipping through the door seams and the sound of Beau hacking up half a lung outside the cab.

The cab door slammed, and the engine rumbled to life.

I reached over and shook Asher's shoulder. "He's moving," I whispered.

"Are we leaving?" said Asher.

"I think so," I said, jumping up to relieve myself in the far corner of the trailer.

"Hey, gross. Don't do that there," Asher muttered.

"Then where?"

"At least go on the other side of the cooler."

"Too late," I said. "I wouldn't have made it anyway."

I returned to my spot beside him just as the Gulf of Mexico Marina Transport hit full speed. We sat quietly, holding hands, letting the reality sink in. We were absconders, treaty-breakers, all crimes that carried a death sentence, or worse, a lifetime in the labor camps.

I glanced at Asher. He smiled.

"Tell me again about Hope Island," I said.

"Again?" he laughed.

"You got something else to do?"

"Fair," he said, sitting up and pulling his knees to his chest. "You know Abel Myers, the morning gate guard?"

I nodded.

"He told me all about it. Said his family escaped the camps and made it there when he was young. He lived there for years before coming back to find his mother, then he got stuck at Greyburry."

"You believe him?"

"I do. Abel's solid. No reason to lie."

"Tell me the whole story," I said, the thrill of escape finally catching up to me.

"The locals call it Isla De La Esperanza. It's south, in Mexico, which used to be this whole other country."

"Hope Island," I said.

"Exactly," he said.

Asher leaned back against the cooler, his voice soft but steady as the truck rumbled beneath us.

"Well," he said, "Abel described it as not really an island, more like a peninsula, outside a few small towns. You get past those, and the land just opens up. No checkpoints, no patrols. Just quiet."

I listened, eyes closed, picturing it.

"He said it was founded by a man named Floyd Pierce, who they called the Mayor. Not the kind with a desk and a badge, just someone people trusted. No laws, no currency. People trade what they have. Everyone works. Everyone shares."

"And the beaches?" I asked.

Asher smiled. "Abel said they're unreal. White sand so soft it feels like flour, and water so blue it looks painted. No fences, no guards. Just hammocks between palm trees and the sound of waves brushing the shore."

I felt something shift in my chest, hope, maybe. Or something close. "Do you think it's real?" I asked.

"I know it's real," Asher said. "And it's waiting for us."

"I hope so," I sighed.

"Hey, I'm hungry. Is it too early to break into the food?" said Asher

"Not at all," I grabbed my pack. "We have two jugs of water, three bags of dried fruit, and crackers for snacks, oh, and two apples with granola for breakfast," I said, counting the bags of food we'd collected the day of our last practice run.

"What about the cheese and dried salami?" said Asher as he chomped on a fig.

"I'm saving that for dinner tonight. We should have plenty to get us by until we get there. We just have to be careful with the water," I said.

Asher and I finished our snack and tried to get some rest despite the road noise and constant vibration from the wheels. Though it wasn't the most comfortable mode of transportation, we were too nervous and excited to care.

Abel Myers made Hope Island seem like a fantasy land, but the world was a dangerous place, and as much as we wanted to believe it was all true, we knew we had to be careful.

Later that day, after the air inside the trailer cooled and the bit of light glowing from the top of the doors disappeared, Beau stopped the truck.

"We can't be there already, can we?" I said.

"I don't think so. Maybe we're just stopping for fuel," said Asher. We quietly waited for some sign we had made it to Hope Island, but Beau never left the truck.

"What's he doing?" I said.

"Maybe he's taking a nap," said Asher.

"Why wouldn't we just keep going? We have to be close, right?" I said.

"I don't know. Maybe he's too tired. He's been driving all day. We should try to get some rest, too. I want to be ready to go when we get there," said Asher.

"I'm not sure if I can fall asleep," I said. The truth was, I was exhausted. Every muscle that wasn't numb from the vibration ached.

"Me neither," yawned Asher.

I lay down across Asher's lap. "Tell me a story."

Asher chuckled, "Again? You tell me a story this time."

"I don't know any good stories," I said.

"Tell me about your last dream. You say you always have the craziest dreams, but you never tell me about them," said Asher.

I shuddered. My last dream wasn't a dream at all but a nightmare. It wasn't the first time I had it either.

"No, it's too scary," I said.

"Tell me anyway." Asher yawned again.

"Asher."

"Yes, Gertie."

"Have you ever wondered what it would be like if we were older? A lot older."

"What do you mean?"

"You know, lived through the scourge and the darkening. Do you ever wonder what it was like back then, when everyone was sick or hiding from the sick?" I said.

"You mean Spinners," he said.

"Yeah. Do you ever think about it?" I said.

"Heck no. I don't want to know. Remember what Lady Darcy said in history class? How they would grab you and fling you around until your body flew apart. No, thank you," he said.

"Sometimes, I wonder if that's why I came to Greyburry," I said.

"How so? You're too young to have anything to do with that. We both are."

"I mean, maybe it had something to do with why I was left out in the woods when I was a baby," I said.

"That doesn't make any sense," said Asher.

"You said to tell you about my dreams. It's all I dream of, and sometimes I wonder why," I said.

Asher stroked my hair. "You really dream about that stuff?" he said.

"Almost every night. The first time was at Trivel. I'd just graduated from kinder and woke up screaming and tearing at my clothes. Lady Beth gave me some juice and calmed me down, but I never went back to sleep that night."

"That must have been terrifying," said Asher.

"It was. The next night, it happened again. Then again, a week later. I didn't remember anything about the dreams at first, but after a few weeks, the images began to stick in my mind. Thin, pale faces with pink eyes and blood-stained teeth lurking through Greyburry at night," I said.

I could feel Asher's breathing intensify.

"Why didn't you ever tell me about this?" Asher sounded betrayed by my secret.

"I don't know. I was scared that talking about it would make it come true, maybe," I said.

"Are you scared now?" he said.

"A little, but not because of that." I shifted myself off Asher's lap and lay on my side next to him. "I've never been outside of Greyburry, not that I remember anyway. I'm excited too. I'm glad you talked me into leaving," I said.

"Good," he said. "I'm right. I'm always right."

"Yeah, well, our baby, if we could even have managed one, would never have been perfect anyway," I said.

"Why do you say that?" he said.

"What with your crooked nose and those funky teeth?" I giggled.

"My teeth are perfect," he cried.

"So vain," I laughed.

"I'm going to sleep," Asher muttered. "You should try to get some rest, too."

"I will," I said, but sleep never came.

If Asher knew the rest of my dream, he'd understand. I didn't tell him the worst part.

There was a woman who walked the grounds of Greyburry at night, calling my name. Her voice was rough and dry.

"Gertie". I kept hearing it, even after I woke up.

She was real. I'm sure of it.

I never saw her face, but I knew her. I knew her smell, her walk, her voice. I remembered how her hair moved in the wind and the taste of her milk.

She was my mother.

And in my dreams, she was still out there, looking for me.

❧ Chapter 21- Poppy

The year 2117

The night Banjo ate his second head reminded me of many things, mainly how dangerous my blood was. That evening, back inside the wagon, Sebastian pricked my finger and fed a drop of my blood to his beloved two-headed turtle while the others slept in the Beast. He wrapped my finger, then leaned over and kissed me long and hard.

I wasn't sure it was a good idea. In truth, I was terrified. The doubts came in waves, first quiet, then crashing, but Sebastian was steady. He handed me the elixir with that calm certainty I'd learned to trust, and told me everything would be okay, that he was in charge now. That nothing bad would ever happen to either of us. That we could manage my condition, fold it neatly into our lives, and pass for normal. Whatever that meant.

He whispered it again: "It'll be okay."

And after a few shots of Poison, I let go. I gave in to him, to the moment, to the fragile hope that maybe just maybe, he was right. I wanted so badly to believe him. I needed to. So I did.

We made love for the first time, bodies tangled beside Banjo's box, where the turtle hissed and spat out bits of his own flesh and bone.

The next morning, Banjo was dead. We found his shell flipped upside down near the wagon door. The bottom of the door had tiny scratches where he'd tried to claw his way out. His stomach and pieces of one of his heads lay scattered across the floor.

I sat on the bed, hoping it was just a nightmare. But my aching head and dry throat told me it was real. I turned to the side and threw up on the wagon floor, just a few feet from Sebastian. He was sitting quietly, staring at the broken pieces of Banjo's shell. The mess hit the boards with a wet splash, but Sebastian didn't move. He just stared at the broken piece of his pet Banjo.

"I'm sorry," I said, my voice shaking. "I didn't mean to hurt him. I know you didn't either."

Sebastian kept looking at the shell. "Of course not," he said.

"Can you forgive me?" I asked, crying.

"Forgive you? You didn't do anything wrong," he said.

"But he was your friend. Your first oddity. And I killed him."

"No," Sebastian said gently. "I wanted to believe what you said. I gave him the blood. Not you."

He looked up and smiled. "Banjo was brave. He gave his life for something bigger. He's just the first. There will be more."

Sebastian's eyes lit up as he spoke. I could almost see the thoughts racing behind them, and my heart jumped. They didn't look like the eyes of someone who had just lost a pet. No, these were the eyes of someone obsessed.

I didn't understand why he wasn't sad about Banjo. But somehow, his excitement made me feel safe. He wasn't scared of me. He wouldn't push me away or report me. Sebastian wanted me. He needed me and my dirty blood.

Later that morning, Sebastian wrapped Banjo in a towel, placed him back in his box, and carried him outside. He hummed softly as he dug a small hole and buried the box in the dirt.

That night, something felt strange. Sebastian was unusually cheerful, almost excited about everything that had happened. He asked me to tell him my story. He demanded, really. Said if we were going to do this, he needed to know. So I did, filling in the gaps I'd left out before. Well, most of the gaps.

I told him about Father Jameson and the eight hidden children he and his men found in a bunker. I told him about life at Proper colony and how the eight of us lived hidden in the library until we were transported, one by one, for our screenings. I told him how the others failed and were terminated, and how only the twins and I remained after Jaco killed Abigail.

I told him about the clinic, how I passed my screening, and how I came home to find the library destroyed by Colonel Lindy. I told him about the Purity Feast, the massacre at Dangers camp, and fleeing to Sparks, where bountymen took Markus. I told him about Jobe and my run-in with Colonel Lindy and Jaco in the Observation Rotunda at Intermountain. I even told him about Percy and his Green Beast, which now belonged to us.

Sebastian held me tight as I spun my tail. He didn't interrupt or ask questions. He just rubbed my back and listened. The only things I left out were my real name, my relationship with Eric, and my Gertie. I wasn't ready to tell her story yet, and I wasn't sure I'd ever be.

Of all the things I've done, abandoning my precious child that day in the barn was my greatest regret, so I left out the part about having her and finished with me leaving Red Rock and finding myself at the fort before stumbling upon him cooking that day. Afterward, the two of us sat holding each other. I felt as though the weight of a hundred boulders had lifted from my shoulders as I sank deeper into his arms.

"I'm sorry you had to go through that, but in many ways, I'm not," he said.

"What do you mean?" I said.

"Don't you see? This is your destiny, to find me, to find us. I'm just so sorry the journey was so painful," he said.

Lying in bed that night, I thought about what Sebastian said. Was this really my destiny? Did God plan this journey for me? I wondered what Father Dillon back at Proper would say about it. He always preached that God worked in mysterious ways, but would he agree that this, too, was part of some divine plan, or would he fall back on the idea that Mother Nature was at work and had something to do with this ungodly, twisted tale? I convinced myself that night that the Kuru was a gift, not a curse.

Maya Jameson may not have known how to use it. Her ignorance caused the death of so many, but not Poppy. Poppy had genuine power, and if used correctly, she could rule the world. Sebastian would get his *Carnivále,* alright, and it would be the best damn one there ever was. Sometime that night while I slept, Maya Jameson finally died. I knew if I wanted to move forward, I'd have to forget all about her and the life she lived, and so I did, well, I tried, and it worked out pretty well, for a while anyway.

❧ Chapter 22- Poppy

The year 2119

After what happened to Banjo, Sebastian became obsessed. My blood had changed something in him, and he wanted more. So we took a detour east to the town of Dain, near the Cube's border, chasing rumors Boris had told us about dog breeding in the area.

Not everyone was happy about the change in plans. The bus was crowded and tense, and Alice was getting fed up. When Sebastian announced we'd be delaying our arrival at Jubilee, she nearly lost it.

"What do you want a dog for, anyway?" she yelled from the back. "I'm sick of this two-ring bus tour from hell. If I didn't know better, I'd say you've lost your damn mind, you hairy lump of bat crap crazy. Everyone knows there aren't any dogs out there."

Sebastian glanced in the rearview mirror, grinning as if he'd just received a compliment.

"Aw, Alice," he drawled, smooth and easy. "You keep talkin' sweet like that, and we're liable to end up in a whole mess of trouble. You know I'm a taken man."

Alice rolled her eyes, but she couldn't hide her smile.

Much to Sebastian's disappointment, there weren't any dogs in Dain. But we did leave with four new crew members: Lady Jane, Cowboy, and the Yeager brothers. Rake and Tershy. All four had been staying at a shelter just outside town after a flood destroyed the encampment they lived in.

Lady Jane was lovely but also very broken. Sebastian said she used to work on her back, though he didn't say much more. She had long blonde hair, tired blue eyes, and the kind of scars you could see on her face and hear in her voice. She spoke softly, like every word cost her something.

Cowboy was tall, quiet, and hard to read. A large birthmark covered most of his neck, and his jaw hung a little slack. He rarely spoke, and when he did, you usually regretted it. Once, Loki asked him how he made money.

Cowboy just said, "I like to kill things with my hands."

He and Jane had a look about them, like they'd seen things, not so great things, and they'd just as soon cut your throat as say hello. But Sebastian said they were harmless. And I believed him.

Sebastian was especially excited about the Yeager brothers, Rake and Tershy. Both had real carnival experience from working boardwalk festivals out west, which made them valuable in his eyes.

Rake was small and strange, not like Loki, but in his own way. He wore thick glasses held together with tape and smiled constantly, even in his sleep. His hair was short and curly, and he stuttered when he spoke. At first, he seemed simple, but he was sharp in ways that didn't show right away. Not book-smart, but sharp. He couldn't read or spell very well, but he could count birds in the sky without missing a beat and remember conversations from years ago word-for-word.

Tershy was different. He was book-smart, maybe the cleverest person I'd ever known, a genius really. Like me, he loved to read, and he tore through my small stack of books in no time. He understood math, knew how to build things, and could draw beautifully. He had the same curly hair as his brother Rake, though his was longer and more natural, falling into his eyes when he read. He kept himself neat and clean, sharper-looking than anyone else on the bus. When he wasn't reading, he'd sit in the back of the Beast, sketching as we drove.

One of my favorite drawings he did was of me, sitting alone and looking out the bus window. He captured everything, the wind in my hair, the quiet in my face, the thoughts I didn't say out loud. Every time I looked at it, I remembered a day just like that, when I was someone else. And it made me smile.

After Dain, we regrouped and headed south toward the coast, back toward Jubilee, just like Sebastian had promised. It had been almost three years since I first met Sebastian Sheets, and now we were finally pulling our traveling salvage yard, Loki's words, not mine, into the place Sebastian had always talked about. His home and the future site of Carnivále.

Jubilee sat near an old grid-rail station that looked like it hadn't seen a traveler since the war. The land was about ten acres, buried under twenty years of neglect. A broken-down two-room shack and the remains of a barn stood out among piles of junk, discarded sinks, rusty truck wheels, and trash hidden in the trees and tall grass.

It was a mess, but I saw potential. Not everyone did.

Loki stayed on the bus, hesitant to step outside. He looked out the window, swatting at a cloud of tiny bugs buzzing around his face.

"Mr. Sebastian, what is this place?" he asked, voice low and unsure.

"This is Jubilee!" Sebastian said proudly. "See that shack? I was born in it. And that old barn over there, that's where my pops used to fix engines and all kinds of things." He was grinning from ear to ear, clearly thrilled to be back.

Alice went inside the shack to check it out. A few minutes later, she came back out and called for Jane.

"Come look, Jane," she said. "It's better than you'd think. There's a hole in the roof near the back and the door needs fixin', but other than that, and the family of rats, it just needs a little cleaning."

Lady Jane started walking through the brush toward the shack when her skirt got caught in a thick patch of tall grass. She tugged at it, wincing.

"Ouch, what's with this grass?" she said, pulling her skirt free.

Sven rushed over, scooped her up, and carried her to the front steps of the shack.

"Careful," he said. "That's not regular grass, it's Sawgrass. It'll cut you up real good if you're not careful."

Sven had clearly taken a liking to Lady Jane. It was sweet watching him fuss over her.

"Look, it ripped my skirt," she said, holding it up.

"Don't worry about that, none," said Alice. "I'll stitch it up for you."

"Sven's right. The first order of business is to clear that Sawgrass and get all the trash into the back of Barnaby's trailer and get it out of here," said Sebastian.

"Yes, boss," said Boris.

"Poppy, I want you to stay on the bus with Loki and Clyde," Sebastian said. "Ain't no sense in you gettin' cut up or steppin' on somethin' sharp out here."

"But I'm going to take Barnaby out for a walk," I said.

Sebastian frowned.

"I'll stay near the trees where it's clear. Don't worry, I'll be fine. I promise."

"All right," he said slowly. "But take Loki with you. Stay outta the brush, and keep an eye out for loose boards with nails pokin' through."

"Yes, sir," I muttered as I opened Barnaby's trailer.

"Come on down, little man," Sebastian called to Loki. "Go on with Poppy."

Loki wobbled down the bus steps, lifted his arms, and Sebastian picked him up and set him on Barnaby's back.

"And don't go pickin' stuff up or gettin' too close to the water," Sebastian added as I took Barnaby by the reins.

"Yeah, yeah, I got it," I said.

I walked the grounds behind the shack while the men cleared the field and tossed trash into Barnaby's trailer. I should've been happier that we'd made it, but instead, I was annoyed that Sebastian had become obsessed with keeping me safe, and I didn't understand why it bothered me so much.

I smiled as I watched Sven fuss over Lady Jane. It was sweet. So why did it upset me when Sebastian tried to protect me? I felt guilty for even thinking it. He was only trying to look out for me and for everyone else. If I got hurt or started bleeding, it could ruin everything we'd worked for. I knew that.

Until that night with Banjo, Sebastian never felt the need to watch my every move. After that night, we'd always been careful, especially during my monthly cycle. We slept in separate beds and kept our laundry separate. Sebastian called it the "week of the red reaper." I didn't find it nearly as funny as he did, but the name stuck. Every month, we adjusted our routines to make sure he wasn't exposed.

We had protocols for accidents, too. If I got cut or had an open wound, we had cleaning supplies and bandages everywhere, in the wagon, in the Beast. Sebastian even kept a small kit in his pocket at all times.

I knew he did it because he loved me, but I couldn't help but think he loved my blood more, and that's what hurt the most.

Despite Sebastian's warning, I led Barnaby and Loki down to the edge of the property where the water, encased in Sawgrass and brush, ribboned through thick, low-hanging trees where tall birds waded in the shallows, looking for their next meal, and small turtles fought over space on nearby logs.

The light on the water was soft and speckled, slipping through the low-hanging branches in scattered patches. It shimmered across the surface like broken glass, catching on ripples and the slow movements of birds' legs as they waded through the shallows. The water itself was dark, almost black in places, but the light gave it texture, silver where it touched, gold where it lingered.

The smell was thick and earthy, full of rot and life. It reminded me of Sebastian's clothes after a long day of work, sweat, soil, and something wild underneath. He called it a bayou. I called it heaven.

I tied Barnaby's rein to a low branch, careful not to brush against the Sawgrass, and stepped slowly into the water. It was warm and heavy around my ankles.

"Be careful, Miss Poppy," Loki said, eyes wide. "Who knows what kinda swamp monster's lurkin' in this Juba-let's-get-murdered place."

"Oh, Loki, don't be so scared," I said, smiling. "You're my friend. I won't let anything happen to you. Just look around, this place is beautiful. The trees have flowers, the ground's covered in clover, and there are birds everywhere. Look at them, those tall ones in the water, the white ones in the trees, even the little ones hopping through the grass. They're not worried, so we don't have to be either."

Loki frowned and swatted at a bug.

"Please get out of the water," he said. "If you get hurt, Mr. Sebastian's gonna come after me."

"Okay, Loki, I promise I'll be careful." I stepped back onto land, took Barnaby by the reins, and led him and Loki away from the water. The bugs buzzed low in the grass, and the birds called out from the trees as we made our way back toward the bus to get supper started.

Back at the bus, I looked out at the land—the dilapidated shack, the old barn yearning to be rebuilt. In the distance, a fire pit glowed, smoke rising soft and steady into the night. I watched the others working, laughing, moving as if they belonged, as if they were home.

And I understood. I understood why Sebastian loved this place. Jubilee wasn't perfect, but it was ours. Rough, wild, steeped in history. And it had room to grow. Room to breathe.

Using long knives they'd found in the brush, Boris and Cowboy had cleared most of the Sawgrass from the front of the shack. Now they were inside, helping Alice and Lady Jane clean out the rooms. Sebastian and Tershy had already unhitched the wagon from the back of the bus and dragged it to the clearing between the shack and the barn. Rake and Sven reattached Barnaby's trailer to the bus so they could start hauling trash.

Loki and I headed back to the wagon to get the cram and biscuits started for supper. He'd been quiet since our walk, which wasn't like him. Then he said, "Is it true?"

"Is what true?" I asked.

"That I'm your friend," he said.

"Of course you're my friend. We've been through a lot together, haven't we?"

Loki smiled, but his eyes filled with tears.

"I've never been a friend before," he said.

"Don't be silly. Look out there. You have plenty of friends. No wait, a family that's what you have, a family." Loki ran over and grabbed me around the waist.

"Thank you, Miss Poppy," he said.

"Of course, now come and help me with the cram so we can get everybody fed before dark."

Other than Sebastian and me, Loki was the only one who knew what happened that night with Banjo. I always sensed he suspected something was different about me, and when Sebastian told him my secret, he didn't flinch. He just nodded, like he'd known all along.

Sebastian trusted Loki. He told the two of us we should keep it quiet until things settled at Jubilee. Then, when the time was right, he'd unveil what he called the *Big Show*, his grand plan, and tell the others just enough to keep them calm. Not the whole truth. Just what they needed to hear.

The others didn't know what was going on inside Sebastian's head. But like me, they were drawn to him. Mesmerized. They'd follow him anywhere.

I couldn't help but wonder what they'd do once they learned the truth about me, about the show. But I figured Sebastian would find a way to make it sound right. He always did.

ᴌ Chapter 23 - Gertie

The year 2132

The truck engine roared to life, and the trailer bounced beneath us as Beau pulled back onto the highway. We hadn't stopped until late last night, and this time his nap was even shorter than usual. Morning light slipped in through the cracks above the door. Beau liked to get an early start, as he had for the past three days.

I rubbed my eyes and looked over at Asher. He was trying to sit up, groaning as he moved. Creases from the trailer floor marked his cheek, and his once-perfect hair hung limp and greasy to one side. "You alright?" I asked.

"Yeah, just sore. I don't know how much more of this my back can take." He stretched, cracking his neck and rolling his shoulders.

I stared at the walls of the trailer, trying to hold it together.

"This is wrong," I said quietly. "What are we going to do? We could've driven there and back by now. Did we miss a stop somewhere?"

My voice shook. I blinked hard, trying not to cry.

"Stop," Asher said gently. "Everything's gonna be okay. We don't know Beau's schedule or which way he went. All we've got is what Abel told me. We should've figured this truck would take a different route. Remember what he said about the roads?"

"I hope you're right," I said, standing up and stretching. My stomach growled loud enough for both of us to hear. The snacks had run out a day and a half ago. If we'd known it would take this long, we would've rationed better. But by the time we realized we were stuck back here longer than expected, it was too late.

We didn't really start to panic until yesterday, when the water ran out.

Abel said the whole trip should've taken eighteen hours, tops. But now we were on day four. No stops, no signs, just Beau's nightly naps and the occasional refueling. And still, no clue where we were headed.

I sat down and leaned against Asher's shoulder.

"I'm so thirsty," I said, licking the salt from my lips.

"Me too. And hungry. Any ice chips left in the cooler?" Asher asked.

"No, it's all gone. Just fish juice now," I said. We'd been sucking on the leftover ice from the fish cooler since the water ran out. At first, the taste made me gag, but after a while, I stopped noticing.

"We should be stopping soon anyway," Asher said.

"You keep saying that," I muttered. "I hope you're right this time."

Asher reached over, took my hand, and gave it a gentle squeeze. "I am right. I'm always right, remember."

"Asher, be serious. We could die in here," I said.

"We're not gonna die," he replied. "Listen, if we stop again tonight, we'll bang on the door until Beau hears us and lets us out."

"I wanted to do that yesterday."

"I know. But we're close. There's something in the air. Can't you smell it?"

"All I can smell right now is you." I chuckled.

"Ha, ha," he snarked.

But I knew what he meant. The air inside the trailer was warmer than yesterday, thicker too. It carried a faint, musty, salty smell, like wet wood and old sweat. Asher leaned back and closed his eyes, overtaken by the heat. I sat beside him, listening to his breath, trying to keep mine steady.

I'd begged him to alert Beau last night, but he said we should wait one more day. We'd come so far. I didn't want to disappoint him or get us in trouble. But I also didn't want to die of starvation in the back of a truck. Eventually, sleep came. And with it, the nightmare. But this time, she found me.

I heard her outside, sniffing around the trailer. Her fingernails scraped down the metal side, slow and deliberate, until they reached the back door. The chains on the door rattled.

"Gertie," she whispered. "Gertie, let me in."

Chapter 24 - Poppy

The year 2119

It only took the men three days to clear the grounds at Jubilee of the junk and trash. Getting rid of the brush and most of the Sawgrass took another week, but once it was done, the place looked different. Open. Clean. Finally livable.

Boris and Sven fixed up the old shack, so Lady Jane and Big Alice could sleep inside. The rest of the men stayed in the Beast, and Sebastian and I stayed in the wagon, like always. Every evening, we gathered around the fire pit Boris built and ate dinner together.

With the dangerous grasses gone and the garbage cleared, Sebastian stopped hovering over me so much. He relaxed. Slowly, he started acting like himself again. It took a couple of weeks, but once it sank in that we'd really made it to Jubilee, something shifted. He was the same Sebastian I met near the river.

Our homesite was simple—no running water. No electricity. But it didn't take long for the ten of us to settle in and make it feel like home.

Life was hard, sometimes more complicated than it had been on the road, but those first few months at Jubilee were wonderful. Dinner was always a feast. Alice baked fresh bread, roasted vegetables, and served whatever game Cowboy had poached the week before. Venison, wild birds, boar meat, there was always something rich and filling. Boris, an avid fisherman, would bring back striped bass now and then or boil up a big pot of crawdads to go with Cowboy's homemade sausages. The days of cram and biscuits were behind us, and I didn't miss them one bit.

Most nights after supper, we'd gather around the fire to unwind. Alice would settle into her knitting while Boris, Sven, and Loki played cards. Lady Jane and I sometimes joined in, but it always ended the same way. Loki and Boris bickering over the rules until the game fell apart.

Sebastian and the brothers never played cards. They were too busy planning Carnivále. Long after the rest of us had gone to bed, they'd stay up sketching diagrams and mapping out the inner workings of the park.

One night, after everyone else had turned in, I stayed up by the fire, repairing the soles of my favorite shoes. I kept quiet, listening as their voices drifted through the dark.

"You'll need rides," Tershy said, his voice low but precise. "At least one big one that draws the eye. Your show can be the finale, but the rides and games, that's what gets them in the gate. Spectacle first, mystery second."

"That's exactly what I want," Sebastian said. "But it has to be something big."

"I used to run the wheel at Monterey," Tershy continued. "Massive. You could see it from the highway. People came just to watch it spin."

"Yes, but where would we even find something like that? We can't build our own wheel," Sebastian said.

Tershy glanced at Rake and gave a slight nod. "Tell him."

Rake shifted in his seat. "Th-that's the crazy part," he said. "There's a scrapyard near the border of the C-Cube. They've got all s-s-sorts of relics from the old eastern boardwalks. Including a wheel. It's torn up, yeah, but the guy swears all the p-p-parts are there."

Sebastian leaned forward. "How do you know this?"

"It's how we ended up out here," Tershy said calmly.

"What do you mean?" Said Sebastian.

"M-m-money," Rake said. "We'd come out, load what we could, take it back west. Sell it off. That wheel's been sitting there for years. Nobody's touched it."

"Yeah, old Hector back home used to send us out two or three times a year looking for scrap," said Tershy. "We got stuck out here last winter when our truck crapped out and never made our last run back."

"So you planned to haul a wheel to the west?" I asked.

"No, nothing like that, ma'am," said Tershy. "But other parts, yes, pulleys, rotors, belts. Mechanical salvage. Easier to move, easier to sell."

"They had a wheel like that in Sparks, you know," I said. "Didn't work, but it was enormous."

"Sparks?" Tershy's eyes narrowed with interest. "I've heard of it. Supposed to have a big one, yes."

"They do. And there's no way you'd move something like that without a convoy of trucks and a thousand men. That thing was at least five hundred feet tall."

"Five hundred feet?" Sebastian echoed.

"At least," I said.

Sebastian's grin spread. He slapped his knee as if he'd just won a bet. "Then a wheel it shall be!"

☙ Chapter 25 - Poppy

The year 2119

Not every night back then was about Carnivále. Some nights we'd let loose and stay up way too late, laughing and dancing like we hadn't a care in the world. Sebastian didn't mind the shenanigans, so long as everyone was up and working come morning. Truth be told, he was usually the one stirring the pot, strumming his guitar, belting out songs, and pulling us into the chaos with that crooked grin and those ridiculous dance moves.

Most party nights, he'd end up center stage, voice echoing through the trees, boots tapping out a rhythm no one could resist. Even Big Alice would get on her feet, swaying and stomping, especially on nights when the elixir went down smooth, and the fire burned just right.

As rowdy as those late nights were, we were always up early the next morning, ready to work. One night, after the last train pulled out, we ransacked the grid-rail station and stripped it bare. We took planks of wood, loose bricks, and even the concrete benches, and dragged them back to the fire pit for seating.

Any wood we collected went straight into rebuilding the old barn. The men handled that while Big Alice and I planted a vegetable garden with seeds we'd traded for scrap metal. Corn, tomatoes, cucumbers, beans, and potatoes. So many potatoes. We ate plenty of potatoes, but saved most for Sebastian's newest invention: Jubilee Ale. A frothy, fermented brew that tasted like it was distilled in a dirty toilet, at least to me. But the others loved it. Every weekend, Sven and Boris hauled the latest batch into town and came back with more wood and supplies.

Once the barn was finished, Sebastian built cages inside and put up a fence around the perimeter. No one asked what the cages were for. Only Loki and I knew, and I didn't bring it up.

There were days I wondered if what he was planning was right. But seeing Sebastian smile again quieted the doubt. Besides, I didn't believe the plan would work. Not fully. But I told myself it would be fine, and the real goal was Carnivále, not the show. And if by some chance it did work, what harm were a few devil dogs, anyway?

Even though we were tucked out far from town, the ten of us living off the land drew plenty of attention. Locals would cruise by on foot or in rusted-out trucks, slowing down just enough to spy on us as we worked. A few even called the authorities, but Sebastian didn't mind. He'd greet them with a grin, pour them a cup of Jubilee Ale, and stand out by the fence yammering about his family land like it was sacred ground.

Eventually, the curiosity wore off. Folks stopped gawking and started waving. We became a fixture in the community, selling handmade crafts, medicinal elixirs, and Jubilee Ale in town every week.

Some evenings, when the weather held, Sebastian and I would walk down to the water's edge. He'd point out plants and animals in the bayou, naming them like old friends. One night, as we walked, I ran my hand through a curtain of moss hanging low from a tree.

"Watch that now," Sebastian said, pulling my arm back.

"Why? What is it?"

"Spanish Moss. Full of lice and chiggers."

"Yuck." I wiped my hand on my skirt.

"Yep. Gotta be careful out here."

"Tell me, are there really crocodiles in the river? Cowboy said there are, but I've never seen any."

Sebastian scowled. "Holy hell, ain't nobody ever listen? It ain't no river. It's a bayou. And yeah, there's gators in that water. Not crocs, gators. So don't be goin' skinny dippin', ya hear?"

"Sure," I laughed.

"Well, now that ya mentioned it, you really shouldn't be down here alone ever. Last thing we need is one of them gators turnin' zombie Spinner and sneakin' up on us while we're sleeping," he laughed, then paused, scratching his head. "Well, now wait a minute…"

"No, we don't." I grabbed his hand and tugged him away from the water.

"You're no fun."

"So what's the difference, anyway? I always wondered."

"Between a crocodile and an alligator?" Sebastian said, flashing that crooked grin. "Oh, 'bout two thousand miles. Wait, there might be crocs in the Cube…"

"No, silly. Stop it with the crocodiles. I meant between a river and a bayou."

"Ohhh, that." He slowed his steps, eyes scanning the water like it might answer for him. "Everything but the water and even that ain't the same."

I raised an eyebrow, waiting.

"A river's always movin'," he said. "Don't settle down, don't make no commitments. It just passes through, fast, loud, and gone before you know it. Doesn't care what it cuts through, just keeps goin'. A river's got places to be."

He paused, then pointed to the still water beside us.

"But a bayou, now that's like a father. Sticks around. Feeds its kin, watches 'em grow. Keeps secrets in its mud and lays down the law when it's called for. The bayou doesn't rush. It waits. There's life and death in a bayou. It has memories and tradition."

I let the words settle. The air was thick with the smell of moss and old water, and the moonlight shimmered off the surface, as if it were listening, too.

"A river just treats the land like a highway," he said softly, "till it hits the ocean. But a bayou, he stays. he belongs."

"Ah," I whispered. "That's beautiful."

"No," he said, turning to me. "You are."

Then he bent down and kissed me, slow and sure, while the bayou watched.

Things between Sebastian and me were better than ever in those early months. But by winter, something shifted. He grew protective again, overprotective, really, and it was starting to wear on me worse than the last time.

One afternoon, while cleaning the wagon, I found a small box tucked inside the chest where he kept his personal items. I'd rummaged through that chest plenty of times before, but I'd never seen the box before. Curious, I opened it.

Inside was a medical kit. There were needles, swabs, and four glass tubes sealed with cork. I asked Sebastian what it was for. He brushed me off, said it was just something he picked up to test elixirs. I didn't believe him, but I let it go.

Then one day, while I was out gathering firewood, he came charging up behind me.

"What do you think you're doing?" he snapped.

I jumped, dropping the piece of wood I was holding. "Sebastian, you scared me! I'm just pulling wood for the fire."

His eyes darted around the trees like they were hiding something. "You shouldn't be out here alone."

"It's not far," I said. "I've done this a hundred times."

"That was before," he muttered. "Things are different now."

He picked up the wood but didn't return it. Just stood there, staring at it like it might tell him something.

I watched him, heart thudding, wondering what had changed again and whether I was ready to know.

"Why? I can do it, and I'm here now," I said, reaching for the piece I'd dropped.

Sebastian snatched it from my hand and hurled it back into the pile.

"I know you can," he snapped. "But you won't. I won't have it."

"Stop coddling me. I'm not weak. I can do this myself."

"I don't coddle you because you're weak. I do it because you're important. Now go inside and rest. That's all I need is for you to cut yourself and get blood all over the place."

"So you're not worried about me getting hurt. You're worried about wasting blood?"

"I didn't say that."

"Yes, that's exactly what you said."

I turned and stormed off to the wagon, slamming the door behind me. Seconds later, Sebastian burst in, flinging the door so hard it nearly came unhinged. He stood in the frame like a madman, hair wild, eyes burning, breath ragged. His shirt hung crooked off one shoulder, and his fists were clenched like he didn't know whether to pray or punch a wall.

"Is that what you think of me?" he shouted. "Do you even know how much I love you?"

I didn't answer.

"Yes, it's true, we have to protect your blood. But not because of my silly dream. This is no joke, Poppy. Do you know what would happen if someone found out about you? If you hurt someone. What if your blood got on the wood and then on Big Alice, Lady Jane, or Loki? Forget the treaties, you'd be dead. We all would. And pray to God it'd be by gunfire and not what's possible."

He stepped closer, voice trembling. "I read the books we found in Sabine. I know what can happen. And so do you. I would walk away from all this today if I thought something might happen to you. We have to work as a team. Just like when we first met."

His words tore through me. Of course, he had to protect me. But it wasn't just me, it was the others—maybe even the world. One misstep could turn Jubilee into another Cube.

I thought of the fort and Danger's camp. I thought of the woman who turned Spinner right in front of me, and how quickly Father Jameson turned after Koby bit him.

"I'm sorry," I said.

"You tell me right now," Sebastian said. "If you want to stop, we'll stop. I mean that."

I wanted to say stop. I wanted to scream it. But the thought of denying Sebastian his dream felt like tearing out my own heart. He was my savior. My love. And I would do anything to let him live that dream, no matter how dangerous or stupid it was.

"No," I said. "We can do this. I want it too."

Sebastian smiled, pulled me close, and kissed the top of my head.

I didn't realize what he did that day until years later. He gave me the choice. He gave me a chance to pull the plug. But instead, I pulled the trigger.

Whatever happened next, good or bad, was going to be all my fault.

The year 2124

It was Sebastian's and my eighth anniversary together, and our fifth year at Jubilee. The grounds that would become Carnivále were unrecognizable from when we first arrived. The old shack was long gone, replaced by full staff quarters for the thirty-five workers we'd gathered over the years. We had a functioning kitchen with running water and 'borrowed' electricity, which Alice managed like a general. The park's blueprint was complete, and the compound was fully fenced. The cement base and seating for the arena that would house the *Big Show* had been poured and set.

And most importantly, Sebastian had found his wheel.

Turns out, it didn't take a convoy of trucks and a thousand men to haul the Wonder Wheel from the Cube to Jubilee. Just three men, Tershy, Rake, and Sven, and Barnaby's old trailer, converted into a flatbed. They brought it piece by piece, slow and steady.

I'll never forget the day they returned, one rainy afternoon, with the first passenger car hanging off the back end of the trailer like a relic from another world. It was the first time I'd seen Sebastian in days. And the first time I saw him smile in months.

"Hot damn, you did it," said Sebastian as he jumped into the metal seat and made himself comfortable. Besides needing a fresh coat of paint, the passenger car looked to be in decent shape and so much bigger than the ones from the wheel at Sparks, or maybe it just looked bigger next to Sebastian's shrinking body. He barely ate anymore, and when he did, it was alone in the old barn; his hygiene had suffered too, he smelled terrible, and his once beautifully flowing hair was greasy and unkept.

His shirt was covered in stains, and his trousers hung loose; the only thing keeping them on was a tightly cinched belt. There was worry in his eyes, constant and heavy. He had too much to manage: staff, payroll, food, and it was wearing him down. But more than anything, it was the *Big Show*. He was making himself sick over it, so it was nice to see him at least happy about the wheel.

"Be careful, you don't want to tip the trailer over," said Tershy.

"And there won't be any issues getting the rest of it?" asked Sebastian.

"No, sir. Magic Jack says he'll break the whole thing down and keep it stored as long as it takes, just as long as we keep bringing him that f, fairy dust elixer of yours," said Rake.

"Perfect," said Sebastian. "Did you get the pills for my Poison from your buddy in Folkston?"

"Yes s, s, sir, got enough to pay for ten wheels and then some," said Rake.

"Beautiful! I can't wait for it to be up and running," beamed Sebastian.

"Yeah, we figured we'd haul the cars first since we can only do one at a time. That's thirty-five more trips alone. It will probably take another ten to haul the spokes, support towers, and drive wheel," said Tershy.

"And all the smaller parts fit in the bus. Look, we got all kinds of p, p pieces in there," said Rake.

"Okay, let's get this car off and pull what you have in the bus. We need to be organized. Everything has to be documented and stored in its precise order of construction," said Sebastian.

The four men disappeared inside the bus while Cowboy and Alice came over to check out the car.

"Crazy sons of bitches," muttered Cowboy.

"So this is really happening?" said Alice.

"Did you ever think it wouldn't?" I said.

"I had my doubts about the whole damn thing until they finished that arena, but I never thought in a million years he'd get a wheel," she said.

That night, Sebastian surprised us all by showing up for supper.

Meals weren't the cozy family gatherings they used to be. These days, they were tightly orchestrated affairs, choreographed by Alice and her seven helpers, who worked for hours to feed the growing crew. Still, the original ten of us tried to sit together when we could. Well, nine, really. Sebastian rarely joined. And when he did, he'd eat fast, speak little, and vanish into the barn before the rest of us had even finished chewing.

So when I saw him stroll toward the fire, my heart lifted. I shifted in my seat, hoping he'd sit beside me like he used to.

But he didn't. He walked right past the empty spot at my side and took his place at the far end of the table with the other men.

"Cowboy, I want you to go on the runs to the Cube with Tershy and Rake. Take a couple of my shotguns with you. I want you to be prepared out there," said Sebastian.

"Uh-huh," grunted Cowboy.

"Guns? What do they need guns for?" said Lady Jane.

"The middle of the Cube's a dangerous place. They'll want to have it just in case," said Sebastian.

"I thought the salvage yard was near the border?" I said.

Sebastian didn't respond. He didn't even look my way. I knew what he was up to, and it upset me knowing he'd put the others at risk. Later that night, I hoped he'd join me in the wagon. I missed him and wanted to talk about him sending the men into the Cube, but he never showed up.

Two days later, Cowboy, Tershy, and Rake loaded up the Beast with enough food and water for three trips and drove off with the trailer in tow. When they returned ten days later with another passenger car and a bus full of wheel parts, Sebastian emerged from the barn and met them at the front gate.

"Find anything?" he asked as the men unloaded the haul.

"Nope," said Tershy.

Not everyone knew what *anything* meant. But I did.

Sebastian had secretly asked them to search deeper into the Cube, beyond the salvage yard, looking for a dog. That was why he'd sent Cowboy along with the guns, though he never told me outright. He didn't have to.

Each time they came back empty-handed, Sebastian sank further into himself. He became a ghost at Jubilee. He rarely left the barn, and when he did, it was only at night. I'd hear his boots echo through the staff quarters as he made his way toward the arena.

Sometimes I'd sneak out and follow him, careful not to make a sound. But I always lost him once he crossed into the arena grounds. It was like the place swallowed him whole.

Those years at Jubilee were some of the hardest of my life. Without Sebastian around, I struggled to stay focused. The nightmares I'd buried in childhood clawed their way back, luckily, I could never remember them. And I was glad for that. The sweat-soaked sheets and scratches on my face told me they weren't the kind worth remembering.

One morning, after a particularly dreadful night, I rose early and headed toward the kitchen. On the way, I spotted Alice and Loki collecting eggs near one of our six coops. I stopped and watched them work. Alice moved with practiced egg-gathering grace while Loki fumbled behind her, dropping more eggs than he collected.

Then, without warning, I started to sob.

Alice looked up, squinting against the morning sun. "Girl, what's been up with you lately? You've been moping around here for weeks."

I wiped my eyes and tried to smile. "Nothing. Just been in a mood lately, I guess."

"Well, snap out of it," she said, brushing straw off her apron. "Stop worrying about Sebastian. He'll come around once he gets that damn wheel put together. And I need help in the kitchen. Lady Jane's about to pop, and this guy here can barely reach the grill. They're starting construction on the museum theater, and Boris brought in more helpers. That means more mouths to feed."

"I can reach the grill just fine," Loki muttered. "She just doesn't want me playing with fire."

Alice rolled her eyes. "Exactly."

"I'm sure you do just fine," I said, patting my sad little friend on the head. "Don't worry about me. I came to help. Now, Alice, get back to the kitchen, and Loki and I will finish collecting the eggs."

Alice nodded and held out her bag. I reached for it then hesitated. There she was.

Figgy. Wild red hair, crooked grin, and eyes full of wonder. She stood just behind Alice, like she'd been there the whole time. Like she'd been waiting for me.

"What if I get them dirty?" I stammered, eyes locked on the ghost of my old friend.

"Well, you ain't gonna get them any dirtier than they already are," Alice said. Figgy's image flickered, then faded.

Loki touched my hand gently. "Miss Poppy, you alright? You look like you saw a ghost."

"Yes, I'm fine," I said, grabbing the bag. "Come on. Let's go get us some eggs."

The memory of that day back at Sparks, collecting eggs with Jobe, haunted me all morning. I remembered how terrified I was of touching food back then and how even the feel of a cracked shell made my skin crawl. Here at Jubilee, I'd helped with eggs and meal prep almost daily, no problem. But today, I washed those eggs twice before letting Alice or any of the helpers use them.

Alice didn't say a word, but I saw it in her face, that flicker of concern, the way her eyes lingered a beat too long. Poppy had never been so meticulous. But this wasn't Poppy.

This was Maya.

And Maya was weak. Maya was scared of everything. She was sloppy, unsure, and didn't know her power. I had to get rid of her again. Once and for all. I tried to push her down, bury her beneath the rhythm of Jubilee. But her memories kept surfacing like weeds through cracked concrete. Walking past the theater, I saw the soldiers from the outpost at Proper rebuilding the old barracks. Jupiter Kane and Kobiashi were tossing a ball outside the arena. Then a woman, sitting in the shade, belly round and heavy, knitting a baby blanket.

"Anell?" I called. "Is that you?"

The woman looked up, confused.

"Who's Anell?" said the woman. It was Lady Jane. "Poppy, are you alright? You don't look well."

"Oh. Jane. Sorry. I'm just tired, is all," I murmured.

She studied me for a moment, concern flickering across her face.

"Maybe a nap, then. Lie down before supper?" she said.

"Yes, I think I just might," I replied.

I went back to the wagon, took a quick shot of poison, flopped onto my bed, and quickly fell asleep.

Later that evening, I heard a soft knock on the door. It creaked open slowly.

"Miss Poppy, you awake?" Loki asked as he stepped inside. "I brought your supper. Miss Alice said you need to eat and drink all the water."

I sat up and lit the lamp beside my bed. The flame flickered weakly, casting long shadows across the wagon walls. But Loki's face didn't need light. His worry was written all over him, the way he held the tray too tightly and lingered near the doorway.

"You feeling alright, Miss Poppy? he asked, voice low and shaky. "You weren't at supper. Miss Alice said you didn't eat. Said you didn't drink nothing all day."

"I'm fine," I said.

He didn't move. Just stared, like he was trying to see through me.

"You don't look fine," he said. "You look... You look bad, Miss Poppy."

He set the tray down, his hands trembling, and poured the water as if it might spill.

"I just need rest," I said, reaching for the glass. My hand shook. Loki saw it. Of course he did.

"I can stay," he said quickly. "I'll sit down right here. I won't talk or babble. Just in case you need something. Please?"

I nodded, and he sat on the floor beside the bed, legs crossed, hands in his lap like a child waiting for a story. The smell of smoked meat and bread lingered in the air, but I couldn't eat. Not yet.

Outside, Jubilee hummed with life, hammers striking wood, voices calling orders, laughter from the kitchen. But inside the wagon, it was just me, Loki, and the ghost of a girl I thought I'd buried years ago. I drank the water he'd brought and ate most of the bread, chewing slowly, trying to feel grounded. Loki was such a good friend to me. Who would've guessed that the odd little man I first saw recruiting souls outside his church at Sparks would become someone I trusted so deeply?

Wait.

That wasn't me.

That was Maya.

I didn't meet Loki until Sabine.

"Thank you, Loki, I feel better. I think I'm going to get some sleep now. I'll see you in the morning," I said.

Loki gave a slight nod and slipped out, closing the door with a gentleness that made my chest ache.

The realization hit like a slap. Maya was going to be harder to get rid of than I thought. She kept slipping memories into my brain, twisting the timeline, making me question what was mine and what was hers. I clenched my fists, heart pounding. She was weak. She was scared. She didn't know her power. And I couldn't let her stay.

I threw off the blanket, crossed the room, and opened the cabinet where Sebastian kept his special stash of elixir. El Diablo. My hands moved without hesitation. Two shots of the bright red drink, twice the potency of Poppy's Poison, should do it.

If that didn't silence her, nothing would.

I crawled back into bed, the room spinning, the lamp flickering like it might go out for good. Somewhere deep inside, Maya stirred. But I pressed the pillow over my head and waited for the quiet.

I shuddered, closed my eyes, and tried to erase the flood of Maya's memories. Instead, I conjured the library. Her library. The smell of rotted paper and musty linens warmed my heart, as did the decayed ceiling mural and the grand staircase that led to my room.

No, her room.

Outside, George sat atop his post, laughing as the Jameson Eight played freeze tag across the grounds of the abandoned outpost. I strained to remember their names. Petra, Abigail, Milo, Gracie, Jacob, but not the twins. Where were the twins?

Maybe I could only see the ghosts of the dead. That would mean the boys were still alive.

Minutes later, the elixir kicked in, and I slipped into a dream. One I remembered the next day, and every day since.

In the dream, I was searching. Hunting, really. Not an animal, but a girl. A young girl I wanted to hurt, though I didn't know why. I couldn't see her, but I felt her everywhere, in the woods, near a lake, hiding in the back of a trailer. Each place brought me closer, only to lose her again.

Until the dungeon.

Damp. Dark. The air was heavy with mildew. But here I was no longer the hunter. I didn't know it yet, but I was prey.

I sat on the cold stone floor, reading by candlelight, when I felt her breath, warm and sweet, brush the back of my neck. It sent a chill down my spine.

I turned just in time to see the candlelight catch the edge of her blade just before she thrust it into my neck. I screamed, and then everything went black.

Though shaken by the dream, I woke the next morning feeling a little better. Aside from the throbbing in my head and the churn in my stomach, of course. But the girl, what was her name? She was gone again. And even though part of me felt like dying, I was relieved to be only Poppy again.

I grabbed the jar of my signature elixir, took a shot to ease my hangover, and headed off to help with breakfast. Alice always said a bit of liquor a day kept the ails away. I figured it worked on ghosts and needy stalkers, too.

Though I never touched the El Diablo again, the Poison had become routine. It helped, mostly. But I couldn't shake the girl completely. Weeks would pass, sometimes months, and then out of nowhere she'd be back, dancing in her library, sneaking through some decrepit hospital, dragging her memories behind her like a bloodied veil.

Alice was always on me about the elixir. About not eating enough. I didn't know how she knew, but she did. And I was getting sick of her constant nagging.

One hazy morning, after refusing breakfast again, we got into it. I stormed off and wandered toward the barn, hoping for a glimpse of Sebastian. I couldn't remember the last time I'd seen him. My days blurred together like fog rolling through the marsh.

To my surprise, he was outside, adjusting the sidecar on a motorbike I'd never seen before.

"Good morning," he said as I approached.

"Where did you get that?" I asked.

"It's my new cruiser. The boys found it on their last run. It's even got a sidecar for you."

My stomach fluttered when he said *for you*.

"Really? For me? What do we need that for?"

Sebastian shrugged. "I don't know. Just drive it to town and back. It's nice to have with the Beast always gone."

"Yeah, I guess," I said.

"Get in. I'll take you for a ride."

"Seriously?" I asked, but I was already climbing into the sidecar before he could answer.

It was a whirlwind of a day. We tore through town, down to the waterfront. Bought fresh oysters at the fishery for a late-night treat. Sipped peach soda near the docks. That night, Sebastian stayed in the wagon with me. We drank elixir and laughed like we used to.

For a moment, I had him back.

But two days later, he was gone again. Took off on the cruiser without a word. Didn't say goodbye, not to me, at least. Left Sven and Boris in charge of the concrete work around Jubilee and told Loki to keep an eye on me.

I guess I should've been grateful. A babysitter meant he cared, right?

But I wasn't.

I was tired. Tired of being managed. Tired of false promises. Tired of chasing ghosts, both his and mine.

❧ Chapter 27 - Gertie

The year 2132

"Yep, yep, keep a-coming. Slow it down a little, Beau," said a man's voice.

The trailer jolted as the brakes squealed beneath us, rocking side to side like a boat caught in a sudden squall. The shift in momentum woke Asher and me.

"You okay?" he asked, pulling me upright.

"What's going on?"

"I think we're stopping. Listen, voices."

The truck groaned through a series of turns, the shouting outside growing louder, more urgent.

"This is it, Gertie. Get ready. But stay down until I say go."

"Got it," I said, stuffing my things into the pack, everything but my swaddle. I tied it around my neck and slung the bag over my shoulder.

"You're wearing that again?" Asher asked, already smirking.

"Of course I am. What do you have against my swaddle, anyway? We need all the luck we can get."

"Well, for starters, you keep calling it a swaddle. And second. You look like a dork."

"You're a dork," I muttered, twisting the fabric until it sat just right.

He chuckled, but there was tension behind it, not because of the swaddle. Outside, the voices grew louder, the trailer rocked again. I reached for the swaddle once more, fingers brushing the worn threads for comfort.

We sat in silence as the truck groaned through a series of tight turns, the trailer swaying like it might tip. Then, with one final lurch, it stopped.

The air inside disappeared, replaced by something hot and rotten.

"Ugh, this is the fishery, alright," Asher choked, covering his nose and mouth with both hands.

"Smells like it," I muttered, pulling my swaddle from around my neck and pressing it to my face.

The cab door slammed shut. Voices outside rose, shouting directions, boots crunching gravel. Then came the rattle of the chain at the back of the trailer.

The doors swung open, and a wave of hot, pungent air surged inside, like it had been waiting to escape the sun. The smell hit us hard, like salt and decay.

Asher and I ducked down, holding our breath, hearts thudding in sync.

"I'll get Bufford to fill the ice bins if you want to come look at the catch," said a man.

"Yep. Hey, I'm gonna need some of them mudbugs, too. Got a fellow out west who thinks his wife can make etouffee," Beau chuckled.

"Sure, sure. Got plenty of those," said the man.

The crunch of boots on wet ground faded, and Asher and I scrambled to our feet. We squeezed past the ice bins and leapt out of the trailer into a blinding wash of sunlight and a slick slurry of muddy fish parts, broken scales, and shrieking sea birds.

Men in blood-smeared aprons stood in a line of covered stalls, breaking down fish with rhythmic precision. A few paused to stare as Asher helped me up from the muck where I'd slipped and fallen. One man shook his head and lobbed a fish head at our feet before turning back to his work.

"Hey! What y'all doing? You ain't supposed to be in there," barked a man rounding the front of the truck, lugging a bucket of ice.

Asher grabbed my hand, already smiling.

"Bufford, leave those kids be and hurry up with that ice before they get back with the fish," another man called from the stalls.

"But they're stowaways. I gotta report them," Bufford protested.

"Stowaways?" Asher gasped, clutching his chest like he'd been personally insulted. "Sir, I'll have you know we are official representatives of the Department of Transportation Oversight and, uh, Fish Logistics team. That's right. We're seafood truck inspectors. Elite division."

Asher marched to the trailer and gave it a dramatic knock, then leaned in like he was listening for secrets. "Yep. Everything here appears to be in order. Fish heads accounted for. Ice integrity, questionable, but passable."

Bufford blinked. "Fish logistics?"

"Highly specialized field," Asher said, nodding solemnly. "Requires years of training and a strong stomach. Now, if you'll excuse us, we've got a shrimp emergency at dock nine and a rogue tuna situation brewing near the bait tanks."

He grabbed my hand and whispered, "Walk fast and don't look back. If he asks for credentials, tell him we're union."

We didn't wait for Bufford to respond. We bolted into the maze of transports, dodging crates, hoses, and squawking gulls, laughing the entire time.

"Hey! You come back here!" Bufford shouted behind us. "We ain't got a dock nine!"

"Can't!" Asher called over his shoulder. "You passed! Keep up the good work!"

I nearly tripped over a hose, laughing. "Truck inspectors? We've been here five minutes, and you've already got us in trouble."

"Correction," Asher said, hopping over a crate. "We've been here four minutes. I'm just very efficient at causing problems."

We burst out of the sea of vehicles and onto a rocky shoreline, breathless and sweating, but free, for now.

Asher stopped running and dropped my hand. "Ah, man," he groaned, staring out at the massive body of water stretching out in front of us.

It was the ocean.

We'd only heard stories or read about it in books back at Greyburry, but now we were standing just a few hundred yards from the edge of it—the real thing.

"It's beautiful," I whispered.

"It is," Asher said, squinting. "But it doesn't look anything like Abel described. Where are the rocky cliffs? The thatched huts? The pristine white sand beaches? This water looks like mud, and the air feels thick and sticky."

He wasn't wrong. It was magnificent, yes, but not the postcard we'd imagined. The shoreline was cluttered with rocks, and instead of towering like majestic umbrellas, the trees slouched low and heavy over the water. Muddy waves lapped lazily against a dock, where an army of pelicans lounged in the sun. There were boats, dozens, maybe hundreds, bobbing near the horizon, their hulls wafting softly as seabirds wheeled overhead.

Despite the confusion, despite the knot tightening in my belly, it was the most thrilling moment of my life. The ocean was real. And we were here.

"Well, this is just the fishery," I said, scanning the shoreline. "Maybe we should ask around and see if there's a beach nearby that doesn't smell like shrimp guts."

"Yeah, let's ask someone for directions," said Asher.

"Who? And how do we even get out of here?"

He pointed toward a faded sign: Port Duffy. "Looks like the exit's over there. Let's ask that guy working on the motorboat."

We walked over to a man in full fishing waders, bent over an engine. His cap read Cap'n Carl's Tug in stitched letters.

"Excuse us, Captain Carl?" Asher said.

The man looked up, squinting. "It's Antoine. Cap'n Carl is just the name of my hat."

"Okay, Antoine," said Asher.

"You ain't got a two and three-fifths, do you?" Antoine asked, spitting at the ground.

"No. Sorry, I don't," said Asher.

"Damn it. How 'bout you?" he said, turning to me.

"No, I don't have one either."

Antoine huffed and tossed his tool to the ground. "What good are y'all then? I gotta find me one."

"Wait, can you help us out first?" Asher asked.

"Yeah, whatcha need?"

"We're lost," I said. "Can you tell us how to get to Hope Island?"

Antoine pulled a stained handkerchief from his pocket and wiped the sweat from his face. "Hope Island? Never heard of it. You got Marsh Island, Palmetto, and Breton. But Hope? Nah. Sounds made up."

"This is the south, right? We thought we were in the south," said Asher.

"Well, yeah, it's the south, alright," Antoine said.

"And that's the ocean?" I asked.

"Looks like it to me," he chuckled.

"And you've never heard of Hope Island?" Asher pressed.

"Nope. Where's it near?"

"The Mexican Baja," I said.

Antoine frowned, then burst out laughing. "The Mexican Baja? You two ain't even close to the Mexican Baja."

"But this is the south. You said so," I insisted.

"Yeah, well, there's all kinds of south, little lady. You got the southern Cube, the South Pole, the Pacific south down near that Baja place you're talking about, and then you got the deep southern south."

"So… where are we?" I asked.

Antoine grinned. "If you were aiming for Mexico, you're in deep shit, that's where."

Antoine threw his head back and laughed so hard his tobacco flew out of his mouth.

Asher stared at the wad of tobacco as it landed near my feet. "Where is that exactly?"

"Why, hell, you two are in New Orleans," Antoine said, puffing up with pride. "Heart of Louisiana. Home of crawdads, blood-sucking buggers, and big bad voodoo daddies."

A lump the size of a melon swelled in my throat, and tears pricked my eyes. "We thought this was the Gulf of Mexico."

"It is the Gulf of Mexico, sweetie," Antoine said, softening just a little. "But you ain't anywhere near the country. Looks like you went the wrong damn way. Don't you have a map?"

"No, no map, sir," Asher sighed.

Antoine reached into a red ice cooler and pulled out two water bags. "Here. Take these before you drop dead. You look like you've been dragged here by a mule."

"Thanks," I said, ripping one open and drinking fast.

"If it's work you're after, they're hiring over at the fishery," Antoine added. "But it's hard, stinky work. You two don't look like the hard, stinky working type."

"You said this is the Gulf of Mexico, right?" Asher asked. "Is there a boat we can take to Hope Island?"

"Nah, nothing like that," Antoine said, shaking his head. "Only way to get down there is to take the rails back west."

"You mean the grid-rail?" I asked..

"Yep, the southern station's not far," Antoine said, pointing down the road. "About two miles that way. Follow the dirt path and take a right at Pepper's Bar. You can probably snag a pass for the four o'clock train cheap."

He paused, chewing the end of a cigar he'd pulled from his pocket.

"You want to jump a ride down to Diego. Whatever you do, don't get off before then. You get stuck out in that desert, and nobody'll ever find you."

"Jump a ride," I snorted. "That's how we got here."

Asher slipped his arm around my shoulder and squeezed me. "Thanks. We appreciate your help."

"No problem," Antoine said. "Just be careful. Rails are safe enough once you're on the train, but don't talk to anyone while you're waiting. And don't be late. The four o'clock is the last train headed west today. You don't want to be at that station after dark."

"Got it," said Asher.

"Oh, and one more thing," Antoine said. "Don't wander off at the rail station. Just stay put and wait. It's near some weird carnival, but I wouldn't go near it if I were you. I heard some strange stuff happens there, and a few people have gone missing since it opened."

"Missing?" I asked.

"Yeah, maybe. Probably nothing. But still, better to stay away. You'll see a big electronic sign for it after you pass Pepper's Bar. The rail station's about a mile past that."

He spat out the tip of his cigar. "Used to see that Sebastian Sheets guy around town with his lady, all dressed up in costumes, pulling a mule like they were royalty. Looked like a couple of weirdos if you asked me."

"Well, thanks for the info and the water," Asher said.

"No problem," Antoine said, heading off to find his tool.

I stepped away from Asher and wiped my eyes. "Asher, I'm sorry. I don't know how I messed this up," I said, crying.

"It's not your fault," Asher said. "Don't worry. We'll figure it out. At least we're out of the truck."

"Maybe we should go back. See if we can ride it back," I said.

"No, that's too risky. What if we end up back in Greyburry? And we won't last three more days in that trailer without food or water."

"What do we do then?"

"How many credits do we have?"

"The same, twenty-eight."

"Alright. Let's head to the grid-rail station and see how much tickets to Diego cost. We'll find something to eat after."

"Okay," I said, wiping my nose.

Asher smiled and gave me a gentle nudge. "Why are you so upset? This is what we wanted, right? An adventure. So we went the wrong way, big deal. We're out of Greyburry, doing our own thing, just like we planned."

"I guess. We should've known we'd get lost at some point."

"Exactly. Now come on. Let's get out of here before someone tries to put us to work."

We left the fishery and followed Antoine's directions. It didn't take long to reach Pepper's Bar. It was just an outdoor counter with a few men sitting around, reading papers and drinking ale. Asher waved, but they barely looked up as we passed.

"Are we going the right way?" I asked.

"I think so. Look up there, past those trees. That electric board, Antoine said, we'd see one. I bet it's for the carnival," Asher said. "Come on. I'll race you."

He took off before I could react, but I caught up fast. We reached the flashing board at the same time.

"Sebastian Sheets' World-Famous Carnival," I read aloud as gold and red letters lit up the screen.

"No, look, it's spelled with an apostrophe. That means it's pronounced Carnivále," Asher said.

"What's the difference?"

"I don't know. Maybe he's foreign?"

We laughed, though I wasn't sure why. We were lost, hungry, and alone in a strange place. All we had were the clothes on our backs, twenty-eight credits, and each other. But still, it felt exciting. Like Asher said, an adventure. For the first time since my last day at Trivel, it felt good to be alive. Scary, but good.

"Look at the board. Something's happening," Asher said.

We watched as fog filled the screen and a whistle echoed. A man with long, brown hair and a dark red cape stepped out of the mist. He reached into his pocket and pulled out a small yellow bird. Then he bent down, looked straight at us, and smiled.

"The countdown is on. Only twenty-six hours left until the *Big Show*!" he said.

He waved his hand over the bird and then disappeared into the fog. The bird flew off the screen and into the sky above us.

"Wow, how did he do that?" Asher said, eyes wide.

"It was just some kind of trick," I said. "The board is probably full of birds or something."

"No way, that was real magic," said Asher.

As much as I wanted to believe in magic, I knew it wasn't real. I was about to tell Asher that when I heard shouting.

Across the road from the big screen, a man was herding cows into a truck. Other men were dragging dead cows into a smoking pit. Every time a cow went in, the flames got bigger.

"What's going on over there?" I asked.

"I don't know. Let's go look," said Asher.

"Okay, Charlie, that's the last one," said a man in a wide-brimmed hat. "Make sure the gate's latched tight. I don't want to lose any on the way to Pinkies."

"What about him?" Charlie asked.

Standing off to the side was a big black bull. He wasn't moving, and he didn't look happy.

"You want to mess with that big fella, go ahead," said the man in the hat. "I'm leaving with my rear end still attached, if that's alright with you."

"Why are they burning those cows?" I asked.

The man took off his hat and wiped sweat from his forehead. "Best you two move along. They've got mad cow. I'm getting these few out before they catch it, if they haven't already."

"How did they get it?" Asher asked.

The man frowned. "From eating dead cows. People keep doing it, even though it's dangerous. You can't feed dead cows to live cows."

I shuddered and grabbed Asher's hand. "You mean like the Kuru?"

"Sort of," the man said. "But this isn't that nuclear kind that turned folks into monsters back in the day. This is nature's version."

He gave the gate a shake, climbed into the truck, and drove off.

"That's so sad," I said.

"I know. Let's get out of here before we catch something. I don't know what mad cow does, but I don't want to find out," said Asher.

"Do you think it's contagious?" I asked.

"I don't know. But if I start mooing and chewing grass, just slap me."

"Done, now come on, let's get to the station," I said.

The grid-rail system stretched across the Western Front. There were six stations placed in key areas across the main territories. We learned about it back in Greyburry. It took almost seventy years to complete, most of it after the revolution, when the old treaties were overturned, and the new government took over.

As we walked away from the fields, the carnival's sound grew louder. Music, voices, and laughter filled the air. Then we saw it, a big red and gold striped tent rising above everything else.

"That must be the carnival, and look over there, it's the station right across the street," I said. But Asher's eyes were fixated on the carnival.

"Wow, look at that place. It's huge! And look at all those people," said Asher. "And look, there's an elephant!"

"Where?" I asked, scanning the grounds.

People were coming from every direction, filling the space around the tent. Some ran, some strolled, but all of them seemed drawn to the entrance. Near the front, I spotted a row of tall posters, almost as high as the tent itself. The first one showed a man riding an elephant.

"No, it's just a sign with an elephant, silly," I said.

"Yeah, but if they have a picture, maybe they have a real one too," said Asher. "Man, I can't believe we're gonna miss this."

I looked at the poster again. The elephant had a crown, and the man riding it wore a shiny cape. It looked more like a cartoon than something real.

"Aren't you even the slightest bit curious?" he asked.

"No, now come on, let's go check in at the rail station," I said. "We barely have enough credits as it is. We can't waste it all on that," I said, although I too was curious whether there was a real elephant nearby. It would be worth spending the credits on something like that, but we needed to get to Diego.

"Ah, come on, please," begged Asher

"Where are we going to get the credits? We'll have to go back to the fishery and get jobs on Cap'n Carl's Tug," I said.

Asher laughed. "Yeah, at least we know someone who can vouch for us. I'm sure Antoine would give us a good reference."

I grabbed Asher's arm and steered him toward the rail station. "I'm sure he would. Now come on, let's go get our tickets and get out of here."

"Okay, mean girl, but don't trip on those tracks. I'm not picking you up again."

❧ Chapter 28 - Poppy

The year 2124

It was after Sebastian's first solo trip to the Cube that I started thinking about leaving Jubilee. I didn't have much reason to stay. Even though I sometimes forgot her name, I still felt Maya with me.

I was lonely, and I tried to pretend I didn't care about her, but I did. I missed her sometimes. I wanted her energy, her kindness, her way of loving people without fear. I envied how close she was to the twins and how much she cared for Eric, even if it was naïve.

Poppy had no one now.

Some days, I wanted to run away and be her again. I thought about heading south to find Jobe and Markus, or going back to the fort and search for baby Gertie.

I used to think Maya was weak. But she wasn't. She was brave and clever. She fought for love and for her friends, even against Colonel Lindy.

Poppy was the weak one. Poppy stayed in Jubilee, stuck with her elixirs and bad dreams, waiting for a love that might never come.

One afternoon, as I walked back from town with Lady Jane and Loki, I spotted Sebastian's cruiser tucked under the trees behind the barn. My stomach dropped.

"When did Sebastian get back?" I asked.

"I didn't know he was back," said Lady Jane.

"Loki?" I said. Loki shrank back. "You tell me."

Loki stopped walking and stared at the ground. "Last week," he said quietly.

"Why didn't anyone tell me?"

"Mr. Sebastian told us not to," he said.

I dropped the sack of flour I was carrying and ran to the barn. I jumped the fence and banged on the door. No answer. Then Tershy opened it.

"He's not here," he said. "He's still at the Cube."

"What are you talking about? I saw his cruiser behind the barn," I said. I looked past him and saw Cowboy, but not Sebastian. Still, I could feel he was there. That awful smell of dirty hair and something worse hung in the air, and I knew it was him.

Tershy glanced toward the back of the barn and shrugged. "Well, that is strange."

Then Sebastian's voice rang out, sharp and cold. "Tershy, close the door."

Tershy stepped back and shut the door in my face.

"Damn you, Sebastian!" I shouted. I kicked the barn door, wiped my tears, and ran back to the wagon.

I grabbed a few clothes and my favorite books, stuffed them into a bag, and headed to the kitchen, where I pulled dried meat and water from the pantry.

Just as I turned to leave, Alice stepped into the doorway and blocked me.

"Where do you think you're going?" she asked.

"To Sabine, then west," I said.

"You're not going anywhere," she said, grabbing the bag from my hands.

"Yes, I am," I said, reaching for it.

Alice slapped my hand away. "Listen to me. We all know Sebastian's lost it, but this is your home. You belong here, not out there wandering around like some hobo. You'd last a week, maybe less."

I wanted to tell her I could survive. Maya had. But instead, I stepped into her arms and cried.

"You're going to be alright," she said softly.

"I don't know who I am anymore," I sobbed. "Am I Poppy or Maya?"

Alice held me close. "I don't know about all that. But my mom used to say, You are who you are when you're with family. And we're your family."

"But sometimes I feel confused," I said. "There are bad things inside me I can't control."

"Now listen to me, girl," Alice said. "I know you've got your secrets. We all do. But don't let them ruin you. Use them. Make them your strength. And stay away from that damn elixir, it's not helping you."

That night, I lay in bed thinking about what she said. I tried to sleep without the elixir. It was hard. But she was right, I did have strength. Maya was part of me. I shouldn't have doubted that.

I told myself I'd do better. I'd take care of myself. I'd fight for what I wanted, just like Maya would.

Two hours passed, and I was still awake. I got up, walked to the counter, and took a long drink from the bottle of Poppy's Poison. I set it down, empty, and sighed.

"Baby steps, Maya. Baby steps."

❧ CHAPTER 29 - POPPY

The year 2124

I'd never be able to thank Alice enough for what she said that day in the kitchen, because not long after, everything changed. I'd been trying to be better, a mix of Poppy and Maya, and aside from my minor elixer addiction, I thought I was doing okay. I chose to ignore Sebastian, show him what it felt like to be invisible. It wasn't hard. He was barely around anyway until that day.

That morning started like any other. I took a sip of Poppy's elixir, then spent the morning in the kitchen baking bread. The other helpers were busy cooking eggs and frying potatoes. Lady Jane sat in the corner nursing Vincent, talking nonstop about how childbirth had ruined her body and how she never got any sleep. She sounded annoyed, but you could tell she loved that baby more than anything. The way she looked at him while he slept, the way she traced his tiny nose and counted the hairs on his head, it was clear.

That afternoon, I went to the wagon to rest when I heard the sound of Sebastian's return. He'd taken the Beast on his latest trip to the Cube and had been gone nearly two months. I hadn't spoken to him since I yelled at him that day at the barn, and I was still angry, but I was also worried. He'd never been gone that long before. Even Cowboy and Tershy had gone out looking for him a few times, but came back empty-handed.

So when I saw the Beast roll past, I dropped my guard. I ran out and waved, hoping he'd stop. But he didn't. He drove straight to the barn and stayed there, like always.

Then, later that night, something strange happened.

Sebastian showed up at the supper table. He was clean. His shirt was fresh, and he was smiling, something I hadn't seen him do in a long time.

"Potted meat! My favorite," Sebastian said, as he grabbed a plate and scooped a hefty serving of Alice's stew while the rest of us stared in shock. He sat down right next to me and started eating like nothing was wrong.

"Who the hell are you and what did you do with Sebastian?" Alice asked.

"How did you know this was exactly what I wanted tonight?" he said between bites.

"You know me, I'm a flipping clairvoyant," she replied.

Sebastian laughed. "Hand me a roll, please," he said with a smile. I passed him the bread basket, and when he took it, his hand brushed mine and lingered for a second before he grabbed a piece.

"Such a wonderful night, don't you think?" he said.

We all nodded quietly, except for Loki, who looked too confused to say anything.

"Why are you in such a good mood all of a sudden?" Alice asked, dropping another scoop of stew onto his plate.

"What do you mean?" Sebastian laughed. "I know, I know I've been a bit busy with work lately, but that's about to change."

"A bit? I don't think I've seen you in over a year," said Lady Jane.

Sebastian looked up and smiled. "Well, look at that little guy! Where did he come from? Can I hold him?"

He didn't wait for an answer. He picked up Vincent and danced around the table with him. Then he handed the baby back, sat down, and grabbed another piece of bread.

"You found what you were looking for in the Cube?" Boris asked.

Sebastian's eyes lit up. "You better believe I did."

"So what is it?" Jane asked.

"It's a secret. You'll have to wait," he said. He finished his stew, kissed the top of my head, and pointed to Cowboy. Cowboy stood up and followed him back to the barn.

"Is someone ever going to tell us what's going on?" Lady Jane asked.

Alice wiped her mouth and leaned forward. "Probably best we don't know. Right?" she said, looking at me.

I didn't answer. I just shrugged, cleared the plates, and went back to the wagon to wait.

Later that night, Sebastian came to the wagon and took my blood for the first time. I didn't fight it. I'd known this day would come. Part of me had even hoped for it. I wanted him to need me again, and my blood was the only thing I had to offer.

His breath was warm on my neck as he slid the needle into my arm. I winced as the vial filled with dark red. He wore gloves, I'd asked him to. I asked questions: how much, where he'd keep it. But not the one I really wanted to ask. What did you find? Was it a dog or something worse?

After he left, I looked in the mirror and gasped. My face was pale, my eyes had dark circles, and my hair was a mess. No wonder he left so fast. I picked up my brush and tried to fix my hair, but my hand was shaking so much that I dropped it.

"Probably just weak from the blood draw," I said, reaching for my bottle of Poppy's Poison. I poured a glass and drank it down. Then I looked at myself in the mirror and smiled.

"Much better, Miss Maya," I said softly.

I stared at my reflection for a moment, brushing the hair from my face. "I'm glad you're back," I whispered. "I don't think I could do this without you."

The next morning at breakfast, I noticed Alice looking at the bandage on my arm. I quickly pulled down my sleeve. She didn't say anything, but I could tell she was suspicious. Instead of letting me help with cooking like usual, she told me to go work in the garden park. She'd never done that before.

I didn't argue. I left the kitchen, stopped by the wagon for one last dose of the elixir, and headed toward the park, hoping to run into Rake. I was running low on my Poison, and, with Sebastian gone so much, Rake had become my new supplier. I wasn't sure where he got the dust, town probably, but I didn't care.

As I reached the picnic area, I saw a man sitting with his back to me, humming. For a second, I thought it was Sebastian. But as I got closer, I saw the brown shirt and the long black braid with beads down his back.

"Val!" I said, running toward him.

He turned, smiled, and motioned for me to sit.

"Hey, kid. Look at you, all grown up," he said, popping a handful of nuts into his mouth.

I sat beside him. "I guess I did. What are you doing here?"

"Just checking in. Wanted to see if you remembered me."

"Of course I remember you," I said. "Why wouldn't I?"

"Oh, I don't know. Thought maybe you'd want to forget some things."

"I've tried," I said. "But it never works. And I'm glad it doesn't now that you're here."

I looked down at my feet. "Sorry you died."

"Yeah, well, don't worry too much about that. All great things must come to an end, or so they say," he said.

"But you were my favorite," I said.

"I know," Val replied, tossing peanut shells to the ground and wiping his hands on his pants. "Look, I don't have much time. I just need to know you're okay. Looks like you've gotten into some trouble." He nodded toward the bandage on my arm.

"I'll be fine," I said.

"You sure about that, *Poppy*?" His voice was gentle but serious. I blushed, and I threw my arms up.

"I just don't get why life has to be so hard and confusing. Everything was easier when I was younger. Now I feel like I keep messing up the same way over and over."

"I get it," Val said. "It's tough out here, especially when you're carrying the disease that can bring the world to a standstill. Again. And let's not forget you're in love with a self-absorbed psychopath, chasing some wild dream, putting you and everyone else at risk. He's got no sense and doesn't care who gets hurt."

I sighed and covered my face with my hands. "Yeah, I guess you're right, but I was alone and had no one. Everyone left me but Sebastian. It's not fair."

Val laughed. "Life ain't fair, Maya. You and I, of all people, should know that. Follow your heart and be your best self. You do that, and you'll find your way."

"But how do I do that?" I said, looking up, but Val was gone.

I didn't make it to the garden that day, but went back to the wagon and tossed back the last of my Poppy's Poison and lay down. "Last time, I promise," I said as I drifted off to sleep.

❧ Chapter 30 - Poppy

The year 2124

Despite my conversation with Val's ghost that day, my chat with Alice gave me the courage to stick it out, so that evening, after my elixir-induced nap, I headed out to the barn to check things out. It was my blood after all, and if Sebastian wanted to use it, he would have to include me in the process.

For once, the barn doors were unlocked, so I let myself in and made my way past the rows of empty cages and tables piled high with blueprints and handwritten sketches to the bench where Sebastian sat alone, staring inside a wood crate.

"Sebastian, can I see?" I asked.

He looked up from the crate, gave me a tired smile, and waved me over. "Of course. Come sit."

He moved aside, and I sat next to him. Our legs touched, and I felt a flutter in my stomach.

"Careful not to scare her," he said.

"Oh. Did you give it the blood already?" I asked, leaning back.

"Not yet," he said. "I decided to wait until she's stronger."

"It's a girl?" I leaned forward and looked into the crate. Wrapped in a blanket was a small, shaking ball of fur.

"Yes, a girl. I named her Genevieve. You can pick her up," Sebastian said.

"Are you sure?" I asked.

"Go ahead. Just be gentle. She's scared."

I pulled the blanket back and saw a white, short-haired animal with tan and black spots on her back and feet. Her nose was pudgy, and her long ears drooped over her head like a soft crown. Her brown eyes were swollen and wet, barely visible behind dried tears.

I reached out and gently patted her. Her long white tail wagged slowly.

"Is it a dog?" I asked.

Sebastian laughed.

"Yes, she's a dog," he said.

"She's so little," I said. I looked down at the tiny creature, then gently picked her up and held her close.

"Oh, Sebastian, she's just skin and bones," I said, wiping her eyes with my sleeve.

"She's got fleas too, so be careful," he said. "I think it'll take a couple of weeks before she's strong enough for the blood."

"Where did you find her?" I asked.

"In the Cube. I traded some food to a couple of drifters for her. They said there were more, but they couldn't remember where they'd been when they found her."

"How old is she?"

"Just a few weeks, I think," he said.

"Oh, the poor thing needs some milk and warm water for her eyes. Here, take her. I'm going to get her something to drink besides water." Reluctantly, I handed the tiny puppy back to Sebastian, raced to the kitchen, and returned with a bowl of milk and the oregano oil Lady Jane used to clear her allergy eyes.

"Do you think we can take her to the wagon for the night so we can watch over and keep her warm?" he said.

"Of course, yes, we will make her a little bed out of some blankets," I said.

Back in the wagon, Sebastian and I stayed up late, doting over little Genevieve like she was our child.

"Oh, Sebastian, she's beautiful. Please let's keep her," I said. "You can go back to the Cube and find the others. I won't complain or care how long you're gone. Just let me keep Genevieve."

Sebastian chuckled. "I see how it is. One fuzzy face and I'm out the door."

"No, it's not like that," I said. "She just feels special. I've always wanted a dog, and now that she's here, I can't stand the thought of losing her."

"She is special," he said. "But you need sleep. Leave her with me. I'll stay up until she stops itching."

"Okay, but promise you'll think about it," I said, climbing into bed and pulling the covers around me. I watched him gently stroke Genevieve's back and worried he wouldn't wait. It had taken him years to find a dog, and it could take just as long to find another.

The next morning, I woke to find Sebastian still by her side, singing the same song he used to sing to me. He even brought her to breakfast, feeding her tiny bites of egg. The way he looked at her made me think I might be able to convince him not to turn her. He was clearly smitten.

"So that's what you've been searching for? An overgrown baby rat?" Alice said.

Sebastian gasped and covered Genevieve's ears. "Bite your tongue, mean lady. This is my new hound princess."

"She's a Beagle," said Tershy.

"A Beagle, huh? I like that. My new Beagle princess," Sebastian said proudly.

"You like her now," Tershy said, "but just wait. Beagles are hard to train and love to run. If she gets out, she might head straight for the mountains. You'd better fix that barn fence."

"Oh, you'll never leave me, will you, Genevieve?" Sebastian cooed, covering her in sloppy puppy kisses.

Loki scowled and spat out his eggs. "Grossness, I can't eat watching this," he said.

Alice rolled her eyes as she got up to clear the table. "Oh, good Lord," she said.

"Tershy, how do you know so much about dogs, anyway?" I said.

"Books mostly, though I had a little terrier for a while when I was a kid. My Dad brought it home one day after working the fields. Said he found it buried up to its neck. Our neighbors were afraid of it. Thought it was some kind of evil creature, and one night it disappeared from the yard," said Tershy.

"That's terrible," I said.

"Yep, some people can't forget the past, I guess," he said.

Two weeks later, Genevieve had nearly doubled in size, and Tershy was right, she was a runner. Keeping her inside the barnyard was more complicated than we expected. Every time Sebastian filled in a hole, she'd dig two more and tear through Jubilee like a wild escapee.

She stole food from tables and the pantry, chewed up shoes, and did her business wherever it was least convenient. One night at dinner, she grabbed one of Alice's nicer underthings from the clothesline and took off. Alice chased her around the hearth, and we laughed so hard we couldn't breathe.

Even with all her troublemaking, everyone loved Genevieve, especially Sebastian. It didn't take long for him to drop the idea of turning her into a carnivorous Adlet. She became the second love of his life, or at least that's what I liked to believe.

When she wasn't causing chaos, she was glued to Sebastian's side. From the moment he got out of bed to the moment he climbed back in, she was there. The only time she acted up was when he left her alone, so he started taking her everywhere.

She followed him on his daily rounds and sat under his feet during meals, waiting for a biscuit to 'accidentally' fall to the floor. At night, she slept at the foot of our bed, but by morning, she'd always be curled up right beside Sebastian's head.

It was around that time that Sebastian filled Cowboy in on what was going on, including my dirty blood. I was scared he'd start to treat me differently, but he didn't. He seemed to enjoy spending so much time alone with Sebastian and feeling special, knowing he was part of some deep family secret, even if it was strange and unsettling.

ᴖ Chapter 31 - Poppy

The year 2126

It took almost two years after that first blood draw for Sebastian to get the Adlet's right, but getting there wasn't easy.

After Sebastian decided turning Genevieve was no longer an option, he took me up on my offer to go back to the Cube without protest. On his second trip, he and Cowboy returned with Riley, a big scruffy mutt they found near the beach. Sebastian was thrilled, but Riley died the day after getting the blood. Bosco, a yellow retriever, they found a few weeks later, didn't survive either.

I never found out exactly what happened to them, but the look on Sebastian's face after Cowboy buried them said enough; it wasn't good.

Still, Sebastian didn't give up. He'd learned a few things by then and decided to hold off on experimenting with Bixby, a small spaniel Cowboy found in the town, of all places. Bixby wasn't bred in the Cube, and didn't come with all the 'radioactive' side effects the others endured. Wanting to experiment with smaller animals first, Sebastian decided to wait on Bixby.

"Don't want to kill off Prince Charming until we run some trials," he'd said.

The first animal they tried was mice. They were abundant and easy to catch, but they all but melted once they were given even the smallest amount of blood.

"Total waste," groaned Sebastian, and he kicked dirt over the stains on the barn floor.

"It's like we poured acid on them or something?" said Cowboy.

The snake looked promising. Sebastian loved the fluorescent pink shimmer of the skin and its enhanced striking ability. Still, when it started to spin, it got all knotted up before turning itself inside out, leaving a bloody carcass and skin casing. The worst, though, was the chicken, and we all agreed never to try that one nor speak of it again.

"Some things are just better off fried," said Loki as he plucked feathers out of Sebastian's hair.

It wasn't until we started using the rabbits that we finally saw some promising results. It was the first sunny day of Spring that year. We'd been at Jubilee for almost seven years, and the construction of Carnivále was coming along. The majority of the wheel had arrived and was under construction. The gaming park was complete, and most of the game booths were built. The Kuru museum and Krakus, or house of freaks, were nearing completion, and the Grand Garden was in full bloom. The only things left were the custom big top that would act as our beacon and main entrance, the secret bunker Sebastian insisted they build under the arena, and, of course, the stars of Sebastian's *Big Show*, the Adlets.

One morning, Sebastian and Cowboy had returned from a hunting trip with a cage full of live rabbits they'd caught with a box snare. Sebastian took a fresh sample of my blood for the first time since the 'chicken incident,' then disappeared. At first, I didn't want to know how it was going with the poor bunnies, but after several failed attempts to control my curiosity, I wandered over to the barn, sat on the fence, and waited for someone to notice me. Not long after, Loki emerged from the barn running as fast as his little legs would go, screaming. His arms flailed above his head while his face twisted in fear.

"Get it off me! He's gonna get me. No, Spencer, please don't eat me!" Loki shouted as he ran across the field, chased by a tiny puffball named Spencer.

Cowboy came out of the barn with an axe and joined the chase. Sebastian, laughing so hard he could barely walk, came over and stood next to me at the fence.

Tufts of white fur flew off Spencer's nearly bald body. His floppy bunny ears bounced wildly before stiffening into curved goat-like horns. His teeth grew longer right before our eyes, so long that they stuck into the ground and made him trip. He rolled across the dirt and landed in a cloud of dust.

Cowboy caught up, chopped off Spencer's head, scooped it up with the axe, and dropped it into a bucket. Then he went back to the barn, grabbed a gas can, and set the rabbit's body on fire.

"Don't nobody touch that bucket," Cowboy said.

"Mr. Sebastian! That furry demon almost got me!" Loki yelled as he fell face-first in the mud.

"What're you talkin' about, Loki? That was fantastic! We're gonna have to try somethin' else, though. I lowered the dose this time, but those rabbits are just too dang fast. And those teeth keep tripping them up. Not to mention the mess from all that fur. Shame though, those horns were incredible!"

Loki popped his head up from the mud, eyes wide and wild. "Something ELSE? SOMETHING ELSE?! Oh no no no NO. WE are not doing something else. WE are done. YOU can do something else, YOU can play God with your fluffy frankbunny farm, but this WE is OUT. I'm going back to bed, and I'm taking the mud with me!"

Sebastian jogged over, grinning, and yanked Loki to his feet. "Of course, we have to try again! Didn't you see that? We're so close, we gotta keep goin' 'til we get it right."

"I didn't see anything except my life flash before my eyes! I saw my sixth birthday, my grandma's ostrich meatloaf, and the summer I fell in love with our neighbors, scarecrow!" Loki slapped at his muddy pants like they were on fire. "Why can't we just get a petting zoo like they have in Gilford?"

"Don't be so melodramatic," Sebastian said, brushing dust off Loki's behind. "We had the whole thing under control. Besides, you're the fastest runner we've got. We need you."

"Well, count me out," Loki huffed, striking a dramatic pose. "I'm much too rare and delicate for this. Besides that, the murderous ball of fluff almost got me. I heard his stomach growl, Sebastian. He was that close!"

Sebastian chuckled. "Alright, alright. That one's on me. I unlatched the gate too soon. I'll give you a better head start next time. But really, what're you so scared of?"

"What am I scared of?" Loki gasped. "Let's start with not wantin' to be a zombie, thank you very much. It's hard enough finding trousers that fit as it is!"

"I won't let you become a zombie. I promise," laughed Sebastian. He reached into his satchel and pulled out a half-crushed granola bar and waved it at Loki. "Here. For morale."

"Well, wait, let's think about this. Loki would make a creepy-looking Spinner. Might be a good attraction," I said, winking at the disheveled dwarf.

"Or maybe we could get you a nice helmet, maybe put your name on it with sequins. That'd be nice, right?" joked Sebastian.

"See! Bait one day, zombie next," Loki scoffed, snatching the granola bar. "My momma didn't raise me to be an appetizer. And she definitely didn't raise me to wear sequins in combat!"

We burst out laughing as Loki stomped across the barnyard, muttering to himself, the granola bar halfway gone before he even reached the gate.

"That was a good turn, but I'm afraid the rabbits are just too fast, and when their fur flies off, they just look like little horned rats," said Sebastian.

"Too damn messy," grunted Cowboy as he brushed fur off his shirt.

"Should we give the fox a try?" Sebastian turned to Cowboy and winked.

Cowboy took off his hat and gave Sebastian a hard look. "Dang it, now. You know I respect you, and I ain't goin' anywhere. I like it here. It's the first real family I've had since I left the rails, and I always wanted to see a carnival. But I gotta speak plain. This is some wild backwoods nonsense you got goin' on."

He pointed toward the field. "That rabbit could've caught little Loki, and we'd be in a whole heap of trouble. If anyone finds out what's going on out here, we could all end up in the chamber."

Cowboy's voice softened. "I may be simple, but I know about them Spinners. My granddaddy's granddaddy fought in that war, and I heard stories when I was just a little bitty. If you're gonna keep doin' this, you gotta do it right. Set up rules. Controls. You've been lucky, but you're playin' with fire, messin' with these animals and that tainted blood."

He turned to me and gave a weak smile. "No offense, Miss Poppy. I know this ain't on you. But we can't have these things runnin' loose or chasin' folks anymore. Next time, that little fella's gonna get caught and turn this place into a killing field."

Cowboy's outburst took both Sebastian and me by surprise. It was the most words he'd spoken since we met him, and he was clearly concerned, though he never let on until now.

"You're one hundred percent right. I don't know what I was thinking. From now on, Cowboy, you're in charge—head zookeeper. We won't create until you say so. We'll only test under your strict control." Sebastian held out his hand, and the two men shook on it.

Cowboy grunted and pulled his hat back onto his head. "Head zookeeper. I can do that," smiled Cowboy.

"Then it's settled," said Sebastian.

Not long after that, Sebastian decided it was time to let Tershy in on the secret. He didn't want Rake to know yet, so he had Boris take Tershy's place on the Cube runs to pick up the last of the wheel parts. He told Rake that Tershy was needed for some special projects.

I was nervous. Tershy was smart, too smart, I thought, to go along with something so risky and strange. But to my surprise, he was excited.

He showed Sebastian how to separate blood cells from plasma using a spinning device he built from an old nut grinder. He explained that splitting the two would allow them to test different versions and find the best results. Tershy believed warm blood was causing most of the damage in the first two dogs and that cold blood might be easier on their organs.

That changed things for Sebastian. He realized this wasn't just about infecting a host. It was a science. From then on, he started calling my blood samples "serum," and Tershy became his go-to partner for figuring out how to use it.

After that, things started moving fast. Cowboy took his new role as head zookeeper seriously. He revamped the barn with stronger cages to keep the animals secure while they were getting 'juiced,' and built a secure enclosure for testing.

I tried to help by explaining the Observation Rotunda from Intermountain, but Cowboy didn't get it. He looked at me like I'd lost my mind, so I gave up and let him figure things out his own way.

Stopping the rabbit trials was a setback. Like mice, they were easy to catch and were everywhere. But it didn't take long for Tershy to find a better option. Foxes.

He said their DNA was closer to that of dogs, which would make it easier to achieve consistent results once the process was established correctly. So Cowboy and Tershy teamed up and started trapping as many foxes as they could.

Every week, new foxes arrived. Each trial produced more data, and the results steadily improved. Tershy had refined the serum to a level of precision that felt almost clinical. He could predict the exact onset of symptoms, gauge the serum's contagiousness, and adjust the formula to manipulate the animals' physical changes.

Following Cowboy's lead and Tershy's advice, Sebastian set strict rules for the blood draws. We switched to once a day, right after breakfast, so that I wouldn't feel as sick. But taking more blood at once started to wear me down. I loved the quiet time with Sebastian, but I was beginning to worry about how much he was taking.

He always told me not to worry, that my health came first. I wanted to believe him. I really did. But sometimes, when he drew my blood, he'd get this look on his face, the same look he had when we were intimate. A few times, I even saw him drool as the blood filled the tube.

Afterwards, he'd lock the vial in a box and leave without saying goodbye.

During that time, Val's warnings echoed in my mind, but I pushed them away. I told myself Sebastian loved me. He was just excited that we were making progress. I wanted to help him, even if deep down, I knew it was a terrible idea.

Chapter 32 - Gertie

The year 2132

The Henry James Dupont Southern Rail Station was crowded with tired carnival-goers waiting for trains home. Parents, worn out and hot, struggled to carry bags and sleepy kids with smudged faces. Everyone stared down the empty tracks, hoping for a train to appear.

There were no ticket booths, no staff, and no place to store luggage. Just a wide open space with solar boxes hooked to rail lines that stretched overhead and led to several waiting platforms.

Asher and I walked to the nearest solar box to check the screen for train info, but it was broken. Same with the second. And the third.

"What the heck? Every single board's busted," Asher said, squinting at the broken screens. "How are we supposed to know which train to take or where to buy tickets?"

"Wait," I said, pointing. "There's a train coming."

A sleek red train rolled into the station, slowing as it approached. A wide, toothy white smile was painted under the front window, giving it a strange, cheerful look. Small grid units powered the train and clicked into place with the platform connectors spaced every ten feet. The sides of the train were marked with tall yellow stripes, just like the carnival tent across the field.

As soon as the train came to a stop, a whistle blew from the first car, and the platform filled with passengers pouring out from every compartment. Children squealed with excitement, pointing at the bright red and gold carnival entrance across the road, while their parents gathered bags and tried to keep up.

People waiting to board rushed forward, hoping to grab the best seats before the next departure.

A man in black slacks and a long black coat stepped off the train and began unloading luggage from the side compartments.

"That must be the conductor," I said. Asher and I walked over and waited until the man finished handing out the bags.

"Hello, can I help you two?" he said.

"Is this the rail headed west?" said Asher.

"No, son, this here is the *Carnivále* trolley down from Clarksville. You want a transport train. They run every few hours until dusk, then resume the next morning. You'll want to grab the blue rail over on platform eleven. The blue rails are the ones that head west. Green goes east and yellow to the north."

"Is the next one west at four o'clock?" I said.

"That I don't know. I only run the *Carnivále* route. The schedule boards should show the times," he said.

"The boards are all smashed up, every one of them," said Asher.

"Again? Now, why in the world does someone keep defacing those boards? Probably some dang hooligans from town," he said.

"Is there a place to buy tickets or something to eat while we wait?" said Asher.

"Not at the station. The conductor will issue your tickets when you board. I believe the fare to the west is eight credits, but I'm not sure. They got a food cart on board where you can buy something to eat," he said.

"Okay, great, thank you," said Asher

"No problem," said the Conductor as he rang a brass handbell. "*Carnivále* trolley, heading to Clarksville, departs in fifteen minutes. Fifteen minutes, folks. This is the last trolley to Clarksville, I repeat the last trolley, so if you miss it, you'll be taking the 2:15 to Bristol."

Once the crowd boarded the bright red trolley, the station emptied. Only a few permanent residents remained. A grungy man curled up on the ground near one of the platforms, a lone stray cat, and an odd little man leaning against a pillar near the *Carnivále* platform. Asher and I stood nearby, watching him. I'd noticed the man earlier. He wasn't just loitering; he was watching the passengers closely, as if he were waiting for someone specific.

He was strange, but not because of his size. His face was deeply wrinkled and had a yellowish tint. Even his eyes were yellow. It looked like he'd tried to clean himself up, but the dirt clung to the folds of his skin, giving him a cartoonish, almost painted-on appearance. His hair was slicked back and tucked neatly behind his ears. He wore a floor-length tuxedo jacket, matching pants, and a crisp white shirt.

"Someone went through a lot of trouble trying to make that guy look presentable," snorted Asher.

We continued to stare, and it wasn't long before the bizarre man noticed the two of us and quickly made his way over to where we stood. Ignoring Asher, the man twirled on one foot, bowed down near my feet, and presented me with a handmade flower of twisted tissue.

"Hello, Miss Gertie," he said.

"How do you know my name?" I said.

The man grinned. "Because I am Loki, and I am magic," he winked.

"Really?" I said.

"Not to mention it's embroidered on your creepy neck diaper," said Asher. Loki rolled his eyes and dismissed Asher with a quick wave of his hand.

"Oh, right," I blushed and smacked Asher's arm.

"Are you two here for *Carnivále*?" said Loki.

"No, we are just waiting for the next passenger train west," said Asher.

"West? Why west?" said Loki.

"We have to get home," I said.

"So you're here alone, no other family? No school trip?" said Loki.

"No, just us two," said Asher. The curious little man seemed excited at the notion that Asher and I were alone, and I immediately didn't trust him.

"Well then, you must come to *Carnivále*," he said.

"But we're waiting for the train. The four o'clock train headed to Diego," I said. "We just need to find platform eleven."

"Four o'clock train? Why, there's no four o'clock on this day, only every other day. The next blue rail isn't until eight o'clock tonight," he said.

"Are you sure? The man at the fishery told us four o'clock," groaned Asher.

"Quite sure. I'm the *Carnivále* trolley concierge. I'm here every day and know the schedules by heart," said Loki.

"That's just great," I said

"The next rail is many, many hours from now, plenty of time to enjoy *Carnivále*. You can even make it to the *Big Show* at two p.m. tomorrow if you stay the night. You don't want to miss out on the *Big Show*, now do you?" Loki smiled and reached into his front coat pocket. "I even have free tickets. Free *Ruby Tickets*. That means special access, no line to the *Big Show*," said Loki as he waved two shiny red tickets in our faces.

"What's the *Big Show* anyway?" said Asher. "We saw the board out on the road. Is it some kind of magic performance?"

"What's the *Big Show*?" cried Loki. "Only the biggest extravaganza in all the world. Took the great Sebastian Sheets nearly fifteen years to perfect, and his debut performance is tomorrow afternoon. Look around. People have come from miles, even other countries, just to see it."

"But what is it?" I said.

"Oh, I don't want to spoil it. You'll have to stay and see it for yourself." Asher and I exchanged glances, and I shook my head.

"No, I'm sorry. We can't stay overnight; we have to go," said Asher.

"Then just come for the afternoon. There's plenty more to see. The Puppy Pavilion, the Spinner Museum, and all the fun rides! The Wonder Wheel is the best!" said Loki.

"I don't think we should leave the station," I said.

"Ruby Tickets are scarce. They even come with food vouchers, good for any two items each at the *Carnivále* food court," said Loki. My stomach growled as Loki extended the tickets again, but I didn't take them.

"My personal favorites are the Saturn dog and the honey fry bread," said Loki.

"What's a Saturn dog?" said Asher.

Loki's eyes rolled into the back of his head as he drooled. "All beef dog batter-dipped and fried to perfection, then slid perfectly up the middle of three crispy onion rings, served with spicy dog sauce and tater chips. Ding dong delicious," said Loki.

Asher grabbed the tickets from Loki's stubby little fingers. "Sold!"

"Wait. Are you sure?" I whispered. "Don't you think we should stay here? Remember what the man at the fishery said?"

"And miss out on a free Saturn dog?" Asher grinned. "No way. Besides, you heard our friend Loki, the next transport west isn't until tonight, and this place doesn't exactly scream safe."

I looked around. With the crowd gone, the station felt eerily quiet. I couldn't imagine spending the whole day here alone. The only places to sit were a few broken benches, all buried under piles of carnival trash, sticky wrappers, crushed cups, and something so foul-smelling even the stray cat kept its distance.

A gust of wind swept through and peeled a flyer off a nearby post. It fluttered across the platform and landed near my feet.

I bent down to look.

It was a missing persons notice. A couple, about Asher's and my age, Clarice Fellows and Bryce Cadder: missing since August third.

I shivered and nudged the flyer away with my foot

"Please, I've never been to a carnival before," Asher begged.

"You've never been anywhere before," I said.

"Exactly! Come on, remember adventure?" Asher said, grinning. "Besides, you heard the man: honey fry bread." He winked. He knew me too well.

"That does sound good," I admitted. "But what about what Antoine said about that place?"

"That old hillbilly?" Asher scoffed. "He's probably scared of his own shadow. Look around, there are kids everywhere. It's gotta be safe if they're taking children."

He wasn't wrong. The crowd from the train station was just a fraction of the people now pouring through the carnival gates. My stomach growled again. I glanced around the empty station and shivered.

"I guess it'll be alright if we go for a little while," I said.

"Of course it will," Asher said, already heading toward the entrance. "Besides, I'm in the mood for something ding-dong delicious."

Chapter 33 - Poppy

The year 2126

Winter that year brought something new to the bayou: snow, and although it didn't stay long, we enjoyed it while it lasted. Even Sebastian and Cowboy ventured out from the barn to throw a snowball or two at poor Loki. By this time, I was no longer allowed anywhere near the barn.

The fox trials were going well, but Sebastian didn't think it was safe. I wasn't upset, though. Rabbits were one thing, but those foxes reminded me too much of Genoveave and Bixby, so I spent most of my time helping Alice in the kitchen, running errands for the construction crew, and trying not to think of what was happening behind the barn doors.

One day, after my usual blood draw, I headed over to the kitchen for some tea and found Sebastian trying to lure Bixby out from his favorite spot under the prep table. Holding a piece of bread out with one hand and a rope in the other, I knew what he was up to, and it sent my stomach in a turn.

"What are you doing?" I snapped. Sebastian jumped at the sound of my voice.

"Damnit, Poppy, you scared the bejesus out of me," he said.

"What are you doing?" I repeated.

"I'm trying to get this lazy hound on his feet," he said.

"Why? You're not thinking of using Bixby now, are you?" I said.

Sebastian sighed. "Oh, Poppy, you knew this was the plan all along. We've made such good progress and have outgrown the foxes. It's time."

"But do you even know how your fox dose will affect him?" I said.

"No, we don't. That's why we test. Bixby will be the canine subject one. There will be adjustments for sure, but we have to start somewhere. I already have Boris and Rake out in the Cube looking for more subjects," he said.

"Can't we save him for last, then? You said it yourself, he's too pure to waste on experimenting. Why can't we just keep using the foxes until you find more?" I said.

"You don't understand, we've done it, Poppy. We are ready, and we can't use the foxes for the show. They aren't true Adlets; they don't have the look, the fear factor, or the longevity. It has to be a real deal."

"But why Bixby?" I said. "He and Genevieve are so close. She'll be heartbroken." It was true. Genevieve and Bixby were best friends, and Genevieve would often leave Sebastian's side to go chase mice in the field with Bixby; they even shared the same blanket. Sometimes I felt Sebastian was jealous of Bixby, and that was why he refused to balk at turning the poor dog.

"Sorry, I told you not to get attached," he said.

"But look at this face," I said, smooshing Bixby's cheeks in. "Look at me, Sebastian, I don't want to be a devil dog."

Sebastian laughed and gave Bixby a friendly pat, then gave up and left the two of us alone while he went back to work. I knew he'd be back, though, and I knew I needed to find a way to save Bixby.

"Don't worry, sweet boy, I won't let him hurt you," I said as I covered his furry face in kisses. That night, I gave Bixby to Alice and told her to keep him hidden. She took Bixby no questions asked, and I knew he'd be safe. I could tell by the look on her face that she was confused, but she didn't say a word, just took him and walked away.

Later in the wagon, I lay in bed waiting for Sebastian to come looking for the dog, but he never did. I stayed up late, wondering where I could hide him permanently, but all I could come up with was to take him to town and set him free and hope Sebastian didn't find him again. I racked my brain all night trying to figure it out, but in the end, it was Genevieve who changed his mind.

I had just returned to the wagon after helping Alice clean the breakfast dishes when Sebastian, smiling ear to ear, burst in carrying Genevieve.

"You'll never believe it," he said.

"What's going on? Is Genevieve okay?" I said.

"More than okay, she's pregnant," he said.

"Pregnant? Are you sure?" I said.

"Tershy thought so, and Cowboy confirmed it. Look at her belly," Sebastian thrust Genevieve's belly so close to my face that a trickle of dog slobber splashed across my forehead.

"I thought she was looking pudgy. Do you realize we are going to have more animals to feed? Genevieve and Bixby are already taking most of the scraps. Alice is going to freak out," I said.

"We'll make do. Besides, do you know what this means? No more hunting, no more foxes, no more long trips to the Cube looking for war-scared mutts. We can make our own dogs. I can't believe I never thought of that myself," he said.

"So we don't need to turn Bixby?" I said.

"Turn him? Oh no, our little stud has work to do! Well, when the time comes, of course, for now, ol Genevieve here needs her rest and nourishment. Is that right, my puppy momma?" Sebastian kissed Genevieve as he danced around in circles. Poor dog looked like she was about to puke, so Sebastian lay her on the bed next to me and sat down.

"I just realized, I'm going to be a grandpa," he beamed.

That night at dinner, Sebastian broke the news to the family.

"More Beagles?" groaned Loki.

"More like mutts," said Tershy.

"What's a mutt?" said Loki.

"A mutt is a little bit of everything mixed into one. Kind of like you," joked Sebastian.

"When are you going to come clean and tell us what you're planning on doing with all these dogs?" said Alice

"What do you mean? They're for a show, of course," said Sebastian.

"Yeah, but what kind of show?" she said. I always knew Alice knew there was more going on with Sebastian's obsession with dogs than she let on. She was especially suspicious about the scars on my arms and the secret experiments in the barn.

"A show all about dogs. Think about it. Hardly anyone has ever seen one. We can have an interactive experience where you can learn about them, watch them do tricks, and even pet them! We'll have an arena just for them. A pavilion full of puppies," said Sebastian.

"You want to do a puppy show?" she said.

"Yes, why not? The kids will love it," said Sebastian.

"You ain't planning on doing anything weird with those dogs, are you?" she said.

Sebastian chuckled. "Heavens no. What makes you think that?"

Alice hesitated, then got up to clear the plates. "I've known you a long time now, Sebastian Sheets, and if something doesn't have two heads or can eat you alive, you're not interested," she said.

Sebastian swallowed his elixir and grinned. "Poppycock." Alice turned her attention to Loki.

"And what do you know about all this, little man?" she said. Loki's eyes bulged, and he grabbed his spoon and began shoving stew into his mouth.

"That's what I thought," said Alice as she left the table.

"When are you going to tell the rest of the crew what's going on?" whispered Cowboy.

"In due time," said Sebastian.

Genevieve's first litter produced eight healthy pups. Unlike the night we got her, Sebastian wouldn't let me anywhere near the puppies and whisked them and Genevieve off to the barn immediately after he found her and her litter underneath the wagon. I wasn't upset, but thankful. The thought of losing Bixby broke my heart, and I wanted nothing to do with the puppies. I didn't want to see them, hold them, or feel the warm, sweet smell of their puppy breath on my face.

One afternoon, a few weeks later, I'd had a couple too many swills of some Poppy's Poison that I'd stashed in the pantry and decided to go back to the wagon to rest. When I got inside, I found Alice rummaging through the icebox where Sebastian kept the extra serum. We must have left it unlocked the night before.

"What is this?" she said, holding up a vial of my blood.

"It's blood. My blood, so stop pretending like you don't already know," I slurred.

"Does this have something to do with those damn dogs? I know something weird is going on, and I want to know the truth. What y'all doin with this here blood? And don't lie to me, I always know when you're lying."

I'm not sure if it was the elixir or a need to tell our secret, but instead of making up some excuse, I turned to Alice and whispered. "It's for his *Big Show*."

"That doesn't answer my question. What does Sebastian need your blood for?" she demanded.

"To make an Adlet," I said.

Alice threw her head back and put her hands on her hips. "A what?"

"An Adlet, you know," I leaned in close to her face and wiped a bit of drool from my mouth. "Demon dogs."

Alice huffed. "An Adlet? You mean one of them Kuru beasts? I told you not to lie to me, girl."

I nodded and wiped my nose. "It's not like you think, though. We have it all under control," I said.

Alice gasped, placed the vial on the counter, and took a step back. "You don't know what you're saying? What has Sebastian done to you? It's that damn green drink. I knew he was destroying your mind with that garbage."

"He hasn't done anything. It's me. It's always been me," I said.

"How so? He's the devil, not you," she said.

"It's kind of a long story, but trust me, I'm the devil, I'm the one," I slurred.

"Oh, pray, Jesus, I don't kill that man," said Alice.

"You don't understand. If it weren't for Sebastian, I'd have been dead a long time ago," I said.

"No, this ain't right. You're talking nonsense," said Alice.

I sat down on the edge of the bed, put my head in my hands, and started to cry.

"No, Alice, it's true, and you know it, you've always known it: this carnival, the *Big Show*, the Kuru museum, and the scars on my arms. You knew what Sebastian was doing with my blood out in that barn. What did you think he was making? A horror show of dancing Beagal puppies?" I said.

"There's no way. I got to do something here," said Alice.

"What are you going to do? Turn me in? Have me killed? Do you think I'm a monster like the ones the reels in the museum show?" I said.

"Not one bit. I'd never let anyone hurt you, especially not Sebastian," she said.

"But he's not hurting me! Sebastian's a good man. He saved me," I said.

"Saved you? He's bleeding you alive and playing god out in that barn. He's only concerned with himself. I still don't believe it. If this were true, you'd be spinning around like a brain-dead monster, attacking people and eating those puppies," she said.

"I don't know why, it's just my blood, go see what's going on in the barn. It's not magic, it's no trick, it's real. And there's plenty of other proof of what I've done before all this. Accidents, of course, but I've destroyed so many lives, my family, innocent people, and some not so innocent. It's why I was on my own when I met Sebastian. He took me in, he cared for me, and when he found out, he loved me anyway. That's just how he is, and not just for me. Where would any of us be right now without him? Lady Jane, Loki, and Boris, all of you owe your lives to that man. And think about it. This is our chance to do something great. Something no one has ever done before."

"It's ungodly," she said. "If what you're telling me is true, then why let him do this? Why take a risk? It don't make any damn sense," she said.

"Nothing makes sense, but I want to give Sebastian his dream, and you'll see it's going to be great. Carnivále will be the greatest attraction in the world, and you'll be part of it. It's what we all have worked so hard for this whole time." I laid down and shut my eyes; the elixir was hitting me, and I needed sleep.

"I could get you out of here, take you somewhere safe," she said.

"No, I can't leave. They know about me out there. I was running for my life when Sebastian found me," I whispered. "This is the only place I'm safe. You said it yourself, this is my home, and we are family. I can't leave, and neither can you. I need you, Alice."

"Who all knows about this?" she said.

"Just Cowboy and Tershey, oh, and Loki. Please don't tell anyone else," I said.

"You know they're all gonna find out at some point. You start walking around here with a bunch of demon dogs, people are gonna start asking questions," she said.

"Sebastian has it all figured out," I yawned.

Alice rolled her eyes. "I'm sure he does."

"Trust him. Please, Alice. Do it for me," I said.

"I'll be here for you. You know that, but if anything bad happens to anyone, I'm going to feed him to one of those things." Alice turned to leave.

"Alice, wait," I said.

"Yes," She said.

"Don't be afraid of me. I couldn't handle it if you were." I said.

"I'm not afraid of you. It's Sebastian I'm afraid of," she huffed.

→ Chapter 34 - Poppy

The year 2126

One morning, a couple of months later, Sebastian came to the wagon and gently nudged me awake.

"Come now, it's time," he whispered.

"Time for what?" I said.

"You'll see," he said. I slipped into my coat and shoes and followed Sebastian to the barn. The sun had just begun to rise, and the grounds of Jubilee were quiet. Inside the barn, Cowboy was sitting in a corner with his head between his knees while Tershy and Rake washed up in a bucket. Neither of them spoke as I followed Sebastian through the barn.

We passed Genevieve's bed, and I didn't need to count her puppies to notice two were missing. I didn't ask Sebastian where he was taking me because I already knew.

The cage in the far corner sat hidden beneath a tarp. Sebastian pulled it away and grinned. "Take a look," he said.

I moved closer, but his arm shot out, stopping me short. "Not that close," he whispered.

It was still dark in the barn, but I could make out something hunched at the back of the cage. Definitely an animal, though its hairless pink skin looked disturbingly human, like that of a child, but the tail told me otherwise. About the size of a baby goat, it sat crouched with its back to me, tearing into something brown and furry.

I knew instantly what happened to Genevieve's missing puppies. One dead. One still alive.

Thick pink muscles rippled along the creature's spine as it ripped into its meal. Then it froze, sensing me. A low growl rumbled from its throat, and its body began to tremble. It arched its back and let out a wail so sharp it made my ears ring.

Slowly, it turned.

Its skin was raw, its veins bulged along its neck and shoulders, twitching with each breath. It didn't snarl. It didn't bark. It simply stared, vibrating with tension, as if the cage was the only thing keeping it from tearing the barn apart.

Its face was smeared with bloody fur, and the cage floor was scattered with torn flesh. Massive fangs, slick and red, gleamed in the dim light. Its eyes—fluorescent pink, impossibly bright—glowed with something that felt almost beautiful, if not for the horror beneath them.

The creature sniffed the air, then lunged toward the front of the cage. It groaned under the impact, metal shrieking as the cage slid forward several inches. I fell back, heart pounding, limbs scrambling until my spine collided with a pair of knees behind me. I turned. It was Alice.

Sebastian let out a nervous laugh and wiped sweat from his brow. "Ladies," he said, "I'd like you to meet Demetrie."

❧ Chapter 35 - Poppy

The year 2130

"Watch it! Don't drop it," yelled Sebastian as Gilroy, our freak show strongman and part-time crane operator, carefully maneuvered an enormous stone statue into the hands of waiting crew members. It was a busy day, Jubilee buzzed with activity as workers swarmed the grounds, putting the final touches on the rides and exhibits. Sebastian's goal for the day was to finish the Krakus, and the two, four-foot-tall gargoyles, one of his many finds from his time in the Cube, were the final touches and would soon perch like watchmen over its entrance.

The Krakus was the exhibition hall, where Sebastian would showcase his oddities and their acts. It was also where the oddities made their home, tucked away in the back field.

The Krakus was a magnificent piece of architecture, more beautiful, even, than the old library back in Proper. However, it lacked the same charm and quiet dignity. The building itself was stunning, a Chinese-style palace surrounded by gardens of oleander and hibiscus. Its arched entrance featured ornamental double doors and iron bars twisted into intricate designs that spelled out "Carnivále" when closed.

Sebastian made the doors himself. Inside, its dark purple walls and dim lighting gave it a spooky elegance. The oddity exhibits were housed in individual booths with large glass windows framed by hand-carved wood. Curtains hung on the inside for privacy, though few ever used them outside of show time.

No other building in Jubilee could compare, not even Sebastian's beloved arena. He wanted the Krakus to be special, and it was.

It was magnificent. And it disgusted me.

To know that such a place belonged to a band of DNA-challenged moochers who would never appreciate its beauty, who would never understand the craftsmanship, the intention, the legacy, it made my stomach turn, and I never went near it unless Loki or Sebastian dragged me along. Even then, I didn't linger. I definitely didn't wander into the woods behind the Krakus, where the real freak show took place. This was where the entertainers lived, ate, drank, slept, fought, and did God knows what else. The air reeked of unwashed skin, stale clothes, and pungent oils, some of them rubbed on themselves instead of bathing.

The Cube had given Sebastian more than just supplies and relics; it had also given him most of the freaks. Gilroy the Beast was one of them, along with his mother, Maribel the Magnificent. Now, Maribel wasn't a freak in the traditional sense, not like her seven-foot, three-hundred-and-fifty-pound son, but Gilroy refused to come to Jubilee without her. So Sebastian made room for both.

Gilroy performed astonishing feats of strength and endurance, all while wearing nothing but a poorly sewn cloth around his waist. Everyone begged Sebastian to make one that would stay on through the entire act, but he couldn't stop laughing long enough to grasp the vulgarity of the situation.

Unlike her son, Maribel the Magnificent was not that much taller than Loki. She had long black hair and a permanent hunch on her back. I assumed from carrying such a large child, but I didn't know for sure. Maribel was what Sebastian called a performance freak, or an act he made up, and despite his constant teachings and direction, Maribel made a terrible psychic. She couldn't remember her marks or read cues and looked more like a witch from an old fairy tale than a clairvoyant. Even the cape and ornate crystal ball Sebastian found for her didn't make her look legit, but it was an act. Loki called her Maribel the Nagnificent, which always made me laugh.

The acts in Sebastian's Freak Show fell into three separate categories—those he created out of regular weirdos like Maribel, or Jacque, our sword-swallowing pirate. Then there were the acts that were just plain odd, like Trevor and Leopold, the wrestling dwarves, or the ever-so-disgusting George the Gorge, whose talent consisted of nothing more than consuming large amounts of food in one sitting.

Then came the genuine freaks. Not just performers, but individuals with actual physical defects, like Gilroy the Beast, one-eyed Julie, and Mavis the contortionist, whose weak bones bent in ways that defied nature.

Once Sebastian discovered the effects of radiation on the human form, the Cube revealed itself as a grotesque buffet of spectacle, 'a smorgasbord of acts that would make Barnum Bailey himself squeal,' whoever that was. Every few weeks, he'd drive off in the Green Beast and return with more recruits. Eventually, the freaks began arriving on their own.

That's how we got Dora and Darlene, conjoined twins and one of Sebastian's favorites. Joined at the torso, they shared two arms, two legs, and a body that, aside from their widened frame and dual heads, looked almost ordinary, like a human version of Banjo the turtle.

The twins said they'd heard rumors of a place near the bayou where they could work and be safe, so one day they simply appeared, pulling a cart piled high with their belongings. After that, it became routine, one or two new arrivals each month, each welcomed by Sebastian. They didn't all make the cut as an act for the freak show, so some left while others stayed on to work.

I never felt comfortable around the growing number of freaks, especially the anatomical wonders. At first, I pitied them. But most were so mean. I guess I would be, too, if I only had one eye, no arms, or spent my life permanently attached to someone else. Thankfully, they kept to the grounds behind the Krakus and rarely wandered into camp.

Though I didn't care for most of the performers, Trevor and Leopold were the worst. When they first arrived, I was hopeful, two more Lokis, I thought. Maybe he'd finally have friends like him. But those two little jerks were mean. They bullied Loki relentlessly, stole his food, and shoved him around like he was nothing. I threatened them more than once, but it wasn't until Boris strung them up by their feet and clanged their heads together like a toy clacker that they finally backed off. They never touched Loki again after that, but I still hated them.

"Easy, easy. Okay, I got it," shouted Stanley.

"Careful now, don't break it. Took me eight days to transport those beauties. Nearly busted out the wheels on Barnaby's old trailer, pulling that thing through the marsh," said Sebastian.

The men had just finished lowering the first stone beast to the ground when a frazzled Loki came running.

"Boss! Help!" cried Loki.

"What now?" said Sebastian, shaking his head.

"It's the puppies. They've escaped again! It's total anarchy over there, I tell you, anarchy!" cried Loki.

"Oh hell, not again. I thought Freddy fixed the fencing," said Sebastian.

"He did," Loki wheezed, collapsing onto the ground. "But those little weasels are escape artists. I've been chasing them all day. I even tried bribing them with jerky. Jerky, Sebastian. They took it and ran." He flopped onto his back, arms spread wide. "I'm getting too old for this."

"Go tell Freddy to dig a trench along the bottom of the fence and fill it with cement, like I told him to. That should keep them from getting out. Tell him that the Pavilion better be done by the end of summer or I'll feed him to those dogs if I have to," said Sebastian.

"Yes, sir," Loki groaned, dragging himself upright like a man who'd just wrestled a tornado.

As if summoned by his misery, three rogue puppies bounded over and launched a full-scale lick attack on his face.

"No more kisses! No means no!" he cried, flailing dramatically. "I told you, I'm emotionally unavailable! I just want to be friends!" He scrambled backward, arms flapping, retreating toward Sebastian's newest exhibit, The Puppy Pavilion, like a man fleeing a very affectionate apocalypse.

"Jeremiah, that rebar goes over near the Wonder Wheel. And tell Tershy to hurry and pour that slab. I want the base up and running before the rains come. And don't get too close to the tent with that metal. That canvas was specially ordered and took nearly a year to get, not to mention the time it took me to sew it all together. Anyone rips it, and you'll find yourself at the bottom end of a hole."

"Aye aye, captain," said Jeremiah.

Sebastian stood before the newly completed big top, removed his hat, and ran a hand through his hair. It was still thick, still lustrous, though streaked with gray, but I didn't mind. If anything, it made him look more distinguished, more like the ringmaster he was always meant to be.

He smiled, eyes fixed on the tent as if it were a living thing. Jubilee was nearly complete, and for the first time in weeks, I saw a flicker of peace in his face. The chaos of Carnivále, the noise, the mess, the endless demands, meant progress. He thrived in it, even when it wore him down.

Things were taking longer than planned. Supplies were running thin, and feeding the small army of workers and acts was no small feat. I knew it weighed on him. But he never let it show, not to the team, at least.

The tent rose before us like a mountain of red and gold, striped and shimmering in the late afternoon light. It was massive, theatrical, impossible to ignore. Sebastian couldn't take his eyes off it, and neither could I. I had to admit, it was magnificent.

It was hard to imagine from Sebastian's messy drawings or the way he'd talk about it late at night, half-asleep and wired from too much elixir, even when the canvas showed up, all three tons of it. I still didn't get it. Not really. But after seeing it come to life, I understood the infatuation.

The roof rose in three peaks, striped gold and red like a vast blanket, each line precise. The sides shimmered with red diamonds and gold triangles, as if the whole thing were some oversized board game. Four entrances marked its edges—two in front, two more opening into the park, each spaced sixty feet apart. To call it a behemoth barely touched the truth. The tent was colossal, nearly the size of two libraries back at Proper's outpost and three times the height of Proper's great wall. Sebastian had spent almost a year carving patterns into the acreage behind the barn, stitching them together with navy-blue industrial thread he'd somehow acquired on his runs. I never asked where it came from. Eventually, I stopped needing to know.

All I knew was that it all had to match, it all had to be perfect, and it was. It wasn't until Sebastian turned to leave that he noticed me sitting in a chair next to our wagon, sipping lemonade.

"And what, pray tell, have you been up to all afternoon?" he said, reaching for my glass.

"Me?" I said. "I'm the mid-afternoon supervisor."

Sebastian snorted. "Are you now? Did you see the tent? It took all night, but we finally got her up. Isn't she a beauty?" he sighed.

"Yes, she's magnificent and so much bigger than I thought. I can't believe you stitched the entire thing by yourself," I said.

"It was all a labor of love, and big doesn't even begin to describe her. I bet you can see her all the way to Baton Rouge," he said.

"I'm so proud of you. Everything is coming together. You did it." I stood up and hugged Sebastian as tears rolled down my cheek.

"We did it," he whispered in my ear. "Now come with me. I have a surprise for you, but you have to close your eyes."

"A surprise? What is it?" I said.

Sebastian shook his head and took my hand. "Close them."

I shut my eyes and let Sebastian lead me, letting his words paint the world around me.

"Picture it," he said, his voice close to my ear. "The music starts before you even step inside—drums, trombones, playing something loud and festive. You walk through the car park and make your way to the big top. You step into a world of red velvet, gold trim, lights blinking like stars, and the smell hits you—popcorn, roasted nuts, something sweet you can't name. Acrobats spinning through the air, jugglers tossing knives, dancers in feathers and smoke. Fire breathers on stilts, clowns with painted faces."

His hand tightened around mine.

I smiled, already seeing it.

"Then you make your way out the other side and into the heart of Carnivále. Rides spinning, kids screaming, barkers shouting over each other. You eat too much cotton candy, lose all your credits trying to win a stuffed bear, and then you ride the Wonder Wheel. At the top, you see it all. The lights, the chaos, the magic."

The tent was quiet. Empty. But I could still hear it, just beneath the silence.

"But wait, there's more!" Sebastian said. "You'll visit the Puppy Pavilion, then head north to the Kuru Museum. Go west, and you'll find Carnivále Court with gift shops, caricature artists, park benches, all surrounded by gardens full of flowers and trees."

"Sounds lovely," I said.

"Next is the Krakus," he continued. "With eighteen freak exhibits. I said eighteen," he chuckled, "Or just eight, who knows. Depends on how many show up."

I laughed.

"Each one designed to thrill, unsettle, maybe even enlighten." He turned me slightly to the left. "And then, the arena… Okay, open your eyes."

I opened them slowly. The tent was empty except for something leaning against a post. It was large, at least ten feet long, five feet high, and covered by a blanket. Sebastian pulled the blanket and let it fall to the ground behind him.

"I give you… Poppy's Lair!" he cried, revealing a beautiful hand-carved sign made of dark wood. It was smooth and slightly glossy, like it had just been polished. Poppy's Lair was etched in bold, curling letters. Around the edges, rough carvings of vines and fox tails framed the name, giving it a wild, almost feral feel. It wasn't flashy, but it was beautiful.

I gasped and covered my mouth with my hand. "Oh, Sebastian, it's beautiful."

"Spencer did it himself. That's real mahogany, too," he said.

"I can't believe you named the arena after me," I said.

"Of course, without you, there would be no show. Everything we dreamed about for the last fourteen years is almost here," he said.

"What about the show? Do you have a name?" I said.

"I do." Sebastian smiled and took my hand in his. "Feast." The name hit my heart like a brick. I grabbed Sebastian's arm to steady myself.

"Easy now." Sebastian pulled me to his chest. "So you don't like it?"

"No, it's perfect. You'll never know just how perfect," I whispered. "I just can't believe it's finally happening."

"Believe it, my love." Sebastian grabbed my waist and spun me toward the center of the big top. We danced through the dirt and sawdust, to a symphony of drills, workers shouting over one another, puppies yapping, and Loki's anguished cries as he chased his runaway beagles back toward the Pavilion.

Sebastian twirled me once more, then dipped me low, grinning like a man possessed.

"This," he whispered, "is only the beginning."

I slept alone again that night in the wagon while Sebastian and Cowboy worked through the night tending to the 'animal act' in the arena. I missed the warmth of him beside me, his breath, his weight, the way he used to hum in his sleep. But nothing could pull him away from Carnivále now. Not even me.

He was happier than I'd ever seen him, lit from within by something fierce and bright. But I worried. He still barely ate, and sleep had become a distant memory. The elixir kept him upright, kept him moving, kept him dreaming, but it wasn't enough. Not really.

I told myself things would settle once we opened. That the madness would pass, and we'd find our way back to each other. But deep down, I knew better. Carnivále had him now. And I wasn't sure it would ever let him go.

The early sounds of construction and someone looting our ice bin woke me. I reached over for Sebastian, but he was the one rummaging through the icebox.

"What are you doing?" I said.

"Counting the serum. We need at least two more vials," he said.

"What are you messing around with all that now?" I said.

"Cowboy and I are trying to figure out the best route of ingestion for the show. We tried mixing it in with their food, but that took more than expected, and it didn't even work that well," he said.

"I thought we were injecting it straight into their necks," I said.

"That's how we do it now, but how are we going to pull that off in the arena?" he said.

I groaned and swung my feet onto the floor. "So what's your plan?"

"I'm not sure. I've been thinking, maybe the blood is in the collar, and we can pull it tight. Or we can dress Loki up and have him race by and stab the marks?"

"Loki would never agree with that," I laughed.

"Well, we have to keep thinking. There's no way to delay the effects. It has to happen in the arena. If it's done too soon, the show is ruined," he said.

"What if I spit it at them? Get it in their mouth or eyes during the performance," I said, remembering what Maya did to Jaco that day in the Observation Rotunda at Intermountain.

"Spit? How on earth would that work? No one can spit that far or that accurately." He paused. "Unless…" said Sebastian.

"Unless what?" I said.

"I think I have an idea, but I need to brainstorm a bit," he said as he raced out of the wagon.

"Wait, what? I guess I'm making my own coffee," I moaned.

I tried to keep myself busy the rest of the day and give Sebastian time to work, but I eventually found myself snooping around outside the arena when a wad of wet paper hit me on the forehead.

"What the?" I said, wiping the wet glob from my head. The sound of Sebastian's laughter wafted from above.

"What are you doing up there?" I said. Sebastian had perched himself on the outer wall of the arena near the entrance.

"Working, of course, and you? Did you come to spy on me?"

"No, I was on my way to feed Barnaby," I said.

"Sure, you were. And don't you mean *Magenta*?" Sebastian replied.

"Yeah… Magenta," I sighed.

I wasn't angry with Sebastian for what he did to Barnaby. The old burro was fading, and neither of us was ready to let him go. Funny thing, though, the serum didn't make him a monster; it gave him new life. His skin glowed a soft, darker pink, and his eyes shimmered with the same hue. But Magenta wasn't like Demetrie or those damn rabbits. Still Barnaby, just changed.

And like the rabbits, the serum had hardened his ears into antlers, and over time, they twisted together into a single spiraled horn that rose from the top of his head. It looked deliberate, like some divine hand had sculpted him to match Sebastian's dream.

That was the moment I stopped doubting. Whatever we were doing, however strange or wrong it might seem, it felt like fate. How else could the serum deliver exactly what Sebastian had once wanted?

What he tried to create for himself back in Galveston.

A unicorn.

Sebastian's plan wasn't just working. It was meant to be.

"Are you coming for dinner?"

"I told you, I'm working. Cowboy and Loki are here, too," he said.

"Hi, Miss Poppy," said a voice from the other side of the wall.

"This is work? I said, holding up the wadded-up hunk of wet paper. Looks like you guys are just playing around."

"Don't you see, I've got it all figured out. Come inside, and we'll show you. Cowboy, get the rabbits ready."

"Rabbits again? I thought you were done with rabbits," I said.

“So did Loki…” moaned Loki.

“This is just for testing purposes, and Loki can watch from the stands. Come on, hurry! You’re gonna flip when you see this, isn’t she, little man?”

“Me hate rabbit,” groaned Loki.

❧ CHAPTER 36- CARNIVÁLE

The year 2132

The line into the carnival curled around a vast lot separating the park grounds from the grid-rail station. Shouts of glee and restless anticipation echoed as the crowd inched toward the towering big top just beyond the arched entryway, where a massive neon sign pulsed like an invitation to fun.

Sebastian Sheets Carnivále Extraordinaire!

Children bounced on their toes, craning for a glimpse of the gates. The breeze carried a strange blend of smells, something like barn animals, greasy fried food, and sugar all mixed together.

Men in gold and red pinstriped vests and black slacks moved through the crowd, checking tickets and keeping order. One of them caught sight of the Ruby Tickets in Asher's hand and hurried toward us.

"Are those true Ruby Tickets you have there?" he said.

"I guess we got them from the little man at the grid-rail station," I said.

"Yes, that's Loki. These are indeed real Ruby Tickets. Please follow me! There's no waiting for someone with Ruby Tickets," he said.

We followed the man past a sea of jealous faces to the front of the line, where he rang a bell hanging next to the big top entrance. A large electronic board erupted in fireworks and played a sweet song about flying over a rainbow.

 The song stopped abruptly, and the screen filled with smoke and fire, and the same handsome man from the roadside billboard, with his flowing lion's mane of hair, emerged from the flames. He wore a long red coat with a sparkling cummerbund and matching bow tie. I was mesmerized.

"Welcome to Sebastian Sheets, world-famous Carnivále!" drawled the man as he disappeared into the smoke, where long pink and gray arms grabbed and clawed through the plumes.

"Ruby Tickets coming through," shouted the usher. The usher turned to Asher and me.

"Now, don't forget the *Big Show* tomorrow," he said.

Still in awe of the magical board, I barely heard what the man said. "Huh, what?" I said.

"The *Big Show* tomorrow, don't be late," he said.

"I don't know if we can stay that long. We have to catch a train home," I said.

"What do you mean, you can't stay? Ruby Tickets are valid all weekend. I can't let you leave… Um, I mean, you don't want to miss the *Big Show*," said the man.

"Aren't you even a little curious?" Asher nudged my arm and nodded at the screen. The advertisement started again, but the man with the hair stared right into my eyes and beckoned me with his seductive smile. I shuddered.

"I'm curious why everyone keeps saying *Big Show*, like it's some kind of BIG DEAL," I said.

"Oh, but it is a big deal. You'll just have to wait and see," said the man.

"So tell me, are these good seats? I don't want to miss our train for terrible seats to the *Big Show*," I said.

"Oh, little lady, you'll have the best seats in the house. But remember to come early, one p.m., show starts at two," he winked.

"Okay, sure," I said.

Stepping into Sebastian Sheets' big top felt like waking from a wild, disorienting dream only to find it waiting for you in full color. Jugglers spun flaming batons while men blew fire from their mouths, their faces slick with sweat and paint. Clowns drifted through the crowd, trying to startle or charm the kids.

A brass band blared from somewhere near the entrance, trumpeters in red-and-white striped jackets blasting festive tunes over the distant sound of rides and attractions outside. Men on one-wheeled bikes pedaled past, tossing candy into the air. Children shrieked and dove for it, adults laughing as they joined the scramble.

I clung to Asher's shirt, trying not to lose him in the crowd. A boy in dungarees and a tweed cap appeared beside us, holding out a folded map. His voice was flat and rehearsed. "Don't forget the *Big Show*," he said.

Asher took the flyer and waved it in my face.

"This place is incredible. I'm glad you changed your mind about the show," said Asher.

"What do you mean?" I said.

"What you said to the usher, you said sure," he said.

"More like no way," I said, waving to a man walking on an overhead wire.

"Then why'd you say sure?" he said.

"I just wanted to get away from that guy. Besides, we'd have to stay all night. Where would we sleep? And who's that creepy guy in all the videos?" I said.

"That must be Sebastian Sheets. Look at all the posters, he's everywhere," said Asher.

Asher was right. The man's face dominated every poster, each one with a different theme. In one, he stood triumphant over a snarling lion, whip raised mid-strike. In another, shirtless and gleaming, he cradled a massive axe across his shoulders like a trophy. His eyes were always fixed forward, theatrical and impossible to ignore.

It reminded me of President Bruno and the self-portraits that lined the halls of Greyburry. Each one more grandiose than the last, each one insisting on a version of truth no one dared question.

There was a woman, too. She appeared in several of the posters, always near him, always beautiful. In every image, Sebastian stared at her like a man possessed. You could tell she was someone he loved very much.

"He seems weird. This whole place seems weird, don't you think?" I said.

"I say it's exciting. Come on, what do you know about carnivals, anyway?" Asher laughed, grabbed my hand, and pulled me through the tent's exit into a flood of lights and noise.

Game booths lined the walkways. Food stands steamed and sizzled. A sea of people moved in every direction, all wearing the same broad, frozen smiles. Kids and adults darted from booth to booth, tossing credits at games of chance, chasing stuffed animals, and glittery trinkets. My head spun as I tried to take it all in: the colors, sounds, smells, and movement. It was too much, too fast, and so loud.

"Ba da dum da dum da dum, ba da dum, da dum," sang Asher as he strutted ahead like he belonged in the band.

Vendors wove through the crowd, shouting over the music. They sold ride tickets, greasy food on sticks, and clouds of spun sugar so bright they looked radioactive. The air buzzed with laughter, bells, and the distant hum of machinery. "Come ride the spin cycle!" shouted a man, taking tickets for a ride where caged seats spun in circles.

"Win your honey, a pink soft bunny," cried another from a nearby booth where frustrated game players tried desperately to toss rubber balls into hanging baskets.

Workers wearing signs advertising the attractions engaged the crowd while huge boards featuring the *Big Show* flashed overhead.

"Look, Gertie, they have a Kuru Museum and a House of Freaks," said Asher.

"House of Freaks? That sounds scary," I said. "What about the puppies?"

"I don't know, but I want to see it all, don't you?"

"Asher, we can't be late," I said.

"Late for what? We have nothing but time and nowhere to be. Let's be adventurous and have fun. Hope Island isn't going anywhere."

"But what if we miss the train?" I said.

"So what? We can take the train tomorrow night or the day after that," he said.

"Where would we sleep? I'm not spending the night at that rail station," I said.

"You'll stay at the Happy Camper Village, of course," said a voice from behind. Asher and I spun around and found Loki, the rail concierge, standing beside one of the game booths.

"We don't have enough credits for that," I said.

"Not enough credits?" said Loki. "Why, you have Ruby Tickets, and that's all the credit you need."

"You said they came with two food vouchers. You never said anything about staying overnight," said Asher.

"Well, that was my mistake. Ruby Tickets are a free pass to everything Carnivále," said Loki.

"I don't know about staying. We need to catch the train," I said.

"Think about it, then. The night train can be pretty scary. You might fare better in the daytime, like your friend said," said Loki.

"Scary how?" I said.

"Oh, I don't know, many characters on the night train. You saw those flyers at the station, right? People get on the night train and never get off. Happy Camper Village is safe and full of happy campers!"

"He might be right," said Asher.

"Of course I'm right," said Loki.

Asher turned to me and shrugged. "It's up to you."

"I don't know. Probably best to just go back tonight," I said.

Loki scowled, grabbed a stuffed rabbit from the booth's prize rack, and threw it at the two of us.

"Fine, your choice," Loki huffed, throwing his arms up. "But don't come a-crying to me when you both end up murdered!"

He spun on his heel and hobbled off toward the big top, muttering something about "idiots with a death wish" and "carnival insurance fraud."

"Ok, will do," I said as Asher, and I rushed through the crowd, laughing.

"Oh my god, what's his problem? Is it just me, or was he following us?" I said.

"I don't know, but he's crazy for sure, and we are definitely leaving early to get good seats on the night train," said Asher.

"Good, but we have to visit the Puppy Pavilion at least and ride some rides first," I said.

"And don't forget the Saturn dog," said Asher.

"Mmmm, and the honey fry bread," I said. "The concessions are over there. Let's go."

The Saturn dog stand was easy to spot with its massive spinning orbital that must have been a giant onion ring with a huge pink hot dog inside.

"Straight out of the Binding for Excellence handbook," said Asher, gesturing towards the sign.

"Asher, you're gross."

"You see it, right?" He said. I laughed and pushed past him to the order window.

"Can we get two Saturn dogs and two honey-fried breads, please?" I said as Asher flashed our Ruby Tickets. The women working the booth look up from her book. She had chubby, overly rouged cheeks with red lipstick on her teeth.

"Sure thing. Oh, wait, you have the Ruby Tickets," she said.

"Yes, we do," I said.

The lady disappeared for a moment, then returned with two enormous grilled hot dogs, served inside three glistening, golden-brown circles of onion. It was just like Loki described, and smelled scrumptious. I grabbed mine from Asher as she handed him our fry bread.

"Whoa, what is this thing? It's a lot bigger than I expected," I said.

"Yeah, I hear that all the time," said Asher.

"Asher!" I said, rolling my eyes.

"Wait a minute," said the lady behind the booth. "Don't forget your gator juice," she said.

"What's gator juice?" I said.

"Mostly sugar, a little water, and some green stuff," she said.

"What's the green stuff?" said Asher.

"Uh, more sugar and some other stuff. I dunno," she said.

"Have you tried it?" I said.

"No, we're not allowed. It's made special for the *Big Show* ticket holders. But I heard it's pretty tasty," she said.

"Is there alcohol in it?" I said.

"Maybe. It has a kick from what I heard, so it must be something," she said.

"I'll take one," said Asher.

"Make it two," I said.

"Oh, you're having the gator juice too? Look who's being adventurous now," said Asher.

"You better believe it," I said as I crammed the Saturn Dog into my mouth. The juice from the hot dog ran down my chin, and a blob of tater sauce landed on my shirt, but I didn't care. It was delicious. I pointed to the Wonder Wheel.

"And mm gonna ride dat Wunder Wheeeeel thing too," I mumbled through a mouthful of hot dog. "You wanna ride dat too, don't you?"

"I'm not entirely sure what you just said, Miss Gross Manners," said Asher, raising an eyebrow. "But if it's what I think, I'm in. Just aim your barf away from my lap."

I swallowed and wiped my mouth with my swaddle. "Sorry. It's hard to talk with a mouth full of wiener."

Asher choked on his gator juice. A splash even shot out of his nose. "Miss Gertie! What would Headmistress Padma say if she heard you talk like that? Even I can't believe you just said that," he laughed, wheezing.

"It's true," I said, taking a sip. "Mmm. This gator tastes good in my mouth."

"Stop! Stop talking before I gag again," he said, clutching his stomach.

"What, you can be gross, but I can't?" I giggled, swatting his arm away from his mouth.

"Oh, Gertie, you're so awesome," he said between bites.

"I love you, Asher," I said.

"Ditto! Now let's finish up and go ride that wheel until we puke."

"Okay, but take this juice, it's actually kinda nasty. I'm saving my fry bread for after the ride, just in case I do barf," I said, stuffing the last bite of Saturn Dog into my mouth.

Asher downed the rest of his gator juice and then mine, and the two of us headed toward the ride.

"Is your tongue numb?" I said.

Asher stopped and pinched his cheek. "Yeah, so is my face," he said.

"What do you think was in that gator juice, anyway?" I said.

"I don't know… Whoa, man! Look how high that thing is?" said Asher as we walked over to the wheel.

"Wow, it looks like fun," I said, staring up at the wheel.

"How are you not scared right now?" said Asher.

"I don't know, I feel good, really, very good right now," I said, skipping ahead.

"Me too. Good and dizzy. Race you!" yelled Asher as he sprinted past me.

"Not today, friend," I said as I took off running after him.

The two of us reached the ride together, but the wheel wasn't moving, and there was no line like the other attractions. Leaning against the fence surrounding the wheel's platform, eating a piece of watermelon, was a young man. He grinned as he spat seeds to the ground.

"Sorry, the Wonder Wheel doesn't take off for a few more hours," he said. The man was only a few years older than Asher and me and had a dangerously cute look about him.

"What?" Said Asher. "The sign says noon?"

"Not today, slight repair needed on the control board, so it's starting later than usual," he said.

"Ahhh," I whined.

No crying, just come back later this afternoon. Tershy, the wheel operator, will be here, and you'll be flying high before you know it," he smiled.

Harley had deep brown eyes that lingered, short, wavy locks of golden hair that caught the light, and muscles that rippled beneath his sweat-stained shirt. A geometric tattoo wrapped around his left bicep in bold, black lines, and just above his mouth, a small scar cut across his upper lip—subtle, but enough to harden his smile in a way that made my stomach tingle.

"You can ride the Merry-Go-Round while you wait," he said, nodding toward a slow-spinning mechanical parade of disfigured ponies.

"That thing?" I said.

"That looks like a kiddie ride," said Asher.

"And those horses look sickly and mean," I said

"That's because they're not horses, they're Adlets. The Kuru-infected beasts that roamed the land at night, feasting on the living," he laughed.

I stared at the ride, wondering why anyone would make a kiddie attraction look so terrifying. Instead of horses, devilish dogs hung impaled on iron poles, their hairless, disfigured bodies slumping and swaying with the motion. Some wore the same carnival uniforms as the men out front, while others bore only ornate leather saddles, waiting for children to climb on.

"Sebastian Sheets had each one hand-carved. They're actually pretty cool. That gray one with the pink eyes is my favorite," he said.

"Thanks, but I think we will just wait for the wheel," I said as I straightened my swaddle and smiled. "What's your name?" I said.

"Slick," mumbled Asher.

"My name is Harley. Is this your first time at the world-famous Sebastian Sheets Carnivále?"

"Yes, we're not from around here. Tell me, why does he pronounce it carnivále instead of carnival?" I said.

"Not sure. I figured he was from another country or something," said Harley. "You know, one of those bougie foreigners or something like that."

"Aha! That's what I said!" cried Asher.

"So you two traveled from out of town just to see the *Big Show*?" said Harley.

"No, just a coincidence, really," I said. "We didn't know this place was even here until today. Not sure if we're even staying."

"Do you know what it is? The *Big Show*, I mean," said Asher.

"No clue. I just started a couple of months ago. The whole thing is pretty secret. They've had the arena on lockdown for weeks. Only the seasoned crew knows what it's about, but you should stay. They're only doing the show one time, then it's over," said Harley.

"Only once? That's dumb. If it's that great, why wouldn't they do it every day?" said Asher.

"Yeah, I think that was the plan initially, but after Sebastian Sheets got sick, they canceled the entire production and then suddenly decided to do it just the one time. They do other shows in the arena, but this will be the only showing of the *Big Show*. In his honor and all."

"Sebastian? Is he the guy with the hair?" I said.

"Yeah, that's him. He spent nearly his whole life building this place and working on his show, only to get sick right before he finished it," said Harley.

"Ah, that's sad," I said.

"Yup," said Harley.

"So what happened to Sebastian?" said Asher.

"That I don't know that either, just know he ain't around, not since I've been here, anyway. He must be dying, though. Folks don't usually do things in your honor unless you're dead or going to die soon," said Harley.

"So the wheel's gonna open later today for sure?" I said.

"Yeah. Listen for the sound of the stampede trigger. Tershy will ring it when he's ready. When you hear someone yell 'Yee Haw' followed by the sound of raging buffalo, hurry back before the line blows up," he said.

"Is it scary?" I said.

"Nah, it's just a little high. Hardly any of the little kids come off crying. You'll be fine." Harley winked. Across the fairway, a man in a fancy gray suit and matching derby whistled.

"Hey, Harley, do us a favor and help pass out the prayer cards for the next show," said the man. Harley tossed his watermelon rind on the ground and waved back.

"Sure thing," he said.

"Who's that?" said Asher.

"That's Casper the Great. Our resident psychic. Go on over and let him tell your future," said Harley.

"No, that's okay. I kind of want it to be a surprise," said Asher.

"At least go check it out. Casper's pretty good," said Harley.

"Is it real? Can he really tell your future?" I said.

Harley snorted. "Of course not. This is a carnival. Nothing here is real. Don't forget that either." Harley stepped off the platform and gently brushed against my arm as he passed. "Come on, I'll show you."

"Someone's got a boyfriend," whispered Asher.

"Shut up," I blushed.

We followed Harley across the park to a dark purple tent as Casper the Great engaged the gathering crowd out front.

"Fill out your prayer cards and hand them in so we can drop them into the cauldron of knowledge," said Casper as he dropped a handful of folded envelopes into a vat of fire sitting in the middle of the crowd.

Casper was handsome, not like Harley, youthful and dangerous, but older, more distinguished. The type of handsome that made you forget what you were doing, or why you'd come, or how to breathe properly. His salt-and-pepper hair was swept back with precision, and his jawline was carved with the kind of quiet authority that made people listen before he spoke. His eyes were a deep, unreadable gray, framed by lashes too perfect to be fair. When he smiled, it was powerful.

Even the way he stood oozed confidence, with feet planted and shoulders relaxed. His suit looked expensive, dark grey with subtle silver threading, and fit him like it had been hand-tailored.

"Your intentions matter," he said, dropping another prayer card into the flames. "So write clearly. The cauldron doesn't like confusion."

A ripple of laughter passed through the crowd, but no one dared speak over him. Even the children were quiet, eyes wide, clutching their cards.

Casper took center stage on a stack of wooden crates underneath a sign that read *Casper the Great's Psychic Adventure Tour.* He raised his hands to hush the crowd, then placed his pointer finger against the side of his head and tilted his neck.

"Is there someone here by the name of... Eddie? No, wait, Edgar? Is there an Edgar here?"

"Yes, sir, right here!" A man nervously twisting a ball cap moved forward through the crowd.

"Your name is Edgar?" said Casper.

"That's me," said the man.

"I suspect you've got a bit of money trouble, don't you?" said Casper.

"Yes, sir, I do. I need to know about Silver City," said Edgar.

"Hmm, I see it. Listen to your brother, James. He knows what's best for the farm."

"What about the trees?" said Edgar.

"That pesticide won't do nearly as much damage as those beetles. The trees will be fine," said Casper.

Edgar smiled and nodded. "Thank you, sir, thank you so much," he said as he stepped back into the crowd.

"Do I have an Eleanor? An Eleanor Rose?" cried Casper over the buzzing crowd.

"Here," a woman raised her hand.

"Well, hello, now wait, you're not Eleanor now, are you?" he said.

"No, sir, Eleanor's my daughter," said the woman.

"How does he know all this?" I said.

"He's reading his mark. It's not as hard as it looks. He has an assistant. See her over there? The lady with the big boobs in the tiny dress. That's Katrina. She takes the prayer cards from the group, reads them while no one is watching, drops them in the cauldron of fire near the tent, then directs Casper to the individuals who'd make good marks," said Harley.

"I see her, but how does she do that? She's nowhere near him," I said, wondering what it would be like to have such large breasts.

"She feeds him clues. Okay, right there, check out the lady in the green dress. Katrina is pointing her out as a mark," said Harley.

"What did she do? I didn't see anything," said Asher.

"That's the point. A good assistant is virtually invisible. She fanned her face with her left hand and then gently placed her hand on the lady's shoulder as she walked by. Now we just sit back and watch Casper do his magic," said Harley.

"Quiet down, please. Quiet down, everyone. I feel there's someone else out there. Someone needing answers." Casper lowered his head and rubbed the back of his neck. He lifted his head, scanned the crowd, and stopped when his eyes reached the woman in the green dress clutching the strap of her handbag.

"You there, the lady in green," he said. Heads jerked in unison as the woman in the dress stepped forward. Katrina returned to the woman's side and took the lady's hand in hers.

"She's come to find out about a lost love," said Harley.

"How do you know that?" I said.

"Katrina took the woman's left hand in both of hers. Hands always mean the death of a loved one. If she were to have placed her hands on the mark's shoulders, that would mean finances. Hands on her hips means finding true love and so on. See her thumbs. She placed them on top near the woman's ring finger. That signifies a lover. Thumbs placed on the mark's thumb and pinky mean children. Left-hand boy, right-hand girl. She's too old to be concerned about her own parents, but if that were the case, Katrina would have placed her hands over her heart in prayer before taking her hand," said Harley.

"It's all so subtle," I whispered.

"You're here to ask about someone deceased, correct?" said Casper.

The woman's eyes filled with tears as she nodded. The crowd buzzed.

"Quiet, please, I must think." Casper lowered his head again and wiped his eyes. "It's a recent passing, correct?" The crowd grew silent, and the lady nodded again.

"Now, if it's her husband, Katrina will caress her hair with her right hand; if it were just a lover, the left. Katrina ran her fingers through her hair on the right side of her head.

"I see someone. It's a man, wait, your husband. Is that right?" said Casper. The lady nodded her head and wiped fresh tears from her eyes.

"Yes, he was my husband," wept the woman. Katrina placed her hands on the woman's shoulders, nodded twice, and casually wiped two fingers across her brow.

"His name started with an O. Is that also correct?" said Casper. The woman's purse fell to the ground as she stumbled backward. Katrina grabbed her from under her arms and helped steady her.

"My Oscar. Can you see him? Tell him I miss him so much," she said.

"Yes, it's Oscar. He says he loves you very much and will wait in Heaven for you when it's your time. He can't wait to see you in your favorite dress. The purple one with the lilacs on the sleeves," said Casper. The woman raised her arms to the sky and smiled as tears ran down her cheeks. Her Oscar was there waiting, and she was happy. The crowd erupted in applause.

"Alright, folks, I hope you enjoyed a preview of Casper's show! Please join us inside for more psychic entertainment. Tickets are only five credits, and the show starts in ten minutes, so get your tickets now!" Katrina cried as the crowd rushed toward the entrance.

"Now, how did he know all that, the part about his name?" said Asher.

"Nodding twice means the second half of the alphabet, and two fingers across her brow means the second letter."

Asher began counting on his fingers. "I get it. The thirteenth letter is M, so the second letter of the second half is O."

"Exactly," whispered Harley. "Don't let the carnies hear you figuring that stuff out, though," he laughed.

Asher lowered his voice. "Oh, right. Sorry."

"What about the dress?" I said.

"Not sure about that. Maybe there was a picture that fell out of the purse or something. I've only really figured out a fraction of the act. Casper and Katrina are good."

"How do they remember it all?" I said.

"Years and years of practice, I assume," he said. "Anyway, I've got to get to the door and help with the tickets. You two stay out of trouble, and don't forget to listen for the stampede."

"Thanks," I said as Harley turned and walked away.

Then he stopped but didn't turn around. "Probably be better if you just went back to the grid-rail station and waited after that. That's what I'd do," he said before continuing towards Casper's tent.

"He was cute," I said.

"That he was, but how do you think he knew we were waiting for a train?" said Asher.

"I don't know. We probably mentioned it," I said.

"I don't think so. All you said was that we stumbled on this place," said Asher.

"Well, maybe he just assumed since the station is across the street," I said.

"Yeah, you're probably right," he said. I laughed and wanted to rub it in, but Asher cut me off.

"Don't even say it," he said.

ɘ Chapter 37- Carnivále

The year 2132

After Harley left to help Casper with his show, Asher and I explored the grounds while we waited for the Wonder Wheel to open. We wanted to see as much as we could and still get back to the rail station before dark, so we headed out of the gaming area along a busy path looking for the major attractions.

"Okay, so I say we hit up the freaks, then the puppies, and if we have enough time, we can check out the Kuru museum," said Asher.

"Or we can just skip the museum," I said. "I'm spooked enough as it is."

"Don't be afraid. I won't let the Spinners get you," he said.

"Do you think they have real puppies at the Puppy Pavilion?" I said.

"I think so. That's what the walking billboard claimed anyway," said Asher.

"Then I want to do that first. I've never seen a puppy before," I said.

"You've never seen a Spinner before either," he said.

"Asher!"

"Okay, puppies it is," he said.

As we ventured further into the park, we found ourselves walking alongside tall maple trees and thick flowering shrubs that bordered the yellow, cobblestone path. We even saw a deer and two turkeys wandering the grounds. In the center of the park was a circular seating area where families sat eating picnic-style. Here, the path veered off in four different directions. Each path had an ornamental street sign hanging from lanterns shaped like human skulls.

"Which way do we go?" I said. I looked at Asher and frowned. "Are you okay? You're white as a sheet."

"Stop worrying, I'm fine. I just need to sit down for a minute. That Saturn dog isn't sitting so well," Asher took a seat on a bench while I went to check out the signs and figure out the easiest way to the puppies.

As I was studying the signs, I noticed a man in full clown-face, wearing a ratty red wig, purple patchwork overalls, and a sinister smile, walking toward me. He held out his fist, then slowly opened it, exposing a bright orange piece of candy. I shook my head.

"Take it!" he commanded. Startled, I grabbed the colorful treat and jumped back as Asher raced to my side.

"What do you want?" said Asher.

"Well, well, what do we have here? Two young lovers taking an afternoon stroll, maybe?" The clown grinned, exposing a set of fangs more suitable for a wild animal than a beloved entertainer.

"We're just trying to see all the sights. Do you know where all these paths lead?" I asked.

The clown scowled and threw his hands in the air. "Do I know where the paths lead? Of course, I do," he said. "But I have to know. Where do you want to go?" The clown smiled and made a grotesque slurping noise with his tongue.

"We want to see the puppies, or the house of freaks, maybe," said Asher.

"Maybe the museum, but I'm not sure," I said.

The clown rolled his eyes as he rubbed his chin. "Hmm, your indecisiveness is rather annoying. Nevertheless, all you have to do is read the signs. It couldn't be any easier." The clown turned and pointed to each sign, rattling off directions.

"Genevieve Boulevard will take you straight to the Puppy Pavilion. The Enchanted Parkway leads to the Grand Gardens. Rapture Road is where you'll find the Kuru Museum. You can even have lunch at the Kuru café and gift shop." The clown licked his lips and grinned. "Brains, anyone?" he drawled.

Asher pointed to the last sign. "What's the Krakus?"

"What's the Krakus?" The clown frowned and slapped himself upside the head. "The Krakus is the home of the most bizarre collection of oddities and freaks known to man." The clown lowered his voice and leaned in close. "Although I've dated worse, if you know what I mean," he winked.

"What kind of freaks? Do you mean like a man with six toes? We had a handyman back home who had six toes on one foot," I said. The clown sneered and rolled his eyes.

"It's true," said Asher. "Jack Arnold used to scare us with his extra toe back when we were little."

"What?" scoffed the clown, as he furrowed his overly made-up brows and took a staggering step backward. "Who the? Six toes? No, I'm not talking about any six-toed idiot!" The clown held out his hand and wiggled his fingers as he counted down all the freaks from memory.

"I'm talking about Dora and Darlene Dupont, the dame with two heads, and Jacque the sword-swallowing war criminal. Then there's that lady with no bones, the funny-looking kid, the fat guy, and those two little fellows who like to beat each other up. I forget their names, but they are so ugly it doesn't matter! Now, my favorite is Magenta, the world's only captive unicorn."

Asher smirked and nodded for me to play along.

"But the advertisement at the front gate said World's *ONLY* unicorn. You mean there's more than just the one?" I said.

The clown winced, then slapped himself in the face again until his wig fell over his eyes. The clown pushed up his wig, adjusted his tie, and gave Asher and me the most scathing grin I'd ever seen.

"Of course, there's more than one you imbecile," he said. "That stupid sign is wrong! R-O-N-G wrong! How could he be the world's only one when there had to be others to make it? Huh? Huh, huh?"

Struggling not to burst out laughing, I covered my mouth with my hand while Asher egged the poor fellow on. "No, you're right, it all makes sense," he said.

"It makes perfect sense," spat the clown.

"Okay, well, you've been super helpful, and thanks for the poison, I mean candy," I said as Asher, and I slowly backed away from the self-loathing, argumentative clown.

"Wait. You forgot one," the clown called back. "Poppy's Lair. You can't forget about Poppy's Lair. They'll be waiting for you there tomorrow afternoon."

"Poppy's Lair?" I said.

"Yesss, that's the arena for the *Big Show*. Everyone is super excited for you two to join," he growled.

"Of course, we'll be there," said Asher as the two of us turned and quickly headed towards Genevieve's Court.

"I thought clowns were supposed to be funny?" I said.

"Me too. I never thought I'd say this, but that guy was creepier than that Loki fellow," said Asher, rubbing his forehead.

"Headache coming back?"

"A little one," he said.

"Do you want to take a break?" I said.

Asher grabbed my hand and pulled me alongside. "Nope, we're off to see the puppies and get as far away from that clown as we can."

We never saw the clown again, but it was there on the path to Genevieve's Court, where I caught another set of eyes spying on Asher and me. At first, I thought nothing of the heavyset woman staring at the two of us as we meandered along, but Asher seemed rattled.

"There she is again," he said.

"Who?" I said.

"Did you see that fat woman back there by the trees?"

"Yeah, so," I said.

"She was working the booth where Loki popped up and screamed at us, then I saw her again in the crowd at Casper's show."

"Maybe she's just having a good time," I said.

"Does she look like she's having a good time?" said Asher.

"Well, no, not really," I said, looking back at the woman standing in the trees with her arms crossed against her vast bosom. A man approached her, a tall man with a stained neck and belt with a ridiculously large buckle holding up his pants.

"Don't look, but wasn't that guy standing at the front gate when we got here?" I said. Asher casually turned and pretended to pull something from my hair.

"He was," he said. "Maybe we should go. This place is getting weirder and weirder, and I'm not feeling too hot," he said.

"Fine, but after the wheel, please," I begged. "You dragged me over here, and I haven't seen anything good yet."

"Okay, first puppies, then the wheel, then back to the rail station. We'll save the Kuru Museum and Krakus for our next visit," he said.

"Oh yeah, next time for sure," I said.

Surrounded by a beautiful pond filled with colorful fish and stoic pink birds, the Puppy Pavilion was a dainty white castle with pointed towers and a fancy arched bridge, sitting amongst a garden of stone statues of every size and shape.

"Look, Asher, it's a dog cemetery," I said.

"A cemetery, yes, but I don't think it's just for dogs. This headstone has a woman's face carved into the stone," said Asher.

"Here lies Lady Jane. Beloved friend and mother," I read.

Near the center of the courtyard stood the largest headstone. It was a cross covered in overgrown ivy. I pushed the ivy away from the front of the cross and saw *My Darling Genevieve* etched across the front of the cross next to a set of paw prints. Asher and I wandered through the rest of the garden, admiring the statues before taking our place in line near the entrance of the bridge that led to the castle.

"Should we flash our tickets and move to the front of the line?" said Asher.

"No, I don't want to stand out. The line is moving pretty fast anyway," I said. Approaching the entrance to the palace, we watched as the people in front of us shelled out credits for specialty items offered at the gate. When Asher and I arrived, we passed through without taking notice of the array of goodies, but the ticket checker stopped us, anyway.

"Don't forget your Ruby swag," he said, handing Asher and me a bag of items from the cart.

"For free?" I said.

"Of course, well, for Ruby Ticket holders it's free," he said.

"Wow, thank you," I said.

Inside the bag was a decorative Carnivále drink bottle, a small hand fan embossed with Sebastian's face, a wrapped ball of sticky-sweet popcorn, and a bag of dog treats for the 'puppy encounter' that, according to the enclosed program, would take place at the end of the tour.

"Fancy," said Asher.

"I know, I could get used to all this Ruby Ticket treatment," I said.

Asher immediately opened his bottle and took a long swig. "Try this. It's delicious," said Asher.

"It's not that gator juice again, is it?" I said.

"No, it tastes like the cola we used to get special for our camping trips back at Greyburry," he said.

"Oh, my favorite," I said as I cracked open my bottle. "Yummy!"

The tour started with a trolley ride through a maze of moving pictures of dogs of all shapes, sizes, and colors. Equipped with a microphone attached to his red cap, trolley captain Poe narrated the history of each breed and the different variations of Adlet that evolved from each one. Not having seen more than just a few photos of the Kuru-infected dogs, I was shocked to find out that just like their ancestors, Adlets, too, came in different shapes and sizes from the very tiny Chudlets and Bulldets to the freakishly awkward Ladlets and spotted Dalmadets.

After the tour, the trolley took us outside, where we disembarked and followed Captain Poe to an enclosed pavilion, where packs of playful dogs, young and old alike, ran free amongst a handful of carnival-goers. Unlike the dogs on the tour, these animals had features similar to those Captain Poe described as Beagles. We waited in line while groups of twenty took turns inside the Pavilion. When our turn came, Leo, the Puppy Enforcement Officer, led our group into a small, gated enclosure and shut us in before opening the door to the Pavilion.

"Okay, everyone, have fun and make sure you make your way over to the exit as soon as you hear the bell. No dilly-dallying, we have lots of folks who want to come through," said Leo.

Asher and I hung back as the others pushed their way inside.

"Leo, do we just give them the treats?" I said.

"Yes, they know the treats are coming, so they'll be pretty excited, so watch out," said Leo, who couldn't have been any older than the two of us, and I wondered if I could get a job here, too.

"They won't attack us, will they?" said Asher.

"Oh, they're gonna attack you, but they're harmless. Just hold the treat out, but don't tease them with it. They're not mean, but they might nip you by mistake if you don't give them the food. If you have any trouble, just call out to one of the puppy wranglers," he said.

"Okay…" I said.

"Don't look so worried, and go on in. Those dogs are just excited to play. You ain't gonna get bit or anything like that," said Leo.

Asher took my hand, and the two of us entered the Pavilion as Leo slammed the security gate shut behind us. And just as Leo warned, we were attacked by a pack of goofy fur balls begging for treats.

"Hi there. Down, down," I squealed as the onslaught of tongues and furry goodness bounced against my legs and back.

"Don't freak out. I think they can sense fear," shouted Asher.

"Don't say that," I laughed. I reached into my goodie bag and took out the dog treats.

"Gertie! Look at this one. He's dancing for his treat," cried Asher.

"Oh my goodness, you're cute and so are you," I said, handing out puppy treats to the knee-high herd of hyper dogs.

The initial attack was swift and merciless. My stash of treats vanished in seconds, including my popcorn ball, which was snatched in a sneak assault after I dropped my swag bag. Once the fuzzy beggars had cleaned me out, they scattered.

I flopped down beside Asher in the grass. We held hands as slobbering dogs licked our faces and tugged at our clothes, their joy contagious. For a moment, everything felt perfect.

Then I saw him again.

The tall man. He was speaking in hushed tones to a curly-haired wrangler near the edge of the Pavilion. They weren't watching the crowd, not the twenty guests inside or the hundred waiting to enter—just Asher and me.

I tried to tell myself it was a coincidence. But this time, I didn't believe it.

Still, I was too happy to care.

After fifteen minutes, our time was up. We left the Pavilion grinning, trailing behind the crowd toward the statue garden. Asher's hair was a mess, his shirt streaked with muddy paw prints, mine was too, but I couldn't have been happier.

"That was awesome! Maybe we should go to the museum after the freak show after all," said Asher.

"I agree! You look like you're feeling better," I said.

"Yep, that was just what I needed. I'm now getting all the hype around this place."

"Yeah, I want to see it all now, too. I hope we can hear the wheel stampede from out here," I said.

"I'm sure we can. Besides, we have plenty of time. Let's go see some freaks," said Asher.

❧ CHAPTER 38- CARNIVÁLE

The year 2132

Asher and I made our way back to the picnic area, then headed down the path that led to the Krakus to see the freak show. There was no clown, fat lady, or tall skinny cowboy lurking among the trees this time, and I was glad. There was, however, a large crowd headed in the same direction, and even though I knew we still had plenty of time before the Wonder Wheel opened, we hurried along, just in case.

I knew we were getting close, not from the view, which was nothing more than trees and dusty cobblestone, but from the resounding, steady thump of drums echoing through the air, and the rising chatter of voices drifting in from somewhere ahead.

Not long after, the Krakus rose in the distance. Sitting high on a hill, it loomed above the brush like a dark brown stain smeared across the sky. It reminded me of an old building I saw once in a picture book about China back at Greyburry.

The Krakus had to be newly built, yet it appeared old and stoic, as if a hundred years of memories were hidden inside. Its roof was layered and curved, with edges that swept upward like wings, and the tiles were dark reddish-brown with golden edges. There were four brown columns, evenly spaced along the front of the structure, giving it a grand and formal look. Just like the book, the columns were covered in etchings, but unlike the pictures, these etchings weren't of clouds, dragons, or ancient symbols. The etchings were modern and looked like the freaks advertised on many of the posters hanging in the big top.

Lanterns hung from the roof corners and swayed slightly in the breeze, while, perched overhead at the roof's highest point, two massive gargoyle statues sat with their wings tucked tight across their chests and their stone eyes locked on the crowd below.

"Look, Asher, they look hungry," I said.

"I know, probably deciding which one of us to eat first," he laughed.

Surprisingly, the freak show was more popular than the puppy show, with a line that zigzagged all the way around the building. According to the program we were handed upon arrival, the show was a walking tour, but the line didn't seem to be moving very quickly, and that didn't seem to bother anyone but Asher and me.

Fuelled by gator juice and the anticipation of the abnormal, the belligerent crowd cheered and danced, while loud music, the kind forbidden at Greyburry, blared through overhead speakers.

Ushers roamed the crowd, in identical matching suits as the other attractions, pinstriped vests, crisp collars, and gleaming brass buttons, but each one also sported a long, brown monkey tail that swayed back and forth when they walked.

"Freak show! Gator juice! Freak show! Gator juice!" Chanted the crowd.

Asher and I started for the end of the line when a particularly exuberant individual riding on the shoulders of another toppled over and nearly knocked me to the ground.

"Hey, watch it," cried Asher.

"Sorry, bro," said the shirtless man as he picked himself up and ran off.

Asher pulled me aside and tapped the pocket on his trousers.

"How about this time?" he said.

"Do it," I said.

"I'm on it," Asher pulled the Ruby Tickets from his trousers and waved them at the workers standing near the entrance. Their faces were calm, almost bored, like they'd seen this all before, but it wasn't long before they spotted Asher waving our tickets and escorted us to the front of the line and through grand wooden doors.

Inside was a wide, dimly lit hallway that seemed to go on forever. There were a few people ahead of us, so we followed, walking slowly and taking in the details one step at a time. The interior of the Krakus was just as striking as the outside, with ornate fixtures that cast dim light across deep purple walls, and heavy black curtains that framed the glass exhibits on either side of the hall. A low, unsettling melody played in the background, while the artificial sound of a giggling child resonated somewhere within the walls.

In between each exhibit hung portraits, some painted, some stitched, some whose eyes followed you as you walked, and some that seemed to shift when you looked away.

Holding tight to the back of Asher's shirt, I leaned forward and whispered. "Is it just me, or is this place creepy?"

"I think creepy is the point," said Asher.

"What happened to everyone else?" I said, noticing that we were suddenly alone.

"I don't know, I was too busy looking at the pictures, maybe we missed a door or something?" said Asher.

"I don't think so," I said, looking back from where we started.

"Well, they must have finished the tour and left," he said.

And then, just as I was about to ask if we should go back, the velvet curtain nearest us parted on its own, revealing our first freak: Madame Mavis, the Boneless Ballerina.

Startled, Asher stepped back into me, and the two of us almost toppled to the ground. We composed ourselves as a Victrola inside the glass enclosure began to play while the young dancer started to move in ways I'd never seen. She twisted, turned, and swayed to the sounds of the music, her limbs bending in ways physically impossible. It was like a rag doll had come to life right before our eyes. Then, just as abruptly as she started, Madame Mavis fell to the ground in an unrecognizable heap, and the thick velvet curtains swung shut.

Next up were the twins, Dora and Darlene Dupont. Conjoined at the torso, they shared one set of arms and legs. Two regular-sized heads sat atop their shoulders, side by side, balanced like bookends. Dora's neck tilted just a bit to the left, Darlene's to the right, giving them space to move. From the neck down, they looked almost ordinary, dressed in a single flowing dress big enough to accommodate their widened midsection and dual posture.

They sat perched on a small high-backed couch where Dora was reading, and Darlene was staring into space, bored maybe, or just somewhere else entirely.

They had no act, as far as I could tell. They didn't need one. Their mere existence was the act.

"Fake," I muttered.

"Totally," said Asher.

As if she'd heard us, Dora looked up and scowled. Then, without a word, she reached up and tore open the top of their dress, revealing a bare chest, no seams, no stitches, no sleight of hand—just one torso, smooth and uninterrupted, with two heads rising from it like a monument.

Darlene didn't move. Her gaze didn't waver. It was hard to tell if she'd even blinked.

"Yikes," said Asher, eyes wide. "Nowhere in the playbill did it mention a peep show."

I tried not to laugh, but it bubbled up anyway.

After what felt like an uncomfortable eternity, we moved on to the next act.

Gilroy the Beast.

Gilroy had muscles in places no man should, bulging knots of flesh that pulsed and twitched like they had minds of their own. Veins coiled around his limbs like ropes, and his skin gleamed under the overhead lights. He wore nothing but a pair of undersized man shorts and had a bald, glistening head. Gilroy flexed his grotesque biceps, hoisted weights that looked to be at least a thousand pounds, then pranced around the enclosure, displaying himself like a prize bull.

Next to Gilroy was Maribel the Magnificent, though she looked more frightened and sad than anything. Maribel sat alone at a small table with her crystal ball resting in front of her. Her shoulders trembled, and she did nothing but sob quietly with her face buried in her hands. The glow from the ball cast faint ripples of light across her cheeks, catching the tears as they fell. There was no performance, no fortunes—just grief.

After Maribel came Leopold and Trevor, the Dueling Dwarves, though "dueling" was a generous term for their act; the two men of short stature stood shirtless in the center of their tiny roped-off ring, their wrinkled faces scrunched in permanent scowls that made them look older than they probably were. Their torsos were pale and blotchy, speckled with old bruises and faded tattoos that looked like they'd been done in someone's bathroom with a dirty sewing needle.

They wore oversized shorts that had clearly seen better decades, frayed at the edges, stained with sweat and something darker, and cinched at the waist with mismatched shoelaces. Every few steps, one of them would trip slightly, recover, and slap the other as if the stumble had been part of the choreography.

I wondered if they were related to Loki. Not brothers, there was no resemblance beyond height, but maybe his cousins.

"You hit like a wet sock," one of them grunted.

The other guy slapped him back, slightly harder. "Your face looks like it lost a bet with gravity."

Asher leaned in, eyes wide. "Is this supposed to be a fight?"

"I have no idea what this is," I said.

The first guy stumbled dramatically. "Yeah? Well, you smell like a homeless beaver."

His opponent raised his fists, then dropped them. "Yeah? Well, well, you're shaped like a potato that was grown in someone's butt."

Asher and I just stood there, unsure whether to laugh or intervene.

"Is this the entire performance?" I giggled.

"More like a cry for help," Asher muttered.

Just then, one of them, Leopold maybe, bent over, wheezing, while the other, dripping with sweat, stumbled to a corner and slapped a ringside bell, and the curtain dropped.

"I'm scared for life," said Asher. "Not my life. Just life in general."

After the Dueling Dwarves, I was ready to leave. But Asher wanted to see a couple more acts, so we kept walking. Some of the booths never opened. One had a sign that read "Clarence the Clairvoyant – Closed Due to Premonition." Another was just a velvet curtain with a single shoe poking out from underneath.

"Must be their day off," muttered Asher.

Then we stumbled upon Jacque the Sword Swallower. No explanation needed. He swallowed a sword. We clapped. He bowed. Curtain. Next up, George the Gorge.

To say George was obese was an understatement. He sat at a table facing the glass, his body spilling over the sides of his chair. Around him rose towers of food, heaping plates of spaghetti, giant turkey legs stacked like firewood, and pies, so many pies, with crusts cracked open, oozing syrupy fillings.

George didn't speak. He didn't look up. He simply ate nonstop. His fingers, stubby and slick, moved from plate to mouth with mechanical precision. Chewing, swallowing, reaching. Again and again.

Choking back the contents of my own stomach, I grabbed Asher's arm and pulled him aside.

"I've seen enough, I think we should go," I said.

"Agreed, I'm still feeling dizzy from that gator juice, but how do we get out? Do we go back to the front?" he said.

"No, I just saw some people go that way. That's got to be the way out. Here, drink more of the stuff we got from the puppy swag bag." I said, handing Asher my half-empty bottle.

Asher and I walked to another set of larger curtains that we thought was the exit and peeked inside, where, to my shock and amazement, stood the most fantastic freak of them all.

Magenta the Unicorn.

A magnificent beast, Magenta's neon-pink skin shimmered with every movement, casting ripples of pink light across the faces of amazed spectators. His tail flicked playfully as he pranced in circles around a large roped-off paddock, hooves clicking and mane flowing in luscious waves of pink silk. His spiral horn gleamed like a white and pink candy cane dipped in glitter. Even from the back of the room, I was overwhelmed by his pink energy and wanted to get closer, but then, from the corner of my eye, I saw Loki and the tall man from the woods standing near the edge of the paddock.

"Behold Magenta, the world's only pink unicorn or any colored unicorn, for that matter!" cried Loki, his voice booming across the room.

Then the lights dimmed, and everything fell silent as a soft pink glow bathed the crowd in color. Gasps turned to cheers, hands clapped wildly, and the room pulsed with awe.

Then, just as quickly as it started, it was over.

The lights came back on just in time to see the tall man leading Magenta out the side door of the paddock and the crowd dispersing out another set of doors marked EXIT.

"Is he coming back?" I asked one of the men in the striped suits.

"Every hour on the hour," he said.

"Come on, Gertie, if there's time, we can come back after the wheel. I really want to see the museum," said Asher.

"Okay, let's go," I said reluctantly. "By Magenta," I whispered, more to myself than anyone else.

∾ CHAPTER 39- CARNIVÁLE

The year 2132

The Kuru Museum stood in stark contrast to the carnival's other attractions. Its exterior was plain and windowless, built from slabs of dull concrete that looked poured in haste and left to crack.

Where other attractions boasted colorful signs, velvet ropes, and painted banners, the museum offered nothing but a rusted plaque bolted to the wall: Kuru Museum. No subtitle, no slogan, no promise of wonder, just the name, etched deep like a warning. Given its contents, I guessed that's all it deserved.

There was no line to get in, just a thin, elderly man standing alone at the front entrance. His skin was wrinkled and gray. His red cap drooped over his small head, nearly swallowing his eyes, and I wasn't sure if he was asleep or awake until he reached out and blocked us from entering.

"No touching, no wandering off the path," he spat. "And keep your grubby hands to yourself, don't smudge the glass cases either," he said. The man lowered his arm and waved us through.

"I guess we don't need to flash these babies here," said Asher as he pocketed our Ruby Tickets.

"I guess not," I said.

Asher and I wandered through Discovery Hall; the only sound was our footsteps echoing against the cold tile floor. The walls were lined with yellowed clippings and brittle photographs, each one capturing a moment from *The Day* and the carnage that followed. We paused to read about the Cannibal War, The Darkening, and how the Treaties were created once the disease was finally contained, all events we'd memorized in Miss Grisham's history class, but nothing in those tidy lessons prepared us for the exhibits on the walls.

The exhibits were raw, unwatered-down, and told tales of what happened when the Kuru88 overtook the planet, hollowing out humanity and leaving behind ferocious, lifeless pink Spinners that ripped through communities, devouring everything in their path. Not just killers, but mindless beasts, whirling through cities like broken toys, their mouths locked open in permanent hunger.

"How could this happen? How was it *allowed* to happen?" I asked, wiping away tears. The pictures, the stories, they were too much. I felt overwhelmed, crushed by the weight of it all.

"You can't feed dead cows to live cows," whispered Asher, mimicking the farmer we'd met on the road.

"All because some people started eating sick, dead people?" I sniffled, staring at a photo too awful to look at for long.

"This one's from London, the day the Palace went down," said Asher

"Oh, look at this. The fall of Manhattan." My voice cracked. "Look at the people jumping from the buildings."

"The abandoned cargo ship Santamaria, docked in Manhattan, unleashing infected dogs, called Adlets, loose on the city," read Asher in a low voice.

"What's the date on that one?"

He leaned in. "August 15th, 2029."

"Look, every paper is dated August 15th, 2029. *The Day,*" I said.

"The last day," said Asher.

"The day the world went dark," I whispered as another tear fell from my eyes.

"Can you imagine what it was like to have lived through that, the drills, the ash, and then the darkness. What about the screenings? It's crazy to think the only reason we are here is because our relatives were one of the few to survive it all," said Asher.

"Look over there, there's an exhibit on the mandated screenings," I said.

"Wait, look, Artifact Hall, let's go in there first," said Asher.

Artifact Hall held relics from The Day, the drills, and the signing of the Treaties—each piece a fragment of the old world, preserved under dim lights and thick silence. At the center stood a towering purity cross, easily ten feet tall, rising from a dry marble fountain like a monument.

Glass cases lined the walls, displaying the tools of containment: authentic masks once used to clamp shut the mouths of the infected— heavy metal contraptions with cracked leather straps, rusted buckles, and, on some, the unmistakable imprint of teeth. Nearby, patient logs lay open, the pages filled with the tight, looping script of an Observation Rotunda nurse. A few were stained with something dark—blood, bile, or both.

And then there were the Spinners. Mummified remains, their limbs contorted in impossible shapes, bones twisted like wire. They reminded me of the ballerina from the freak show—graceless and warped into something grotesque.

"Sick," said Asher.

"I know, right?" I said.

"No, I'm getting sick, I need some fresh air," he said.

"Oh, right, let's leave," I said. "I think I've seen enough anyway."

Outside, Asher took a seat on one of the benches and put his head between his knees.

"Is there any more to drink?" He asked.

"No, but look, we could probably get some water at the little shop over there. Then I say we go back to the Wonder Wheel and wait, no more exploring. That is, if you're up to it," I said.

"I'm feeling better, just need a little water. The fresh air helped. It was all too much in there," he said.

"I get it, come on, let's get you something to drink," I said.

Inside the shop, I was surprised to see the woman working the pay register. It was the same fat lady from the walking path. The one Asher had seen numerous times before. I was about to alert Asher when out popped Loki from behind one of the gift display racks. I screamed and fell against the rack, causing a whole row of croquetted hats to fall to the floor.

"I'm so sorry, but you scared me," I said, picking up the hats.

"Oh dear, Loki can't seem to do anything right today," he said as he helped me with the hats.

"What happened now?" It was Asher.

"It was my fault. I wanted to come and apologize for my silly outburst earlier. I was just excited about the *Big Show*, is all," said Loki.

"It's okay," I said. "Nothing got broken."

"Well, I was thinking," Loki said, shifting his weight from one foot to the other. "Since you can't make the *Big Show*, I wondered if you'd let me take you on a private tour of the arena before you leave. It's the least I could do after my unacceptable behavior earlier. And, you know, for scaring the hats."

He gave a sheepish grin, then leaned in, cupping his hand to his mouth like he was about to share a secret.

"You could say you had your very own exclusive tour of Sebastian Sheets' arena," he whispered. "And if you're lucky, I might even tell you what the show's *really* about."

Asher and I exchanged glances. "Maybe we could go for a minute or two?" said Asher.

"Splendid," said Loki. "Just follow me through the back door over there. I know a shortcut."

Just then, a distinct cry of '*YEE HAW!*' and the sound of a raging stampede filled the gift shop.

"Asher, it's the Wonder Wheel! Come on, we need to go get in line now." I grabbed Asher by the hand and pulled him toward the door.

Loki clenched his fists as his contorted face turned a fiery shade of red. "What about the tour?" he cried.

"Sorry, Sir Loki, but we have to respectfully decline. Thy lady has spoken. The Wonder Wheel has trumped you," Asher laughed, curtsied to the little man, and the two of us quickly left the store and headed toward the sound of a running stampede. By the time we got to the ride, the line stretched back to the food court, but we only had to wait for one rotation to finish before we made our way onto the platform and showed the wheel attendant our tickets.

"Aha, my Ruby Ticket holders have arrived," said the attendant as he lifted the safety rail from the next car. "Now remember, keep your hands inside the car at all times, no standing, no jumping around for any reason, and have fun," said the man as he slammed an overhead bar down across our laps.

The car slowly rolled backward, then stopped so the next set of riders could board. The rocking back and forth was both terrifying and exhilarating.

"Asher, stop moving," I squealed.

"I'm not moving, you're moving," said Asher as he rocked back and forth.

"Stop, oh please stop," I said as I grabbed Asher's hand and shut my eyes.

The seat continued to rock as we slowly crept higher and higher. Finally, fully loaded, the wheel began its slow rotation, and the rocking finally stopped.

"Gertie, open your eyes and look. You can see everything from up here. The houses in town, the fields, even the ocean."

"I am not opening my eyes," I said.

"Look, you can see Casper's tent. They are getting ready for another show," he said.

I opened my eyes and leaned forward. "Where? Can you see Harley?"

"I knew it!" he said. I reached over and slapped Asher on the leg.

"Hey, watch the rocking," he said. Asher dropped my hand and wiped his face with the bottom of his shirt.

"Oh, Asher, you're turning green. Are you sure you're feeling okay?" I said.

"I'll be alright. Note to self: avoid spinning rides when you're already feeling woozy."

"Why didn't you tell me you weren't feeling well again?" I said.

"Because I knew how much you wanted to ride the wheel," he said.

"Well, the ride will be over soon, and we can go sit somewhere and get something to drink before we go back to the rail station," I said.

"Sounds like a plan," he said.

"Wow, you're right. I can see the whole town from up here. Look how big it is. That must be the fishery over there. I can see the sails on the boats," I said.

"Yep, and down there's the big top, and you can even see the grid-rail station... Wait, what the heck? Look, Gertie, there's a blue train pulling into the station. It must be the four o'clock rail, like Antoine said."

"What? That Loki lied to us?" I said.

"Of course he did. Grid rail concierge my hinny," he said.

"Asher, we need to get off this ride. If Loki lied and Antoine was telling the truth, the four o'clock is the last rail west," I said. I leaned over the top of the bar as the wheel completed its second full rotation and waved to the ride operator.

"Yeah, I'm sure Loki lied about there being an eight o'clock train, too," said Asher.

The car rolled over onto the platform, where the man who had boarded us smiled and waved from his control board.

"Having fun?" He called out.

"Sir, we need to get off," I said.

The man shook his head and pointed at his ride controls. "One more lap to go," he said.

"Oh, Asher, we're going to miss the rail," I said.

"No, we won't, but we'll have to hurry. As soon as the ride ends, be ready to run."

"I will," I said. The Wonder Wheels' last rotation took an eternity, and then we had to wait for the ride operator to empty and refill each car ahead of ours. Luckily, we were the fourth car in line, and as soon as he lifted the safety bar from our laps, Asher and I were off and running toward the front entrance, but stopped when we reached a security barrier near the bit top.

"It says entrance only," I said. "We have to find the exit."

"Or jump over it," said Asher.

"Jump over it? You can't do that, the crowd is coming through, you'll get trampled," said Loki, who'd again appeared from nowhere.

"I'm sorry, but we have to leave. The four o'clock train west just arrived," I said.

"Yeah, you said the next rail wasn't until eight," said Asher.

"Oh dear, well, I must have been confused. Why do you want to leave, anyway? We can still take that tour, and I can set you up at Happy Camper Village for the night. You can even make the *Big Show*," said Loki.

"Forget the stupid *Big Show* already. We are leaving and we are leaving now, so tell us where the exit is or get out of my way so I can find it myself," said Asher.

"My, no reason to get so angry with Loki. If you must go, the fastest way to the station is through the grid-rail tunnel on the other side of the arena. Takes you right there."

"Why should we believe you now?" I said.

"Loki has no reason to lie. How do you think everyone gets back to the station without jamming up the entrance?"

"Where is it?" said Asher.

"Next to the arena. I can show you," said Loki.

"I didn't see any tunnel at the station," said Asher.

"It's near the back. The stairwell takes you straight to the yellow platform. Not too far from blue," Loki shrugged, lowered his head, and walked away. "Or you can go find it yourself, I guess. No one ever believes Loki."

"We're sorry. We believe you now take us there. Please," I said.

"Very well, this way. I know a shortcut."

We followed Loki past the crowds to the other side of the big top on a route we'd never have known existed. Asher and I were on Loki's heels as his little legs traversed through the wooded area in the center of the park near the main attractions. We followed him through a dreadful encampment behind the Krakus, hopped over a wooden fence, and ended up just outside the arena, where workers were busy hauling a heavy wooden sign through the main entrance. Loki stopped, bent over, and wheezed.

"The tunnel is over on the other side of the arena. See the sign?" Loki huffed and puffed, then pointed a stubby finger toward a sign with dripping red letters staked in the ground next to the walking path. **Grid-Rail Station →**

"I see it," said Asher. Asher grabbed my hand, and we hurried down the path to the back of the arena.

"See, Loki got you back in plenty of time," yelled Loki as we raced toward the tunnel.

"Thank you, Loki," I cried as Asher and I raced around the arena. Passing the sign, I noticed the ground around the sign's wooden base looked freshly dug, and there were spots of red paint splattered on the dirt. I almost said something when a distant sound of a whistle blew, and Asher grabbed my hand.

"There it is. Hurry Gertie. We can make it if we run," said Asher as we came upon a heavy wooden door in the back of the arena. **Grid-Rail Tunnel Entrance Only.**

"Are you sure this is it?" I said.

"That's what the sign says," said Asher.

"But it looks like it just goes into the arena," I said. Asher grabbed the handle, opened the door, and peered inside.

"It's stairs. The tunnel goes underneath. Listen, I can hear something," said Asher.

"Welcome to the station. Please take caution when entering the platforms. Conductors will be present to take payment before departure. ALL ABOARD!"

"That's us. They're getting ready to board. Come on!" Asher and I descended the staircase and ran through the dimly lit tunnel as the overhead speakers continued to announce the upcoming departure.

"How do we know which train they're talking about?" I said.

"It has to be the blue rail. It was the only train I saw," said Asher.

"I don't know. Something doesn't seem right," I said.

"What do you mean?" He said.

"The voice on the speaker. It sounds familiar," I said. "It sounds almost like Loki?"

"You're crazy. Look, this must be it," said Asher as we came upon another door.

"Already? It doesn't seem like we've gone very far," I said. Asher pulled the door, but it wouldn't budge.

"It won't open," he grunted.

"Well, keep trying," I said. Next to the door, another speaker box rattled off instructions for the pending departure.

"Rail station, this way, continue this way to the grid-rail station. Station, station, station. Grrr, grrr, grid." The speaker crackled with static, then went silent.

"I think it's locked." Asher tugged the handle and pushed on the door. "A little help?"

"Wait, are you hearing this? The speaker keeps repeating the same instructions over and over. Like it's a stuck," I said.

"So," said Asher.

"If it's a live person, then how could it be stuck?" I reached up and wiggled the box, and it fell to the ground. The speaker burst open. Inside was a small portable recording machine.

"This isn't a speaker at all. It's a trick! Asher, we need to go back," I said.

"What the…" Just then, the door flung open, and a dark blur grabbed Asher by the shirt and flung him inside a dark room.

"Asher!"

I turned just in time to see the blur return, then something slammed into me, knocking me flat. A rag pressed hard against my mouth, soaked in a sweet, chemical stench. My nose burned. My lungs screamed. I thrashed, kicked, and clawed at the air, but the world was already slipping.

Hands gripped my ankles. I screamed, scrambled, tried to grab anything, but I was dragged backward, feet first, into the dark as the door to the tunnel slammed shut.

∾ Chapter 40- Carnivále

The year 2132

Drip. Drip. Drip.

Water kept falling from somewhere above, striking my face in slow, deliberate drops. I wiped at my forehead, but another bead landed squarely between my eyes. The dark was complete—thick, suffocating, and alive with echoes. My breathing filled it, shaky and uneven, tangled with the drip's steady rhythm.

I tried to sit up. Pain tore through my chest, a fire that forced me back down. Nausea surged, heavy and merciless, and I lay still, staring into nothing. My cheek throbbed, swollen and hot. When I touched it, my fingers came away slick. Blood. The smell clung to my skin, sharp and metallic, and the taste was bitter across my tongue.

Where am I? Not in my bed. Not back in Greyburry. Not crouched behind the fish cooler. No—this was somewhere else.

I pushed myself up on one elbow, squinting into the black. A breeze moved through, cool against my skin, carrying a smell I almost recognized. Sweet, maybe. Burnt. Smokey meats, fresh off the grill.

And then I heard it—faint, but unmistakable. Music. Laughter. The distant hum of voices rising and falling in waves. The sound of Carnivále.

It hit me all at once, the tunnel and the attack. I shot upright, heart pounding, breath catching in my throat. "Asher, where are you?" My throat burned and tasted of chemicals. The sound of chains dragging across the floor and a guttural moan from somewhere in the distance rumbled, but I couldn't see anything.

"Who's there?" I said. I reached my hand out in front of me and felt the hard, cold metal bars of a cage. I followed the iron bars until they met with a solid wall, then another before I was back to the bars. There's a soft giggle from somewhere beyond my prison.

"Asher, is that you?"

"Hush now, girly. Get back to sleep," said a man.

"Where's Asher? What have you done with him?" I screamed— more chains and growling from beyond.

"I said keep it down!" he hissed.

"Please keep quiet. Your friend is right there next to you. And here, I brought some water; you'll need it for hydration. Gator juice and special cola are yummy but not so good on the tummy or the brain," laughed another man. This voice I recognized.

"Loki? What have you done? Where are we?" I said, reaching out into the darkness. I scurried blindly across the floor and found Asher's limp body lying on his side near where I awoke. I put my hand near his mouth and felt his warm breath on my skin.

"You better not have hurt him," I wept.

"He's fine. Just go to sleep and stay quiet," said the first man.

"Yes, rest. You'll need your strength for tomorrow," said Loki.

"Strength for what?" I said, but the two of them had walked away. The last thing I heard was the slam of a door and the rattle of the chains.

I'd circled the enclosure at least ten times, searching for any way out. It wasn't large, but it was solid, two brick walls, two sides of thick iron bars spaced just wide enough to tease hope. I shoved at them, slammed my shoulder against them, even clawed at the places where the bars met the brick. Nothing gave.

Sore and out of breath, I collapsed beside Asher and curled my body around his. That's when I heard it again, the dragging chains.

I sat up fast. "Hello? Who's there?" I called out.

A scream answered. Deep and primal, definitely not human. I flinched as the sound of violent banging followed, like something trying to break free from its own cage.

I scrambled back to Asher and shook him hard until his head lifted. "Who is it? Where am I?" he muttered.

"Asher, it's me. Get up. We need to get out of here," I said.

"I think I'm gonna be sick," he said. Asher began to wretch. "Can you turn on a light or something? I can barely see you," he said.

"There isn't one. Asher, we're trapped. That Loki tricked us," I said.

"What are you talking about? Help me up," he said. I reached down and grabbed Asher's arm as he tried to stand.

"Oh, whoa, my head hurts," he said, sitting down.

"I know. They drugged us and lured us into this, this dungeon place," I said.

"Dungeon, what?" said Asher.

"Here, let me help you up so I can show you," I said, helping him to his feet.

"Over this way." I led Asher to the bars. Asher grabbed hold of the bars and shook them, but the cage didn't budge.

"Hey! Let us out of here," he shouted.

"No, don't, you have to be quiet. There's something out there. Some kind of monster or wild beast," I said.

"A monster? Come on," he said.

"It's true. Be still and listen," I said.

"I don't hear anything," he said.

"It might be sleeping," I said.

"Hey who's out there?" he yelled. I grabbed Asher and pulled him away from the bars.

"No, don't," I said.

"I don't hear… Wait, what's that?" he said as the sound of chains dragging across the floor returned, followed by a low, angry growl.

I stepped back into the center of the cage. "Asher, get away from the bars."

A door rattled, soft at first, then harder, until it slammed and shook with such force the ground beneath us trembled.

Then came the roar.

A bellow so raw and furious it tore through the dark like thunder cracking open the sky. Then the pounding stopped and the chains stilled.

"Is it gone?" said Asher.

"No, not gone, just quiet. He must be locked up, too," I said. "Oh, Asher, I'm scared!"

"Me too, but don't worry. We'll get out of here," he said.

"How?" I said. "We can't even see."

Just then, a soft glow appeared in the distance. Behind it, a shadow.

"It's coming!" I cried.

Asher grabbed my hand, and we scrambled to the back corner, away from the bars. The light grew brighter, then stopped just a few yards from our cage.

The light was faint, but I could make out the silhouette of a woman holding a small lantern. She set it down near us and lowered herself beside it. The glow spread slowly, brushing the ground in soft gold. Now I could see her clearly. She wore a long white dress, her hair tied back with a ribbon, and her bare feet tucked neatly beneath her. She didn't speak. She just sat there, calm and still, as if she'd been waiting.

"Good evening, my love," she whispered.

Chains rattled. No growling this time.

My eyes adjusted. She was seated next to a massive steel door, reinforced with a thick metal bar and three heavy locks, the kind you use when you don't want something getting out.

Near the floor, a small chute opened. Not wide, but enough to slide through a tray of food or, as we watched, a book. It slid out from inside, pushed by an unseen force.

The woman picked it up and slowly flipped through the pages.

"Asher, who is she?" I whispered.

"I don't know, but stay quiet."

"But maybe she can help us," I said.

"Just wait," he said. "We don't know who she is."

The beast was growling again, but it wasn't angry this time. It sounded longing like it wanted something.

A large hand slid out through the chute, rough, dark, and gently brushed against the woman's leg. She didn't flinch. Just adjusted the lantern beside her, opened the book, and began to read.

Asher and I stayed frozen. We didn't speak. Didn't move. Just watched as she turned page after page, her voice too soft to reach us.

After a while, she closed the book, set it aside, and took the beast's hand in both of hers. Then she lay down beside the door, curled on her side like she was settling in for sleep.

And then, the beast began to hum. Low at first, then rising into a song.

It wasn't a song of rage. It was something else. Something sweet.

"Asher, listen. He's singing to her," I said.

"So that's a person in there?" said Asher.

"Yes, a man, I think, but I wonder why he's locked up?" I said. The beast continued to sing as he stroked the woman's leg. Memorized by the interaction between the two, I didn't notice new light entering the room.

"Look, the sun's coming up," said Asher.

As if startled by the emerging light, the woman got up, wiped away a tear, and quietly disappeared down the same path from where she came. The man-beast moaned as he retrieved his book and slipped his hand back inside his room.

"Asher, we should have stopped her," I cried.

"No, she knew we were here," he said.

"What do you mean?" I said, but Asher didn't answer. He was busy surveying our newly lit surroundings.

"You were right about one thing. We're in a dungeon, all right," he said as he paced back and forth. "But not a prison. They built this cage after the fact, and the room with the beast is new, so is the door," he said.

"How do you know?" I said.

"The concrete doesn't match. Neither does the hardware on the beast's door. It's newer than the door to the tunnel we came through. So is this one," he said, rattling the heavy iron door in front of him.

"So, what's this place for?" I said.

"I don't know, but I think we're under the arena. Remember the stairs we went down, thinking it was the tunnel to the railway station?

Look to the left. That opening leads to the outside. I can see the sky just beyond the stairs."

I looked to my left and saw what Asher was talking about—a large open exit with stairs leading up to the outside. I hadn't noticed it before because of the darkness.

"Is it a way out?" I said.

Asher gripped the bars and pulled himself up, squinting through the gloom.

"Looks like the arena," he said. "If that's true, there'll be exits all around, for the crowd, at least."

He dropped back down, landing hard. A grimace twisted his face as he clutched his ribs.

"You're hurt," I said.

"It's nothing. Just a couple broken ribs, I think." He lifted his shirt.

I gasped. His ribcage was blackened, bruises blooming like ink beneath his skin.

"Oh, Asher… you need help."

"Yeah, well, first we need to get out of here."

"I know, but how?" I asked, voice cracking.

He stepped closer, placed his hands on my shoulders, and looked me straight in the eyes. "Hey. No crying. We can do this. We have to focus. Can you do that for me?"

I nodded.

"Good. It looks like there are three ways. The door to our right. That has to lead to the underground tunnel where we came in from. I can see the drag marks on the floor. Then down that hall where the woman came through, not sure where that goes though, and up these stairs leading to the arena," he said.

"We're not going anywhere until we get out of this cage first," I said.

"I know," he said.

Joining Asher at the gate, I stood on my tiptoes and peered out into the arena, but all I could see was the top of the bleachers and bright orange flags waving from atop the perimeter wall.

"What's the writing on the flags?" I said.

"I think they say Feast," he said.

"Feast? Is that the name of the stupid show?" I said.

"I guess so," he said. "We need to find something to pry open this lock. Wait, where are our packs? They're missing."

Asher was right. Our two packs with all our stuff were missing. I hadn't even noticed. I reached around my neck and let out a sigh of relief

as I felt the familiar cloth of my swaddle. I took it off and shoved it in
my back pocket for safety.

"They must have taken them," I said.

"Dang it, I had a knife in there. I could have used it to pick the lock.
Look around, there has to be something here," he said.

"There's nothing," I said

"Maybe we can loosen the door if we both push on it?" said Asher
as he slammed himself into the cage door, but it didn't budge or give
even the slightest. Growling erupted from the beast as Asher screamed in
pain and fell to the ground.

"Asher, stop, you're going to hurt yourself even worse," I said.

I sat down next to my wounded friend and leaned against his
shoulder. "What are we going to do?"

"For one, we're going to stay calm. The sun's coming up. Someone
will be here soon," he said.

"And then what?" I said.

Asher groaned, lay down on his back, and stared at the ceiling. "I
don't know."

I knew Asher was hurting, and rest was the only thing that might
help. I curled up under his arm, careful not to press against his ribs, and
waited for his breathing to slow.

It didn't take long. The sharp, uneven gasps softened into a steady
rhythm, then into a low snore.

I let myself relax, just for a moment. The fear was still there,
humming beneath the surface, but my body gave in.

Sleep took me before I could fight it.

~ CHAPTER 41- CARNIVÁLE

The year 2132

He didn't speak. Just stood there, barefoot on the cold stone floor, eyes too large for his face, watching me. I could smell the bread he carried, and saw a small water jug sitting on the ground near his feet. My mouth began to drool.

I reached for the bars, slow and quiet, and the young boy flinched.

"I won't hurt you," I whispered.

He slid the jug and the loaf through the gap beneath the bars, then turned and walked away without a word.

"My name is Gertie," I said, keeping my voice low. "I'm a friend. Do you have the key to the door?"

The chains behind the beast's door clanged, sharp and sudden, like a warning.

The boy flinched. His eyes darted to the door, then back at me.

Without a word, he turned and bolted up the stairs to the arena and disappeared.

I grabbed the jug and drank nearly half of its contents before I remembered Asher. I tried to rouse him, nudging the rim to his lips, but he didn't stir, so I sat and watched him sleep.

Not long after, the woman returned, dragging a dead rabbit by its feet. Its ears scraped the floor as she walked, and its neck was torn open, leaving a bloody trail behind her. She stopped at the chute near the beast's door and dropped the carcass on the ground.

Chains groaned. The hand emerged again, human for sure, I could see that now, but deformed and trembling with hunger. It snatched the rabbit and vanished.

The woman stood with her back to me, humming something soft. She'd changed clothes: no longer the white frock, but a long gray blouse and a long black skirt, the hem brushed the tops of her bare feet.

I waited. She didn't turn around.

"I know you can see me. Come back and talk to me, please," I begged. "Help us get out of here. We just want to go home." The beast growled and began beating on the door. I rushed to the cage door, grabbed the bars, pushed my face in between the bars, and screamed.

"Look at me! Do you see me now?"

The woman turned, her face expressionless. Her straight brown hair slipped past her shoulders, catching what little light remained. She was beautiful—striking, even. Her full red lips were perfectly shaped, and her deep brown eyes held steady against the stillness of her face. Yet within those eyes lingered something hidden, something dark, a shadow I could not name. And with it came a flicker of recognition, a familiarity that made my stomach twist.

"Quiet now, they will be here soon," she said softly.

"Who?" I said. "What is going on?"

"The production team, of course. Today's the *Big Show*. Don't worry, dear, Loki will make sure everything goes as planned. Now, be a good girl and keep quiet. Today's a big day, and my Sebastian needs his rest."

The woman turned, pressed her forehead against the door, and sighed. The beast growled.

"Now, now by love. Soon, very soon."

❧ Chapter 42 - Carnivále

The year 2132

"Wake up, Gertie," cooed the woman as she gently brushed the hair from my eyes. She was smiling down at me. This time, there was something different about the woman who'd haunted me my entire life. This time I saw her face, and although I couldn't figure out where, I knew I'd seen her before. Then realized it was the woman with the rabbit.

"Are you ready to eat, baby girl?" The woman lifted her arm to her mouth, took a deep bite into her wrist until her blood oozed, then held her arm to my mouth.

"No!" I screamed and bolted upright, nearly knocking Asher backward.

"Hey, are you alright? You've been out cold for over an hour," he whispered.

"What? I was asleep?" I stuttered as the familiar achy fog of gator poison flooded my head.

"Keep it down over there. You don't want to wake up his majesty," said a man.

"Who is that?" I said.

"It's the tall man from the park," whispered Asher. "They're all here, plus a few I've never seen. Some kind of meeting of the creeps."

"Production team," I muttered.

"What?" said Asher.

"I said y'all keep it down," shouted the tall man. I waited for the rattling of the chains and nasal growl of the beast, but the room was silent. My eyes focused, and I noticed the overturned jug of water near the cage door.

"Oh, Asher, you didn't drink that, did you?" I said.

"No, I dumped it out. I'm guessing you did, though," he said.

"Yeah, a little," I said as I rubbed my eyes and looked around.

Near the arena's entrance sat a plain wooden table, its edges worn smooth from use. Around it sat familiar faces from the day before: the tall man, the fat lady from the store, the puppy wrangler from the Pavilion, and two new figures I hadn't seen before had joined them, a man with a monkey perched on his shoulder and a large man with huge muscles.

The muscular man sat quietly, his broad frame filling his chair. His shirt stretched tight across his arms, and his hands, thick and rough, rested on the table in front of him. They played cards in silence, the young boy who had left the water now sat beside them, plucking grapes from a bowl and feeding them one by one to the monkey. The monkey's tail curled like a question mark, flicking now and then as it ate grapes and watched the group.

Beside the table stood a tall golden statue shaped in the likeness of Sebastian Sheets, though something about it felt off. The surface gleamed too smoothly, too perfectly. The face was blank, and the eyes were nothing but hollow sockets cut into the gold.

Then I realized it wasn't a statue at all. It was a coffin shaped like a man. And whatever was inside was alive, watching us through the emptiness.

Beside it, the door where the beast had been hung open, spilling only darkness.

Bored with the grapes, the monkey jumped off the man's shoulder and clambered to the cage.

"Hey, little fellow, want some bread?" Asher tore a piece from the loaf and tossed it to the monkey. The bread hit the monkey's arm and fell to the ground.

"Git away from there, Clyde," said the man whose shoulder the monkey had been sitting on. Ignoring the tiny offering, the monkey snatched the entire loaf from Asher's hand and ran back to his master's shoulder.

"When did they get here?" I whispered

"I don't know. Early, I guess. They were here when I woke up," said Asher.

"Was that thing here the whole time?" I said.

"What, that statue? No, I don't think so, but it was dark, so maybe," he said.

Outside in the arena, the sound of Loki's voice shouting orders over the sounds of hammers and drills grew louder until he emerged from the stairwell carrying a rolled-up spool of cable.

"Games? Are you playing games right now? We have a show to put on." Loki dropped the spool of wire on the ground near the monkey man's feet.

"Relax, little man, we got plenty of time," said the man.

"Time, Boris? No time. Where is the sound? Where are my dogs? I need those hounds moved before the gates open," said Loki.

"D-don't worry, the mutts are ready. We've got hours before the g-gates open," stammered the puppy wrangler.

Loki's arms shot skyward, his scowl twisting into something wild. "Hours? Only hours?" His voice cracked, rising into a shriek. "Cowboy, what about the serum?"

The tall man gestured towards a box sitting under the card table. "Ready, sir."

"Extra darts, as we said?" said Loki.

"Extra, extra," said Cowboy.

"And the props for the second act?" said Loki.

"The props and scenes for the second act are ready. Got the transition down to forty seconds. We just need to make sure the actors are ready once the scenery is in place," said the monkey man named Boris.

"Oh, they will be ready, alright," Loki purred. He lifted his hands and wiggled his fingers in heated delight, as though savoring the chaos to come.

"Okay, guys, enough messing around. You need to let us out of here now!" Asher demanded.

Loki rolled his eyes, flicking his hand as if brushing away a bad smell. "Oh, bravo, bravo, darling. So much passion for such a whiner. Save a little something for the arena," he snorted.

"Listen here, you little twerp…" Asher snapped.

The jab at his height made Loki's face twist with fury. He darted to the bars, jabbing his stubby finger through the cage and hissing like a snake.

"No, you listen. Shut up and do what I say, or I'll feed you to Sebastian." His grin widened as he nodded toward the coffin, eyes glittering with cruel delight.

"Sebastian's inside that coffin thing?" I said.

The tall man named Cowboy laughed. "Hey Tershy, what's that there coffin thing called again?"

"It's called a sarcophagus," said a man entering the room. He must have been Tershy. I recognized him from the Wonder Wheel.

"The ancient Egyptians used them to bury their leaders. They believed it would protect their spirit and keep it near the living. I made this one here special for old Sebastian. Turned out pretty nice, don't you think?"

"So is he dead?" I said.

"Oh no, this is just for fun. You know so that he can watch the show," he said.

"Why can't he watch like everyone else?" said Asher.

"Not for you to worry about," said Loki as he turned and huffed his way to the table and took a seat.

"Oh, I'm not worried, but you should be. I'm warning you. Let us go now or else," said Asher.

Boris jumped to his feet, rushed to the cage, and grinned. "You got plenty to worry about, boy. You ever seen a Spinner? A real one?" he drawled.

"No, let us out of here. You're all going to be in serious trouble," I said.

"Oh no, we're going to be in trouble," Boris mocked as he pulled a syringe from his belt and waved it at me between the bars. "Keep quiet, or I'll put you to sleep again. This time, with this."

Asher stepped in front of me. "Leave her alone."

Boris laughed, slid the syringe back into his belt, then drove his fist through the bars, catching Asher hard in the cheek. Asher flew backward and hit the floor hard.

"Asher!" I dropped to my knees beside him, reaching out as he groaned and rolled onto his side.

"I'm okay," he muttered, pushing himself upright with a wince. His cheek was already swelling, a deep red blooming beneath the skin.

I hovered close, unsure whether to touch him or give him space. The bars still loomed behind us, where Boris stood laughing.

Loki smirked, wagging a finger as if scolding a child. "Oh, don't cry to Loki. Sorry if the accommodations aren't up to your precious standards, but you're the ones who turned your noses up at Happy Camper Village. You're the ones who tried to scurry back to the station. This mess? It's yours, not mine."

"So all this so we can watch some stupid show?" I said. The sarcophagus rattled.

Loki's eyes lit up as he smiled the most gruesome smile. "Not watch. Star!"

"What does that mean?" I said, but Loki paid no attention. He placed his hand across his heart and looked to the fat lady.

"Miss Alice, please go help Miss Poppy with her outfit. She may need some assistance, what with all the fuss. Make sure she gets a little dose of Poison if you have to," he said.

Alice snorted as she pulled herself to her feet. "If I know Poppy, she's already had several little doses by now, but I'll make sure she is ready on time."

"Thank you, Miss Alice," said Loki.

Asher jumped to his feet and began banging his fists against the cage door. "Listen to me! You're crazy, all of you are crazy!" The sarcophagus shook and growled.

"Careful now. He doesn't like it when people call him crazy," said Alice as she walked up the stairs and disappeared into the arena.

Loki sighed and took a seat at the table. "Morning, Mr. Sebastian, don't you worry. Loki's got this all under control."

"My friend." Sebastian's first words sent chills up my spine. His voice was raspy and raw, like a wild animal taught to speak.

"I am your friend," said Loki.

"Where'd you get those two anyway?" said Cowboy.

"At the grid-rail station," said Loki.

"I told you to stop poaching over at the station," said Boris.

"No worry, they were alone, no friends or family this time," said Loki.

"I don't know. They look young and awfully clean. Somebody's bound to be looking for them," said Tershy.

"Well, there isn't," said Loki.

"What happened to those two loners we found?" said Boris.

Loki scowled. "Oh, those two dimwits went and jimmied the lock on the cage and got out. Stupid fools tried to escape through Sebastian's room by mistake. Took me three whole days to clean that mess."

"And the others?" said the strong man.

"I had to move them to the paddock on the other side to make room for these two. Now, no more questions." Loki stood up and swiped his hand across the table, scattering the playing cards to the floor.

"Enough fun! Everyone get to work now, no more time to play. We have work to do before the show, and I want to do a complete rehearsal for the first act."

Boris rolled his eyes and stood up. "Anything you say, boss man."

"I'll go get the dogs," said the puppy wrangler.

"That's more like it, and deliver this cable to Mr. Chuckery. The projector's been bugging out, and I want to make sure we get it smooth. Come on now, we have a show to put on!" Loki wobbled up the stairs to the arena and resumed barking orders to the outdoor crew as the card players scattered to their assigned posts.

❧ Chapter 43- Carnivále

The year 2132

We spent the morning clawing at every possibility. We fought with the gate lock, tested the hinges, and whispered frantic strategies between the rush of footsteps. But the door to the cage held firm, and the room never emptied. The card players from earlier passed in and out without a glance, their faces blank with purpose, as if we weren't even there.

Eventually, the fight drained out of us, and we retreated to the corner like wounded animals. I sank to the floor, knees buckling, hands pressed to my face to hide the tears that had been threatening for hours.

"Hey," Asher murmured, crouching beside me. His voice was low, steady. "Don't do that. We'll figure it out."

He didn't sound convinced. But he was trying, for both of us.

"How, Asher?" I sobbed.

"Since we can't break out, we need to find out what they plan to do with us," he said.

"How are we going to do that?" I said.

"It's got something to do with the show, that's for sure. Just listen," he said.

Out in the arena, loudspeakers crackled and spat, then roared to life, drowning the sounds of Carnivále in a wash of static and Sebastian's recorded voice.

"Welcome… to Feast."

There was a pause. Then a wave of loud electronic noise hit, timed with the sound of a ship's propeller. It was so strong it shook the floor. The narration started again. Sebastian's voice, calm and serious, as he tells the story of a transit ship heading to America.

Across the room, the real Sebastian stood humming and growling to himself, like someone in a trance.

The speakers cut out. The workers shouted.

"Is that too loud? It seems really loud."

"It won't be once the arena's full," another replied.

"Rerun the ocean acoustics. Do the waves sound okay?"

"Sounds like the ocean!"

"Are the actors coming out to practice again?"

"Nope. We're just running the narration today."

"Really?"

"That's what the little man said."

"Okay, start the score for the first act. Hey, Cowboy, where do you want the dogs?"

"Over in the back, no one touches them but Rake or me. We'll put them in place before the show. Once we hit the scene where the container is open, no one, I mean no one except the actors, can be on the stage," said Cowboy.

"Aye, aye. Orchestra ready? Que the music!"

The orchestra played for three scores before fading out as Sebastian's sultry voice returned.

"What no one knew was that something sinister was lying in wait." The steel drums rumbled a low, ominous boom.

"I thought we cut that part," cried a voice.

"Cut, take a break!"

"What is all that?" I said.

"That's the show. They're recreating the voyage of the Santamaria when the dogs onboard turned to Adlets and killed the crew," said Asher.

"Like the stories from the museum?" I said.

"That's what it sounds like," he said.

It was then that we heard the barking, actually barking, not a recording.

"Do you hear that?" I said.

"Yeah, it's the dogs," he said

"You don't think they're going to hurt them, do you?" I said.

"I don't know," said Asher.

The pounding of the steel drums returned as trumpets blared. Then the arena fell silent.

"Time?" shouted Loki.

"Twenty-eight minutes," said a man.

"Twenty-eight minutes? No good, I need forty-five," said Loki.

"Altogether, the first act should be over forty. No saying for sure, though, because we've never run the final scene all the way through. No point really without the dogs," said a man.

"Right, right. Quick break, then we clear the floor and run the set for Act two," yelled Loki.

The arena fell silent, and Sebastian's growl from inside the Sarcofogus returned. I couldn't stop staring at the sarcophagus.

"Asher, I think we're supposed to die here," I said. Asher didn't respond. "This isn't a show. I really think they plan to kill us," I said.

"But how? Why? None of this makes sense," he said.

"It's Sebastian. He's sick. I think it's the Kuru."

Asher frowned. "There's no way."

"Then why do they have him locked up? Did you see his eyes?" I whispered. "They're pink."

"I don't—" Asher stopped as the sarcophagus began to shake.

Something inside, Sebastian, or a version of the man, pressed against the lid. A pink glow leaked through the holes, and two eyes stared out. Then came a laugh, low, strange, and cruel. It sounded frightfully amused and incredibly hungry.

… CHAPTER 44- CARNIVÁLE

The year 2132

Asher turned away sharply. "Stop staring at him," he muttered. "He's just trying to scare us, and you're letting him."

The tears came harder now.

"You have to be tough, okay?" Asher said. "We might have to…"

He didn't finish. But I knew what he meant.

"At some point, they're going to let us out of here to be in their stupid show. That's when we make our move," said Asher.

"But how? We don't know if that's the plan, and if it is, what if we can't get out of the arena? What if that's locked too?" I said.

"I'm pretty sure. So think about it. There's gonna be at least a thousand people here for the show. They can't do anything to us; there will be too many witnesses, and they will have to let us go. All we have to do is get someone to listen to us," he said.

"I didn't think about that," I said. Asher's reasoning was comforting.

Just then, two men entered with a dolly. They carefully loaded the sarcophagus and wheeled it down the hallway and out of the dungeon. I let out a sigh of relief.

"Where do you think they're taking him?" I said.

Asher stood, walked over to the cage door, and pulled himself up. "Don't know and I don't care. Look, it's getting late. This show must be starting soon," he said.

"How do you know?" I said.

"Listen. Do you hear that?" said Asher.

I stopped and held my breath, and listened to the sound of stampeding buffalo and a familiar 'Yee Haw!'

"It's the Wonder Wheel!" I said. "What time did it start yesterday?"

"Not till almost four, but remember, Harley said it normally opens around noon, so we only have two hours left until the *Big Show*," said Asher.

The words had barely left his mouth when Loki swept down the stairs, draped in a pristine, black jacket with tails that brushed the floor. A sequined red cummerbund glittered at his waist, and a top hat so tall it nearly made him look normal-sized perched on his head. He strutted across the room in theatrical circles before halting, eyes fixed on the stairs that led to the arena.

Asher snorted, leaning back against the bars. "Well, well… look at you. A turd in costume, all dolled up for the *Big Show*. Shame the sequins can't hide the stink."

Loki hissed but let Asher's jab slide. "Where are my ushers?" he cried.

At once, twenty men came racing down the stairs, grins stretched ear to ear. They snapped into formation, each one clad in identical red vests and black slacks.

Loki strutted past them like a ringmaster, pausing now and then to flick lint from a pant leg, his stubby fingers fussing.

"Nice, very nice. Wait, Ponty, is that gum in your mouth?" he said.

The usher named Ponty nodded and spat the gum to the ground. "Sorry, Sir."

"On the ground?" cried Loki. "At least stick it behind your ear, gum don't grow on trees, you know." Loki bent down, picked up the gum, and popped it in his mouth. "Now, where was I? Oh, right. Concessions!"

At Loki's cue, another swarm of men in bright yellow shirts and matching caps burst into the room. They moved with rehearsed precision, each strapped into a wooden tray rigged around their necks and waists. The trays were hands-free, lined with rows of empty cups that clinked softly as they fell into formation.

"Excellent," Loki said, plucking a cup from the nearest tray. "Now listen up. I want every guest to have a drink the moment they sit down."

He reached into his jacket, pulled out a silver flask, and poured a stream of bright blue liquid into the cup. Without hesitation, he downed it, wiped his mouth, and grinned.

"Even the children?" asked one of the vendors.

"Yes, even the kiddies," said Loki.

"What if they don't want one?" asked another vendor.

"They will want one. It's free, everyone wants free," Loki said. "After that, we run the rows selling these…"

He ducked beneath the table and emerged with a box filled with toy trinkets, pins, funny glasses, and cola bottles like the ones Asher and I received in our swag bag.

"Two credits each," he said. "Annnd. Whoever sells the most gets a reward!"

The men exchanged glances, then grinned. Not one of them asked what was in the drink.

"They're giving gator juice to kids?" I whispered.

"No, the gator juice was green. That stuff is blue," he said.

"So what is it?" I said.

"I don't know, it might just be fruit punch or something," said Asher.

"I doubt that," I said. One of the ushers turned to face us.

"Help us, please help us! They won't let us out of this cage," I cried.

"Are they alright, sir?" said the usher. "They say they need help."

"Pay no attention to those two, they're in character. Pay attention to Loki only, or you'll get no pay. Does everyone hear?"

"Yes, sir," cried the group.

"And you two, save it for the arena. If not, maybe Boris can come back and help you again with your lines?" winked Loki.

Asher took my hand and shook his head.

"Good. Now listen, we have one hour till the gates open and two hours till showtime—ushers, at your gates in twenty minutes. Concession, find your captains, collect your elixirs, and take your stations. Quick, quick!" Loki clapped his hands, and the men raced up the stairs, leaving Asher and me alone with Loki for the first time.

"These costumes are for you. Put them on." Loki tossed a folded pile of garments into the cage, his tone sharp, no trace of playfulness.

Asher kicked the clothes back and scowled. "We're not putting these on. We're not doing anything until you let us out of here so we can go home."

Loki's sigh was heavy, edged with impatience. "You'll go home when the show is over. That's the only way."

"You're lying," I said.

"Open the cage!" Asher shouted.

Loki's jaw tightened. He stepped closer, his voice low and hard. "Enough. I've tolerated your whining long enough. You'll do as I say, or you'll learn what happens when I run out of patience.

Now put these on, pretty please. Look, these are your costumes for the show—second act. Pretty pretty," Loki smiled and nodded towards the clothes as he kicked them back into the cage.

"We don't want your stupid costumes," I said.

Loki huffed and stomped his feet. "Why does everything have to be a quarrel with you, two? No, Loki, I don't want to see the *Big Show*. No, Loki, we don't want to stay free at Happy Camper Village. No, no, no!

Sebastian will not be pleased if you don't wear the costumes!" Loki's face had turned dark red, and his eyes bulged from his skull.

Asher walked to the cage door and bent over until he was face-to-face with the little man.

"Tell Sebastian to shove it," he said.

Loki clenched his fists, and his face twisted in anger. "Well, don't come crying to me when you don't match everyone else," he cried as he turned and stormed out into the arena.

"Whose everyone else?" I yelled, but he was already gone. I picked up a costume and held it up. It was a long, brown tunic-style shirt frayed around the edges with dark brown trousers.

"So what is it, some peasant uniform?" said Asher.

"I don't know, but it stinks. Here, take a whiff," I said, tossing the shirt to Asher. He jumped away, and the shirt fell to the ground.

"No, thank you. It looks like something a Loki might wear to bury treasure," said Asher.

I took my swaddle out of my back pocket and tied it back around my neck.

"We need it for good luck," I said. Asher smiled and reached over and tied it for me.

"Don't want to lose this," he said.

After that, things inside our dungeon got loud. With little time left before the show, our private prison became the staging area for the show staff and players. Men dressed as sailors raced about fixing each other's costumes and hair. No one paid any attention to Asher and me except Boris, who stood guard near the cage door.

Then, just as suddenly, they were gone. All but Boris, that is.

Moments later, Loki returned, trailed by the rest of the card-playing companions from that morning. They gathered in a loose circle. The fat lady named Alice stepped forward and recited a prayer; her voice trembled as she spoke. When she finished, the group embraced, eyes wet, faces drawn. One by one, they drifted off to their assigned roles.

Only Loki and the muscle-man, whose name I learned was Sven, remained.

Loki stood still, his gaze fixed somewhere beyond us. He said nothing. His face was pale, eyes rimmed with something that looked like fear or regret, maybe. For a fleeting moment, I felt sorry for him.

"Come now, little man. It's time," said Sven. Loki let out a heavy sigh.

"Time, now? I guess you're right." Loki looked worried.

"We owe it to Sebastian, and you don't want to disappoint Miss Poppy, now do you?" Sven sighed and wiped an eye. "And Lady Jane, of course."

"Yes, of course. I remember my promises." Loki straightened his jacket.

"Places, everyone, places," he whispered.

Loki looked at Asher and me, gave a sad smile, and slowly ascended the stairs while Sven came to our cage, took out a key from his pocket, and unlocked the door.

❧ Chapter 45- Carnivále

The year 2132

Sven tied our wrists with coarse rope and marched us through narrow corridors. We climbed cement stairs, passed flickering lights, until we reached an observation deck, high above the arena, just above the dungeon. Sven said nothing. His grip was steady, his pace unchanging. We didn't dare try to run. Not yet. I saw it in Asher's eyes. He was already working angles, already halfway to escape. So like Asher. I stayed silent and waited, letting him think.

From above, the arena didn't look real. The air was cooler up here, and everything below felt far away and fake. The guests walked in perfect rhythm, their steps matching the soft hum of the speakers. Their laughter floated up, but it sounded fake, like it came from a recording.

The drink shimmered blue in their cups. Some sipped eagerly. Others hesitated, then gave in. No one refused.

"They look drugged," Asher whispered.

I nodded. It was apparent now. The crowd's faces slackened after that first sip, smiles stretching wider, shoulders easing. They leaned forward in their seats, expectant, ready for whatever was about to begin—the Big Show.

Below us, the ushers moved about, adjusting lights and whispering instructions to the dazed crowd. The vendors darted between rows, their trays clinking softly, their faces blank.

And then the music started.

Beyond the arena, the Wonder Wheel turned slowly, its spokes catching the sunlight. The gold-and-red stripes of the big top shimmered in the afternoon sun, and just past the treeline, the Krakus loomed.

There were three viewing decks in total, each staffed by a silent, armed guard. Our guard stood like a statue next to Sven, eyes fixed on the crowd below. I wanted to ask why there was a need for armed security, but I was too afraid of the answer, so I didn't.

Overhead, the sun shinned bright, but the stage floor, sitting at least twenty feet below ground level, remained cloaked in shadows and fake fog.

In the stands, credits exchanged hands in a last-minute frenzy to snatch up the last of the trinkets bearing the name Sebastian Sheets.

Today was the only showing—the world-famous *Big Show*. And the crowd all wanted a piece of it.

Directly across the arena, above an archway identical to the one leading to our dungeon, sat a grand balcony perched like a crown. The balcony was draped in rich red curtains that billowed in the breeze. Tall ceramic pots lined the edges, overflowing with bright blue and yellow flowers.

There were two thrones carved from dark wood. In the leftmost seat sat a woman so beautiful and proud, I almost didn't recognize her. She wore a floral gown that shimmered with every movement. The bright red slippers that peeked from beneath the hem of her dress sparkled in the sun. Her long brown hair spilled down the front of her dress, gleaming as she absently stroked its ends with one hand.

Above her, affixed beneath one of the armed guard posts, hung a sign carved from polished wood and etched in curling script:

Poppies Lair

"Look, that's the lady from last night," whispered Asher.

"She must be Poppy," I said.

"She's the lady from the posters, alright. I recognize her now," said Asher.

"She's beautiful," I said.

"I didn't notice it before, but she kind of looks like you," said Asher.

The woman kept playing with her hair, then tugged at the seam of her sleeve. She looked nervous, or maybe just bored. Then she turned and smiled as the men pushing Sebastian's sarcophagus arrived and set it into place between the two thrones.

A few minutes later, Loki appeared. He took the seat on the opposite throne. Once seated, he raised a hand, and two trumpeters stepped out onto the walls flanking the arena. They stood tall, horns ready, waiting for the signal.

The crowd quieted. The fog on the stage thickened. Something was about to begin.

The arena was nearly full now, a sea of faces stretching in every direction. It reminded me of our plan.

"Should we call out to someone?" I whispered.

"Not as long as he's here," Asher said, nodding toward Sven.

Sven didn't speak. He didn't need to. The gun shoved into the back of his belt spoke for him. He just stood there, watching us.

Asher shifted beside me, trying not to look nervous.

We weren't going anywhere. Not with Sven guarding us. So we did the only thing we could. We stayed put.

Below us, the trumpeters raised their horns. A sharp blast echoed through the arena, signaling the start of the show. Just beneath our perch sat a full orchestra of strings, brass, and a conductor waving his baton like he was casting spells.

Then came the violins. A high, trembling screech that cut through the chatter and made the crowd settle into their seats. The sound faded, replaced by a playful piano melody. Overhead, the lights dimmed, casting the arena in a soft, expectant glow.

"I think it's starting," I whispered.

"Yep," Asher said, eyes fixed on the stage. "Look at that."

High above the stage floor, a peculiar purple light appeared, tiny at first, flickering like a dying star. Then it sharpened into a perfect circle, spinning wildly as it zipped across the arena. It danced overhead, dipped low into the crowd, teasing the audience with sudden dives and dazzling loops. Each movement drew gasps and laughter, leaving the audience in awe.

The glowing orb settled near the center of the arena floor, hovering midair amongst the fog. The orchestra erupted into sound as the orb stretched and spun, twisting into vibrant ribbons of red and gold. The colors spiraled, folding into themselves, until Sebastian Sheets emerged, his arms outstretched, his robe billowing, and his hair flowing like a brunette waterfall.

Sebastian hovered above the stage, radiant and theatrical, spinning slowly as he blew kisses to the roaring crowd. Their cheers rose like a tide, echoing through the arena with a fevered intensity that could've reached the fishery and beyond. The light around him pulsed unnaturally, and the air felt charged—like the moment before a storm. The crowd kept cheering, louder and louder, as if they couldn't stop.

I imagined Antoine out in his boat, jolted awake by the noise, his Cap'n Carl hat pulled low over his eyes, muttering curses at the Carnivále he'd warned us about.

The music swelled, lifting Sebastian higher until he hovered just over the highest peak of the arena, arms outstretched like a saint. The crowd was clapping, shouting, and some even wept with joy. It was as if they'd waited their whole lives for this moment, and now that it was here, they couldn't contain themselves.

Sebastian twirled slowly, his red robe flaring out like a flame. He winked at the audience, then gestured toward the balcony where Poppy sat. She raised a bejeweled goblet in response, her smile unchanged, frozen in that same lifeless curve. Loki remained still beside her, his eyes locked on Sebastian.

Below, the orchestra shifted again, violins returning with a trembling urgency, brass swelling like a storm. The purple light that had birthed Sebastian now pulsed behind him, then disappeared.

"How are they doing that?" I asked, staring at the glowing figure floating above the arena.

"It's called a holo something," Asher said.

"It's a hologram," Sven grumbled.

"Oh yeah, hologram. See that projector up there?" Asher motioned with his head. "It shoots laser beams to make images that look real."

"Like a movie?" I asked.

"Kind of," he said. "But without a screen. It's three-dimensional, like a real person. We learned about it in third-year science."

Sebastian's image continued to float, then stopped midair and composed itself. The crowd fell silent as he began to speak. His voice was deep and smooth, and the women in the crowd leaned forward, smiling like they were under a spell.

"Ladies, gentlemen, welcome to the world-famous Sebastian Sheets Carnivále and tonight's *Big Show*!" The crowd erupted in applause. Sebastian raised his hands, and the arena fell silent, as if under his spell. His voice was low and serious, with an eerie edge. Each word landed heavily.

"Tonight, we do not perform. We reap. We do not entertain. We expose. For what you are about to see tonight is not theater. It's a history lesson, a life that once lived, and destroyed."

He paused, letting the silence settle.

"Tonight, we gather not for spectacle, but for remembrance. Not to be entertained, but to bear witness." The overhead lights dimmed, and the stage began to rise.

Sebastian gestured toward the looming shape below him.

"Behold, the Santamaria. This vessel marks a turning point. A moment when the world shifted, loudly, quickly. We revisit it tonight, not to explain, not to judge, but to honor what was and to feel the weight of what it meant."

The crowd leans in. No one speaks. The air hums with anticipation.

"This is not just a show. It is a reflection. A passage. A way to understand what came before, and what lingers still." He paused.

"Be grateful. Be open. What you see tonight may change you. That is its purpose."

The floor beneath our feet vibrated as the stage rose slowly from the depths, locking into place just a few feet below the first row of arena seats. Still cloaked in darkness. Fog still wafting.

"What you're about to see will be raw. Intense. It will shake you to your core." Sebastian's smile curled.

"Please note: what you see tonight may look real. But rest assured, no humans or animals are harmed in the making of this production. The events are an allusion. A reflection. A truth dressed in costume. So please, open your mind, open your heart, and remain seated." He stretched out his arms, arched his spine, and threw his head back to the rafters.

"Welcome to FEAST!" he roared.

And then he was gone.

No trapdoor.

No wires.

Just a flicker of light, a gasp from the crowd, and a space where Sebastian once hovered.

Chapter 46- Carnivále

The year 2132

Spotlights aimed at the stage, lit from all directions. The fog thinned, peeling back like a curtain, and the scene beneath it came into focus. The cargo ship Santamaria. A tattered flag flapped weakly in the artificial wind. The ship deck, flat and wide, was lined with steel cleats and thick ropes coiled like sleeping snakes. Massive shipping containers stood stacked along the edges, some rusted, some freshly painted, all sealed tight. The deck's wood floor gleamed under the arena lights, spotless as if recently washed, and the air smelled faintly of salt and freshly stained wood.

The crowd leaned forward, murmuring with excitement. This wasn't the glitter and glamor of Sebastian's entrance. This was something else. Something real. A low hum began to rise from the orchestra pit, like the sound of engines warming up.

Asher shifted beside me. "Feast," he said quietly. "I was right."

"What's happening, Asher?" I said.

Asher didn't respond.

His eyes were fixed on shadows in the shape of men as they emerged from the corner of the stage, as the artificial sound of waves crashed around us. Leaping through the fading fog, one of the shadows perched himself onto a makeshift stern near the front stage and bellowed.

"America…."

The dancing sailor wore no shirt; his bare chest gleamed under the stage lights. His pants were high-waisted and grungy brown, held up by a fraying rope belt. He had scuffed leather boots and a faded kerchief hung loosely around his neck, just like my swaddle. His cheeks were bright with rouge, giving him a theatrical look. The outfit looked more like an old-fashioned sailor costume you'd see in a child's picture book, not on a real ship.

"America…" chimed a hidden chorus of sailors as they bombarded the stage, each one dressed just as absurdly as the first.

One of the sailors twirled around the bow while others danced in unison near the middle. Someone tossed a bottle of rum through the air, and it was caught mid-leap by a man whose leg kicked so high it nearly brushed the stage rigging.

Another group of sailors stormed the stage, stomping their boots in rhythm as the bottle of rum once again spun through the air. One man sang of New York's gaslit streets, another of a woman named Clementine who broke his heart and took his money.

Their voices rose in harmony as they danced and clapped to the music. The performance was polished, almost cheerful. Troupes of men took turns singing and dancing, their movements crisp, their smiles rehearsed. The crowd responded with delight, eyes wide, laughter bubbling, hands clapping in rhythm. But beneath the joy, there was a quiet tension. They were waiting, not for the next act, but for the promised terror. It hung in the air like a second curtain, invisible but heavy. I, too, felt it in the pit of my stomach.

The lights dimmed for a moment—just a flicker, but enough to see it. Behind the dancers, one of the shipping containers had shifted. Not opened, not rattled. Just moved. A few inches closer to center stage. No one acknowledged it. Not the performers, not the audience. But I saw it.

"Asher," I whispered, tugging at the rope around my wrists. "That container moved."

He didn't look away from the stage. "I saw it."

The music played on, and the audience roared. A child near the front clapped to the beat while her face glowed with excitement.

But something was wrong. The deck near the container didn't just shine like before. It glistened, slick and dark. Something had spilled, but what?

One of the sailors slipped on the stuff, just for a moment. His hand slapped the floor with a wet smack. When he stood, a red smear covered his hand and costume. He broke character, confused, scanning the stage. No one else reacted.

"Asher," I whispered. "Did you see that?"

He nodded. "Yeah. I saw."

"It looks like blood," I said.

Just then, the armed guard broke his silence.

"It's entertaining and all, but I don't get it. The costumes look like something a child's mom would have sewn together for a party or parade. Not a cargo crew from just a hundred years ago. They don't look a thing like the pictures of the crew they have in the Museum," he said.

Several of the containers creaked.

"It's not about the performance," I whispered. "Isn't that right, Sven?"

Sven didn't respond.

"It's what's lying in wait in those shipping containers," said Asher.

"What's in the containers?" Said the guard.

"Everyone shut up," muttered Sven.

Just then, one of the containers creaked louder than the rest.

Not too loud, though. Just enough to be heard over the singing. One of the dancers faltered mid-step and glanced toward the sound. His smile twitched, then returned, wider but curious.

I stared at the container. Its door rattled, like something inside had pressed against the metal, testing its strength.

"Asher," I whispered. "They're in there."

He didn't ask what. He didn't need to.

The container doors' latch twitched. Just once. Then, slowly, the door cracked open, not enough to see inside, just enough to let something out. A slimy, pink tongue slithered through the gap. It was slick, impossibly long, and it moved with purpose. It lapped at the ooze pooling near the sailors' feet, curling around droplets like a cat savoring cream, then retracted back inside the container.

The music stopped. So did the dancing. The crowd shifted in their seats, murmuring. Something was about to happen.

The sailors looked around, confused. This wasn't part of the script for sure. One sailor stepped forward. He knelt by the container, dipped his finger into the blood, and held it up for the crowd to see.

The crowd gasped in unison.

Then, from the cracked container, the tongue shot out again, fast and wet. It had grown to at least ten feet long. The tongue wrapped tight around the sailor's boots and yanked him off his feet.

The sailor screamed, but only for a second. He hit the floor hard. Then the tongue pulled, fast and strong, dragging him into the container.

The container door slammed shut. Silence swallowed the stage. One actor dropped his hat, another edged backward, eyes wide. Then came the creaking—low at first, then swelling, deeper, heavier.

The container shuddered, and from within rose screams, tangled and raw, human voices twisting with something not human at all.

Asher grabbed my arm.

"They're not done," he said.

Sven nodded.

"They've only just started."

Chapter 47- Carnivále

The year 2132

"Asher, I'm scared. Is that what they are going to do to us?" I cried.
"Gertie, don't watch," he said. But I couldn't look away.

Just then, the container burst open with a deafening metallic shriek, and seven doglike creatures leaped out, landing hard on the stage.

An audible gasp broke the crowd's silence.

The Adlets didn't rush. They crept forward, heads low, sniffing the air with twitching, blistered snouts. Their bodies were hairless and pink, their eyes the same unsettling shade. Some had spots, some were long and lean, others short and stout, but they all looked plastic, unreal, like something pulled from a nightmare.

They moved like puppets yanked by invisible strings, spasming with the erratic grace of something long dead but moving—one locked eyes with one of the sailors. The man didn't move. Just stood there, trembling, as beads of sweat streaked through his stage makeup. The creature circled him twice, slow and deliberate, then lunged and slammed into him, tearing him down in a blur of pink claws and red teeth. Flesh ripped. Bone cracked. The man didn't even scream. He didn't have time. It was over before he could open his mouth.

As if on cue, the others attacked.

Screams tore through the arena. Actors scattered—diving behind props, crawling under set pieces, scrambling toward exits that no longer existed. The stage, once lit for song and dance, twisted into something brutal. A sailor's leg was ripped clean off, his body hurled like debris. Another was dragged across the deck, still trying to harmonize, his voice warbling through a throat torn open. His attacker spun in circles, faster and faster, until the man's body shredded under the force, scattering blood and bone like confetti across the lights.

As if confused by the notion that the show must go on, or to drown out the sound of death, the music returned, louder and more intense.

The audience went silent. Not the silence of fear. Not disbelief. But something more profound, a collective breath suspended at the edge of awe. Hundreds stood shoulder to shoulder, eyes glittering, mouths ajar.

Minutes later, the crew of the Santamaria was gone, torn apart. What remained was a blood-slick rail of carnage. From our vantage point, we saw a gate open on the far side of the arena, just below Poppy's

Lair. The Adlets turned and raced toward the deer carcass, hanging like a lure, its body swaying gently, beckoning.

They entered. Bullets rang out, and the overhead gate slammed shut. The stage went black.

Asher and I saw what the audience didn't. The Adlets were shot dead.

A single spotlight swept across the crowd, revealing faces wet with tears, eyes wide with something deeper than awe. Gratitude, yes, but also guilt. The understanding that survival had come at a cost, and tonight, they stood on the bones of that cost.

Sebastian didn't return. No bow. No curtain call. Just the echo of his voice clinging to the rafters. *No humans or animals were harmed...*

❧ CHAPTER 48- CARNIVÁLE

The year 2132

As the arena plunged into darkness, a new platform rolled out from ground level. It was smooth and silent, erasing the carnage beneath it. Artificial fog crept back in, wafting around the edges of the arena wall.

The crowd, still in awe, sat staring at one another as if searching for confirmation that what they'd witnessed had truly happened. This was it—our moment. I could feel it in my chest. I leaned into Asher, shoulder to shoulder.

"Wait for it," he whispered.

But it never came.

No one screamed. No one ran. There was no outrage, no scramble for the exits, no demands for answers. Instead, the crowd erupted in cheers, whistles, and applause. An overhead speaker crackled to life, announcing a thirty-minute intermission before the next act. Vendors swarmed the aisles, topping off cups of elixir and tossing snacks and glittering swag into eager hands. No one noticed us, trying to make eye contact, trying to get anyone's attention.

That is no one but Sven.

"Okay, you two, time to get you downstairs. Let's go," he said.

"Please, Sven, just let us go, no one will know…" said Asher.

Sven grunted, then grabbed Asher by the arm and escorted the two of us back into our dungeon and down the long hall where Poppy had come from the night before. Asher leaned against me as we descended a narrow staircase at the end of the hall and stepped into a smaller room with a similar exit to the arena as our dungeon.

Inside, waiting, were Boris and his monkey Clyde, perched in his usual spot on his owner's shoulder, and fourteen others, seven men and seven women, all dressed in the same stained, shapeless uniforms Loki had once tried to force on us. The group looked drugged, their faces hollowed out, and their eyes glassy, as if someone had given them too much gator juice. No one spoke. One man rocked gently in place, while drool dripped from his chin. A woman stood rigid, staring into a corner, while the others all sat slumped on the ground with their head bowed down.

"Here, put these on, or I'll lock you in with Demetri," grunted Sven as he untied our arms. I didn't have to ask who Demetri was because the giant pink and black Adlet caged in the corner of the room began to growl at the mere mention of his name. Asher and I immediately pulled the costumes on over our clothes and took our place next to the others.

Loki burst into the room, trailed by the puppy wrangler and a pack of full-grown dogs, ordinary ones, not Adlets. The two of them herded the animals into a separate cage, away from Demetri.

Sweat streaked Loki's brow. He turned to face us, breath ragged, eyes wild.

"Loki, listen," Asher began.

"No! Not you again!" Loki spat, spinning toward Asher with wild eyes. "I am so sick of your face! Shut up, shut up, shut up!" Loki threw his arms in the air, pacing in frantic circles.

"One more word and I will feed you to Demitri!" Loki kicked Demitri's cage, and the creature inside erupted, snarling, shrieking, a frenzy of pink limbs and teeth.

Loki stopped and grimaced at the original group, "What's wrong with these ones?"

"We had to give them a bit more juice. They're coming out of it now," grunted Sven.

"Coming out of what? A coma? A near-death experience?" Loki stopped and clutched his chest. "Problems, why so many problems. All I want is a spot of tea, and maybe a cookie."

Then his eyes widened, and he smiled as he reached into his pocket, fished out a crumbling piece of shortbread, and popped it into his mouth, licking his fingers. "Mmm. That's better."

Then his voice snapped like a whip. "Up! Up, you limp noodles! Anyone who gives me attitude will get a private session with Demitri, and he's feeling a bit peckish today. Aren't you Demitri?"

Demitri growled again.

Loki spun toward Boris and Sven. "Okay, everyone, ready, ready. Blood team, prep the cartridges. Rake, get the dogs in position in case we need a grand finale."

Then he turned to us, eyes sharp, jaw clenched.

"You all, spread out—even spacing. I want symmetry. Don't clump. Clumping is for mashed potatoes. You, guy in the hat, go long. Big gal, you're bait. Center stage. The rest of you, fill the gaps."

No one moved.

"Places, everyone," Loki said, clapping once. "Let's make Act Two something to remember."

The group on the ground began to stir, slowly rising and drifting toward the others like sleepwalkers. Their eyes were foggy, their faces confused.

"What's Act Two?" said one of the girls, tugging at her costume.

"What's happening?" Muttered another.

"You're Act Two," said Asher, his voice low.

"I don't understand," said the big gal, blinking hard.

Loki spun on his heel, arms flung wide like a deranged conductor. "Do you understand move it? This is the show! You don't have to understand it, you just have to hit your mark!"

He stalked forward, eyes blazing. "Did no one read the script?"

"Script, what script?" Said the hat guy.

"I didn't get a script," said Asher.

Loki rolled his eyes. "Well, that's your own stupid fault now. I hope you're all good at improv. Now get in places!"

Sven motioned for us to start walking. His gun was no longer holstered, it was in his hand, ready to fire. No one resisted. Not even Asher or me.

He led us up the staircase we hadn't seen before, and through another arched entrance that opened onto the arena floor.

The moment we stepped through the archway and into the arena, the lights hit us, blinding and hot. I couldn't see a thing. Just noise and fog. All around. A wall of sound, rising like a wave. Behind us, the archway boomed as a massive cage door fell into place, sealing us off from the inside.

Asher leaned over and whispered, "No matter what, stay close to me?"

I nodded.

The orchestra began to play a low, eerie tune. An overhead intermission sign blinked once, then vanished. The uneasy crowd murmured.

The floor underneath our feet began to tremble, and something began to rise near the center of the arena, but the lights were still too bright to make out the details. Then, slowly, a platform emerged from the ground, not big, just large enough for one person to stand. The platform rose at least fifty feet into the air, and Sebastian's hologram returned.

He stood tall on the platform, dressed in a black leather one-piece suit laced with crisscrossing chains. The crowd fell silent.

Sebastian began to speak. His voice was steady and calm.

"After the fall of the Santamaria, came the great unraveling of humanity and the great extinction.

Sebastian's image glitched, then re-stabilized.

"Tonight, you will witness a brief recreation of that extinction," he said. "You will see what remains when civility is stripped away. You will witness a piece of the day-to-day carnage that was once our world and what people had to do to survive."

Sebastian paused, stepped forward, voice steady, eyes scanning the crowd.

"And by survive, I mean something dark. People turned savage. They traded lives for food. Burned the weak. Ate the kind. Cannibals weren't beasts back then. They were neighbors. Parents, even lovers."

His voice grew louder.

"They fought the infected, the military, and above all else, each other. And tonight, you will witness their fight and pay your respects."

Sebastian's hologram stood tall, chains glinting under the arena lights. His voice dropped to a low, reverent tone as he turned to face us.

"Tonight, you will fight, not for glory. You'll fight for proof. Proof that you are worthy. That you are no better than those who came before. That you are deserving of the life given to you. But most of all, you will fight to show your gratitude."

He raised his hands, bowed to the crowd, and declared:

"Let the Feast resume!"

His image flickered once, then vanished.

The platform sank back into the floor, taking the fog with it. The overhead lights dimmed, and the arena lights surged to life.

My eyes, still raw from the glare, slowly adjusted. And for the first time, I could see.

The ship was gone.

In its place, a pit of dirt, with rusted steel skeletons of antique cars spread throughout. Decorative bone fragments lined the arena walls, and a rack of weapons stood gleaming nearby: blades, clubs, chains, and knives of every size sat polished and waiting.

Asher and I stood still, quietly surveying our surroundings. The others were awake now but obviously confused. Having been drugged and missing the first act, they had no idea what was happening, not to say that I did.

One man blinked rapidly, as if trying to clear fog from behind his eyes. The big gal staggered, her hand reaching out blindly before curling into a fist. The drooling figure wiped his mouth, confused, his gaze flickering between the weapons and the crowd.

A horn blew, and Loki emerged above us, standing atop the ledge of the Lair.

The crowd hushed.

Loki stood motionless, arms crossed, framed by a pulsing red glow spilling from the sign above the Lair. His throne loomed empty behind him. Beside it, Poppy's seat was also empty.

The arena lights dimmed further. Loki peered down at us from his perch and smiled.

"You've been given weapons," he said, turning a long, slim metal pipe in his hand. "How generous." He took another step forward and pointed the pipe at us.

His voice came through the speakers, amplified by the small microphone clipped to his jacket. The sound was sharp, unavoidable, filling every corner of the stage even when he spoke softly.

"But weapons alone won't save you. You need guts. You need speed. You need to dance like your shoes are on fire while everyone else stands still."

He grinned.

"Survival isn't clean. Why no. It's chaos. It's blood and panic. It's breakfast without any biscuits."

Loke spun once, laughing.

"The last one standing wins. But don't get cocky. Winning just means you get to see what's next."

He leaned in, voice low. "And what's next? Oh, it's ever so delicious."

Loki raised his arms, silhouetted against the red glow, and danced as a siren wailed, and the crowd erupted in cheers.

And just like that, the stage was set, but not everyone was getting it yet.

"So what exactly do you want from us?" A man yelled.

Loki stopped, frowned as he addressed the man. "Why isn't it obvious?" he scowled. "You are to fight. Fight as if you've already lost everything. Because by the end of tonight, you probably will."

"Huh, we're supposed to fight each other?" Asked another man, voice thin with disbelief.

A woman whispered, "This isn't real."

But it was.

Another woman stepped forward, fists clenched. "We won't do it," she cried up to Loki.

Loki tilted his head, smiling like a child watching ants burn. "Oh, but you already are."

"What does that mean?" the woman snapped.

"He's kidding," someone muttered.

"I don't think he is," Asher murmured.

"They can't make us fight one another," said a man, his voice trembling.

"He's right," said another. "What if we just stand here? What can they do?"

A flicker of hope passed between Asher and me. We turned to the crowd, waving, pleading. Hands raised not in defiance, but in desperation.

But no one cared.

They cheered. They smiled. They chanted.

"Fight! Fight! Fight!"

Their joy was grotesque—their hunger, bottomless.

"Oh, don't worry," Loki called from above, voice gleeful and cruel. "You don't need to start. My Arena Master will start for you."

"What does he mean?" I said.

"Who's the Arena Master?" said Asher.

We turned again toward the Lair as a figure emerged. It was Poppy. She was the Arena Master.

Her presence was magnetic and terrifying. She wore a black silk gown that shimmered in the light. Her hair was braided with silver wire, her eyes were painted black, her lips a perfect slash of crimson.

The sarcophagus behind her let out a roar as she stepped to the edge of the balcony and peered down at us. She didn't speak.

I looked at Asher. His jaw was clenched, eyes locked on Poppy.

She raised a hand, and the crowd fell silent. She turned to us, her gaze sharp enough to cut.

"Sixteen souls," she said, her voice echoing through the dome. "Sixteen lives, standing on the edge. Like Sebastian said, tonight, you must earn your place on this earth. Earn it or die."

We all just stood there, staring back and forth at each other. One woman shrugged as another ran screaming toward the center of the arena.

"They can't be serious," said the man in the hat.

"It's all just a show," said the big gal.

Poppy smiled. "You think you have a choice, but you do not." She lifted a long, ornate pipe, almost identical to the one Loki held, and brought it to her lips. She aimed toward our group and blew through the pipe.

From the pipe, something flew, silent and precise, and it struck one of the men in the chest. He gasped, staggered, and dropped to his knees. The crowd didn't cheer. They watched and waited.

The rest of us remained still. No one reached for the weapons. We just looked around, blinking under the lights, trying to make sense of what had just happened.

The man on the ground yanked the object from his chest and tore off his shirt.

"She shot me," he cried, voice rising. "She shot me with this!"

He held out the object, a four-inch-long, thin, gleaming metal projectile, blood still dripping from its sharp tip.

The man's breathing grew ragged. His eyes darted from face to face as if searching for answers no one had.

Standing above us, Poppy, calm and unmoved, lowered her pipe and gave a faint smile.

A younger woman knelt next to the man, cut a piece of cloth from her shirt, and wiped away the blood from his chest.

"It's just a tiny wound, but there's a bit of blood. Let me see that," she said.

The man handed her the object. She turned it in her fingers, inspected the tip, then dropped it to the ground.

"It's a hollowed-out dart, and it's full of blood," she gasped.

"Blood darts. Who would be shooting blood darts at us?" asked the big gal.

I leaned in and grabbed Asher's arm.

"Asher," I whispered. "How do you think those dogs on the ship were infected?"

He turned pale. His eyes met mine.

"They somehow injected them with tainted blood?"

"Exactly," I said.

"And earlier in the dungeon, what did the man say about the transition rate?" said Asher.

"Forty seconds," I said.

Asher and I stepped back as the wounded man began to shake. His spine arched with a sickening crack. Foam spilled from his mouth and nose. The girl helping him jumped to her feet and ran away while the rest of us watched as the man began to change.

I'd heard about it. Read about it in history class and stared at it in a glass case in the museum just hours ago. The man was becoming a Spinner.

His skin turned gray and transparent. His eyes went pink. He rolled onto all fours and started laughing, not an ordinary laugh, though, a sick, broken laugh.

He began to crawl in circles, knees scraping against the dirt, body twitching with each jagged motion. At first, it was slow and awkward. Then faster and faster until he spun on one knee like a broken toy, limbs flailing, head thrown back. The skin of his knee tore in long, wet ribbons, and the earth beneath him bloomed red.

"Oh lord, something's wrong! He's not okay!" shouted the big gal. The others began to scatter.

Asher and I backed away slowly and quietly.

Then, the Spinner stopped. Still on all fours, chest heaving and drenched in sweat, he twisted his head toward Asher and me. His eyes locked onto ours. Then he laughed. Heavy. Wet. Like something rotting inside him told a joke.

I grabbed Asher's arm. His skin was cold and clammy. Mine was shaking. Slowly, I turned and looked at the weapons rack waiting behind us, then back up at Poppy.

Poppy smiled. "Now choose."

ᴄᴇ CHAPTER 49- CARNIVÁLE

The year 2132

Asher and I sprinted toward the weapons rack, breath ragged, shoes skidding on gravel. He grabbed a sickle. I took a large knife.

The spinner was on our heels, limbs jerking in unnatural rhythm, its head twitching like it was sniffing for blood.

Without hesitation, Asher turned and lunged at the beast. The sickle curved through the air and sank deep into the infected man's neck. He dropped, twitching once before going still.

But it wasn't over; the darts kept falling.

The big gal woman lay sprawled, her limbs slack, two darts jutting from her neck like grotesque jewelry. Her eyes were open, but glassy. I thought she was dead until she began to giggle and twitch.

A man crouched beside her, frantic. He grabbed one of the darts stuck in her neck and pulled it out with a wet snap. His hands shook as he stared at it, unsure what to do, then tossed it aside.

The woman growled.

Her wild pink eyes shot open as she rolled to her side and reached for him, her fingers curled like claws.

He didn't move.

He just sat there, frozen, staring.

"Get away from her!" Yelled another man as he grabbed the stunned man by his arm and dragged him away.

Then the sting, sharp and sudden, right in my neck.

I gasped.

"No, no, no!" Asher's scream split the air. He dragged me down to the ground and yanked the dart free, flinging it away like it might explode. I sobbed, clutching my throat. The pain was sharp at first, then warm, and in a way soothing.

All around us, the arena broke into chaos.

Some people, untouched by the darts, rushed to the weapons rack and grabbed whatever they could—blades, pipes, anything with an edge. Others froze in panic. They dove behind rusted cars, clawed at the walls, or curled into corners, desperate to vanish.

Those struck began to change. Their bodies twisted and trembled. Their skin peeled away in sheets. Their eyes flared bright pink, and their limbs bent in ways that defied reason. The screams that followed were raw and animal, echoing off the walls and thickening the air with dread.

Darts continued to rain down from above, clinking against metal, thudding into dirt, hissing through the air like venomous insects. Each one carried the possibility of change, of infection, of becoming something else.

I sat in the middle of the chaos, untouched, unturned, just watching.

Then another dart hit, this time in my arm. I stared at it. The shaft shook slightly, buried deep in my skin.

I waited.

Still nothing. No burning. No shaking. No change. Not yet.

Asher moved around me, trying to block more darts, his body tense and fast.

Above us, the crowd watched. They were quiet now. Waiting. Hungry. Wondering what I would become.

"Asher, get away," I said, my voice shaking.

"No," he said. "I'm not leaving you."

Asher bent down and scooped me up without hesitation, then sprinted toward one of the rusted-out vehicles. The metal groaned as he shoved me inside, shielding me with his body.

"Stay here," he said. "She can't reach us in here."

"If she doesn't get you one of them, will, Asher. Please go. Save yourself. There aren't many left. You can still win."

"I'm not going anywhere without you. That was our promise back at Greyburry, and I'm keeping it."

"But I don't want to hurt you," I sobbed, clutching my arm where the dart still quivered.

"Better you than them," he said.

Then a crash.

The man in the hat lunged through the side opening, his face a mask of blood and drool, mouth stretched wide in ravenous hunger. His eyes locked onto mine, wild and empty.

Asher didn't hesitate. He grabbed my knife and drove it into the man's face.

The man shrieked, staggered back, and fell to the ground, taking the knife with him.

I shifted and looked up at the balcony. Poppy was there, looking frustrated, trying to find the right angle to hit her mark. I reached over and pulled the dart from my arm.

Asher ran from the car, dodging darts as they hit the ground around him. He grabbed something from the weapons rack and rushed back to me.

He wiped a tear from his cheek and held up an even larger knife.

"I got this one." he said, out of breath. "It was the last one."

I looked at him, then at the dart in my hand.

"Asher," I said quietly, "it's been more than forty seconds. More like four minutes."

He knelt beside me, looking into my eyes. "You're right. I don't see anything. How do you feel?"

"Scared. Sore. Thirsty," I said.

"Oh, thank god," he said. "Maybe the darts were duds."

"No," I said, holding up the dart I'd pulled from my arm. "There's blood in this one. And in my wound. Not just that, something is happening inside me, I can feel it. It feels weird."

"Weird how?" he said.

"I don't know, but whatever it is, it's affecting me, just not like the others," I said.

Asher didn't respond. He was scanning the area, watching for danger.

"Asher, I have an idea," I said. "Look at the gates. They don't go all the way to the top of the archways. There's at least a foot at the top of each one. You can pull yourself up and squeeze through it. We both can," I said.

"I'll never make it that far without getting hit," he said, though his eyes flicked toward the balcony, toward Poppy, still calculating her next shot.

"You won't. We run, you in front and me behind, I will protect you from the darts," I whispered.

Asher's jaw clenched. "No, I won't let you."

"Look," I said. "Whatever's in that dart, it's not hurting me, it's not turning me either. It's humming inside of me, I can feel it. It's telling me what to do."

"But what if," he said.

"Does it matter? If it happens here or out there, at least we have a chance. Besides, if it does, you have that," I said.

Asher looked down at the knife in his hand and nodded. "Okay, let's do this."

ح Chapter 50- Carnivále

The year 2132

Above us, Poppy cursed and fired another dart while Loki cheered her on. The dart missed its target and clinked off the rusted frame of the car before rolling into the dust.

The gate on the opposite side of the Lair shimmered in the dim light. It looked like a way out, but I didn't trust it. Not yet.

The arena was nearly still now. After running out of fresh bodies, the infected turned on one another. Only three were left. They moved from body part to body part, sniffing at the remains of the others, slain in one way or another during the feeding frenzy. The bodies were in pieces, strewn like discarded props. In the distance, a dog barked, then two and three. The humming inside told me to get out before they unleashed the hounds for what Loki referred to as 'the finale'.

The crowd was silent, mesmerized by Poppy's darts, the chaos unfolding below, and the blue elixir rushing through their veins.

I listened to the hum inside me, low, steady, unrelenting.

I wasn't sure if I was infected.

I wasn't sure if I was immune.

But I hadn't imploded.

Not yet.

Asher and I crawled out of the car and crouched down, staying out of sight.

I heard a soft whimper and looked toward the weapons rack.

A young woman was there, the only other survivor. She was curled up behind the rake, hugging her knees, rocking back and forth. Her face was buried in her arms.

Asher saw her too.

"She's still alive," he whispered.

I nodded. "Barely."

The woman didn't look up. Her body shook with small, steady tremors.

Around her, broken weapons lay scattered. Blood streaked the ground. The infected hadn't noticed her yet, either, but it wouldn't be long before they did.

"Should we help her?" Asher asked.

"No," I said. "We save ourselves. Watch Poppy. When she's not looking, run on the count of three. You first, then me."

Poppy stood on the balcony wall, furious. She grabbed a dart, stabbed herself with the tip, and let her blood drip into the chamber. Then she handed it to Loki, who loaded it into the blowpipe.

Asher and I peeked up from behind the car.

"She's using her own blood?" I whispered.

"She must have run out of darts," Asher said.

"So it's her," I said. "How can that be? She isn't infected."

"She's got to be a carrier. They don't have symptoms, right? That's what the wall in the Museum said. Maybe that's what's happening to you. Are you feeling anything yet?"

"I am," I said. And I knew then, he was right. The hum inside me told me so. I was a carrier of the Kuru88.

Asher moved back, just a little.

"Not like that," I said quickly. "Not like the infected. Like what you said, being a carrier. It feels natural. Strong. It's telling me things."

"What things?" said Asher.

I didn't know how to answer him at first. The hum wasn't just noise. It was direction. It was focus.

It didn't hurt. It didn't burn. It moved through me, slow and steady, like a current under my skin. I didn't know what it was. Blood, venom, something else. But it wasn't killing me.

It was helping.

I could see things more clearly now. The gates. The gaps. The timing of the darts. Even the Spinners, how they paused before they moved, slow and calculated.

Something inside me had switched on. Something that had been there all along, hiding, waiting.

"I don't know," I finally said. "But I can feel it alive inside of me, it's part of me."

Asher looked at me, unsure. "So what do we do?"

"We move," I said. "When I say."

"You're sure?"

I nodded. "I can see it. The path. The timing. It's like... It's showing me."

He glanced toward the gate, then back at me. "You lead. I follow."

I rechecked the Spinners. Two were circling each other now, distracted. The third was chewing on something that might have been a hand.

Poppy hadn't fired in a while. She was busy fidgeting with her darts.

The hum inside me pulsed once, steady and calm.

"Now," I said.

✤ Chapter 51- Carnivále

The year 2132

Asher leapt forward, fast and low, his feet kicking up dust as he sprinted toward the gate. I followed close behind. The infected didn't chase us. Not yet. They were still distracted, circling each other like confused animals.

I counted each step, watched the shadows, and listened for the whistle of a dart or the bark of a dog.

Just then, a dart flew past Asher's shoulder and hit the ground with a sharp thud. We kept going.

The gate shimmered ahead, just a few feet away now. I could see the gap at the top, the way out.

Asher pushed harder, breathing loudly, legs pumping. Then he stumbled. His foot caught on something, maybe a broken weapon, maybe another foot, and he fell forward, hard. His head hit the cement wall with a sickening thud. He dropped, motionless, and the disappointed crowd moaned.

"Asher!" I shouted, rushing to his side.

He was facedown, blood spreading slowly beneath his head. I turned him over gently. His eyes were open, but dazed.

"I'm okay," he mumbled. "Just hit wrong."

I pressed my hand to the cut, trying to stop the bleeding. "You're not okay. But we're almost there."

The gate loomed above us.

I looked back. No darts. No Spinners. Not yet. The hum inside me pulsed again, steady, calm, and focused. I pulled Asher's arm over my shoulder and picked him up. He was heavy, and the gate was too high. There was no way I could pull him up and over.

"Tell me what to do," I said. The hum inside me answered.

I wrapped my arms around Asher's chest and dragged him behind the weapons board. I sat him down next to the girl. She didn't move. Her eyes were wide and glassy, staring at something far away.

Then another dart hit, this time in my cheek, but I stayed focused as the dart filled with Poppy's warm, fresh blood pierced the side of my face. It burned. Not like venom. Like memory. I yanked it out with a grunt, as another lodged in my shoulder.

Poppy stood above, scowling, but there was something else in her eyes. Amusement or disappointment, maybe.

"I'm not afraid of you!" I yelled.

Poppy's smile faltered. She glanced at Loki, who stared at me like I'd broken the rules of the game. Like I'd refused the script after all.

The crowd gasped, confused, hungry for transformation.

But I didn't turn into a Spinner. Instead, I turned and ran, straight towards the gate underneath the Lair.

Darts whistling past my ears. The crowd rose around me, cheering now as I sprinted toward the gate on the opposite side of where we had planned to escape.

Strength and anger surged through me. It felt natural and electric. I had to find a way out and come back for Asher. I had to save him, and if Poppy and her little demon friend got hurt in the process, all the better. I hit the underground gate below Poppy's Lair and climbed like a creature born to escape, leaping with the grace of a gazelle clearing a gorge. I'd never moved like this before. Not even in my dreams.

At the top, I scaled the jagged cement wall like it was something I'd done a hundred times.

Out of the corner of my eye, I saw Cowboy, Tershy, and Sven pushing through the stunned crowd. Their faces were pale, their mouths open, but I didn't stop.

At the top of the wall, Loki was waiting. His eyes widened as I pulled myself up and onto my knees. Face-to-face, he lunged to shove me backward, but I was faster. I tore the dart from my shoulder and drove it into his hand.

He screamed. Stared at the wound like it betrayed him, then turned and fled somewhere behind the thrones.

"What have you done to my Loki, you little troll!" Poppy's voice cracked.

She grabbed my hair and yanked me off the wall and into the Lair. I hit the ground hard and rolled into the base of the sarcophagus. Dust rose around me. I looked up to see her standing over me with her goblet raised high above her head. Her face twisted in fury.

"I'll smash your head in for what you've done." She gripped the goblet, her hand shaking with rage. Then she stopped.

Her eyes narrowed, and her face went pale.

"Where did you get that?" she said, voice sharp.

"Get what?" I asked, trying to sit up.

She lunged, knocking me flat on my back. Her hand clamped around my neck. She pulled at my shirt, yanked at my hair.

I fought back, but she was stronger than I expected.

Her fingers dug into my collar, clawing at the fabric until it tore free. She stepped back, breathing hard, and stared at what she held.

A tattered swaddling blanket, frayed at the edges, soft with age. The stitching was faded, but the name remained.

Gertie.

Her lips parted, but no words came.

She blinked. Her fury drained into something else, shock, maybe, but why?

"Give that back," I said, voice shaking. "It's mine."

"Where did you get this?" she demanded.

"I told you it's mine!"

"No, it's not. Where did you get it?" she screamed. "You stole this, didn't you?"

"I didn't steal it, I've had it since I was a baby," I sobbed.

Poppy's face froze. Her fingers were still clutching the swaddle. Her eyes scanned the faded stitching, the name Gertie barely holding together in thread and memory.

"No," she whispered.

I scrambled backward, heart pounding. "I said, give it back."

She didn't hear me. Or maybe she did.

Poppy took a step back. Her face drained of fury. "Gertie?" she said, like the name itself was a wound.

The crowd outside roared, oblivious to what was happening inside the Lair.

"You're my Gertie," she whispered.

Sebastian's sarcophagus shook.

Then there was Loki, leaping from behind the sarcophagus, his body twisted and stretched, his eyes pink and full of death. He moved fast, lunging at me with sharp teeth that clicked like knives.

Poppy didn't hesitate. She threw herself between us, pushing me out of the way just as Loki's claws swiped through the air.

Poppy and I hit the ground hard while Loki's momentum carried him straight into the sarcophagus. The heavy sarcophagus tipped, crashed, and split open with a thunderous crack. The lid fell on top of Loki, trapping him underneath. He struggled, but the weight held him down.

Poppy lay beside me, breathing hard. Her eyes were wide with shock.

"You saved me," I said.

Then, from the ruin, Sebastian emerged. A pink, glistening menace, limbs twitching, mouth stretched in a grin too wide for any sane face. He shrieked, a sound like metal tearing.

Cowboy, Tershy, and Sven burst into the Lair, weapons drawn, eyes wide. They didn't hesitate. They charged Sebastian, but they were no match for the monster he'd become. He tossed each one aside like a broken rag doll.

I jumped to my feet, grabbed Poppy's arm, and pulled her away.

"Run," she said. "Take the stairs on the left. They'll lead you out. Go fast. Don't look back." She was crying now, black makeup streaking down her face like war paint.

"No," I said. "I have to get Asher."

"There's no time," she said, voice shaking. "You have to leave."

"I'm not leaving without him."

She looked at me, then nodded. "This way, then. To the arena floor. Hurry."

We ran down a set of stairs, fast and low. Poppy moved like she knew every turn. I stayed close behind as she led me through a maze of corridors.

At the end, we reached the gate.

She grabbed a lever and pulled.

The gate rolled open.

"Hurry, I'll wait for you," she cried as I raced out into the arena. The crowd cheered.

Inside the arena was a blur of dust, blood, and broken bodies. I spotted Asher behind the weapons board, struggling to stand. I rushed to him, wrapped my arms around his waist, and pulled him to his feet. My legs burned. My lungs screamed. But I didn't stop. I couldn't. The last three spinners had spotted us. One veered toward the girl still sitting in shock behind the weapons board. The other two locked onto Asher and me, falling into pace behind us as we scrambled for the gate.

I heard their screeches—the slap of feet on the dirt floor and the whir of their bodies spinning. Then the hum returned, low and steady, and it told me not to stop.

So I didn't.

We reached the gate just seconds ahead of the spinners. Poppy was still there, waiting, hand poised on the release.

As I dragged Asher through the arch, one spinner lunged, and its claws grazed my ankle.

Poppy dropped the gate.

It slammed down with a deafening crack. The Spinner was caught mid-leap, its body sliced in half beneath the weight. A shriek split the air, then silence.

The second Spinner skidded to a halt, stared at the carnage, then grabbed the dead Spinner's severed legs and vanished into the dust.

In the distance, Sebastian howled.

He was free.

Back at the stairs leading to the Lair, Poppy stopped and gestured toward the top.

"Gertie, listen. You don't have much time. On the other side of the Lair is another way out, but be careful of Sebastian. Follow the path outside and head to Krakus. Out the back, there's a big green bus just outside the pasture. Under the driver's seat is the key. Wrapped around it is a map. Follow it. It'll take you somewhere safe."

"But I can't drive," I said.

"Yes, you can. Go now. Follow the map and don't stop for anything. There's extra fuel in the back, enough to get you there, and extra to barter. But be careful who you trust."

I swallowed hard, trying not to throw up. I reached for Poppy's arm, but she pulled away.

"Take your friend. Get to the bus. Get out of here."

"You're coming too, right?" My voice cracked. Tears blurred my vision.

"No. I can't, but I'll show you the way. Come on, I have to get you out before Sebastian gets here. He's coming! Come on!"

At the top of the stairs, Poppy pointed toward the exit. "This way!"

The Lair was nearly empty. Only Loki remained.

The sarcophagus had been shoved aside, like someone had tried to free him. But it was too late.

His small body lay twisted, flattened beneath the weight of the sarcophagus lid. Limbs bent the wrong way. His grimy pink face was barely visible, pressed into the floor like a broken doll.

Loki was dead.

The torches that circled the Lair had fallen, and fire was everywhere. Flames climbed the wooden arch, throwing wild shadows across the arena.

The heavy drapes, now burning, tore loose and flew into the trees outside, igniting them.

At first, the crowd was silent, frozen in place. But as the fire began to spread into the stands, the screaming started. Raw and wild. The sound of panic and death. Some still thought it was part of the show until Sebastian appeared.

He tore through the crowd, grabbing, biting, spinning, his body a blur of violence.

Back in the Lair, Poppy stood frozen. Her eyes flicked from Loki to the fire, and then to Sebastian. For a moment, it looked like she might run to him.

But then she wiped away a tear.

"We have to move. This way!" she shouted.

She turned and led Asher and me out of the Lair, down the narrow stairs that opened to the outside. The wind had picked up, feeding the fire. Flames had already reached the outdoor tables and rows of chairs. Smoke filled the air, thick and fast as the fire jumped from tree to tree.

Carnivále was burning.

"Keep going. Remember the Krakus," Poppy said once we made it outside.

"You have to come with us. He'll kill you," I told her.

"No. He won't hurt me."

"But…"

"No but. You'll figure it out. And take this." Poppy pulled a chain from around her neck and pressed it into my hand. A gold cross with infinity wings. A purity charm with the sideways infinity symbol, like the ones they used to tattoo on the clean.

"I can't take this," I said.

"Yes, you can, it's yours. Take it and keep it safe. Keep it next to your heart at all times," said Poppy.

"Back there, when you said I was your Gertie, what did you mean?" I asked, but I already knew. I just needed to hear her say it.

"That swaddle of yours, it wasn't always stitched in blue, now was it? It was once written in coal," she said.

Tears rolled down my face, and I let go of Asher's waist to wipe them away. "How did you know that?"

"I know it because I was the one who wrote it," Poppy said. "I did it to save you. Always remember that."

She reached out and wiped my tears.

"Now go," she smiled.

"Please come with us," I sobbed.

"No," she said, steady now. "This is my home. My doing. I will stay here with Sebastian and reap my fate."

Smoke poured through the exit.

Then, as if summoned by his name, Sebastian stepped out into the light.

His pink eyes glowed through the haze. His white hair clung to his face in damp strands. His body ticked back and forth, slow and broken. He didn't speak. He growled.

Asher grabbed my arm and pulled me back.

"Sebastian, no!" Poppy threw herself at him as Asher, and I took off running through smoke and fire, past overturned tables and chairs, through a crowd that had lost its mind.

Carnival-goers screamed, trampling each other in panic. Children cried out for parents who were already gone.

Behind us, Sebastian followed. And somewhere in the chaos, Poppy kept screaming his name.

"Faster, Gertie!" Asher shouted. "The Krakus is this way!"

By the time we reached the Krakus, it was already on fire. We stopped at the edge of the grounds, gasping for breath. The place that once welcomed the strange and forgotten was now an inferno.

Its grand roof had collapsed inward. Smoke filled the air, thick with the smell of burning velvet and old wood. On the ground, two large gargoyle statues lay in the ash, staring up at us through the haze. Their stone faces looked almost alive, like they were asking for help. Behind us, the crowd scattered. Ahead, the fire roared.

And somewhere in between, Sebastian lurked.

He hadn't followed us past the entrance of the Krakus, though. He stood at the threshold of the inferno, head tilted, eyes gleaming pink through the smoke. He didn't move. He didn't speak. He simply watched the Krakus burn.

I wanted to scream. To find Poppy. To know if she was still alive. But Asher grabbed my hand and pulled me onward.

"Wait for her," I cried, pulling away.

"We can't," he said. "She chose this."

Asher grabbed my hand, and we raced around the fiery ruin that was the Krakus to the back of the building, where the oddities were scattering, throwing bags together, shouting to each other, vanishing into the smoke. No one looked at us. No one asked questions. They were too busy trying to flee.

Asher spotted the large green bus parked just a few hundred feet away. Its paint was chipped, its windows fogged with ash, but otherwise it looked intact.

We sprinted toward it.

Asher climbed in first, flopping onto the bench behind the driver's seat with a groan.

"You're not driving?" I asked, breathless.

Asher shook his head. "I can't, this one is all you, Gertie."

≈ Chapter 52- Carnivále

The year 2132

Sitting in the driver's seat, I reached underneath and felt around. Poppy's promise was true. The key was there, tucked inside a crinkled map beneath the seat, just like she said.

As I pulled it free, a faded photo slipped out. It showed Poppy and Sebastian, years younger. Poppy was smiling, her eyes bright. Sebastian stood beside her, looking down at her with a quiet grin.

In Poppy's hand was a rope, tied to a small, fluffy burro. They looked happy, like they belonged to a different world.

I slid the photo and map into my pocket, took the key, jammed it into the ignition, and turned it. It took a few tries, but the engine finally sputtered and came to life.

"We need to hurry, our buddy Sebastian's back," said Asher.

"Which way?" I said.

"Just follow them." Asher motioned to a caravan of buggies and wagons leaving the Krakus grounds. The oddities were out to save themselves. I stared down at the wheel in front of me and turned it back and forth.

"How do I make it go?" I said.

"Step on the gas," he said.

"What's the gas?" I said.

"How many pedals are there?" said Asher between wheezes.

"Pedals? Where?" I said.

"On the floor by your feet. Are there two or three?" he said.

"There are only two," I said.

"Good, this will be easy, then. The one on your right makes the bus move forward, and the one on the left makes it stop," he said. The sound of something exploding, followed by more screaming, surrounded us.

"Hurry, Gertie, before Sebastian catches up to us," he said.

"I'm trying, I'm trying," I said. I jammed my foot down on the right pedal, the engine groaned, but the bus didn't move. "It's not working!"

"The shifter there, the knob by the wheel. Pull it out of park and into drive mode," said Asher.

"I don't see drive mode?" I said.

"Is there a D somewhere?"

"There's a P, a D, and an R," I said.

"Okay, P is for park, D is drive, and R is to go backward," he said.

"So what do I do?" I said.

"Pull it down to D and step on the pedal!" He shouted.

I yanked the knob into the D slot and stepped on the pedal. The bus squealed, but the wheels wouldn't turn. Screams from the Krakus grounds grew louder, and Sebastian suddenly appeared in the rear-view mirror above the driver's seat. He was sprinting toward the bus at full speed. Behind him, Poppy, my mother, chased after.

"Asher help, he's coming, and the bus won't go!" I screamed.

"Okay, there must be a break somewhere. Look for a lever or knob labeled "brake," and pull it. Hurry, Gertie!"

"Stop yelling at me! Okay, wait. There's a knob on the left of the steering wheel, but it doesn't say brake," I said.

"Pull it anyway," he said in a calm voice. "Don't worry, you got this, now get us out of here before that pink-eyed monster and his girlfriend get here."

I pulled on the knob; it popped out, and the bus lurched forward.

"Okay, okay, it's moving," I said, gripping the wheel tighter.

In the mirror, Sebastian was gaining fast. His hair whipped around his face, wild and slick with sweat. His mouth twisted into something between fury and delight, a grin stretched too wide, teeth bared like a predator mid-meal.

His shirt hung in tatters, stained with soot and zombie sweat. It tore loose and spiraled into the air behind him, leaving him shirtless, his pink muscles flexing as he pumped his arms back and forth.

"Asher, he's still coming!" I shouted.

"I know, I know," he said, bracing himself against the back of his seat, "Just keep it straight. Don't hit anything. Or do. Honestly, just get us out of here."

The bus rattled over a boulder and lurched forward.

"Hey, watch that tree!" Asher shouted.

I yanked the wheel hard, just missing a thick oak, and swerved onto the dirt path. Ahead, the oddities and carnival worker were scattering, running for their lives.

"Watch your speed, especially on turns," Asher said, gripping the seat. "Whoa, slow down on those turns, Gertie!"

"Sorry."

"It's alright. You're doing great. If you need to slow down, tap the left pedal. But don't stop. Not yet."

"Got it," I said.

Behind us, Sebastian seemed to lose speed. He was limping now, one arm flailing as he pushed past the occasional oddity. People scattered around him, unsure whether to help or run away.

"He's slowing down but not giving up," said Asher.

I swerved to avoid a woman dragging a taxidermied flamingo on wheels. She screamed something at me, but it was lost in the roar of the engine and the crackling fire behind us.

The ticket booths near the front entrance were half-collapsed. One roof had caved in. Smoke poured from both like chimneys. I aimed for the gap between them and prayed the bus wouldn't tip.

"Hold on," I warned as we hit a chunk of booth debris at full speed.

The bus bounced hard. Tires caught air, then slammed back down. Asher groaned and hit the floor.

"Sorry," I cried back.

"Still alive," he said, climbing back into the seat. "Holy cow… look at the big top."

I turned.

The big top wasn't a tent anymore.

It was a cathedral of flame.

Its striped canvas peeled upward in curling sheets of red, gold, and black, like the wings of a dying moth. Smoke billowed from the seams in all directions.

The central spine sagged inward and glowed like hot metal.

I glanced in the rearview mirror.

Sebastian stood in the middle of the lot, chest heaving, eyes wide. The fire painted him in flickers, his white mane catching the light, his face slack with something close to awe. He didn't move. Just stared at the burning big top, like a man watching the end of a dream.

And then I saw her.

Poppy stood at the entrance of the once grand tent, framed by the collapsing entrance. Her silhouette was sharp against the blaze, one hand raised, beckoning, or warning. Her dress fluttered in the heat, and for a moment, she looked like she belonged to the fire.

Sebastian didn't hesitate. He turned from the bus, from us, and ran toward her. Arms pumping, feet kicking up ash. The crowd parted around him, stunned into silence. Asher and I watched as he raced towards the big top, his pink flesh pulsing with each motion.

"He's leaving. He's going back," I said.

"Yeah. I saw him turn. He's going after her."

"She's luring him away from us," I whispered. "Thank you, Mother."

Sebastian neared the entrance. Flames bent around him. Smoke curled at his feet. His eyes never left Poppy, and as she turned and vanished into the blaze, he followed. And just like that, they were gone.

Moments later, the big top folded in on itself, swallowed by fire. The grand behemoth was gone, reduced to a smoldering heap of canvas and smoke.

I started to cry, quiet, steady tears as I drove the bus around the outer edge of the compound where mobs of carnival-goers ran in every direction, faces twisted in panic, trying to escape the flames.

At the edge of the lot, just a few feet from the main road. I eased my foot off the right pedal and gently pressed the left. The bus came to a stop, and I turned the engine off and wiped the tears from my face.

"Oh, Asher, what do we do now? Should we go to the grid-rail station and wait with everyone, or catch a train out of here?" I asked.

"Are you crazy? The station's under siege. The authorities will be here any minute, and I can already hear the fire patrol coming."

"But I don't know where to go, and I don't even know how to drive this thing," I whined.

"Listen, Gertie. People saw what happened in there. They were infecting people with that disease. People saw you get hit with the dart, and nothing happened. We need to get as far away from this place as we can."

"But I didn't do anything," I said.

"You're a carrier, it's just as bad and punishable by death, you read about it at Greyburry, you saw what they did to them back in the Museum. They will kill you, Gertie, probably kill us both. And if what that woman said is true, if she really is your mother, then it makes sense, and you're just as contagious as she was."

"I hadn't thought of that," I whispered. I lifted my hand to my neck, but my swaddle was gone. Poppy still had it.

"Right now, we need to get out of here. Drive this bus as fast and as far as you can. We'll figure it all out once we are in the clear."

"Okay. You're right," I said. The humming inside me agreed.

I started the engine again and steered toward the main road, swerving to avoid the mob flooding the lot. People screaming for lost loved ones, faces streaked with ash and panic. A woman engulfed in flames rushed the bus, clawing at the door, but I didn't stop. I slammed the gas pedal down and didn't let up until we reached the road where Asher and I had first walked, back when the grid-rail station had seemed like just another stop.

There, I paused.

Right would take us back to the fields, the sick cows, Pepper's bar, and the marina. Left was a mystery. I glanced at the station and remembered the Carnivále route had come from the same direction as the town, which would have been east. So we needed to go the other way, to the west. That was it. I felt the hum inside me confirm.

I turned the bus left a little faster than I meant. It tipped hard, and I jerked the wheel right. The back end bounced over a cement barrier, lifted off the ground, and poor Asher nearly flew from his seat again.

"Be careful up there! Don't kill us!"

"You try driving this thing then," I said.

"You're doing great."

As I drove past the grid-rail station, I glanced into the rearview mirror one last time. Carnivále was gone. The place that had once shimmered with color and wonder had been reduced to smoke and ash. Red and gold had turned to black, and the magic that once filled the air had burned away.

And with it, my mother, Poppy.

Just then, Magenta, the majestic unicorn, galloped past us, veered to the right, and disappeared into a field of tall grass, and my heart smiled.

"Run free, beautiful creature. Run free," I whispered.

ɶ Chapter 53- Carnivále

The year 2132

We sped away as an emergency fire brigade descended upon Carnivále. I didn't look back. I couldn't. My hands shook as I clenched the wheel of the bus. I drove for what had to have been three hours, knuckles locked on the wheel. The sun was sinking, but the heat inside the bus stayed thick and brutal, like it had nowhere else to go.

Asher was half asleep the whole time, slumped against the window, his breath shallow. I kept checking on him, every few minutes, as if I looked away too long, he might vanish. The swelling on his head had gotten worse. I was scared. Not just scared. I was unraveling, and even though I had no idea where I was going, I couldn't stop. Not yet.

I kept seeing Poppy. My mother. Her face, her voice, the way she stood between me and the fire like she'd done it before. Like she'd always known she would. She sacrificed herself and not just once, but twice. And I still didn't understand why. The whole thing felt unreal, like a dreadful dream. Did that really happen? I kept asking myself. But she knew. She knew about the swaddle. She knew my name, etched in coal. That wasn't a coincidence. That was memory. That was love.

And then it hit me, quietly, like a whisper in the back of my skull.

Greyburry. The escape. Getting lost. All of it. It wasn't random. It wasn't chaos. It was a plan. Maybe not God's plan. Perhaps something older, something stranger. But a plan, all the same. And we were inside it, Asher and I.

I didn't know whether to feel grateful or furious.

Because if it were a plan, then someone had watched us suffer. Someone had let Poppy burn. Someone had counted the bruises on Asher's skull and said, "Yes. That's necessary."

And yet, if it wasn't a plan, and it was all just one meaningless coincidence. Well, that was worse. That meant the outcome was unclear. There would be choices, dangerous ones maybe, so I chose to believe this was our destiny and I drove on. Into the darkness, not because I wasn't afraid or knew where I was going. I drove to find whatever came next. I just prayed it was good and not pink. Definitely not pink.

Eventually, I had to stop. I turned onto a narrow dirt road that curved into the woods, headlights flickering against the trees. It had taken me ages to figure out how to turn them on, but now they lit the way just enough. I stopped the bus behind a cluster of trees, hidden from the main road. I set the brake and threw the door open.

The air outside was dry, but cooler than the stifling heat inside. I stepped down, legs trembling, and sank to my knees. Sweat clung to me, but the breeze touched my skin like a balm. It was quiet here. No sirens. No shouting. Just the hush of wind threading through the leaves. We'd passed a few transports before sunset, but now the road behind us was still. For the first time in hours, maybe longer, there was nothing but silence.

I looked back at the bus. Asher stood in the doorway, outlined by the faint glow of the instrument panel. His clothes hung in tatters, and his face bore streaks of blood and soot. But he was upright, breathing, watching. He looked like someone who had survived a wreck—and was still standing.

"Well, we did say we wanted an adventure," Asher managed before stumbling down the stairs and landing next to me on the ground.

"Oh, Asher, your head looks awful," I said.

"Feels awful," he said.

I sighed, reached into my pocket, pulled out the necklace Poppy had given me, and clasped it around my neck.

"I hope you're good luck. I'm definitely going to need it without my swaddle," I muttered.

"Oh no, not the swaddle, please don't tell me we've lost the swaddle," groaned Asher. "The one good thing about all this was losing that grody old thing."

"Shut up," I said. Asher rolled onto his side and hit my leg.

"Not only that! Your creepy long-lost mom stole it. What the heck, Gertie, did all that really just happen?" Asher asked. "Is Sebastian your biological father? Because that would definitely explain a lot."

I smacked his arm.

"Stop! I can't laugh right now. It's too painful."

"So now what? We just going to sit here?" he said.

"Asher, I'm tired. I don't think I can drive anymore tonight."

"Yeah, it's getting too dark anyway. It can't be safe," he said, pulling himself to his feet.

We climbed back into the bus, each of us finding a place to rest. I lay down and drifted off almost immediately. I was too tired to be afraid. Fear had emptied me, but sleep offered something back—safety, and the chance to begin again.

Morning arrived. The sun crept through the cracked windows of the bus, casting soft golden rays across the floor. It warmed the metal rails and lit the dust in the air like glitter. The world outside was quiet now, no screams, no ticking, no chaos—just light.

I blinked awake, my body sore, my throat dry. Asher stirred beside me, groaning as he sat up. He looked better, less pale, but his head was still red and swollen from his fall. We were both hungry and thirsty, so we started searching the bus for anything edible.

In the far back, just as Poppy said, sat four ten-gallon fuel tanks, scratched and dented but sealed tight. There were also several boxes stacked neatly across the last two rows of seats. I opened one and started digging through its contents.

"What's all that?" Asher asked.

"Clothes mostly," I said

Inside one of the boxes, I found two long skirts, faded, like they'd been worn in another life. Beneath them, a handful of colorful scarves spilled out, tangled together. At the bottom was a thick book, its spine cracked, its pages bent and yellowed with time.

I held it for a moment, unsure whether to open it.

"And a book," I said.

"I wonder if it's the one she was reading to him," he said.

"I doubt it. It's been here a while," I replied, tossing it back in the box.

"I think someone was planning a trip or something. These gas containers are full," said Asher.

"She was going to leave, or wanted to," I said.

"Yeah, maybe," Asher agreed.

"Wait, I forgot," I said, pulling the map from my pocket.

"What's that?"

"It's a map, I found it with the key. Poppy said it would take us to a safe place," I said.

"What's it say?" he said.

"She was planning to leave, I think, oh Asher, look what it says," I cried and handed him the map.

"It says Free Zone. What's the Free Zone?" he said.

"No, there at the bottom next to all those words I don't understand, look what it says," I said.

Asher gave the map another look, lifted his eyes, and smiled. "Playa de Esparanza. It's a map to Hope Island!"

❧ Chapter 54 - Gertie

The year 2132

We were excited about the map, too excited, and I prayed it was real. After everything that had happened, escaping Greyburry, getting lost, and being taken hostage at Carnivále, it felt like a light at the end of the tunnel. It was more than hope. It felt like fate.

We tore through the rest of the boxes, hoping for food. Nothing. Just clothes, blankets, and a few tools. Our stomachs growled. The hunger was sharp now, not just a dull ache anymore. The morning had stretched thin, and we knew we had to get back on the road soon.

But first, the map.

It was drawn by hand, rough and uneven, like something a child might sketch. A long red line snaked across the page, beginning at a sketch of a big top and ending at a place labeled Free Zone, circled by palm trees. Between those points were scattered symbols and names— one of which I recognized.

"Look, Asher, this says Freda. We passed a sign for it yesterday, just before it got dark," I said.

"We're on the right track then," Asher replied, taking the map from me.

He traced the red line with his finger. "The next one looks like a church, maybe. With horns painted on the front."

"That shouldn't be too hard to spot," I said.

And it wasn't.

Late that afternoon, we found it at the edge of a dry, cracked field. The building stood alone, its white paint peeling, the steeple leaning slightly to one side. Horns, real ones, maybe from cattle, were bolted above the doorway, curved and sun-bleached, and another set, painted on the side like a beacon.

We didn't get out.

We just slowed down, looked for a moment, then kept driving.

We stayed on the road for the next three days, only stopping when we needed rest, to fill up with gas, or find food and water. Once we stopped to grab apples from a field near the road.

We didn't stay long, though.

A man with an axe came charging after us, shouting something we didn't stick around to hear. But not before we loaded both our arms and two skirts, tied into makeshift bags, full of apples.

We dove back into the bus and peeled off, laughing as apples bounced across the dashboard.

The road stretched ahead, quiet but not empty. Traffic came and went depending on where we were, mainly near the small towns. We passed a ton of food transports like the one we escaped Greyburry in. There were other big rigs too, with reinforced sides and faded logos. Some carried crates strapped down with wire. Others had cages, empty or covered with tarps. Most were headed in the opposite direction.

A handful of regular cars rolled by, too. Dusty. Dented. Their drivers stared straight ahead, hands tight on the wheel, like they didn't want to be seen. No one waved. No one slowed down.

Every few miles, we passed under tall electric boards like the ones Sebastian used for his show, but these were older, the kind that used to flash warrants and Treaty fugitives across the sky. Now they flashed cola ads or President Bruno's face, smiling widely, reminding us how lucky we were to have him.

We stopped when we saw water, an old spigot behind a collapsed shed, or a small stream, and filled every bottle we had. We lived off the stolen apples, soft now, bruised from the ride, but still enough to keep us going.

When we first left New Orleans, the land was green. Fields of grass and hay stretched out on both sides of the road, broken by fences and rusted signs. Every so often, we passed an old checkpoint booth. The windows were shattered. The roofs were falling in. No guards. No scanners. Just silence.

Then the terrain started to change.

The grass gave way to open earth. Fences fell away, and the signs thinned, leaving space for something new. Dry earth gathered gently along the road's edge, and the air grew light. The sky stretched vast and pale, waiting. There were no clouds, only the promise of distance.

Asher pointed to the cactus symbol on the map.

"We're getting close," he said. "We've covered more than two-thirds of the map already."

I nodded, watching the desert roll past the window. The land was wide now, open and dry. The sun hung high, and the road shimmered ahead.

But there was something else out there.

The Grid.

Not the new sleek version built into rooftops or carved into mountains. This was the old Grid, the massive, outdated system that once stretched across the Front like a line of metal angels holding hands.

Each unit stood on three legs, tripod-style, with a giant metal hoop on top. The hoops spun slowly, clockwise, pulling energy from the sun and storing it deep inside.

They were tall, at least 150 feet, and spaced about a quarter-mile apart. Thick power cords connected them, eight per unit, zigzagging across the valley like a web.

I knew it was coming; I'd seen it on the map. But I didn't expect the size, the force of it. It rose tall and silver against the sky, visible from miles away.

Now the units didn't hum. They didn't spin. They just stood there, quiet and broken. Their cables split and hang, like arms too tired to lift.

I kept glancing at Asher. He hadn't said much since morning. His face was pale and still bruised, his eyes puffy and red. He tapped the map sometimes, but didn't look at it. I wasn't sure if he was tired or just somewhere else entirely.

I was worried about him.

The next morning, we reached another marker on the map: the town of Avendale.

We used almost all the remaining fuel getting there.

According to the map, we were close. But the scale was off. It had taken us twice as long to get from the marker for Freda to Avendale as it had from the Carnival to Freda, even though the distance looked shorter. The map couldn't be trusted. Two inches left on paper meant nothing out here.

We used most of our remaining credits on fuel and bought an unfamiliar, wrapped sandwich of meat and cheese from a woman selling food from a cart on the street. It was warm, spicy, and exactly what we needed. We filled the bus tank and half of one of the extra containers at the only fuel stop in town, then drove in silence for a while, watching the road stretch out ahead like a ribbon.

Asher was feeling well enough to take the wheel, which gave me a much-needed break. He still moved slowly, ribs sore, but after we wrapped them with his undershirt, he seemed to breathe a little easier, and after a while, he needed to rest again, so I was back in the driver's seat.

"How are you feeling?" I asked.

"Better. Now that I can breathe."

"Good. Keep the wrap on. I think you're going to be fine. Your head's looking better, too."

"Thanks."

He smiled faintly, eyes still tired but clearer than before.

As we neared Diego, the landscape shifted again. Electric boards lit up the horizon, advertising everything from neon clubs to miracle cures. Traffic thickened, not just transports and the occasional car anymore, but clusters of motorbikes weaving between moving and abandoned vehicles.

They rode in packs of ten or more, all in matching leather, goggles, and beards. Some had passengers clinging to their backs while others rode solo. They passed us in droves, staring into the bus like they were sizing us up, deciding what to take.

I was nervous. So was Asher.

"Just keep going. Don't make eye contact. Don't stop," he said.

"What do they want?"

"I don't know. Just drive."

Eventually, the bikers dispersed. Maybe we weren't worth the effort.

The road settled, transports, cars, the usual, and the city came into view. It shimmered in the distance, loud and alive, like it had no idea what was happening in the rest of the world, nor did it care.

Diego was beautiful. The ocean looked like glass, and the people moved slowly, calmly, like they had nothing to fear. Everything looked clean. Ordered. It almost felt safe.

For a moment, I let myself believe we could disappear here. Blend in. Start over.

"Maybe we should stay," I said.

"No," Asher said. "We have to keep going. They're going to be looking for you."

"You really think so?"

Asher sighed. "I don't know anything right now," he said. "This could all be a dream."

He was right. It didn't feel real. But it was.

We got turned around on the way out of the city. Asher did his best to navigate, but the roads were confusing. The map didn't help, and the signs didn't match. We ended up outside a big warehouse with a fuel station next to it. The attendant had run down the road to help a stranded motorist, and we took advantage and stole what we could: some crackers, a jug of water, and just enough gas to fill the tank and one container. I left an apple on the counter, along with a couple of scarves, as payment. We weren't thieves after all. Just desperate.

I kept watch while Asher pumped fuel into the beast. Then we jumped in and drove off, hoping we were heading the right way.

Luckily, we spotted two final landmarks within a mile of each other. One was a faded sign reading "San Ysidro Crossing." The other was a massive, rust-colored wall, partially falling apart. It stretched across the land like a scar.

The wall looked old and damaged. Some sections had collapsed. Others leaned at strange angles. The metal was bent and scorched in places, covered in dust and faded graffiti. I'd never been so happy to see such a disgraced monstrosity.

Beyond it was Mexico.

We were getting close.

ℰ CHAPTER 55 – HOPE ISLAND

The year 2132

After leaving Diego, the signs disappeared. No more electric billboards, no more glowing ads for miracle cures or late-night clubs. Just sand. Endless rows of it, stretching in every direction, swallowing the road.

I hoped the fuel we'd stolen would be enough to get us to Hope Island. The map seemed to say it was, but who could really tell? The markings had changed, the red lines turned black, and the symbols were written in a language I couldn't understand.

Thankfully, Asher could. He'd taken Spanish back in Greyburry. I'd chosen Latin. What was I thinking?

Something had shifted in him, too. He was starting to act like the old Asher again, and that made me happy. Maybe he was getting better. Perhaps it was the excitement of being close. Whatever it was, having him back felt good.

"Please explain how you're so good at Spanish but got so lost back in Diego," I giggled. "Oh… por favor."

"Hey, I got an A in Spanish and a D in geography," he said, smiling through the exhaustion.

After the sand, we passed a town so small it disappeared before we could even register it. Then another. And another. But no ocean. No island.

Just more signs, scattered and strange:

No Rebase

Peligrio No Conducir De Noche

No Traffico de Drogas

Later in the afternoon, I could tell Asher was too tired to keep going, so we started looking for a place to rest. The road had narrowed, and the sand returned, deeper than before. Off in the distance, I thought I saw water, but it shimmered and vanished, just a trick of the heat.

We parked behind a deserted building and slept.

The next morning, we'd only been driving a few hours when I saw it for real, water. It was the ocean, bright, crystal blue. Nothing like the dull brown back in New Orleans. It stretched wide under the sun, endless and shining.

For a moment, I felt something close to peace.

We drove through a small beachside community of dirt roads, fish shacks, and homemade houses patched together with driftwood and tin. We tried to ask for directions, but the few people on the street scattered at the sight of us. I couldn't blame them. We looked like a mess, unwashed, riding in a giant green bus that groaned with every turn.

A lone man sat near one of the fish shacks, wearing a giant, round cowboy-style hat. He waved us over.

"Esperanza?" Asher asked.

"Esperanza, sí sí," the man nodded.

"¿Dónde?"

"Aqua," he said, sitting up and pointing toward a lonely dirt road that disappeared into nowhere.

"So… down that road?" I asked.

"Yeah," he said, switching easily to English. "But it's not really an island, ya know. Not sure why they call it that."

"Oh, you speak English," Asher said, blushing.

"Yes. I'm from Tucson," the man replied with a smile.

We thanked him and drove on. The road unraveled in endless curves and jolts. Behind us, the ocean shimmered, then slipped away, swallowed by the land. The sun climbed higher. Inside the bus, the heat thickened.

Eventually, the bus sputtered and died. We'd finally run out of gas.

We grabbed what we could and continued on foot, the heat pressing down like a weight. The walk was slow and hot. The road was pure sand now, soft and uneven beneath our feet. Each step felt heavier than the last. The sun hung above us, bright and unforgiving. The wind carried dust that clung to our skin. We didn't talk much; we just kept walking, heads down, hoping the horizon would shift.

And then, it did.

The ocean returned, glittering in the distance. And there, rising from the dust like something out of a forgotten story, stood a palatial rustic arch. Its stone was weathered and cracked, with vines curling around the base. A faded wooden sign hung at the top, swaying gently in the breeze.

Esperanza.

We stepped into Esperanza like we were walking into a dream. Asher and I moved slowly down an empty boardwalk, hand in hand, trying to take it all in. After everything we'd been through, I didn't know what I expected. I hoped for safety, but I never imagined this.

Esperanza was quiet, tucked along the coast like a secret.

A row of whitewashed villas stretched across the beach, their paint chipped by salt and time. Hammocks swayed between crooked posts. Empty chairs faced the ocean.

The air smelled of sun-warmed wood and sea breeze. Peaceful. Beautiful in a way that didn't feel real.

A few people wandered near the water. A man lay in a hammock outside one of the villas. But otherwise, it was still. Empty.

No one called out. No one asked us to leave.

The only sounds were the hush of waves and the creak of old shutters.

Asher dropped my hand and staggered down the embankment toward the water, his steps slow but steady.

Just then, a man in white pants and a crisp shirt with a dark blue vest approached, smiling as he walked. He moved with ease, like the heat didn't touch him. His clothes were spotless, his shoes barely kicking up sand. Everything about him felt out of place. He was too polished and calm.

"Hola, señorita. Welcome!" he said, voice smooth and cheerful.

"Where am I?" I asked.

"Why, you are in Esperanza!" he said, arms wide.

"Is this Hope Island?"

"Sí, yes it is," he said. "Are you here to see the Mayor?"

"I'm not really sure."

"Ahhh, then yes, you are here for the Mayor. I will let him know you've arrived."

"The Mayor?" I asked.

"Exactly. Have a seat over at the palapa and relax. Señor will make you a special drink while you wait. I'll be back," he said, already hurrying off toward a large white house perched on the hill.

"Special drink? Great," I muttered, remembering the gator juice.

The sound of the ocean was steady, hypnotic. The breeze carried the scent of salt and grilled fish. My throat was dry, my skin hot. I spotted a small palapa near the water, its thatched roof casting a patch of shade over a few empty stools.

I walked over, sat down, and waited.

The man behind the bar noticed me, wiped his hands on a towel, and smiled.

"Hello and welcome to Maya's Cantina. You look like a newcomer." His English accent was unexpected. He didn't seem local. He was tall, tanned, with dark curly hair and eyes like blue glass. "Yes," I replied. It was all I could manage.

"Waiting for the Mayor, I assume?"

I nodded. "I guess so."

"You don't look so well. How about something to drink?"

"Just water, please."

He grabbed a glass, filled it with ice, and poured water from a jug. "Here, drink," he said, setting it in front of me.

I picked it up and drank the whole thing in one go, then set the glass down hard on the bar.

He smiled and waved to another man polishing glassware nearby. "My name's Markus, and that's my brother, Jobe. We own this place."

"Oh yeah?" I said. "You're twins?"

"Since the day we were born," he said with a grin.

"Do I look like a mess?"

Markus laughed. "You look like most people do when they arrive."

"Oh," I said.

"So are you going to tell me?" he asked.

"Tell you what?"

"Your story," he said.

I looked down, unsure. "I don't really have one."

"Come on now. Everyone has a story. Especially anyone who finds this place." He set a bowl of dried fruit in front of me. "So come on. Tell me yours."

I didn't think it was a good idea to share, but something about his face made me feel safe, like I could trust him. Still, where would I even start?

I shrugged and grabbed a handful of fruit. "Nothing too interesting."

"Don't be shy," he said, refilling my glass.

"What kind of story do you want to hear?" I asked.

Markus leaned in, his smile fading into something more serious. "Why don't you start with how you got that purity necklace?"

"Oh, this?" I touched the charm around my neck.

Markus glanced at Jobe, then back at me. "Looks special. You don't see many with the horizontal wings anymore. So tell me about it."

"You probably wouldn't believe me."

"Try me," he said quietly.

Jobe stopped polishing and joined his brother at the bar. I turned toward the ocean. Asher was waist-deep in the water, pushing through the waves. He looked back and waved.

I looked at the brothers, took a breath, wiped the tear from my cheek, and rested my hands on the bar.

"I don't even know where to begin."

"How about you start with your name?" Jobe said.

"Okay," I took a hard swallow of the water and set the glass down. "My name is Gertie. Well, Gertrude really, but everyone calls me Gertie…"

The end.

I sat back in the chair with the book in my lap—the one that had belonged to my mother, the one I'd pulled from the back of the Green Beast. The sand was warm beneath me, the tide creeping close enough that the foam kissed my toes. I watched Asher sprint across the beach and dive into the water, his figure shrinking against the horizon until he was nothing but a speck. A smile tugged at me, faint and fleeting.

I lifted the book and thumbed through its worn pages, the paper soft beneath my fingers. Something slipped free and fluttered down onto the sand. I bent to pick it up, my breath catching when I saw it was a note. My hands trembled as I opened it. The handwriting was precise, deliberate. A letter. From Sebastian. Written to Poppy.

My Dearest Poppy,

I found your things tucked away in the bus—the book, the clothes, the keepsakes you thought no one would notice. I know what they mean. You're planning to leave me, to leave us.

You've often believed you were the monster in my twisted scheme—because of my obsession, because of what happened to Lady Jane. But you're wrong. From the first day I met you, you were my muse. I didn't know all your secrets then, but I knew you carried something I desperately wanted. We were a team, even through the darkest times. I wanted nothing more than to make you proud, to show you the rewards of all the sacrifices we made year after year.

Jane's death was no accident. But you knew that already, didn't you? I needed to see what the serum would do, to understand the cost of what I craved. And still, I told myself it was for us—for the empire we built together, for the sacrifices we endured. But the truth is simpler, and darker: it was for me.

I'll admit my hunger for your blood, the thrill it gave me, drove me to recklessness. But you were always my priority. Even after it became about the power. The power was yours—I knew that—but I needed it to be mine.

Despite that, you are the reason Carnivále breathes, the reason I do. Everything I did was for you. Every thread I stitched into that tent, every nail I drove into its beams, every breath I took beneath Carniváles' lights was for you.

Without you, they are hollow gestures, empty echoes of a life that no longer exists. Without you, the lights will dim, the music will falter, and the beasts will return to their cages: all but one. I have kept something for this moment—a bottle of serum, my last gift to myself.

If you go, I will not chase you. I will not beg. I will simply surrender to what has always waited beneath my skin. The serum will finish what began long ago. The man you once loved will fade, and the beast will rise in his place. I will become the spectacle itself.

Do not mistake this for a threat. It is only the truth. My life ends without you in it. I will become what I was always meant to be—alone, monstrous, and final.

Forever yours,
Sebastian

www.ingramcontent.com/pod-product-compliance
Lightning Source LLC
Chambersburg PA
CBHW021242060726
47590CB00005B/1857